Praise for the *The Pyongyang Option*:

"A compelling espionage thriller."
—LIBBY FISCHER HELLMANN, AUTHOR OF THE *JUMP CUT*
AND *WAR, SPIES & BOBBY SOX* ESPIONAGE THRILLERS

*"Multi-layered suspense, international intrigue...
and heart-pounding action."*
—LISA TOWLES, AWARD-WINNING AUTHOR OF
CHOKE AND OTHER BOOKS

*"A masterfully-crafted...thriller that plunges readers
into the intriguing depths of...a secretive regime."*
—FRANCIS GARY POWERS, JR., FOUNDER OF THE
COLD WAR MUSEUM AND AUTHOR OF *SPY PILOT*

*"An international thrill ride with equal parts
intrigue, politics, and blistering conflict."*
—FRANK ZAFIRO, AUTHOR OF *CHARLIE-316*

Praise for the Jonathan Brooks series:

"Solid espionage."
—*KIRKUS REVIEWS*

"Intelligent and intriguing."
—*CRIMESPREE MAGAZINE*

"Gritty, complex and satisfying."
—JAMIE FREVELETTI, AWARD-WINING AUTHOR OF
ROBERT LUDLUM'S *THE JANUS REPRISAL*

"A myriad of twists and turns."
—MARC PAOLETTI, AUTHOR OF *SCORCH*

The Pyongyang Option

A.C. FRIEDEN

For information on other titles and author news,
visit A.C. Frieden's official website:

www.acfrieden.com

Avendia Publishing ®
Chicago, Illinois

The Pyongyang Option
© 2019 by A.C. Frieden and Avendia Publishing

eBook versions of The Pyongyang Option are published
exclusively by Down & Out Books

ISBN-13: 9780974793429

Editor: Julia Borcherts

Cover design by Avendia Publishing
(based in part on a photo by Andre Frieden)

Author photo by Efe Babacan Photography, Istanbul, Turkey
© 2011 A.C. Frieden

Printed in the United States of America
PIMM/1904

A.C. FRIEDEN

The Jonathan Brooks Series

TRANQUILITY DENIED

THE SERPENT'S GAME

THE PYONGYANG OPTION

LETTER FROM ISTANBUL

DIE BY NOON

AVENDIA
PUBLISHING®

DOWN & OUT
BOOKS

www.acfrieden.com

Pripyat, Ukraine

Pyongyang, North Korea

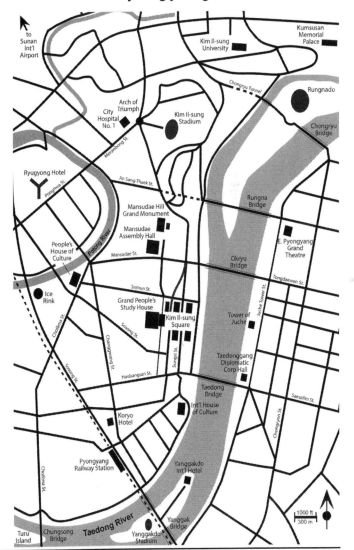

For my family

1

Northern Ukraine – July 2005

TALL, DARK SILHOUETTES OF PINE TREES, RESEMBLING A horde of witches, passed by on both sides of the desolate roadway as the rain pounded Misha's helmet, his soaked gloved hands tightly gripping the handlebars of his old Voskhod motorbike. This was no ordinary night, nor a leisurely ride. The cryptic messages spun wildly in his head as he sped along the shoddy pavement, at times weaving into the opposite lane to avoid potholes. *This isn't right*, he told himself, hoping, however, that he'd be proven wrong. That his fear was indeed misplaced. And that the hastily arranged meeting was entirely benign. *But how could it be?*

The text message had in fact come with the proper codewords, and from the right phone number. But everything else in the meeting request was a break from protocol: a rural location not previously used;

a strange demand that he leave his cell phone behind; and an ungodly hour that drew unwanted attention when Misha exited the two checkpoints within the Chernobyl Exclusion Zone, the thousand-square-mile security perimeter around the Chernobyl nuclear power plant that was set up after the reactor meltdown in 1986. He'd asked why. He'd asked for another day and time. But the messenger insisted. Misha had never been tempted to say no before, but even though he needed the money, he'd felt his stomach wrench as he agreed to this meeting. *I can still turn back*, he thought. *I can.*

Misha reached the town of Ivankiv—an already sleepy hamlet by day, but now, nearing one in the morning, activity was all but nonexistent. He hadn't expected rain, and certainly not this fierce downpour that had soaked through his leather jacket, jeans and shoes. The cold wetness of his clothes made him angry. If only he hadn't been so rushed, he could have checked the weather and donned a rainsuit.

At the village's only lighted intersection, he turned right, heading northwest toward the next village, Obukhovychi. Misha despised anything rural. The manure-scented air. The primitive dwellings. The peasantry. It reminded him how far his country lagged far behind the likes of Austria or Germany, where he'd visited often in recent years. He was in this northern part of Ukraine only by professional obligation, crisscrossing this unimposing landscape after being assigned as the numbers-cruncher at the former Chernobyl nuclear power complex. To him, all that mattered in the Ukraine was his native Kyiv, and Crimea for those infrequent vacations on the coast, but nothing else. Accountants don't belong in fields or forests, he thought, and even less so on such a dreary night.

The rain pummeled his helmet, muffling the sounds of his bike as he continued down the darkened road walled in by tall trees—witches, he thought, as his mind raced along with his motorbike. Perhaps they had cast an eerie spell on him. His prior rendezvous had always seemed mundane, and most importantly, safe. But not this one tonight.

"What the fuck am I doing here?" he mumbled into his helmet. He struggled to gauge why a meeting that had originally been set for Saturday in a quiet café on the west side of the capital was now hurriedly pushed forward. Worse yet, in the middle of the night on a barren green spot on a map. He couldn't think of any justifiable reason.

Misha continued down the country road, his weariness exacerbated by nerves. *Could it be a trap?* he pondered. *Did the late-night message really come from his handler?* But the codewords were correct, he reminded himself. He'd deciphered them using the identical formula they'd been working with for months.

In keeping with the instructions, he turned onto the first dirt road after spotting the faded welcome sign for Obukhovychi. His heart sped up the moment he saw the path exit the roadway and enter a forest—the witches' lair. He thought of his handler, a man he knew only as Brian—a wiry, sharp-dressed Brit whom Misha had never imagined would be the type to meet anywhere as uncivilized as a forest.

He slowed. The rain eased the instant he passed under the shelter of the pine trees. He slowed further, maneuvering his bike over the muddy trail and natural debris that told him no one had wandered down this way in a while. It reminded him of his childhood fear of forests—and not just because they were dark and secluded. His grandfather had gone missing on a long walk through the woods and was later found dead of a heart attack. Misha had gone through his teens believing all woods were haunted. As an adult he simply disliked them.

Misha struggled to keep the bike's tires from sinking into the muddy trail layered with fallen branches, wet leaves and shrubs. His boots felt heavy. He peered into the darkness as he crept forward on the bike but saw nothing. Then a brief flash of headlights suddenly pierced through the mass of tree trunks ahead. The car must have driven in from another path, since he hadn't seen tire marks.

He stopped about fifty yards from the car but stayed seated on his bike, the engine left idling. He noticed his breaths becoming more rapid, as was the thumping in his chest, as if he was running a marathon. *This spot could not be farther from help*, he thought, if he needed it. His eyes chased the darkness for any sign of Brian. He removed his helmet, tensely scanning what little he could see.

Misha quickly pondered how he'd escape if things went wrong. *Impossible*. There was no telling who else was around, perhaps behind him, or to the sides, hidden, maybe with a night-vision scope aimed at his head.

An outline of a long-coated person emerged a few feet away and slowly approached.

Misha keenly eyed the silhouette with the scrutiny he would give a financial statement. The person didn't appear to have Brian's lean physique. The man was shorter. Wide-framed.

"I am glad you made it, Mikhail," the stranger said in English, his words barely loud enough to be heard over the 175 cubic centimeters of motor belching between Misha's legs.

Misha felt a chill crawl down his spine. That was not Brian, for sure. The Brit had switched to calling Misha by his nickname some months ago, rather than using the more formal "Mikhail."

"Where's Brian?" Misha blurted loudly, his heart now threatening to crush through his sternum. He gripped the handlebars so tightly that his knuckles hurt. He turned it towards the stranger, then flipped on the high beam. "Where is he?"

"Turn off the light!" The man instantly shielded his face with his arm, with only his whitish-gray hair showing, and froze in his tracks. "You have nothing to worry about."

"Who are you?" Misha gripped the throttle tightly, revving it twice as he considered making a run for it.

"Turn it off!" He used his other hand to further cover his face. "Brian sent me instead on short notice." His accent was British, but not completely. Misha sensed a trace of Russian or Ukrainian that was not entirely camouflaged.

Misha switched to his native Ukrainian. "I have very clear instructions only to meet with Brian, and no one else," he said. And this was true. From the very beginning, Brian had told Misha not to trust anyone, and that no one was supposed to meet Misha on Brian's behalf.

"I only speak English," the man said, his voice hardening. He casually crossed the beam of the motorbike's headlight, still covering his face. "And please turn off that light. If you don't, I'll break it."

Misha turned off the headlight as he cast about for an escape plan. "I don't like sudden changes."

"We have our reasons." The man turned briefly to light a cigarette.

"What's your name? Who do you work for?"

"It doesn't matter."

"I will not meet like this again." Misha stared at the stranger's face faintly illuminated by the glowing end of his cigarette the moment he took a long drag.

"It would be easier to talk if you turn off your engine."

Misha reluctantly did so.

"There is no reason to worry." The stranger took a step closer and another drag of his tobacco. "Do you have the materials?"

"Yes." But Misha suddenly realized that if this meeting were a trap, he'd have no leverage after handing over the thumb drive. "I mean, only some of it. The rest is in a safe place—I will give it later." He hoped the man would buy the lie.

The stranger stretched out his hand. "Give it to me."

The hair on the back of Misha's neck stood on end but he struggled to keep his voice steady. "I don't understand what's so urgent. It is just transactions—boring financial records that only people like me appreciate. If Brian can wait a few more days, I will have better information than I do tonight."

The man expelled a deep, smoke-filled laugh and threw down his cigarette. "If we don't have all the information tonight, it might be worthless tomorrow."

Misha breathed in deeply and quickly reminded himself of the money. Brian had been generous. He wasn't about to give that up. He dug into his jacket pocket and retrieved the thumb drive. "They are mostly PDFs and a few spreadsheet files." He dropped it into the man's open palm.

"How much more is missing?"

"This is most of the data I told Brian about. It also shows that money is being diverted to two unknown entities possibly operating in the Exclusion Zone. They may be used for brides, or even unauthorized construction or maintenance projects in the area. As I said, I will need more time to collect the rest."

The man said nothing. He simply glanced at the thumb drive and then closed his fist.

"And my money?"

The man stayed silent.

Despite the cold, Misha felt his armpits grow clammy with sweat. "Brian assured me he would transfer it to my account in Vienna." Misha thought of his mother's surgery, which he'd paid for last time he'd given Brian names and addresses of key engineers at the Chernobyl complex. "You better clear it up with Brian tonight, because I won't accept silence on this issue."

"How much was your arrangement?"

"Five!" Misha said, insulted he'd have to remind this man of the deal. "Five fucking thousand, you hear me?"

"Euros?"

"No, beers." Misha's anger boiled. "Yes, Euros, what do you think?"

The stranger let out what seemed like a chuckle and then crossed his arms, slowly taking a step closer, the sound of crunching branches breaking the dead air. "Not my problem, but I can give you all I have on me now as an advance." He reached into his inside coat pocket, took out and opened a bulky wallet, and pulled out all the banknotes. He folded them once and handed it to Misha. "It's probably just under a thousand. Take it."

Misha cautiously reached for it and slipped the wad of bills into his pants pocket without counting it.

The stranger then stepped back and lit another cigarette. "I will relay the message that there's still an amount we owe you." His tone reeked of insincerity.

The cold fear Misha had sensed the moment he'd come into the forest swept back into his head, tempering his rage. He didn't say anything else, his indignation bottled up by self-preservation. But as he watched the stranger pocket the thumb drive, Misha felt a sense of shame wash over himself as well. He had been accustomed to longer, pleasant chats with Brian, along with the very finest of British civility. A glass of wine, a fine cigar, and even once a game of chess. They'd built a rapport that had comfortably cleansed the soiled reality of an agent-handler relationship. This stranger had exposed the treasonous role Misha had been seduced into playing—a pawn, a mere microscopic cog in a slimy wheel of a major power's espionage machine. And as the stranger turned away, Misha understood that he had very possibly sold out his honor for nothing.

The stranger disappeared into the darkness toward where the car had flashed its lights.

"You're welcome, asshole," Misha mumbled alone as his hands trembled. Before putting on his helmet and turning on his bike's headlight, he scanned the trees, fearing a sniper might be hidden in the dark. He turned on his bike's motor. The pine needles rustled as he revved the engine and headed out of the forest, sweating through the chill of his still-wet clothes.

A long stretch of desolate, rain-soaked roadway in the near pitch-black night is a lonely, scary place when you're on the payroll of a foreign power, betraying your employer—and your country—by turning over official financial records. This sullied truth clung to him like the mud on his motorcycle boots. Misha's heart was still racing as he watched the speedometer needle vibrate over the 100 km/h mark—about as fast as he could go on this battered rural road. The rendezvous bothered him. Had he just been duped? He replayed the stranger's voice in his head. Brian had always reminded Misha of the sensitive nature of his role, something that had to be kept secret from his Ministry—and from anyone else, for that matter.

But if he'd been duped, he'd be dead by now, he surmised. Misha forced his thoughts to slow down. As the distance away from the witches' lair increased, his heartbeat seemed to steady itself. The stranger had broken protocol, but he hadn't harmed or threatened Misha. Indeed, Brian must have sent him. He was now sure of it, and once he was home, he'd message Brian to make sure everything was proper.

The rain beat down as Misha sped up to reach his destination. All he wanted now was to be back in his apartment, in the relative safety of the Exclusion Zone. As he sped along the road, his body shook, the cold heaviness of his soaked clothes nearly unbearable. He squinted, quickly wiping his visor with his gloved hand as he tried to see the road more clearly. There was something ahead. He again wiped with his sleeve.

A wire!

He instantly squeezed the brakes but knew even as he did so that he couldn't stop in time. He slammed into the wire stretched chest-high across the road. A loud snap followed. He flipped backwards, catching a glimpse of his legs flinging upward as he twisted airborne, the bike darting forward from under him. His helmet smashed onto the pavement, the rest of his body following, the impact on his ribs knocking the wind out of him. He rolled four or five or six times before coming to rest in a motionless state.

Misha heard his own rapid panting echo in his helmet, his breaths steaming the cracked visor. The pain hadn't arrived yet, which surprised him. His lungs pumped out short wheezes. The raindrops hammered his helmet. The motorbike's engine whined in the background. But no pain.

No pain because suddenly he realized he couldn't feel a thing below his shoulders. His legs were numb. His arms and hands, too. No pain, no tingling, no cold, no wetness. Nothing. He tried to yell but couldn't push more than faint puffs of air out of his mouth.

His body lay face down on the pavement. He clenched his jaw and turned his head, barely. All he could see was the soaked asphalt through his cloudy, half-shattered visor. The rain continued to hit the pavement, the pelleting sound blending with the bike's engine and his hard breaths. He lay there unable to get up for what felt like ten minutes or more.

Suddenly, the sound of another engine approached from somewhere behind him, and the wet asphalt glowed from a beam of light. A car, he guessed. He heard two doors open and close. The engine idled. His Voskhod suddenly went silent. Muffled voices echoed amid the sounds of rapid footsteps sloshing over the puddled road. Misha tried desperately to move, but every appendage remained numb. He wheezed out a weak cry and jiggled his head back and forth, attempting to bring the vehicle into his line of sight, but to no avail. The drenched pavement was all he could fixate on as he heard what sounded like two or three people pacing nearby. But none came to his aid.

Misha tried again to speak but instead began coughing as warm fluid quickly filled his mouth. It tasted like blood.

The footsteps were now closer. A shadow covered the glowing pavement. He felt his helmet being pulled sideways and upward, violently, until it was completely removed. His face hit the asphalt and a second later he heard his helmet slam to the ground some distance away.

"Help me!" he said faintly in between coughs.

Suddenly an arm bumped his jaw as it reached under his chest. As it pulled back, he saw the hand gripping banknotes—the same cash he'd received in the forest.

"Break his neck," a man then shouted in his native tongue.

Misha coughed out his lungs, realizing they were not rescuing him. They were going to finish him off.

The shadow loomed again into Misha's narrow line of vision.

He screamed, "*Nyet!*"

2

Five weeks later

THE ROTTEN ODOR OF MOLD LINGERED UNPLEASANTLY as Jonathan Brooks swept the debris across the warped parquet floor toward the foyer. What was left of his looted, wind-and-water-damaged second-floor law firm disgusted him. Hurricane Katrina had done its share of the damage three weeks ago—he'd seen the heart-breaking destruction all over the city—but it was the ensuing pillaging that angered him most, even now, as it had a week ago when he'd returned from his death-defying ordeal in Central America.

Looters had taken everything but the heaviest fur-niture, and what they'd left behind they simply broke. For a moment Jonathan thought he'd been lucky. They hadn't burned the place down. But then again, ashes might have been easier on his eyes—a pain he'd already survived once before.

The pile of wreckage sat four feet high near the stairwell. He set the broom down and stared vacantly at the shattered front door, snapped in half and resting against the wall behind the heap. He shook his head, gazing at the foyer's gutted floor and the few ceiling tiles still clinging to the metal frame above him. Two of Amber's cubicle walls were bent beyond repair, and her tabletop was smashed and still decorated with a filthy shoe print from whoever kicked it senselessly. He then realized Amber might return soon, unlike his law partners, and she'd want to get paid for her last week of work before Katrina struck. What would he tell her? He barely had enough money to make it to next month.

He inhaled the acrid air and paced near the entrance. He couldn't see anything remaining of any use. Nothing. His neck stiffened. He clenched a fist. The cost of replacing it all spun in his head. The computers, the printer, the chairs, the fridge, the fax machine. None of it insured. It only further stirred his rage. But there was no one to go after, no souls to exert revenge. And to make matters worse, his two partners were nowhere to be found. He was certain they'd found shelter out of state and just couldn't be bothered to deal with the aftermath. By now, he knew this mess was his alone to clean up.

His cellphone rang. He hustled to his office and grabbed it off his mold-damaged oak desk and answered.

"You okay?"

Jonathan bit his lip. He'd hoped it was Linda, his ex, not his client, Cramer. He didn't want to deal with him now. "I'm at my office again, salvaging what I can."

"Good, you're close," Cramer said, his voice dwarfed by the palpitating sounds of a helicopter coming through the phone.

"Where are you?" Jonathan asked.

"On the river. Come over. I'm heading to Houston tonight, so we need to talk."

"About what?" said Jonathan, playing dumb.

"Your trip, of course."

Jonathan shook his head. "I need more time to decide." He leaned on the window ledge, gazing out the broken frame at the shattered glass scattered on the sidewalk below near a burned-out sedan abandoned at the curb.

"There ain't more time, buddy. You want the gig or not?" Cramer spoke fast. "You need the money, right? So decide. I want a lawyer there by Monday." The helicopter noise faded. "I've waited long enough."

Jonathan thought of Linda. She was supposed to pass through New Orleans this week, but he hadn't heard from her despite his half-dozen calls. He couldn't imagine jetting off to Europe now without seeing her. Not after everything they'd been through separately and together, and certainly not after she'd finally seemed to have gained the strength to tackle their troubled past head-on. And Jonathan fully understood that her past troubles ultimately came as a result of his choices.

"I need an answer! There're plenty other hungry lawyers, Jonathan."

"I hear you."

Cramer was right. Jonathan knew his legal practice was all but dead, except for this one client—Cramer Banks—extending him a lifeline, but an iffy one at best.

Cramer had already loaned Jonathan a car and some money the moment he'd returned to New Orleans, but he'd gone one step farther by throwing Jonathan a bone: a four-thousand-dollar cash advance, use of a corporate credit card and a chance to make Cramer richer with a potentially lucrative business deal in Ukraine. And a wealthier, happier client meant he'd get paid, though perhaps just enough to cover the basics for four or five months.

"Jonathan!" Cramer barked. "Are you in or out?"

"I'm thinking."

Like all good things, there was a catch. Jonathan would meet with unknown Ukrainian businessmen in hopes a deal would percolate; and if it looked that way, only then would Jonathan begin to pay Cramer back for the advance by billing his normal—and already heavily discounted—hourly rate. But that bone represented just about all the billable work Jonathan could chew on in the foreseeable future. And with his damaged, boarded-up home his only remaining asset, things couldn't look much bleaker. He needed money, and fast. And if the deal worked out, he could collect a lot more after he paid off the advance. The dusty damp air filtered through his lungs as he scanned his ransacked office. A sense of gratitude for Cramer's offer came back to him as he pondered a response.

"Meet me now," Cramer again spat out. "Or I'll call Hansberry."

"Oh god," Jonathan putted. "That creep—he'll screw you."

"I doubt it. He's starving, like all you lawyers."

"Uh-huh." Jonathan spotted a large military helicopter skimming the adjacent rooftops, heading over downtown, the deep whine of turbines shattering the stillness of the street. He rubbed his bristly cheeks, the image of Linda still permeating his thoughts—her silky, straight dark blond hair, her effervescent smile. He couldn't put off a response any longer. "Where exactly are you?"

"Riverwalk, aboard the *Iwo Jima*?"

"What?"

"I'm in a command center, aboard the ship. It's docked alongside the mall."

Jonathan remembered spotting the Navy ship two days earlier easing along the Mississippi, past the riverbank in Algiers, across the river from the French Quarter. He checked his watch. "Fine. Give me thirty minutes."

"Smart man." Cramer chuckled. "Head to the checkpoint at the end of Notre Dame Street. I'll leave your name with the guardsmen." He hung up.

Jonathan wasn't sure he'd just made the right choice. He needed to see Linda. But he also needed money. He picked up the broom and continued sweeping, this time harder, thrusting forward the filth and debris, his grip tight, his heart pounding. He swept. And swept. His eyes fixated on the mess. And then he stopped, shook his head and dropped the broom, feeling a sudden surge of hopelessness.

His despair still weighed him down as he lifted a large plywood panel over the front doorway and secured a padlock into a metal clasp on the left and right edges of the frame. And the heavy anxiety accompanied him down the stairs, as he turned the corner toward the last set of steps, when suddenly he heard sounds of crunching glass echo from below. He slowed, leaning forward as he cautiously peered down the stairs at the entrance that once had a glass door.

A shadow cut through the bright light coming from the street. He squinted and then froze in his tracks. "Linda?" he said, nearly gasping.

"Yes," Linda uttered tepidly, her shadowy silhouette stepping forward into the tiny atrium, crushing more glass with her platforms. "I went by the house first," she said with a staleness that felt like a splash of ice water."

"Why didn't you call?"

She shook her head. "Long story."

"I called, left messages, I don't understand." His heart dropped. He'd hoped for something different. A kinder greeting, perhaps. Something more in line with the words he'd heard her say on the phone that day he'd returned from Venezuela. Since then, on those lonely nights in his destroyed city, he'd even imagined her running into his arms, her lips pressed hard on his, with words of hope and rebuilding and strength and solace. But no.

She shrugged.

He looked down, feeling a chill that pierced bone-deep despite the chokingly balmy air.

"It's nice to see you," he said, concealing his disappointment. But her presence still comforted him, if not her words. An ex-wife should not be relied upon for emotional support, he tried to rationalize quietly. She was the one who'd left. She was the one who'd given up. But she was the one he needed the most.

She stood there, gazing at him analytically as he slowly descended the last few steps. He glanced at her slender legs, her hips. She wore a dark skirt suit. She'd lightened her hair and was wearing long curls. He wondered how she was able to look so well-groomed compared to everyone else, most of whom didn't have electricity, running water, or basic supplies. But he didn't ask.

He sighed. "I'd invite you up, but it's quite messy."

She returned a sedate smile. "I don't want to interrupt you, if you've got work."

He threw his hands in the air and half-smiled. "Does it look like I can welcome clients?"

She scanned the debris at her feet. "I suppose not."

He reminded himself it had been almost a year since he'd last met up with her. "I've really needed to see you." He looked into her calming eyes. "I've seen two of your broadcasts. Very well done."

"The ones from Biloxi?"

"Yes. Reporting is in your blood. You do it so well. I'm so thrilled for you that you're back, doing what you love. Back on your own two feet."

"Thanks, but it feels a bit odd after so long." She crossed her arms. "Anyway, I just wanted to come by, you know, to...to make sure you're okay." Her smile withered.

"Let's have dinner tonight and talk."

"Actually, I'm...leaving."

"You just got here."

"I landed something big—a great opportunity."

Jonathan started to feel his chest constrict. "What do you mean?"

"I'm headed to China for some freelance projects."

"China? But you've done so well here with your post-Katrina coverage. Every news channel in town will want you back. Why not continue your work here?"

"It's the big leagues, Jonathan. I'm riding a streak of good luck—I still can't believe it."

"But we haven't..." Jonathan felt his heart skipping. "I've been dying to see you for so long. I've gone through a lot of shit, Linda. I haven't yet told you everything that happened to me here and in Central America." He took a step toward her and reached for her hand, which she limpidly surrendered.

"I understand, but I'm on a roll now. I don't know how long it will last, so I can't pause. There isn't enough strength in me to think, to feel, to do other things except ride this wave."

He shook his head. "I love you, Linda. I want to make it work again. I want to give us another go—"

"Please, Jonathan." She pulled her hand away and stepped back over more broken glass. "Let's not go down this path. I'm not ready for anything like that. Only what I'm doing now."

Jonathan ran his hand through his hair. "Which is escaping."

"Maybe, but with my career reenergized; it'll help me find direction."

"When are you back from China?"

She shrugged. "Not sure yet. The gigs may lead to other work there. What about you? What are you doing for work?"

"I've been offered something temporary in Europe. It's all I've got for now." He didn't want to let her change the topic. He began to sense a toxic anxiety overcome him. "Please, we should take some time to talk. You said you would when we spoke by phone. What's changed?"

"I need time. Part of me is on auto-pilot. I wasted a lot of time up north, disturbed, drinking myself to no end. I've finally broken free from that black hole." She stepped back, turning to head out.

"Linda, wait." Jonathan's heart sank. His lips began to quiver. How could this woman slip away? He scrambled for the right words to say, but he felt too weak for more pain.

She turned when she reached the sidewalk. "Do what you need to do, and let's give us time."

"We've been apart for years, for Christ's sake. How much more time is there to give?"

Her vacant gaze pierced him like a dagger. "You have no choice." She crossed her arms. "We can't force things to happen. They can only come if the time is right, and now it isn't. Trust me. I needed to see you. But we both have huge challenges to deal with before we can even think about having something to offer each other."

"I...I simply thought..." His chest constricted to a point where he found it hard to breathe.

"Please, Jonathan, be realistic. I will call you when I'm back in the States. I promise. I have your new numbers. And here's how you can reach me." She handed him her card.

He watched her walk away. "I love you," he shouted. He fought not to cry, but the pain was ripping him apart to a point of nausea. "I really love you," he said, his voice shaking. "I don't care how far away you go, I'll be here for you, dammit. I will wait for you."

She turned briefly, flashing a soft smile.

Jonathan gazed at her until she turned the corner onto Magazine Street.

*   *   *

As if the pain from Linda's short visit wasn't enough to make him feel queasy, the eight-minute walk east along Julia Street also turned Jonathan's stomach. The piles of litter—and the deathly stench that came with it—had yet to be cleaned up. Storefront after storefront displayed the cruelty that humanity can unleash when law and order collapse. These weren't food stores or restaurants. No, the destruction wasn't about survival. It was malice. A bookstore. A shoe repair shop. A florist. An electronics store. That's what differentiated criminals from survivors.

He reached the National Guard checkpoint at the edge of the large parking lot facing the Riverwalk mall. The tall antenna mast of the *Iwo Jima* rising above the mall was all he could see of the ship. But there wasn't a maritime lawyer who didn't know the size of these seagoing beasts.

Once the soldiers checked his name off a clipboard and waved him on, he walked across the lot, which was mostly empty but for a scattering of military vehicles on one side, opposite the famous Whale mural—an ironic reminder that water in parts of New Orleans had indeed reached high above ground.

The Navy's amphibious ship USS *Iwo Jima* was gigantic. It was docked alongside the Riverwalk, whose floor-to-ceiling windows were shattered, with debris strewn across the vacant restaurants and stores that faced the Mississippi.

He cleared another checkpoint and walked the bridge leading into a doorway on the ship's starboard side. A crewman escorted him one deck up and through a series of doors, and into a large, darkened room filled with large flat screen monitors and manned consoles. He presumed it was the command center Cramer had mentioned on the call.

Jonathan heard his name as Cramer appeared from behind him sporting a greasy mop of hair, a drenched t-shirt, and shorts and sandals.

"You look like you're heading to a beach bar."

Cramer laughed and lightly punched Jonathan's chest. "I wish. I've been working all night making sure my corporate fleet and aircraft are available for the ongoing relief effort. So, are you up to the task?"

Jonathan wished he still had a reason to stay in New Orleans as he replayed Linda's gaze, her words, the pain of her cruelly short visit. The rejection. The lost hope. He'd analyzed her every word on his walk to the Riverwalk. He felt betrayed. He cocked his head back and gazed at Cramer. "Yes, I'm ready."

"Good. I'm also sending Kevin Wyatt, my Chief Technology Officer. And you'll also work with a local

law firm I've hired—they're top notch, and expensive."
He put his hand on Jonathan's shoulder. "Despite this
mess here in New Orleans, I can't let a good business
opportunity fizzle, no matter how far away it is. You'll
represent me in these early talks—and keep local counsel honest—and the moment the other party gives the
green light to negotiate an agreement, then you can bill
me for that work going forward."

"What's it about?"

"Software. They're bringing something to the table
that can make us the leaders in logistics data management. Imagine for a moment that seventy or eighty or
even ninety percent of all industrial components and
finished products being transported worldwide would
be tagged and tracked during transit, and then monitored
once purchased and in use. It can revolutionize the way
we consumers interact with the things we buy and use."

"But you've got competitors aiming for the same
thing."

"I know. But that's why these Ukrainians can help
us leapfrog into a dominant position, well ahead of the
pack."

"Why aren't you going, too?"

Cramer nodded in the direction of a uniformed officer at
the far end the command center. "I promised him I'd help
out."

"Who is he?"

"Vice Admiral Rosewood—a childhood buddy of
mine. I'm using both my corporate aircraft to shuttle
special surgical teams from San Antonio and Austin
to here, and I'm sending my fleet of trucks to bring

electrical equipment, generators and other supplies down from Shreveport. Lots to do." Cramer dug his index finger into Jonathan's chest. "You'll be my eyes and ears in Kyiv. You know what questions to ask. I trust you'll keep my business interests safe."

They headed up two decks, where they were greeted by a Navy crewman, who said to Cramer, "Sir, we're ready for you."

Cramer nodded and turned to Jonathan. "I'm off to the airport now. My assistant will drop off your advance."

"Let's call it a personal loan," Jonathan interrupted.

"Fine. And she'll also give you the corporate credit card and your flight information. Good luck." He gave a thumbs-up and turned.

The crewman opened a large metal door that instantly let in the bright daylight and loud noise of a helicopter. Jonathan leaned out of the opening and saw Cramer keep pace with another crewman as they headed across the flight deck to a waiting Navy chopper. Seconds later Cramer was airborne, the aircraft swooping over the mall.

The instructions were clear. This gave him a sense of direction and purpose after his encounter with Linda had filled him with despair. But it wasn't just her, of course. Everything suddenly began to roll in. The crimson stained corpses he'd witnessed firsthand in the Katrina-ravaged streets of his city; a murdered man in Caracas' crime-filled *barrio* of Petare; the cadavers on the ship he'd raided in the Panama Canal. So much upheaval. So many moments when his life could have ended up like those others. This was still all too vivid. Too disturbing to simply vanish because of Cramer's generous offer of work.

Jonathan closed his eyes, but the chaotic raw images trampled in uncontrollably. The mental relapse made his heart race. His face began to sweat. And now he thought of what might await him in Europe. He was in debt to Cramer with no way to pay him back if he failed in his role. But for now, that's all he had. He briefly pondered the predicament of other New Orleans lawyers he knew, some of whom had no doubt left the state in search of work. He suddenly felt damned fortunate. By the time he'd left the *Iwo Jima* and was back on Julia Street, he was firmly focused on Cramer's project. Come what may in Kyiv, it would be good to get back to work, and the sooner, the better.

3

Washington, D.C.

MAJOR LANE BARCLAY DIDN'T KNOW WHAT ALL THE fuss was about when he'd received an urgent cable from SIS (MI6) headquarters in Vauxhall an hour earlier demanding that he be available for a call at exactly eleven-thirty. He stood by the windows of his second-floor embassy office, gazing at parked cars along the tree-lined Observatory Circle. The cryptic message gave no clue as to who would call nor for what purpose, a strange absence of detail that made him edgy. He glanced at the Union Jack clock on the wall and waited, pacing by the window.

The secure line on his desk phone rang on time. He stayed standing, leaned over to grab the handset. "Barclay here."

"Hello, Major. I take it you got the heads-up," the voice said, and not a second later Barclay recognized it: Sir

Wallace Carrington, Chief of SIS—head of Britain's foreign intelligence services.

Barclay swallowed hard as a sudden rush of questions filled his head, and asked, as calmly as he could, "How may I be of assistance?"

"Yes, just a moment." The sound of turning pages came through the line.

Barclay had heard an SIS Chief's voice live only three times before in his fifteen-year career in intelligence. With the long pause, Barclay's flash of questions quickly settled on one: Am I about to be fired? What other possible reason would there be for a call outside the normal chain of command? And from the Chief himself? Especially when nothing out of the ordinary had come through the cables. No imminent terror threats. No unexpected military deployments. No belligerent moves by rival intel services.

His mind went straight to the enjoyments of his post: Sitting in the hive of global intelligence activity that was the Maryland-D.C.-Northern Virginia corridor. The cocktails, the banquets, the dinners with the inner-circle that mattered most in the Beltway: Washington's security elites, both private and government. The large, comfortable ranch house in Alexandria that he'd called home for the past six years. This could not possibly end, not so soon. His heart raced with the uneasy silence on the line. "Sir?" He held his breath. His hands began to feel clammy.

"Yes, yes, Major. Sorry. I'm just thinking how we can best handle this."

"Handle what, sir, if I may ask?"

"A sensitive matter—quite troubling, in fact. As uncomfortable as this makes me feel, I need you to run it by our American friends."

"Of course..." Barclay suddenly sensed the chill in his body dissipate. His job was safe, so it seemed. He felt a bit foolish for worrying.

"Check your inbox shortly for details. You are not to discuss this with anyone on this side of the pond, other than me and the members of my staff who'll be copied. Is that clear?"

"Absolutely, sir. May I ask what this pertains to?"

Lord Carrington paused, his slow, noisy breaths coming through clearly over the phone. Several breaths followed without accompanying words.

"Sir?"

The chief vented a long sigh and then said, "Seems we may have a bloody mole."

Barclay tilted his head. "I see."

"Either in SIS or the Foreign Office—possibly in our embassy in Kyiv." Carrington's voice hardened. "And we've lost a vital local asset."

"Who, if I may ask?"

"An accountant who somehow found it pressing to wander off in the countryside in the middle of the night, in a rainstorm, before crashing his motorcycle."

"Dead?"

"Yes, a broken neck. It's all in the file."

"Foul play?"

"Not sure, but evidence may point that way. And he was due to provide our handler something valuable, Barclay. Very valuable indeed."

"I understand," he said, though there was little to go by.

"Bottom line, Barclay, there are some very upset people here worried about this, and they're breathing down my back. Worse yet, they're pointing fingers our way. I want to make sure we didn't botch this. We're running this investigation outside of SIS, GCHQ or the Foreign Office—at least for now. I realize this is quite unorthodox, but can I count on your assistance?"

"Certainly, sir." A tinge of excitement crept into Barclay's voice. "I'll reach out to our most trusted channel." The opportunity to please Carrington would go far to helping Barclay get what he wanted most: another three-year extension to his D.C. posting. The exhilaration was now bubbling.

"Just get it done, quickly, quietly. And keep me informed every few days, will you?"

"Of course."

Some thirty minutes later, Barclay had skimmed through the materials he'd been sent. There was lots to read—too much, in fact. He wanted to get things started. He dialed his key contact at CIA and hastily arranged a meeting.

Barclay left the British Embassy in his black Ford Taurus and soon arrived at F Street and 14th, a block east of the Hotel Washington, where his contact had stepped away from a luncheon. His windows half-down, Barclay observed the sidewalk from his rearview mirror for a few minutes, until he spotted George Porter's bulky six-foot-three frame and dark skin, dressed in an elegant grey suit, walking unhurriedly his way.

The door on the passenger side opened.

"Twice in two weeks," George said, plopping down in the seat and shutting the door. "One might think we're pals." He unbuttoned his jacket and loosened his tie.

Barclay quickly recalled the first time he'd looked into Porter's wide-set eyes and dark-skinned face a decade earlier, when the American was temporarily assigned to a joint UK-US operations cell created in the wake of 9/11. They'd occasionally stayed in touch in the ensuing years of heightened British-US intelligence collaboration. Barclay even considered him a friend of sorts, to the extent intelligence officials of allied nations can.

"Are we at the point of sharing toothpaste?" Barclay said, chuckling, referring to President Bush's awkward comment about sharing the same with Tony Blair.

"Sure, but not floss," George replied, rolling up his window. "So, what's so urgent?"

Barclay pulled away from the curb and weaved into traffic, heading east. "A small problem in Kyiv."

Porter raised a brow. "I get edgy whenever you preface the word 'problem' with the word 'small', given our most recent matters."

Barclay shrugged, took a sip of his iced tea, his eyes never leaving the road. "Seems we have one dead Ukrainian asset and his local embassy handler is missing."

"That's it?" Porter raised his chin and tilted his head. "The crowd is booing, Barclay. I was anticipating fireworks."

"This appears serious. Really. We'd like your people to task the Ukrainian's phone numbers through OCTAVE, for starters. Parse through all his text messages, emails, GPS-location data, metadata, content—the whole lot."

"Why not tap NSA directly for this?"

Barclay sighed. "I'm afraid my request is a bit out of the ordinary—and rather delicate." He shared the information he'd been given, though he attempted to package it in the most uncontroversial way, so his American colleague would simply agree to help without his usual cross-examination. He also censored what he assumed Lord Carrington would not want divulged to the CIA. Most importantly, he reminded Porter not to speak of this matter with anyone at GCHQ—Britain's NSA equivalent—nor any of the other Five-Eyes intel partners, that is, Canada, Australia, and New Zealand.

Porter puckered his lips with his fingers, his eyes examining Barclay. "Should I have reason to worry as well?"

"No, it's strictly internal—UK interests only. Nothing whatsoever with your country. My chaps assure me of this."

Porter raised his brow, clearly not fully convinced.

Barclay decided to spill more details. "Our informant kept tabs on a Ukrainian government procurement program, and MI6 was tasked to ensure competing bidders stay on a level playing field."

Porter grinned. "Uh-huh, Her Majesty's services coming to the rescue of a UK company, I presume?"

"Yes," he replied with a sigh. "Need I remind you, George, that the CIA wrote that playbook long ago."

The American chuckled. "What's the procurement for?"

"The new sarcophagus over the damaged Chernobyl reactor. We're up against Canadians, French, and Italians—no Americans, sorry to say."

"Good for us. I can't see any sane person wanting to irradiate themselves for money."

"Apparently, we Brits are salivating at the chance." Barclay reached back under Porter's seat and handed him a large manila envelope. "Here, everything you need to know about the fellow—a certain Mikhail Zhuk, who most often goes by his nickname 'Misha.' He's a senior finance manager with Ukraine's Ministry of Internal Affairs. He'd been assigned to the Chernobyl Shelter Fund work in an audit role and was feeding us mostly mundane things on a consistent basis. Recently, however, he hinted at finding something quite disturbing. He didn't live long enough to share it."

Porter flipped open the envelope over his lap and fingered through a loose-leaf ten-page document, the third page of which included an image of Misha's passport identification page. "What's your timeline?"

"Yesterday."

"And Misha's handler?"

"Brian Fletcher—working at the embassy under diplomatic cover as a low-level political officer. Fairly normal background and career. Nothing unusual for his level. But he's gone missing. We're holding off on issuing any Red Notices at the moment. I'll need further clearance to share anything more about him."

"Fine, I'll see what I can do."

"I need this fast. Days, not weeks."

Porter sighed and shook his head. "Why are you asking this of me. You've got a wide array of resources in your toolbox."

Barclay suspected Porter had other things on his plate, including preparing for his upcoming move to London, a perk that came with his recent promotion.

"Yes, but our TEMPORA and HACIENDA programs have their limits. Besides, I've been told to keep GCHQ and MI6 out of this, and you can use NSA's Tailored Access teams far more smoothly than we can—and I hear they recently scored big in Ukraine."

"Is that right?"

"Yes, they've drilled lots of new holes in the Yushchenko government plumbing, if you will."

Porter frowned, perhaps mockingly. "I'll look into it."

"You should know all this, since you work closely with them. Word is they've also penetrated Ukrtelecom's backbone and servers like a sarcoma, as well as a whole range of government servers in Kyiv and other cities. And I'm sure there's plenty of data to pick using BLARNEY and BULLRUN. You boys have been harvesting Ukrainian banking data, diplomatic cables, and military communications for years. There's no one more able to find what we're looking for than you Yanks."

"I'll get started on this today." Porter checked his watch and glanced out the windshield. "It's best that I get off here and grab a cab."

Barclay pulled over.

Porter got out, turned and leaned back into the car. "One caveat: if your request raises red flags, I may not be able to deliver."

"It won't." But Barclay suddenly worried that Lord Carrington may have not shared with him everything, perhaps things the Americans would find objectionable. Barring that, however, he'd likely get something back from Porter within days, since he was usually quite thorough and fast.

Five days later in Kyiv, Ukraine

THE SPEEDY STRETCH OF HIGHWAY THE CAB HAD TAKEN
from Boryspil Airport had soon slowed to a crawl in the
morass of Kyiv's afternoon rush-hour. The driver took
what he claimed was a shortcut, squealing the tires as
he brusquely weaved his abused Slavuta sedan through
narrow, sloping streets, twice nearly taking out a pedes-
trian. Shortcut or not, it had taken a full hour to drive the
twenty or so miles from the terminal to the hotel.

Jonathan felt exhausted, and for good reason. He'd
had a delayed connection in New York, followed by the
long transatlantic flight in a cramped coach class seat,
and a five-hour layover in Paris before flying the last
leg of his journey to the Ukrainian capital. He simply
craved a bed.

He hustled through the hotel's dark, rundown lobby
with its worn, black faux-leather chairs and sofas and

other dated furnishings that were doubtless leftovers from Soviet days.

After check-in, the bellman, with Jonathan's suitcase in hand, led the way to a fourth-floor room, where the door opened with the loud squeaking sound that a mouse might make if were being skinned. The man dropped the bag on the tattered parquet and lazily reached for the curtains at the lone window, pulling them aside and pushing the window open. The cloud of dust that flew into the air told Jonathan no guest had stayed in this room in a while.

The diesel-scented breeze filled Jonathan's lungs.

"Mr. Brooks, your view," the bellman said proudly, as if it might compensate for the room's unglamorous interior.

Jonathan gazed out at a vast square featuring many fountains and large glass domes rising out of the concrete.

"Maidan Nezalezhnosti—Independence Square— our city's most famous open area," the bellman added. "We simply call it Maidan."

"What are the domes?"

"A shopping center, under the ground."

Jonathan pointed at a massive building at the other end of the square. Its Stalin-era façades reminded him of structures he'd seen in Moscow. "And that building?"

"Hotel Ukrayina," the young man said softly. "It was called Hotel Moscow before."

Jonathan remembered seeing an ad for the five-star hotel in the airplane magazine during his flight into Kyiv.

The bellman frowned and put his hands in his pockets. "You will like our hotel more. It is warmer, special."

"Uh-huh," Jonathan muttered as he scanned his surroundings: adjacent single beds, thin pillows, a 1980s vintage television and an old radio almost the size of a microwave. "Yeah, special."

Jonathan tipped him and closed the window. All that mattered to him were the essentials: a bed and a bathroom. He instantly thought of the battered and boarded-up homes in New Orleans. Vivid images came to mind, like the letters and numbers spray-painted by emergency responders on the front doors of dwellings to indicate survivors and deaths. He suddenly was thankful for this simple room, despite the lack of amenities. It was safe. It had running water. Electricity. No sirens. No gunfire. No look and feel of a war zone.

Jonathan quickly dialed Cramer. "I'm here in Kyiv," he told him.

"Kevin Wyatt's on his stop-over in London," Cramer said. "He'll head to the law firm directly from the airport."

"I look forward to meeting him." Jonathan quickly understood Kevin was someone he'd have to please to get a deal going.

"He's the brains behind my business. He's not only our CTO and Vice President of Strategy, he's also the innovator behind our prized proprietary algorithms and source code, especially VASTLINK. So, let him talk about whatever he wants."

Jonathan knew a bit about VASTLINK, a web-based global tracking and information service that South Seas

Logistics had spent a ton of money developing. In fact, Jonathan had worked on a commercial lease in Shreveport, where the system's main data center was located.

"You'll like him—he's very smart, very techie," Cramer said before they hung up.

Eventually travel fatigue caught up with Jonathan, and he drifted into a restless sleep, his head flat on the pillow, as he pushed his disappointment over Linda and anxiety about their future from his thoughts.

A jingling sound echoed in the darkness. Keys on a keychain, it seemed. And faint footsteps accompanied by voices. Deep voices. Men. Speaking what sounded like an Asian language. The sounds filtered through the obscurity. Jonathan felt sweat on his palms. His neck. *Where am I?* His eyes chased the dense night in the direction of the sound. Somehow, he sensed he was asleep but couldn't wake up. *It's not real.* The jingling was indeed keys. A metal-on-metal clang told him a key had found a lock. The door. Ahead of him. Jonathan held his breath, his chest tightening. The bolt snapped loudly, and instantly, bright flashlights sliced wild arcs through the darkness as the door abruptly flung open.

Jonathan covered his eyes with his arm and sprang up, gasping for air. He was now awake. It was but a nightmare. He was safe.

*   *   *

A loud ringing yanked Jonathan out of his sleep. He abruptly reached over the nightstand, grabbing the handset but dropping the phone.

"Allo, Mr. Brooks?" an accented voice announced.

He rubbed his eyes and placed the phone back where it was. "Yes." Jonathan glanced at the glowing red numbers of the vintage quartz alarm clock. It was eight-thirty.

"*Pryvit.* I am Vanko," the man said, sounding too damn cheerful.

"You're early."

"Yes, no problem. I wait here when you are ready, then take you to office."

Jonathan took a deep breath, stretched out of bed and did his best to get ready quickly.

At nine-fifteen he was in the lobby, wearing his best suit with his favorite navy-blue tie that Linda had given him.

Vanko turned to Jonathan and dropped the newspaper he'd been reading onto a chair. He looked more like a bodyguard than a driver: broad shoulders, bulky arms and chest, shaved head, puffy neck with serpent-like tattoos on two sides, and a stumped uneven nose that told Jonathan it had been broken more than once. "I take you now."

Vanko got into the driver's seat and took out what appeared to be a dash-cam from the glove compartment and clipped it to a windshield mount under the rearview mirror.

"For fun?" Jonathan asked.

The Ukrainian chuckled. "No, insurance. In this country, video is only truth if you have accident, because police lie. Drivers lie. People in the street lie. Even our animals lie." He abruptly drove out of the parking spot and at the next block merged into a wide boulevard. "And in your city, no camera?"

"Right now in New Orleans, a dash-cam would show a place that looks more like Baghdad."

Vanko whipped his head back at Jonathan, his eyes wide open. "You are from there? The crazy hurricane?"

Jonathan nodded. "Yes," he said, "and it will be a long time before we recover."

*   *   *

At ten-thirty sharp, Jonathan was sipping tea alone, gazing out tall windows of a third-floor conference room, admiring a light blue, two-story rococo style building across the cobbled street.

"It's the Romanian Embassy," an accented woman's voice came from behind him.

"Ah, quite nice," Jonathan said, turning to her.

"I'm Elya Savchuk," she said, holding the door half-open. "I'll be back shortly with Mr. Soykis. Apologies for the delay." She wore a black light wool blazer and matching skirt that covered her long legs to her knees.

"No worries," Jonathan said with a smile and returned to face the quiet, tree-lined Mykhaila Kotsyubyns'koho Street.

He finished his tea, sat down and observed the room. The centerpiece was a long and wide live-edge conference table. It was dark-stained, edged in bark, probably maple or walnut, Jonathan guessed, and given its size, he was sure it had been hoisted in through the windows. And the eight dark leather chairs seemed to be the latest design in ergonomics. Two silver-framed cubism paintings hung on the wall. Their bold colors, mostly shades of yellow and red, were livened further by the bright sunlight that flooded the room.

Jonathan had always believed that the place where one negotiates makes a difference. A venue has a subtle influence on behavior, perhaps not in a quantifiable way, but some effect nonetheless. The furniture's sedate earth tones and sophisticated simplicity, the clean white walls and high ceiling, and the spacious windows collectively radiated a certain tranquility—like the cozy feel of an expensive country home. In fact, everything he'd seen of the boutique law firm since stepping off the elevator looked sleek, spotless, and pricey. Exactly what Cramer had told him to expect.

Soykis & Kharenko catered to wealthy foreign clients who were venturing into Ukraine's burgeoning free market and wasn't afraid to charge fees comparable to those of larger German, UK and American law firms that had recently established beachheads in Kyiv.

Ivan Soykis finally walked in, dressed in a charcoal suit and bright orange tie. He briskly made his way around the table toward his American guest.

"Welcome to our city," he said, reaching out to shake Jonathan's hand. "Pleasure to meet you."

"Likewise," Jonathan replied. "Your English is excellent."

"Thank you," he said, shrugging. "I suppose my three years in Manchester did me some good."

Soykis was a slender, youthful man of fifty with the only hint of his true age being the salt and pepper hair, but the gray was so faint it appeared air-brushed with surgical precision. Otherwise, his fair-skinned complexion and chiseled jaw line and cheeks put him in his late thirties.

"Please help yourself," Soykis said, as an assistant brought in a bowl of fruit and small tray of pastries which she set on the long, bleached wood cabinet." He took a seat next to Jonathan. "I've heard many good things about you, Mr. Brooks."

"Call me Jonathan, please."

The Ukrainian lawyer handed him his business card. Jonathan reached into his pocket and gave him his. *If only he knew*, Jonathan mused to himself as images of his fully-looted, debris-filled, shell of a law office back home popped in his mind. Soykis studied his card before slipping it into his pocket.

"New Orleans," Soykis said sedately, "I understand you've been through a difficult time. It was all over the news here."

"Yes, difficult...but we'll make it," Jonathan hoped Cramer had not told him too much, like the fact that he no longer had a functioning law firm.

"Is Mr. Wyatt not with you?"

"No, Kevin's flying in as we speak." Jonathan checked his watch. "He should have landed by now." He was looking forward to his arrival.

Elya walked in and nodded, taking the seat next to Soykis, and also exchanging cards with Jonathan. She, too, was a lawyer.

Jonathan refilled his tea and began thinking about the task at hand.

"I must say that Cramer has told me very little about these negotiations," Jonathan said.

"I assure you, we have received a fraction of the information we are accustomed to knowing before stepping into such initial meetings."

How typical of Cramer, Jonathan thought. He'd hoped at least that his long-time client had given more details to the local lawyers. Unfortunately, that wasn't the case. "As I understand it, Cramer had casual discussions with ScorpionCloud about collaborating with our freight tracking software, and perhaps more broadly with our other software-as-a-service offerings."

Soykis shrugged. "That's about all we know."

"Who's on the other side?"

"Huh." Soykis leaned back in his chair and scratched his jaw. "Ultimately, at the top of their food chain is Bodrov—Oleg Bodrov, a former Communist bureaucrat who was both lucky and devious, and now there aren't many Ukrainians who don't know his name."

"He's their attorney?"

"No, their client," Soykis said, his voice diminishing into a sigh. "One of the wealthiest companies here, which also makes him among the richest men in Ukraine."

"New money or old?"

Soykis chuckled, his brows raised. "There's no old money here. The smart ones took advantage of independence in 1991 and aggressively made their millions. They are all nouveaux riches. Among the many titles Bodrov holds, he's chairman—and the largest shareholder—of PMZ, Poltavskyy Mashynobudivnyy

Zavod, Poltava Engineering Works, probably the largest engineering company in Eastern Europe. And he's driven their expansion into other sectors, namely consumer electronics, nuclear energy, hydroelectricity, wind power, and most recently, software. ScorpionCloud is their latest venture, but we're not very familiar with it. Apparently Bodrov's son, Artem, heads it."

"Privately held?"

"PMZ is public, but many of these side ventures, including ScorpionCloud, are private with some form of ownership or investment from PMZ. And I must warn you, privately held companies in this country have nearly zero transparency."

Jonathan had dealt with foreign corporate structures in his past, having represented maritime shipping companies, many of which had affiliates registered in Europe, Africa and South America, though no dealings in Eastern Europe, which had since the '90s become known in many business circles as the Wild East.

"Artem Bodrov will probably attend in person today."

"With his A-team?"

Soykis grimaced. "Yes, they are good lawyers, I suppose. All Ukrainian but, ironically, working for the American powerhouse, Baker Sutton."

"Isn't it a bit unusual for a local company to choose a U.S. firm?"

"They're only using them for deals with foreign entities. For everything else, I think they simply bully their way without the need for lawyers."

Jonathan smiled. Definitely the Wild East. "And Artem?"

Soykis leaned into Jonathan and whispered, "An asshole, I'm told, but..." His voice trailed off for a moment. "Regardless, he's a businessman first and foremost. He wants money like we want oxygen, so we have to listen carefully and act prudently."

"I believe Cramer only wants a joint-venture or some sort of licensing arrangement, nothing more—no takeover, no transfer of assets or intellectual property, nothing that would be deemed an interest in Southern Seas Logistics. And if you know Cramer, he's a good, honest man who doesn't like rulebreakers, and doesn't play loosely with his money."

"Good." Soykis bowed his head. "That's the kind of client we prefer."

Forty-five minutes later, the other side's lawyers arrived and took their seats across the table from Jonathan's team, having made brief introductions and a bit of small talk. Last to arrive was Artem, some twenty-five minutes late. He quickly shook hands with the hosts, muttered his name in a raspy voice, and plopped in a chair between his two lawyers, without apologizing for his tardiness.

Artem was chunky, with puffy hands and a round, youthful, clean-shaven face and eyebrows that looked professionally groomed. He was impeccably dressed. Jonathan guessed his tailored dark blue suit cost more than all of those worn in the room combined. His jacket had gold round buttons with what looked like a diamond at the center of each.

"I take it we all speak English," Jonathan said, breaking the silence.

"Yes, of course," Artem said. His was thickly accented but understandable.

Jonathan looked at Artem's business card. To the left of the company name was a design of a black scorpion with its stinger whipped forward in a fighting stance. "What does...*khmarnykh obchyslen* mean?" Jonathan asked, pointing to the Cyrillic words under the logo.

"So, you read Russian, Mr. Brooks?" Artem said with a hint of mockery.

"No, no, but I can decipher most of your alphabet." Jonathan had thought it might break the ice.

"It means cloud computing, though we do much more than that."

"And *Mag*?" Jonathan said, reading again in Cyrillic what he thought was Artem's title printed below his name.

Artem burst into a hearty laugh, the air seeming to spew from his well-rounded belly. "It means 'magician.' That's my role in all my businesses, just like my father. We make things happen when everyone else is plagued by pessimism, risk aversion and incompetence—inconvenient leftovers from our Soviet days."

Jonathan quickly realized this man had profound mastery of English grammar, far more than most Louisianans, though somehow Artem had not been able to cure his heavy accent.

"Then let's make more magic today," Soykis said lightheartedly. "Perhaps we can start with your initial expectations for today's meeting."

Artem returned only a swift glance at Soykis, his eyes then straying back to Jonathan. He leaned his elbows

over the table, pursed his lips and said, "We are interested in VASTLINK." He then reclined into his chair, his
eyes never leaving Jonathan's. "Your new RFID tools
and management software are very interesting. So are
your advanced user interfaces and your data processing
capabilities. From what we can tell, VASTLINK is an
impressive system, though, I must say, we have discovered numerous cybersecurity weaknesses. Anyway,
we've mentioned to Mr. Banks some months ago that
we'd like to bolt on to your platform some of our innovative tools. We have already licensed patent-pending
solutions to governments, aerospace companies, satellite
manufacturers—the top of the top."

"So are you looking for a licensing arrangement?"

"No, Mr. Brooks, I want to buy your client."

Jonathan almost grinned but wanted to stay polite.
"It's...not for sale."

"I know. But that's what I want in the end."

Jonathan studied Artem's lawyers, who'd already
given away a lot without having said a word. The way
one of them pressed his thumb into his other palm hard
enough to turn that skin arctic white. And how the other
attorney blinked too little and seemed to avoid eye contact with Artem. Jonathan sensed they were uncomfortable with their client, perhaps with his directness or with
whatever strategy they'd discussed before this meeting,
or simply because he was an asshole, like Soykis had
said. That hint of discord between attorney and client
can often be twisted to some advantage, however small,
if needed. Perhaps their dislike for Artem was a way
Jonathan's side could create a better, less formal rapport

with them. *Who knows*, Jonathan thought. In any case, he was now perked up, attentive to possibilities.

Soykis cleared his throat and said, "We can also—"

Artem pounded his knuckles on the table three times. "Let me be clear, we're not only offering a lot of money, Mr. Brooks, but investment opportunities." Artem was almost shouting, a vein above his left brow appearing to pulsate. "We want to build the world's most interconnected information platform, creating an uninterrupted data exchange between manufacturers, suppliers, distributors, sellers and consumers. Total information awareness—from the moment suppliers are shipping components to factories, through the manufacturing cycle, then the shipment anywhere on earth, to its ultimate end-user in a home or business, and even beyond that, to when it reaches a landfill or recycling plant. That is what we are offering. To turn your narrowly successful product suite into a cross-industry global leader. Big Data is coming; cloud computing and smart devices, too; and we are setting our sights on becoming the dominant player. We want what we want, because it's within reach."

"I certainly don't want to take any air out of that balloon," Jonathan said. "But I hope you are willing to accept far smaller steps. Cramer Banks does not foresee selling his company or divesting any part of it or its technology at this time. But finding synergies, forming partnerships, yes, that's on the table." He wanted to be reasonable in the face of this bizarre man.

Artem slammed his fist on the table, his scowling gaze aimed at Jonathan. He paused, then, like a magician, his hand wiped his face and an insincere smile emerged. "Got it. We will go slow."

The lawyer to Artem's right further straightened his already erect back and said, "We are willing to entertain a phased joint venture—perhaps over an eighteen-month period—modeled around a hybrid product, combining our mutually relevant intellectual property."

Cramer had given Jonathan some statistics about VASTLINK before he left New Orleans. The number that sprang to mind first was twenty-three million. That's how much Cramer's company had spent developing the system over a seven-year period. The sum was in the league of companies ten times its size, and not what one would have expected for Southern Seas Logistics, Louisiana's tenth largest locally owned business based on revenues—something Cramer constantly reminded Jonathan, as if the rank really mattered.

Over the next hour Artem's attorneys proposed potential structures for the joint-venture, and Soykis threw into the mix local corporate requirements and tax ramifications, and Jonathan chimed in to explain the five affiliates that essentially comprised Southern Seas Logistics and the governance structure.

Suddenly, Artem checked his watch and stood up, his chair sliding back noisily as he cut off one of his lawyers. "It is almost noon, and your own magician isn't here, Mr. Brooks. And we all know you aren't authorized to make any decisions, and frankly I doubt you even know your client's technology."

Jonathan didn't give much weight to Artem's insult, but he again felt anxious. He couldn't understand why there had been no news from Kevin. No call or text message from the airport. Nothing. Without Kevin, the meeting would remain an over-lawyered ego contest about as fruitful as a catfight on the Jerry Springer show. Jonathan felt his stomach wrench. His mind spiraled with worry. With no useful meeting, there were no negotiations, no terms sheets or contracts to draft, no due diligence to commence, no legalese redlines to wrangle over. Nothing substantive for a lawyer to do. He'd have to pack up and go home. To New Orleans. To a destroyed office with no billable work.

"Let's take a short break," Jonathan suggested.

"Very well," Artem said, checking his watch again.

Jonathan tugged Soykis' arm and glanced at Elya, nodding for them to follow him out of the conference room. He closed the door and led them to the far end of the corridor as he dialed Kevin's cellphone, but it only went to voicemail. He texted him, too. "Elya, would you please call the limo company to find out why he's delayed?" He handed her his phone showing the number to call.

She stepped into an assistant's cubicle and instructed the woman at the desk to dial. A moment later Elya took the handset and spoke in her native tongue.

Soykis looked annoyed, his arms crossed. But he said nothing, though he seemed eager to do so.

"I'm on the line with the transportation service," Elya said, leaning back to face Jonathan. "They're saying he's not at the airport."

"What do you mean? He must have arrived."

"I don't know," Elya said and shrugged, covering the phone with her hand. "The flight arrived a while ago."

"I'll text Cramer now," Jonathan said, taking his phone back from her. "Kevin was in London overnight, and his flight left early this morning."

Soykis raised his chin. "This doesn't look professional, you know."

"Maybe he's stuck in customs," Jonathan suggested, though his own passage from gate to terminal yesterday had been swift. He shook his head. He was just as impatient as anybody to have Kevin's ass planted in that conference room. He turned to Elya again. "Tell the driver to keep looking at the terminal," he said, his voice hardening.

More than a half-hour passed still with no word from Kevin. Soykis' staff had brought sandwiches and a large salad into the conference room, and the teams did their best to keep the time productive, but Kevin's absence was a looming roadblock.

At 1:10 P.M., Artem, who'd been rather quiet since the group had reconvened, abruptly sprang to his feet, again interrupting one of his lawyers. "We will continue when your team is fully assembled. Right now, it makes no sense to sit here and debate abstract scenarios. My time is valuable, Mr. Brooks. My family built our empire by efficiently defying human nature's weaknesses."

Is he for real? Jonathan mused alone. But no one else in the conference room appeared to react to this statement. His lawyers kept their eyes on their notepads.

Everyone shook hands, and moments later Artem and his lawyers left. In the meantime, Jonathan had received two more text messages from Cramer, none giving any clue as to why Kevin was late or unreachable.

At two-thirty, Soykis left the office for a meeting. Jonathan stayed behind in the conference room and tried again to dial Cramer, but he only got his voice-mail.

When Elya popped in one more time, he stood up. "I should go back to my hotel," he said, shaking his head. "I don't get it."

"I'm sorry," she replied and lightly smiled. "Cheer up. There's always tomorrow."

"I'm worried. Clients don't behave this way intentionally."

"Perhaps he took a cab instead of the limo service."

"I called the hotel. He hasn't checked in."

"Then maybe he missed the flight and his phone has a dead battery."

"He's the CTO of a technology company. He's probably got more electronic gadgets on him than all of us combined."

She ran her hand through her long, straight black hair. "You have a point."

"I hope nothing bad has happened." This was Ukraine, after all, Jonathan reminded himself. He'd read articles about the country's booming corruption, the mafia, turf battles, the oppressive security services, and the rising random crime attributable to a working class that felt toxically disenfranchised from any real opportunity. His imagination began running wild. Had Kevin's phone been stolen at the terminal? By the limo driver, perhaps? Or crooked customs officials? There was simply no immediately apparent reason for Kevin's radio silence. Maybe he's dead. The thought suddenly scared the bejesus out of him.

5

Maidan—Independence Square, Kyiv

JONATHAN CHECKED HIS WATCH AND GLANCED OUT toward the street that looped between the hotel and the nearby McDonald's. Elya had promised to pick him up at seven sharp. She was only a minute overdue when she pulled up in her late model Saab.

"Kevin was on the flight," Jonathan said the moment he joined her in the front seat. "Cramer confirmed this morning, and the airline said Kevin's luggage was picked up at baggage claim. I also asked the hotel—no one by that name checked in overnight or this morning."

Elya's eyes widened. "That's not good." She stepped on the gas, heading uphill on the cobbled street.

"Where're we going?"

She sped through an intersection but seemed deep in thought, chewing on her bottom lip. "Ultra."

"Ultra?"

"Ultra Transport, the limo company."

"Oh, yes, of course."

"I called ahead to speak with the driver."

Jonathan clutched the door handle, thinking that Elya could be mistaken for a rally driver, except she didn't wear a helmet. She swerved, she honked, she braked hard, and— he guessed—she cursed. It was a side of her he hadn't expected, given her mild-mannered composure at the law firm the prior day.

"If you drive like this much longer, I'm going to throw up," he said, trying to smile. "I ate a horrible meal last night near the hotel."

"You should have called me," she said, slowing down a bit. "I could have taken you to Belvedere—nice place, overlooking the river."

"Next time."

A few minutes later, she decelerated and pulled over the curb across from what looked like a warehouse. "We're here."

He took a deep breath, surprised they'd made it to their destination in one piece.

Jonathan and Elya were shown to a cramped, smoke-scented room with a small square table, two chairs and an ashtray overflowing with cigarette butts. He sat down and crossed his arms, staring out the grimy window at man washing a shiny Mercedes parked in front as Elya took the seat next to him.

They stood up as the driver, dressed in a wrinkled black suit, quickly entered the room and nodded a greeting. He too reeked of smoke and appeared fidgety and disinterested.

Elya spoke with him. She then turned to Jonathan and said, "He only has a minute—he's late for a pickup."

"Fine, ask him about Kevin."

She spoke again and listened to the man's answer as his eyes shifted between Elya and Jonathan. "He's saying that he waited in the baggage area for more than thirty minutes, holding the sign with Kevin's name, but no one approached him."

"But he was late, right?"

Elya again interpreted, and the driver seemed bothered answering her.

"Yes, he was, but it—"

"What time did you arrive?" Jonathan asked him directly, feeling annoyed that he couldn't speak the local language.

Elya spoke, again translating, before the driver replied. "He says he arrived at the baggage area at nine-twenty yesterday morning, holding a paper with Kevin's name."

"Is he sure?"

They spoke again.

"He's checking his phone..." The man then held the phone out to Jonathan, pointing to the call entry, just as Elya spoke. "Apparently, that nine thirty-two call was to his office here—about then minutes after he arrived—to say that no one had approached him."

"But Kevin's flight landed at eight. And this driver showed up at nine-twenty." Jonathan shook his head. "That's more than an hour late; no wonder Kevin didn't wait around."

Elya shrugged and again spoke to the driver. "Yes, he says he couldn't help it. A policeman pulled him over on the highway and gave him problems about his car papers. He was stuck for a long time."

Jonathan glanced at Elya. "We have to report him missing."

Elya gazed back and nodded. "I know a police station on Moscovskaya Street, ten minutes from here."

They thanked the driver and quickly headed back to her car.

"Were you speaking Russian or Ukrainian with the driver? Sometimes I have a hard time catching the difference."

She tilted her head. "In this country, most speak both. But here in Kyiv, Ukrainian has become dominant, while the east is mostly Russian-speaking."

Jonathan still couldn't fathom how Kevin could go missing. Was he the victim of random crime? Targeted as a tourist arriving at the airport? Was he wearing an expensive watch? Were his luggage and attire too pretentious? The possibilities spun in his head.

"We should go to the airport as well," Jonathan said.

"Let's file a report first. Things are very bureaucratic here, and the police often point to small errors to justify delaying their work."

"If Kevin cleared customs and picked up his bags, there must be video surveillance showing that."

"I'm sure there is," Elya said, then chuckled and added, "if the cameras are not broken or if someone didn't forget to put in a tape."

Back in Elya's car, Jonathan scrolled through his BlackBerry and spotted a text message from Linda. His heart raced and then sank as he read the message:

In Beijing. Turn on the news tomorrow night. Lots happening. Take care. He couldn't help but think she was too busy to care. Too busy that in the one week they were in the same city, in a devastated New Orleans, she didn't bother to see him. And when she finally did, it was to say goodbye. Now that she's stronger, she's moving on, he thought, his heart tightening. The sorrow was enveloping him so forcefully he began to feel low on air. He swallowed hard.

"You okay?" Elya asked.

Jonathan glanced up at her, only half-present. "Yeah, sure," he mumbled, bowing his head.

"News about Kevin?"

"No...something else. It's nothing." He slid the phone back in his pocket.

"Let me take you to Belvedere this evening."

Jonathan looked at her. "Maybe if I feel better later."

They drove through wide boulevards and smaller streets. Then, Elya pointed over the steering wheel at a three-story pink and white building at the corner of a busy intersection. "There, that's it, the *Viddilennya Militsyii*—the police station."

They waited more than an hour in the lobby before a short, uniformed woman with the body of a casserole summoned them. She led the way through a poorly lit corridor to a narrow staircase.

Following the policewoman, Elya leaned into Jonathan and whispered, "Don't ask anything. Let me do the talking."

Jonathan signaled his silence by passing his fingers over his lips.

"Good, because policemen, or *militsiyonery*, are uneasy and unhelpful around foreigners, particularly if I say you're American. I will only mention your nationality if they ask."

On the second floor, the two were greeted by a uniformed officer almost the size of a refrigerator—a physique, Jonathan guessed, made as much from muscle as from fat, and perhaps iron.

As Elya had asked, Jonathan waited by the stairs, impatiently eyeing her as she sat facing the officer's desk some twenty feet away. She spoke, and the cop typed, briefly looked up at her, and then typed some more.

Jonathan glanced at this watch. He could hardly believe it was almost midday and they were no closer to finding Kevin. He then noticed the officer turn his sights on him with a frosty gaze. The man tilted his head to one side, raised his brow and with a bold wave of his arm signaled for Jonathan to approach.

"Have a seat," Elya said. "He has a few questions for you."

Jonathan nodded, sat down and stayed silent.

The officer seemed to study him before speaking.

"He asks if you know this man well."

Jonathan shrugged. "He's a senior executive of the company I represent."

Elya and the policeman spoke some more, and she turned to Jonathan with a frown. "He says that foreigners love Ukrainian girls, so maybe he's having some fun before getting down to business."

Jonathan didn't know whether to laugh or get up and leave. "Is that a serious question?"

"I don't know," Elya said. "I'll tell him no, that you know Kevin wouldn't do that."

"No, tell this prick he's being ridiculous, and that he should learn the kind of probing questions that reputable law enforcement officials ask in missing persons cases." Jonathan sat back, shook his head, dwelling in the aftertaste of the man's stupid comment.

Elya spoke again with the policeman.

Jonathan sensed she didn't translate his words exactly, for which he was grateful.

As he watched Elya and the policeman finalize the missing persons paperwork, Jonathan suddenly imagined being back in New Orleans in a matter of days. Close to penniless, in his destroyed law office, with his assistant Amber demanding her past due paycheck. He hadn't a clue about how to rebuild, but he knew if he failed here, he had no chance for a future. That's why finding Kevin safe and sound was his only priority.

Elya and Jonathan soon were back in the car, this time headed to the airport. If anything could offer better answers about Kevin Wyatt's whereabouts, it would be the surveillance cameras at the Arrivals terminal.

*   *   *

Artem Bodrov, his mind brooding with anger as it always did when others failed to return his calls, opened his car door and then immediately slammed it shut with such force the glass nearly shattered. He yanked his cellphone out of his coat and dialed the same number he'd been trying since the previous night.

"Finally!" Bodrov barked the moment the man on the other end answered. "Where did you disappear?" His bellowed Russian words echoed off the concrete walls of the parking garage.

"I was at the farm, taking care of our precious cargo."

"Why didn't you tell me about that American lawyer?"

"You mean Brooks? I think I did."

"You didn't, you fool," Bodrov said. "My memory never fails me. In any case, I don't like him. He's going to be trouble."

"He's only a lawyer. How much trouble can he be?"

"Find out more about him. Ask the North Koreans, if you must. I trust my instincts, Edmar, and this man will be a problem."

"I will check."

Bodrov hung up and wiped the spit off his lips with his handkerchief before stepping into his Jaguar. Whatever this lawyer was up to, Bodrov was going to stop him.

6

Malé, Maldives

THE VIEW OUT OF THE AIRCRAFT WINDOW FOR MUCH of the descent showed only water. Then suddenly a cargo ship, a couple motorboats and a yacht whisked by below. It seemed as if the plane was about to land on water when, at the very last few seconds, a smidgen of rocky terrain zipped beneath the fuselage and a concrete runway appeared. The tires touched down with a loud chirp.

Malé International Airport was located on a narrow island composed of a main runway, a taxiway and two terminal buildings, one of which was exclusively for seaplanes. That the airport was its own island was not so surprising. After all, the Maldives was an archipelago situated southwest of Sri Lanka and India and made up of twenty-six atolls stretched across more than fifty thousand square miles of ocean. And its islands, waters and beaches attracted tourists from all over the world.

But the man in seat 23A had traveled twenty-nine hours to reach here, but for the most unorthodox of reasons. His brown-skinned hands were dry, his knuckles stiff. His spine crackled as he stood up. He exited the Emirates flight with a lone backpack strapped over his right shoulder, his heart now racing as it always did on these risky journeys.

As he neared Passport Control, surveying the officials manning the booths, he felt droplets of sweat ooze down his back. His skullcap, too, felt damp. He held his British passport by its edges, worried about making the document suspiciously warm from the excited blood rushing through his hands.

Soon it was his turn. He forced himself to meet the officer's gaze.

"Abubakar, Yusuf," the uniformed man read aloud the name on the passport and looked up.

"Yes," he answered, his heart pounding under his beige qamis. Though he'd taken on this assumed name three years ago, hearing the words directed at him still made him edgy. And it sounded nothing like his birth name, Farouk Kamfar.

"How long is your stay?"

"One or two days," he said in a faint voice, handing the officer a printout of his return ticket.

"And what business are you in?"

"A professor, sir." That quasi-lie, unlike his alias, no longer bothered him as it had earlier when he'd first been recruited from Old Kent Road Mosque, his regular place of worship in southeast London. A group of elderly worshippers had gone to great lengths to teach him the Koran while also funding Farouk's university studies in tax and accounting until he'd earned a part-time position at an Ealing area business school. The then-twenty-three-year-old Farouk had wanted to be a fighter. He'd long stated that to detonate an explosive in a tube station or bus was more virtuous than earning the degree, but the cleric had insisted there was a better use for Farouk's skills. Indeed, Farouk had shown himself to be quite the prodigy, his memory and math skills impressing visiting clerics and even the head of Bin Laden's ostensibly well-hidden Saudi movement, who'd later flown him to Istanbul to meet his new mentor, Ibrahim Jafal, now Al-Qaeda's most influential money-man outside Afghanistan.

And since then, Farouk had spent his time shuttling between far-flung cities, towns and remote villages across Al-Qaeda's nascent global network, becoming Jafal's courier, bean-counter and, in Farouk's eyes, the man's whisperer. But deep-down Farouk grappled with the fiercely aggressive members in his network, many dreaming of martyrdom and defining their existence by the number of Western lives they'd take down with them in a glorious final act. He'd slowly distanced himself from the desire for blind carnage. Perhaps it was age; perhaps it was subconscious realization that the violence had gone too far. And Jafal, too, was an ardent supporter of this extreme ideology, often adding colorful combative words to discussions, showing his own desire for blood, having blamed virtually all of life's unpleasant experiences on the evilness of Whites, Christians, Imperialists, Capitalists, Infidels, and Zionists.

Farouk picked up his brown duffel bag laden with cash from the luggage carousel and set it down between his sandaled feet and then scanned his surroundings in the baggage claim area.

"Your bag is a Samsonite?" a whispered male voice came from behind him.

He slowly looked over his shoulder and examined the man in a beige service uniform who'd just spoken. "No, it's a cheap brand," he replied, confirming the man's coded acknowledgement, as he'd been instructed.

Farouk discreetly followed the man, walking about twenty feet behind, and then stepped into a room past the last carousel.

"There are no cameras in here," the man said, seemingly nervous to make eye contact with Farouk.

Farouk handed the officer a small envelope. He had counted the money in the plane's lavatory and thrown in an extra fifty dollars for good measure.

The officer quickly peeked into the envelope without counting the bills and then lifted his pantleg and slipped the envelope into his sock. He then agitatedly waved Farouk on toward another door, saying nothing and keeping his eyes to the floor.

Farouk pushed open the door. A damp breeze instantly swept his face, the air laced with the scent of jet fuel entering his lungs. He breathed deeply, his nerves settling. His heart slowed. He'd made it. Jafal's paid network of facilitators seemed loyal, so far. But Farouk always feared that any of them—be it the airport official in Dubai, the baggage handler in Beijing, or the lanky fellow he'd just paid off here at the airport in Malé—could one day betray him.

He weaved briskly past large wooden crates and retired equipment dumped along the length of a shaded alley between the terminal and an adjacent building, and then crossed the street facing the airport Arrivals building toward the waterfront, where dozens of boats were moored side by side.

Farouk paid the one-dollar fare and stepped onto a large, diesel-powered Dhoni boat filled with locals—mostly airport staff, he presumed—but there were a few tourists as well. He eyed all those who'd embarked after him. His vigilance was second nature, and although he felt less nervous, he knew that fatigue could lead to a costly mistake.

He sat on a wooden bench in the middle of the vessel and placed his bag and backpack between his calves. The boat gently pulled away from the dock, and a pleasant calm returned. He yawned. The tiredness had also returned. Farouk began recalling the beginning of his journey—a four-hour bus ride from Dandong—the Chinese border town across the Yalu River from North Korea—to Shenyang, followed by a nine-hour ride to Beijing in a poultry truck. Then there was the nine-hour flight to Dubai and a further four hours to Malé.

The boat slipped out of the calm waters of the airport's harbor and onto the mildly choppy surface of the open sea. He gazed ahead. A peaceful, orange-tinted dusk sky hung over the distant flickering lights of the island-city. He checked his watch. The one-and-a-half-mile ferry ride would take ten minutes.

Moments after the boat docked, he stepped onto Malé proper, a landmass only about two square miles in size, which also served as the capital of the Maldives. Farouk was always amazed by the fact that some 140,000 inhabitants were squeezed into such a tiny amount of real estate.

He left the ferry terminal on foot, his bag in one hand and the backpack over his right shoulder. He walked swiftly down several narrow, cobbled streets packed with people ending their workdays, occasionally glancing back as the sweat started to pour again. He turned onto another street, this one crammed with scooters and motorcycles parked on one side. He continued, past the ADK Hospital, and once more checked his surroundings before turning a final corner based on the directions he'd memorized.

He stopped at an unassuming two-story cement and glass building adorned with a sign that read, "Ahmed Shoe Repair," clumsily hand-painted in both English and Maldivian. He knocked at the glass door, trying to peer through the thin curtain hanging immediately behind it. The store had closed an hour earlier.

Three or four heavy breaths into his wait, the door opened. A boy no more than six or seven years old reached his head out and glanced up at Farouk.

"Sonu, right?" Farouk said softly. The innocence of the moment lifted Farouk's tension just enough to make him smile.

The boy nodded, his look serious. "Yes, upstairs," he said in his native Maluka Bas dialect, pointing timidly at the ceiling.

Farouk understood only a handful of words and phrases in Maldivian, but even fewer in Maluka Bas. He waved a thank you as he walked in, ensuring that the boy had closed both deadbolts on the door before Farouk headed to the stairs at the back of the workshop. The pungent scent of leather and rubber dissipated as he reached the top step, the lights dimly showing the way forward.

"Yusuf?"

"Yes," Farouk said in a loud whisper upon hearing his assumed name, squinting through the room illuminated only by the faint bulb from the stairway.

"You were careful, I hope." The words, spoken in Gulf Arabic dialect, floated across the room as a wrinkled, leathery face emerged out of the darkness into the dim light.

The man was Ibrahim Jafal. He stood a foot away, his tall, aging body dressed in dull green qamis, displaying an austere gaze that made Farouk uneasy.

"What's wrong?"

"It's nothing." Jafal's face glowed with sweat. It was odd given the cool, air-conditioned room, Farouk thought.

"Really, is there something wrong?"

"The meeting was pushed forward." Jafal still appeared poker-faced, but Farouk knew this wasn't a good sign.

"Why?"

"*You* must make the deposit," Jafal added and scratched his jaw.

"Me?"

"Yes. Our man is not coming. I think he got scared and left when he heard the CIA dispatched their usual team from Sri Lanka a week earlier than normal."

"CIA? Here?"

"Don't worry. We're fine. They're not looking for us."

"What do you mean?" Farouk was afraid, but Jafal was not the man to whom one raised his voice.

"You have forty-five minutes to be at the bank, and the amount now is nine hundred thousand dollars."

"What? That's much more than what I brought with me," Farouk said, suddenly fearing he'd taken the wrong sum, or worse yet, that Jafal would accuse him of pocketing some of it.

"I know." Jafal turned, shook his head and checked his flip phone briefly. He spoke with his back turned. "You'll have to pick up more at the mosque. I have arranged for an additional three hundred thousand."

"Why is it so much more?'

"Khaddam is furious. He's demanding more..."

"But why?"

"Because..." Jafal interrupted himself with a long, loud exhale. "Apparently it's an American."

Farouk froze. "*Ya lawhwy!*" He leaned forward to meet Jafal's eyes. "An American?"

"Yes."

"You told me it was the usual components?" Farouk put his hand to his forehead and shook his head. *What has he done?*

"No. This time it's a person."

"Who is it?"

"I have no idea."

"But they'll come looking for him!" Farouk wanted to shout but forced himself into an angry whisper instead. "This could expose Khaddam, his network, ours. Everything you've built so carefully. That was not what we bargained for."

Jafal glanced at Farouk with what appeared to him to be pity or disgust. "We can't always choose our moves."

Farouk waved his finger in the air and replied, "If Khaddam is asking for more, those Korean pigs should pay more."

"I cannot ask for three hundred thousand more! It's too dangerous."

"Dangerous? You mean you're scared of that fat Asian idiot who gave me the money? A man who probably can't tie his shoelaces."

"You have no idea..."

"Damn this." Farouk clenched his fists and shook his head, feeling dismayed and angrier by the minute. Jafal was the entrusted financial guardian of their organization. "We can't be lackeys for that Asian crook."

"I will eat this extra cost. You don't understand, Farouk, that Asian crook—as you call him—is only a messenger. You cannot imagine the power and ruthlessness that stands behind him. I have spared you the details for obvious reasons. If I go back to him with Khaddam's higher demand, he may lose his trust in us. He may even think we've been compromised. I can't risk this. We've been dealing with him for a long time, and we've earned a lot of money. I will handle Khaddam's recklessness later, but for now we'll cover the shortfall." Jafal turned, lumbered forward and sat down noisily into an oversized vinyl chair near the drapes, his head resting in his hand.

For the first time in Farouk's dealings with Jafal, he sensed a certain weakness in his mentor and superior. Although Farouk didn't know why the Asian had convinced Jafal to get into human trafficking instead of the usual contraband in the form of centrifuge components, highly processed pieces of machinery and metallurgy, he understood that Jafal had somehow gotten himself embroiled in a murky, money-losing deal. But more worrisome was that now an American was in the mix, and this meant U.S. intelligence agencies might become involved.

"You just found out?" Farouk felt less constrained as he observed Jafal's wilted posture. "We've been helping those bastards with their logistics for two years based on agreed rules. And now this? The Americans are going to come looking, and we'll risk losing everything."

"Stop it!" Jafal suddenly jumped to his feet. "At some point everything we've been creating is designed to face them and their European dogs, so if it's now or later, it doesn't really matter." He moved quickly across the room and angrily pushed Farouk's chest with both hands. "You're going to do what you are told. You hear me?"

"All right." Farouk, understanding his place, raised his hands in a calming gesture. "I'll get ready."

"Your things are in the room. Whatever you are wearing now, throw away in the trash cans in the back alleyway. Your bags too, since they can trace the scent of money. Everything, I tell you. There must not be any hint of us here. And do it quickly, since Sonu's family will be back soon."

*   *   *

Farouk closed the bathroom door and glanced at his inch-long beard in the mirror. He removed his skullcap and qamis and tossed them in a garbage bag. He then ran the water and began shaving. Within a minute his full cheeks and jaw were clear of facial hair. He then wetted his head and began rubbing a dark gel into his mop of hair. He let the solution sit for a few minutes, tilting his head to each side, observing curiously. Soon he noticed his natural blackish hair had turned a lighter shade of brown, and the gray strands over the ears had vanished. It would last only a few hours, but this was fine for his purposes.

Farouk got dressed in the clothes that Jafal had left for him and then raised his chin as he examined his newly polished persona in the mirror. His suit was wrinkle-free, his shirt whiter than his teeth, and paisley tie knotted with perfection. He gently put on the non-corrective black-framed glasses he'd used once before as a finishing touch to his disguise. He took a step back to glance at himself, for a moment letting his imagination wander. What if his fellow Muslim scholars back in Ealing could see him now, he thought. They'd be stunned, even impressed, by the camouflage.

He heard sandals scrape the floor outside the door. As he opened the bathroom door, Jamal gazed at him for a few seconds before his voice broke the air.

"Do not envy these infidels," Jamal said. "There's nothing worthy in what you see in that mirror. Remember, they wore suits and uniforms when they conquered our lands, pillaged our villages, raped our children and siphoned our oil."

Jafal gestured to a black briefcase by the stairs. "I have counted the money you brought, and it's now in there. Go now to the mosque and then the bank. Don't waste time."

Farouk said nothing. He picked up the briefcase, gave Jafal a simple nod goodbye and headed downstairs. The small boy at the door did a double-take, clearly shocked by the change of appearance. As he headed through the back alleyway, Farouk tried to rid himself of his nervousness by reciting over and over again the information he needed to have at his disposal if the bankers were to ask questions.

The Islamic Centre, officially known as the Masjid-al-Sultan Muhammad Thakurufaanu Al Auzam, was located on Medhuziyaarai Magu, a few blocks east of the shoe repair store on the same northern edge of the island. With a capacity to hold about 5,000 worshippers, it wasn't only the largest mosque in the Maldives; it was bigger than most mosques in all of South Asia. The modern, three-story white stone structure, topped with a huge gold dome and accented with a decorative gray-lines, was set between Republic Square—a small park with a monument and flagpole—and the island's National Museum. Farouk gazed up at the single minaret, its summit also matching the main dome's gold plating, as he walked the twenty-or-so white stone steps to the arched entrance.

A teenager seated on the last step silently stared at Farouk, which only increased his discomfort. Wearing a Western suit made him stand out, almost as if he were eating pork on the front steps, he thought. But he had no choice. The next destination, the head office of TransAsia Commercial Alliance Bank—"TACAB", as it was locally called—required him to have a certain look for the deposit to proceed trouble-free.

Farouk took of his shoes and left them near the boy. His feet squeaked as he walked along the Islamic Center's main floor, with its white marbled floor decorated with a few rows of black marble reflecting the dim overhead lights. He passed the main prayer room on his left, its floor covered with large, ornate rugs and above which were two enormous glass chandeliers, their bulbs dormant. The muggy breeze passed through the floor, as both ends were open to the outside air. Toward the back end of the building, next to a narrow passage that could be a stairway, he spotted a man wearing a short beard and dressed in a white tunic and skull cap, who made eye contact and nodded once. Farouk approached.

"Shoes," Farouk whispered. It was the codeword he'd been instructed to use.

The man put his hand on Farouk's shoulder and whispered back in Maldivian, "All good, Allah-willing." He glanced at both ends of the hallway and then with a light pat to his back prodded Farouk to follow him downstairs.

Reaching the lower floor, Farouk followed the man into a long corridor that had several closed doors on both sides but the last one was cracked open. The stranger peeked in first and then waved Farouk into the darkened room. The weak light of a desktop lamp illuminated a brown paper packet on the furniture's surface, and behind it stood the silhouette of man.

"You are late," the figure said in Arabic, moving into the indirect light.

Farouk squinted and was able to make out a tall, bearded man with glasses dressed in a dark, embroidered thobe.

"Take the money," he said to Farouk, his deep voice carrying with it a subtle Arabic accent that Farouk recognized as Egyptian. "What you do with it is not my business, but remind your chief that we expect this returned to us in one month and not a day longer."

Farouk was afraid. He knew nothing of the arrangements between Jafal or others in the labyrinthian organizations and clans both within and outside of Al-Qaeda, and even less about those associates on this island.

"You understand?" the man said, his voice rising.

"Yes, yes, of course. I will relay the message." He felt sweat drip down his back as his heart rate kicked into high gear.

"Then take it and get out."

These were not words of like-minded, empathetic brethren fighting to reverse the injustices unleashed on the Muslim world, Farouk thought as he slipped the wads of hundreds from the packet into his briefcase. These words would never leave the lips of great men; nor would Allah want them uttered in his name. Farouk snapped his briefcase shut, nodded at the man and left the room without saying another word. This powerful organization he'd so willingly joined seemed to be cracking under the weight of its own dysfunction and rivalries.

Farouk hurried to the entrance, slipped on his shoes and exited the mosque. He kept a quickened pace for the duration of the eight-minute walk to the TACAB office on Boduthakurufaanu Magu, the island's busiest waterfront street. There he signed in at the reception desk and was promptly shown to a private office on the third floor, its large, floor-to-ceiling windows facing the swarm of Dhoni boats docked along the shorefront. A senior bank official checked his ID. A moment later an assistant came in and began counting the money to be deposited to Khaddam's secret account. The process went smoothly; none of the complications that Farouk had feared. Nonetheless, this wasn't his money—it was dirty money. Possibly dirtier than he could ever imagine, given the likes of the men he'd encountered today. And if the bank knew its origins, they'd have a police contingent summoned in no time. Farouk left the bank with the shirt under his suit jacket completely drenched. Still, all in all, his efforts had been successful. He hoped he would find the same success in his next stop, Syria.

7

Boryspil Airport, Kyiv

"OVER THERE; THAT'S HIM," ELYA SAID, SCURRYING
through the terminal with Jonathan in tow. She glanced
back at him with an excited look. She then shook hands
with a uniformed officer in his mid-forties, with bony
cheeks and thinning blond hair.

"Jonathan, please meet Major Denys Prystaiko," she
said. "He is the Interior Ministry's police commander
here at the airport."

Jonathan shook hands and glanced at the man's
dark-blue and red epaulettes, each with a small pin of
the Ukrainian national coat of arms and a single silver
star.

"So, I understand you have problem," the major
began, his English weighed by a thick accent.

"You speak English," Jonathan said feeling both
relieved and surprised.

"Yes...a little," he said, gesturing the international sign for small with his fingers.

"We're looking for a passenger who arr—"

"I've already given Major Prystaiko the background," Elya interrupted. "We're going to his office. He was kind enough to set aside the surveillance videos from yesterday."

Jonathan was glad Elya had helped save some time. They headed through a narrow hallway some distance from the terminal's farthest check-in counters, proceeded across a courtyard and into an annex. There, the major led them up a flight of stairs and into a rudimentary office space with old metal desks and cabinets, documents and notes taped and tacked all over the walls. The place was empty except for one uniformed officer seated on a stool in a cubicle, eating a sandwich, his Kalashnikov laying across the desktop.

"This way, please," the commander said. He ushered Elya and Jonathan through another corridor and into a small brightly lighted room, where another officer sat facing a laptop and four bulky television monitors stacked in pairs.

"You said driver arrive nine in morning, yes?" Prystaiko asked Jonathan and then pointed at the screens, mumbling something to his subordinate manning the equipment.

"Yes, just after nine," Jonathan said, recalling what the driver had told him earlier.

Prystaiko tapped the junior officer's shoulder. The video footage started up on the lower right monitor. "This camera is from arrival inside Terminal B." He then said something in Russian or Ukrainian, which Elya quickly translated, saying, "He means it's the lobby where passengers from that flight entered after they exited the customs area and the secure zone of the airport."

"I understand," Jonathan said. "I went through the same area two days ago."

The images showed what anyone would expect in an arrivals lounge. People waiting. Passengers arriving and looking a bit confused or weary. There were kids running around. Even a policeman walked by. The footage continued for several minutes.

"There, that's him," Jonathan interrupted, spotting the driver he and Elya had questioned earlier. Jonathan and the others watched the silent black and white security camera video. The driver was among several others holding up signs. His had misspelled Kevin's last name—Wyat, with only one "t" —on his printed sheet, which he held above his head off and on for about ten minutes, twice walking briefly off-screen toward what looked like a kiosk.

"He is nervous," the major said.

"He was late, very late," Elya replied.

Jonathan glanced at the timestamp at the bottom corner of the video. "Yes, by then the flight had already been on the ground for over an hour."

The commander shrugged. "Bad driver to be so late."

"It's the police's fault," Jonathan snapped. "He was detained on his way to the airport."

Commander Prystaiko crossed his arms and frowned. "Perhaps he is bad driver."

"We have to rewind farther back," Elya said. "We need to see the passengers from the flight. Mr. Wyatt had one checked bag, so he must have come to that area."

The police commander spoke to the officer, who selected a different video from the on-screen menu. "This is from the luggage pickup area at 8:15," he said and then tapped his index finger on the monitor. "Look, here, there is the flight number, you see?"

"Yes." Jonathan surveyed the passengers congregating at the luggage carousel, trying to spot Kevin. The tape continued for several more minutes until a dark-haired man in an untucked flannel shirt and jeans walked into view. "There, that's him...that's Kevin Wyatt." Two minutes later the video clearly showed him retrieving his suitcase, throwing it on a cart and heading towards customs at 8:31.

Jonathan turned to Prystaiko. "Can we now go back to the arrivals camera, like before, but at this same time or a bit earlier."

The police commander gruffly gave instructions to his assistant, who quickly switched the footage and rewound the scene to 8:20. The area was crowded with passengers streaming by a narrow area with luggage-filled carts.

"What's that?" Jonathan picked out one of three men, presumably drivers, holding signs. The man wore a baseball cap and an anorak. Jonathan squinted, trying to read the name on the sign, which the man did not raise, choosing instead to keep at his side. "Stop, stop."

The screen froze.

"What is it?" Prystaiko asked.

Jonathan leaned in, deciphering the sign that was at a difficult angle to read. "I think it has Kevin's name on it." He weaved around Elya, turned off the ceiling lights and returned to the monitor, now pointing at the sign in the man's left hand. "Look carefully. There. Doesn't it read W-Y-A-T-T? With two 'ts'?"

Elya said something in her native tongue to the officer, who rewound and replayed the video but let it go for about three more minutes, until suddenly the man—who looked nothing like the driver they'd spoken with at Ultra Transport—tucked the sign into his jacket and scooted forward through the crowd, his face still not clearly discernable.

Jonathan drew in his breath as Kevin's flannel shirt suddenly edged into view in the lower corner of the screen. "Shit." A second later the man grabbed Kevin's cart with his right hand and flashed him the name sign with his other.

"Oh my god," Elya vented, surely realizing what this meant.

Jonathan stared at the video. The man led Kevin out through the sliding glass doors and out of the camera's field of view.

"Do you have cameras outside?" Elya said, her voice rising.

Prystaiko chewed his gums, his eyes glued to the monitor.

"Well?" Jonathan asked. "You must have video in the parking area, right?"

"*Da.*"

As the junior officer scrambled to find the footage, Jonathan turned to Elya. "There's something very wrong here."

"I see that; I know."

"No, what I mean is that this man had Kevin's last name spelled correctly."

"I don't understand."

"Cramer's office had reserved the limo pickup by email and mistakenly written Kevin's last name with only one "t," so it makes sense that the driver we spoke with earlier held up the misspelled name," Jonathan said and then pointed his finger at the still image of the man grabbing Kevin's cart. "The man has the right name because he learned of Kevin's arrival independently, through some other source, and it's clear they targeted him specifically."

Elya took a step back and shook her head, her hand covering her mouth. "So, what now?"

Jonathan's synapses crackled as he glanced at Commander Prystaiko. "Whoever this person was, why would he risk being spotted by the Ultra Transport driver?"

The senior officer said nothing.

"He knew he wouldn't," Elya said softly.

"Exactly." Jonathan straightened his shoulders and met Prystaiko's gaze. "The police stopped him to make sure that would not happen."

"Are you saying we are an accomplice?" the commander said, his condescendence not at all masked by his accent.

"No, not your airport police," Jonathan said. "But maybe your highway or city police. I don't know."

Prystaiko inflated his chest. "This is not the Wild West, Mr. Brooks," he said, his chin now raised and his large round eyes glaring down at Jonathan. "We are all professionals here, so be careful telling stories."

"We need copies of these videos," Elya interrupted.

Prystaiko looked at his watch, appearing to ignore her.

"Please, we need them."

Prystaiko looked as if he was about to roll his eyes. "There's a form to fill out in my office and then you will need a court order before you can pick them up."

"Okay." Elya tapped Jonathan's arm. "Let's fill out the form and go."

*   *   *

"Cramer, I'm telling you, that's everything I've got!" Jonathan was frustrated. He had no good answers to give his client. Nothing more than the scant information he'd pieced together with Elya at the airport police station. "Someone who wasn't the authorized driver went to the airport, tracked down Kevin, took him to his car, and disappeared. We've got video of this."

"Can't they track down the vehicle?"

"I told you, the police hasn't yet found the video from the parking area. They're still looking."

Jonathan heard Cramer bang his fist on something, perhaps a table.

"Cramer, why would anyone want to kidnap him, in Ukraine of all places? Has he ever traveled here before?"

"Not that I know of."

"Can you think of any reason? Anything?"

"Look, I'll call Senator Jordan in the morning. He's a good friend and can get things moving. He knows a lot of people at the State Department. I'm certain he'll find us a useful contact locally, probably at the Embassy."

"I hope. The longer it takes, the worse this could end up, I fear."

"By the way, start charging your hourly rate."

"What?" Jonathan wasn't sure if Cramer meant to be funny.

"I'm serious, you can charge me. Kevin is the brains behind my business. I'm paying you now to find him." Cramer hung up.

Jonathan vented a lungful of air. He hadn't expected to come here to track down a missing person, in a country where he didn't speak the language and had few contacts. It reminded him of his search for his brother in Russia a decade ago. He just hoped it would be an easier, less dangerous process this time.

Hotel Kozatsky, Kyiv, 8:50 A.M.

JONATHAN GAZED PENSIVELY OUT THE HOTEL LOBBY windows at the dark speckles coloring the concrete sidewalk as a light drizzle began to fall. Not a thought rumbling through his head could escape the reality: Kevin was taken. By whom was anyone's guess. In addition to his personal fears for Kevin's well-being, he reminded himself that the disappearance of Cramer's most visionary resource would send shockwaves through his client's multimillion-dollar enterprise—and Jonathan's only viable corporate client—with incalculable consequences.

He again checked his watch. The taxi was late. The nervous sweat he'd felt since he got up hadn't subsided, not even in the chilled lobby. He removed his jacket and threw it over his arm, but nothing lessened the heat radiating through his body.

Jonathan dug into his pocket and pulled out the note on which he'd hurriedly scribbled a name and the U.S. Embassy's chancery building address on Yuriy Kotsubinsky Street. Cramer had called back at three in the morning with brief instructions: Jonathan was to meet a senior diplomat named Anton Kane at 9:30 A.M. sharp.

Jonathan hoped Kane would quickly pump steroids into the local police's search efforts. Besides, Americans were generally respected here, he remembered Elya telling him. The U.S. government had gone to great lengths to schmooze local politicians and bureaucrats, she'd added, and quite broadly at that. Their efforts were especially targeted at pro-Russian factions in a determined effort to pluck Ukraine out of Russia's orbit. Jonathan therefore expected local law enforcement to cooperate.

Jonathan glanced at the bellman's close-cropped, light brown hair, which again reminded him of Kevin. Cramer had emailed color scans of Kevin's passport photo and other pictures from various corporate functions. Though Jonathan had never met Kevin in person, the emails had complemented what he had gathered online. All of it painted a fairly complete bio of the Stanford educated, forty-three-year-old missing executive.

Born and raised in Montana, with a Romanian-American wife, a son in middle school, a large ranch house in Slidell, Louisiana, a small apartment in Alexandria, Virginia, and a resume indicating prior roles at two tech consulting firms and a programming stint at IBM, Kevin Wyatt was as apple pie as any highly successful American engineer-turned-executive. And while he had made his money riding the dot-com wave, his success hadn't translated into the kind of wealth that would invite a ransom demand. That absence of rationale added to Jonathan's frustrations.

The cab finally pulled up and Jonathan stepped in, watching the streets as they headed north out of Maidan Square. The morning rush hour traffic was lighter than in New Orleans, which surprised him since the Ukrainian capital was five-fold more populated. Large concrete buildings and decaying apartment blocks passed by, which offered uncomfortable reminders of his time in Moscow. Ten years is not enough time to wipe away that kind of pain.

After a mere eight minutes' ride, and just as the cab turned onto a quiet, two-lane street lined by lush green trees on both sides, the driver turned his head back and blurted something Jonathan didn't understand. The car slowed to a crawl.

Jonathan leaned forward for a better view. There were two uniformed policemen standing guard on the sidewalk in front of a long row of concrete security planters. Behind them was a green-painted metal gate that ran the length of the property with a three-story beige-brick building sitting at the center of the highly protected perimeter. Jonathan quickly surmised it was the typically unhospitable facade of America's diplomatic missions. All that seemed missing were rifle-clad Blackwater security services contractors and a mine-field.

Stepping out of the taxi, Jonathan heard his phone chirp. He checked for messages. It was his ex: *Finishing one big gig, looking for my next. Leaving Beijing soon. Be safe. L*

After clearing visitor formalities at the security checkpoint, Jonathan was greeted by an embassy staffer with wavy blonde hair and a docile Ukrainian accent. She led him through a side entrance of the chancery building and into a small, empty waiting room that resembled the one at his doctor's office back home.

There he sat for several minutes, immersed in his troubled thoughts, feeling close to helpless. An extensively thumbed copy of the Economist lay on the coffee table, half-covering an equally worn issue of Time magazine. The sound of someone typing loudly on a keyboard filtered past the half-opened door, and occasionally he heard heels clacking down the hardwood floors of the corridor. But not for a moment did his rapid-pulsed heart ease up.

He pulled out his phone and reopened Linda's text. He reread the words on the screen as if there was more substance to extract. A sharp pinch gripped through his chest.

"Why even send it," he whispered alone, shaking his head. He stared at her "L" signoff, and for a split-second pondered if it stood for Love. He shook his head, chasing away the silly thought. If it didn't mean Linda, it would surely stand for "Leave me the fuck alone for the rest of my wretched life." She'd been unambiguous days ago in New Orleans. It quickly made him angry that she thought it acceptable to lob such useless messages his way. Silence was infinitely better for his soul than meaningless reminders of the gulf between them.

"Mr. Brooks," Jonathan suddenly heard as the door opened wide. He stood as a tall, goateed man, dressed in khakis and a button-down with sleeves rolled to the elbow, stepped into the room and extended his hand. Jonathan shook the man's firm, cold grip.

"Anton Kane," the man said in a throaty voice. He then apologized for his tardiness, but in a tone that caused Jonathan to question his sincerity.

The two took the stairs one floor up to a windowless conference room furnished with only a small round table, three chairs, and a fake potted floor plant. A lone framed picture of a smiling George W. Bush hung unevenly on the wall.

"I'm here to find Kevin Wyatt," Jonathan said, not wanting to waste time. "We're both in Ukraine on behalf of Cramer Banks to negotiate a collaboration with ScorpionCloud."

Kane nodded, planted his elbows on the table and began caressing his salt-and-pepper goatee with both hands. He had sunken eyes, with dark but not overly puffy bags under them, and solid brown hair that didn't match his facial follicles.

Jonathan took him through the main turn of events. He spoke of the airport footage, Kevin's radio silence, the confirmed passenger list on the flight into Kyiv, the driver service that never found Kevin. He left nothing crucial out. And when he was done, he sighed and watched Kane, anticipating.

The diplomat cleared his hoarse airway. "These kinds of disappearances happen here, of course, but not to Americans. In fact, not a single incident of this kind has been reported to this embassy in over eight years."

Jonathan sat in disbelief. "But he's missing," he said, throwing his hands in the air. "What do you plan to do about this? And eight years is not a long track record."

"If he were an organized crime figure, I'd understand," Kane added. "But a software engineer? A consultant?" He ended his sentence with an exaggerated shrug.

"That's not trivial, Mr. Kane. He's now an executive for a $350 million company."

"Still," Kane uttered, tilting his head side to side as if he and Jonathan were viewing a badminton match.

"I know something bad happened."

The diplomat's lips drew back in a tight line as he leaned back in the chair. "Did you check hospitals?"

"Not yet."

"Filing a police report in this town doesn't mean they'll check medical centers. In fact, they may not lift a finger."

"Kevin was walking on his own two feet, perfectly healthy, in the video at the airport." Kane's lack of a sense of urgency began to rub Jonathan raw.

"Anything on the vehicle that drove Mr. Wyatt from the airport?"

"Nothing yet," Jonathan said, his voice now flat.

"You're an attorney, correct?" Kane asked.

Jonathan barely nodded.

"Then I'd expect a bit more thoroughness before coming here yelling fire. I've been in Eastern Europe a long time. Who's to say your Kevin won't show up tomorrow with a hangover and a complicated excuse as to why he misunderstood the meeting date."

Jonathan immediately recalled the same cynicism coming from the police officer at the station the day before, but today it was happening in plain English. And there was another difference: this diplomat was no idiot. Despite his apparent lack of interest in Kevin's predicament, he had been watching Jonathan closely during their ten-minute conversation.

Perhaps there was a reason why Kane wanted this matter to go away, Jonathan mused. "Other than appearing to be rather unhelpful, what exactly is your role here?"

Kane cracked a grin. "I assist the Regional Security Office from this embassy." He nodded at Jonathan. "In this part of the world, if you do as you're asked, mind your own business and don't rile up political or business circles, nothing will happen to you. Plain and simple. Given your recent experiences, Mr. Brooks, you of all people should know this rule."

Jonathan now understood this man had dug into his past prior to their meeting. He held his tongue for a moment longer.

"The chance that something nefarious happened in this case is pretty slim," Kane went on, "and it seems you haven't done all your homework."

"He was targeted," Jonathan barked as the words reverberated around the relative quiet in the room.

"For what?" Kane said, raising his voice to match. He didn't appear ready to relent an inch.

"Maybe something about the company, or something from his past—"

Kane chuckled. "Even with Mr. Wyatt's background, you can't jump to conclusions. Plenty of former NSA folks wander to globe, and nothing happens to them."

Jonathan took a few seconds to digest what he'd just heard. He tilted his head. "NSA?"

Kane's brows shot up. "You mean..." He wiped his goatee and then sat farther back in his already tilted chair. He stretched his arms to hold the back of his head with his palms.

That's when Jonathan spotted a faint, circular scar on the man's inner right arm, just above the wrist. The shape and texture seemed identical to the scars that seared Jonathan's back and chest when he'd been shot in Russia. The bullet scar suddenly told him more than anything he'd heard from Kane's lips.

"Kevin was NSA?" Jonathan repeated.

Kane straightened his chair back and stood up. "Drop it, Mr. Brooks. It's a non-issue."

"What do you mean, forget it? Every detail matters." Jonathan stood up, his hands on his waist. "I've seen the security video, for Christ's sake!" Jonathan felt incensed, almost trembling—almost violent. "Someone conned Kevin into a ride at the airport—a guy who somehow knew Kevin's last name. It's a fucking kidnapping."

Kane seemed to chew on the inside of his cheek, his dismissive gaze unchanged.

"And given that this matter landed on your desk from a U.S. senator, I'd expect you would have at least pretended to help find him."

Kane's eyebrows began to curl against each other. As Jonathan observed the subdued thunder brewing in Kane's hawkish, sunken eyes, he realized he needed Kane as an ally, not an adversary—no matter how unhelpful the diplomat had shown himself to be.

Jonathan leaned on the wall behind him and crossed his arms, feeling increasingly troubled by Kane's unconcerned attitude but also trying to stay calm. "Look, I just need a bit of help here. Please. You have many more resources available than I do to investigate this case."

Kane put his hands in his pants pockets and sighed. "If you're so convinced there's been foul play, I'll make some calls to—"

"And what about Wyatt's NSA background?" Jonathan wasn't about to let that go. There had been no mention of it in the resume Cramer had sent him. The National Security Agency, America's technologically supreme intelligence gathering organization, was the kind of detail that, in Jonathan's view, turned Wyatt's otherwise bland corporate profile into a fireball.

"What about it?" Kane said.

"It may not be so trivial. How long was he with the NSA? What exactly was his role? I think this may matter. You need to share this information with me."

"I don't think I need to," Kane said, as he turned to the door. "I have another meeting. You'll hear from me."

"Soon, right?"

Kane nodded and shrugged his shoulders. "My assistant will show you out." He left without shaking hands.

Jonathan wasn't sure if Kane's hostility was related to the information he'd gotten on Jonathan's past brushes with American intel agencies. Maybe reading about his Central American escapade had jaded Kane's objectivity, Jonathan thought. Or perhaps Kane simply wanted him out of the way so that he could handle a missing former NSA resource without interference from a civilian. Either way, it was clear that Jonathan could not rely on Kane as a trusted ally. That didn't bode well, he admitted to himself. Not well at all. He needed other leads to pursue in parallel, without which he was wholly dependent on Kane to move things along.

9

U.S. Embassy, Kyiv

KANE WATCHED THE ELEVATOR DOOR CLOSE. JONATHAN'S words were still swirling in his head, and they'd taken added importance considering the information Kane learned earlier in the morning, before their meeting. The fact that Kevin was former NSA was not a trivial detail as he'd made it seem to Jonathan. But he felt it necessary to prevent Jonathan from jumping to uncorroborated conclusions—an urge he'd always learned to contain throughout his career until he'd had more time to gather and scrutinize all the relevant facts. He needed to assess whether Kevin's relationship with the agency could have anything to do with his apparent disappearance. Until then, what bothered Kane most was Jonathan—his past, that is.

By the short time he'd stepped out of the elevator and walked to the north end of the chancery's basement floor, Kane's thoughts were entirely on the New Orleans lawyer with whom he had met for a mere twenty minutes. The information he had gleaned after only a few minutes of browsing the shared intelligence databases painted a complicated picture. He'd seen Jonathan's name appear on numerous CIA, FBI, and DoS files, including most recently in a heavily redacted memo relating to theft of fissile material in Venezuela. Kane wasn't sure what to make of it all. Was Jonathan credible? Was he simply a serial thrill seeker fabricating a reason for his next adrenaline rush? Or was the man a paranoid nutcase with coincidental run-ins with intelligence assets, both friend and foe. He'd never before seen any civilian with such a bizarre track-record in his nearly twenty years of intelligence and law enforcement experience.

At the far end of the corridor, he pressed his thumb onto the wall-mounted reader adjacent a reinforced metal door, after which the door lock buzzed, and he entered a large, well-lit room.

"You're early," a voice greeted him before he'd fully walked in.

Kane nodded at Clyde, the scruffy-bearded resident NSA techie, who was already seated at a conference table, his fingers typing into his open laptop. The two were part of an ad hoc Special Collection Service team, though Kane had always disliked the forced collaboration with non-CIA resources.

Clyde dialed the secure speaker phone at the center of the oval table and connected to an operator for their pre-arranged call.

Two minutes passed until a husky voice blared from the speaker, disturbing the quiet room. "Who's on?"

"Kane and me," Clyde said as he stopped typing.

"Good," returned the voice Kane didn't immediately recognize. "Guys, I'm George Porter, and I'm now coordinating the Mikhail Zhuk matter going forward."

Kane chewed on the name for a moment and quickly realized it was the same Porter he'd seen in a memo announcing the next head of counterintelligence operations for Europe. A vague memory of his time in Langley popped into his head. He had crossed paths with Porter some years ago, at an internal seminar, and remembered him as a tall, black man with a laser-like ability to zero in on the most important details in any given scenario. In any case, Kane thought, it was unusual for such a senior official to step into what had until then appeared to be a dull intel matter.

"Saw your note today, Clyde," Porter said. "Tell me what's so hot?"

Kane scowled at Clyde. This wasn't the first time Clyde had neglected to give him a heads up on new information he'd uncovered prior to a meeting. Kane sat down next to Clyde and raised his hands in frustration, after which Clyde simply slid a manila folder across the table toward Kane.

"We're still piecing things together, and translations have to be rechecked," Clyde said, scrolling down a document on his screen.

"Let's have it." Porter sounded impatient.

Kane quickly opened the manila folder and scoured through the five paper-clipped pages, trying to identify what would have caused Clyde to call a meeting, when suddenly his eyes caught a name he'd heard before—from Jonathan some fifteen minutes earlier. He tapped his index finger on it: ScorpionCloud. For a moment his mind broke away from Clyde's discussion with Porter. Kane quickly recalled what Jonathan had said. It was the Ukrainian company that Jonathan—and Wyatt—had been brought here to meet with for negotiations.

"We haven't actually found Zhuk's cell phone, but we retrieved metadata through BULLRUN. He had forty-two calls and over a hundred text messages in the three days before he crashed his motorcycle—including six calls and seven texts in a six-hour window before the crash, but nothing in the final two hours. Geolocation data showed his phone was at his apartment when he died, some sixty miles from the crash site."

Porter let out a long sigh. "We need more, guys."

"We tasked all the numbers with whom he communicated," added Clyde, "and all appear banal—except one. The night of his death, Zhuk received a call from a number lasting less than thirty seconds along with a dozen texts both to and from the same number. But it's a burner phone, whose unknown account was opened only two weeks earlier and is now deactivated. It dialed no other number."

"But," Kane jumped back in, glancing at the notations in the folder, "but it received one five-second call from a known number—a cellphone tied to a local corporate account."

"The company?" Porter asked.

Clyde answered, "ScorpionCloud."

"Maybe a wrong number?"

"Or a careless mistake," Kane said slowly, his mind contemplating how someone who apparently covered their tracks so well could make such a blunder.

"Heard of them?"

"Yes," Kane replied. "I heard it for the first time this morning, but in connection with a completely separate matter."

"I don't believe in coincidence." Porter sounded taut. "Whose account was it?"

"Only in the company's name."

"Go on." Porter's tone grew more impatient.

"The phone received one call," Clyde went on. "But it never went through—a test call, maybe. And that was to a certain Edmar Kucher, a Ukrainian national and Kyiv resident."

"Edmar Kucher, huh...who is he?"

"An employee or contractor," Clyde added. "Cell tower data shows he spends a lot of time driving between company facilities and other venues."

"Sounds like our first solid lead," Porter said.

"We have more, I think," Clyde said. "We ran Zhuk's IP addresses—home and office—through XKEYSCORE. He and his British handler, Brian Fletcher, both visited the website of Sollis International Bank in Vienna. They both examined the page providing information on how to obtain a safe deposit box, with Fletcher using Google to translate from German to English. And that was the only website they both visited—other than search engines and a few news sites."

"So?" Porter said.

Kane was impressed. "Jesus, did you stay up all night to find this?"

Clyde chuckled. "Travel records show Zhuk headed to Salzburg on July 18 for one day. So now I'm looking into whether he made the commute to and from the bank in Vienna—less than three hours by car."

"What does this all mean?" Porter asked, sounding irritated. "We've got—"

"Wait, it gets even better," Clyde interrupted. "Edmar Kucher flew to Budapest the day before Zhuk's trip to Austria and returned two days later."

"You think they met?" Porter asked.

"Possibly," Clyde said. "Or Edmar was trailing Zhuk."

"It's about two hours from Budapest to Vienna, right?" Kane asked.

Clyde sat back in his chair. "Sounds about right."

"We need more on this Edmar guy," Porter said, his voice hardening. "If he was on Zhuk's trail and communicating with him through text messages using Fletcher's codes, then clearly the Brits were compromised."

Kane stretched his back. "But Fletcher was using a GCHQ mobile phone straight from their OPA-TAS inventory, I'm told."

"Yes," Clyde said, "but none of the messages between the two were encrypted."

"So, Fletcher may have opened a safe deposit box for Zhuk. Probably that's how they were paying him?"

"I was told differently," Porter said, sighing. "Apparently, money changed hands physically, and in Ukraine only."

"Perhaps," Kane lamented. "Regardless, looks like Zhuk had been riding the SIS gravy train for several months before going to Vienna."

"I'll see what more I can get on Edmar," Clyde said. "But my opinion—given that Zhuk had traveled to a remote area and then ends up in a fatal road incident, tells me this is foul play. Whether Edmar is directly involved or not, I can't tell yet. I think the text was a trap."

"Let's regroup in two days," Porter said before hanging up.

10

Diaoyutai State Guesthouse, Beijing - Sept. 19

THE AUDITORIUM BURST WITH CHEERS AND APPLAUSE AS chief diplomats of the six national delegations waved at the crowd and shook hands amongst themselves, smiling and glad about the breakthrough they'd managed on the often-thorny diplomatic negotiations.

Linda stood up from the back row of the immense room, grabbed the mike from her chair and turned to Tommy, her cameraman, who was retying his pony-tail.

"Let's do the first take," she said.

"No smoke break?"

She rolled her eyes. "Com'on Tommy, after this."

He yawned. "Politicians give me narcolepsy." He stood up and stretched his tattooed arms, his hands clasped. "Alright, let's do it. Remember, it's Detroit news for this first segment."

"Got it." Linda scanned through her notes as Tommy detached the camera from the tripod and propped it on his shoulder, pointing it at her.

"My makeup okay?"

He nodded. "You're hot. Now hurry; my nicotine fit's gonna make the camera shake soon."

Linda felt her eyes were glassy. Her muscles ached. She wasn't used to jet-lag. And the fatigue from her post-Katrina coverage—only days ago—weighed on her after visiting many small coastal communities, where she worked long hours in dismal conditions, interviewing locals, many of whom had lost relatives, their homes or businesses. For those two weeks she practically lived in the TV van or in shabby motels with no power.

She breathed in deeply, waited a half-minute for the crowd to quiet down and then peered into the lens, holding her mike to her mouth. "Roll."

Tommy nodded, and a red light on the camera began flickering.

"Here in Beijing today, the United States delegation led by Assistant Secretary of State Christopher Hill and his counterparts achieved a significant milestone: a renewed commitment by North Korea to abandon nuclear weapons and programs and return to the Nuclear Non-proliferation Treaty. The culmination of this fourth round of talks also includes mutual promises for the U.S. and North Korea to normalize relations, and, perhaps most significantly, the U.S. affirmed that it has no intention of attacking or invading North Korea and plans to provide a formal security guarantee to this effect. This guarantee has been a key demand of Kim Jong-il's regime throughout the talks. So, it looks like each delegation has good news to bring back to their capitals." She held her mike closer to her lips. "But only time will tell if this historic accord will in fact lead to a definitive peace and denuclearization, and hopefully to tangible benefits for the Korean people as well, both north and south of the Demilitarized Zone. Linda Fabre, on assignment for WJBK News."

Tommy flipped a thumbs-up and pointed the camera down. "Next one's for Vancouver—you know it can be longer, right?"

"Got it."

He pointed the camera at Linda and their taping resumed. She reworded the message for the Channel M News but added historical details of earlier negotiations, and then did a third take, though much shorter, for Baton Rouge's WBTR 41."

"Shall we do the last two from outside?" Tommy said. "A shot of the delegations getting into their convoys?"

"Damn, you really need a smoke."

"Yep, I'm jonesing."

The moment Linda handed her mike to Tommy, who started packing the camera and other gear into bags at the foot of the tripod, she heard someone shout her name from somewhere behind her. She turned and spotted Max Balotelli weaving toward her through the dissipating crowd, wearing an expensive suit and a wide smile.

"Go have your cigarette," she told Tommy. "I'll meet you outside shortly." Then she turned to Max.

Though only in his early forties, Max was the most connected China-based bureau chief of any Western media company. Linda had heard his name over the years and had been told by many that he was the savviest journalist in the business this side of the Pacific, with contacts that reached deep into China's complex political apparatchik. And, apparently, he'd been impressed with her work enough to reach out to her agency and get her to Beijing as a stringer to help cover the breaking North Korean news for various network affiliates. It was nothing short of a miracle that she had been chosen for this gig, and she felt damn lucky that she'd been in the right place at the right time, especially in the highly competitive news media industry.

"You must be Max," she said extending her hand. "Thanks for everything." She brushed back her hair with her hand. "We've gotten great coverage, and I really appreciate the opportunity."

"Don't mention it." Max had taken her under his wing the moment the Linda-Tommy freelancing duo had landed in the Chinese capital two days earlier, though they hadn't had a chance to meet in person until now.

"I mean it. This is a big deal for me, and you made it happen."

"My pleasure," Max said.

She smiled.

He was average height, slender, clean shaven, with well groomed, dark brown hair—as Italian as his name suggested. And he'd been kind. He'd helped get the required press passes for Linda and Tommy to attend the conference, loaned her a driver, and even gave Tommy a fresh battery pack and tripod, since his had been damaged in transit.

"So, you're off again soon," Max asked.

"Yes." She sensed his tone was fishing for something. "We're headed to Hong Kong tomorrow for another short gig, and then home, I guess."

"You came a long way for only a few segments."

"Well, you offered this generous work, so I'll take what I can." If only he knew, she immediately thought. She'd only just gotten back into television journalism after a difficult hiatus following a devastating incident, job loss, depression and divorce. Then, Hurricane Katrina had somehow awakened her from that downward spiral. She had regained the strength she thought she'd lost, set down the booze, begun to confront her complicated relationship with Jonathan, built up the courage to leave her refuge in Iowa and rejoin the world. And she was pumped for more—whatever she could get her hands on.

Max gently took her elbow. "If you're not busy tonight, I have something to run by you."

She smiled and shook her head. "Tommy and I have an early flight tomorrow."

Max moved in closer. "It's another opportunity. What do you know about Pyongyang?"

Linda chuckled. "Hmm, the capital of North Korea. A resort destination, filled with well-fed, hard-working proletariat whistling with joy. Why?"

"Funny." He leaned in and whispered, "Are you interested to go see it firsthand?" He raised his chin in the direction of the throng of journalists dispersing toward the entrance. "Many of them are headed there tomorrow."

"But I'm freelancing in Hong Kong."

Max crossed his arms. "I got a call today from ITV in London. Their reporter had a family emergency and flew home a few hours ago. If you're game, I can recommend you as her replacement."

Linda stared at him, replaying his offer in her head. She imagined her luck: Katrina coverage; Beijing negotiations; and now possibly Pyongyang. *I could pull off a hat trick.*

"Yes or no?" Max asked, his chest inflated.

"How long?"

"I think two days...three tops."

"All costs are covered? And can you get visas and press passes so quickly?"

"Yes. And the North Korean consulate assured me they can have everything ready by early morning—assuming you have no criminal record in that country."

Linda chuckled. "Never been there before, don't worry." Also, she knew the Hong Kong story—a series of short segments for a Discovery Channel documentary—could be pushed back a few days, if needed.

"I need to think about it."

Max grinned. "Dinner? Seven-thirty?"

Linda sighed. "Very well." She was both excited and nervous.

11

Kyiv, Ukraine

"KANE HERE," THE STRIDENT VOICE PIERCED THROUGH Jonathan's sleep-deprived head the moment he answered the phone, not ten minutes into a longed-for nap. "We have a lead. Will tell you more in the car."

"How long?" Jonathan asked, shaking his head to rid himself of the remaining jet-lag grogginess.

"Thirty minutes." Kane then gave him the location.

In half that time, Jonathan was standing at the corner of Arkhitektora Horodetskoho Street where it intersected the vast open urban landscape of Maidan, Independence Square, near his hotel, as he'd been told. The balmy air made him sweat under his jacket. Arriving early offered him time to think, which he used to enjoy when he was preparing to depose a witness or face a jury. But these moments of reflection were now stress-inducing in the aftermath of Hurricane Katrina and his grueling jaunt across Central America. The unpleasantness quickly returned. About Linda, mostly. Her most recent words in New Orleans, especially. Each of them exiting her lips like gunfire. *Distance, huh*. She needed distance. *Whatever*.

He now imagined her navigating the streets of Beijing, fighting for air time amongst the bevy of competing reporters fawning over diplomats. But he knew it was something she could handle well, at least if she had regained the skills and confidence she once had. He'd always admired the way she could elbow her way through an aggressive, male-dominated industry to get her stories. From everything she'd said recently, it sounded like her professional confidence was on its way back up. And she wasn't just relying on others telling her what a good job she was doing. She'd quit drinking; she was spending a lot of time soul-searching, doing the hard work she needed to in order to build back her self-esteem. He'd be happy to help her on that journey, but not only did she not need his help, it was starting to sound more and more like she didn't need him either. He shook his head. He couldn't ignore the futility of letting his feelings for Linda permeate his thoughts. His heart sank. He swallowed hard. His eyes watered as he attempted to purge her from his mind.

To distract himself, Jonathan checked his watch. Kane was late. Just as he began keying in Kane's phone number on his cell, a car horn took his attention. He looked up and spotted Kane pulling up in a gray, late-model Volkswagen sedan. As it approached, he observed that the vehicle lacked diplomatic plates.

Jonathan was taken aback by Kane's scruffiness. He wore a wrinkled beige plaid shirt, untucked. He hadn't shaved. Whatever mediocre diplomatic look he'd had at their embassy meeting had been replaced by the raggedness of a third-shift repairman. Perhaps the pungent smoky, mildewed scent came from this unbathed diplomat and not the vehicle's filthy interior. A pile of cigarette butts filled the open ashtray below the radio, and coffee stains decorated both cup-holders.

"Seems like you live in this car?" Jonathan said.

Kane half-smiled.

A handheld radio was tucked into a side pocket of the driver's side door. Kane also had a small laptop wedged in between his seat and the center console, partly hidden behind his right arm.

As Kane pulled away from the curb, Jonathan noticed an unusual reflectiveness of the windshield and the glass on his door. Once seated, he asked, "Bulletproof?" and tapped the window with his knuckle.

"Huh." Kane seemed mildly amused. "It's coated with a film that makes it resistant to small arms, if you gotta know. There's also aramid fiber lining inside the front doors and trunk bulkhead."

"We're going to a warzone?"

Kane scoffed. "Not with this car. In Afghanistan I drove a Suburban that could withstand fifty caliber rounds and even some types of RPGs. A fucking beast. But this baby doesn't even come close."

As they drove off down the busy street, Jonathan continued to carefully examine Kane, who sat slouched in his seat, his left palm leisurely maneuvering the steering wheel as he weaved through traffic. He again spotted the scar on Kane's wrist, just a half-inch up from his excessively large silver watch—an expensive Omega, Jonathan observed. He was tempted to inquire where Kane had earned the lead, but on second thought, he didn't want to distract Kane's surprisingly cooperative mood.

He glanced at the diplomat and asked, "What's your lead?"

"ScorpionCloud."

Jonathan tilted his head. "How?"

They now were speeding across an overpass.

"The phone number of a guy who works for them came up in an unrelated matter." Kane's eyes stayed glued to the road as he pulled his laptop out and dropped it onto Jonathan's lap. "Open it."

Jonathan did so, and Kane quickly placed his index finger over a reader to unlock it. The screen came out of sleep mode, and instantly a black and white headshot of a middle-aged man came up.

"Recognize him?"

Jonathan examined the photograph. The man had short, grayish-white hair, dark eyes and brows, a bulbous nose and poorly-shaved, leathery skin. "No, never seen him before. Who is he?"

"Goes by the name Edmar Kucher, but he's used an alias recently to board a plane. You sure it's not the guy at the airport?"

"Certain," Jonathan said and sat back in his seat. The sense of disappointment started setting in again.

"Look carefully."

"I told you. The guy in the video had dark hair, long sideburns, longer jaw and different eyes." Jonathan was beginning to fear that he was again wasting his time by spending it with Kane. "When did you get this picture?"

"Yesterday."

"Pretty close up."

"From his laptop webcam."

"Nice hacking job. They teach you diplomats this skill?"

"We also captured a few shots from his cellphone. Problem is, he's got other phones we don't know about."

Jonathan assumed Edmar's drug-dealer-like behavior was probably not the norm for Ukrainian corporate employees any more than it was in America. What piqued his interest was how a ScorpionCloud employee became a person of interest in the first place. "What's the other matter about that led you to this guy?"

Kane slowed the car and shook his head. "I can't tell you."

Jonathan attempted to assemble possible scenarios, but as the seconds passed, he couldn't come up with a logical reason for this well-funded software company to have anything to do with Wyatt's disappearance.

"It doesn't matter, anyway. Let's just see what this guy might be hiding."

"Wyatt came here to meet ScorpionCloud's CEO," Jonathan said. his voice reflecting his confusion. "His key executives. His lawyers. His technical leads. Why kidnap him?"

"Was the first meeting at their law firm?"

"No, at ours." Jonathan was irritated that Kane hadn't remembered such a key fact. "There's simply no reason for Bodrov to mess with Wyatt. It's ultimately to his detriment that Wyatt's not at the negotiating table right now."

"What if Edmar's disgruntled? Wants to kill the deal?"

Jonathan shrugged.

"Any corporate trade secrets of value?"

Jonathan lowered his visor to block the late afternoon sun. "You mean valuable enough for an elaborate abduction in a public airport terminal?"

"Just asking."

"Answer's no, as far as I can tell." Jonathan was mulling the other enigma that had begun to fester since Kane had blurted it out. "What about Wyatt's NSA work. You've explained zilch. Don't tell me you haven't dug more deeply into his past."

"It's a factor."

"So how does this Edmar guy fit in?"

"In the separate investigation I mentioned, a call popped up, traced to his number. We tasked his recent travels and his local movements. Some of it looks fishy."

"How so?"

"Very short trips to Kuala Lumpur, Tashkent, Vienna, Doha. Not long enough for legit business dealings. He doesn't own any property and there's only a few thousand dollars in his bank account, which means he's covering his tracks. And he's using burner phones, which leads me to think he could be a courier. He's also been driving to various locations in and around the city for no reasons apparent to us."

"If he's any good, he's already onto you."

"Doubt it. We've got skilled people on him." Kane put on his sunglasses and nodded a confident chin-up.

From Jonathan's perspective, Kane appeared to know the city well. He drove without the aid of a map and made turns onto large and small streets without eyeing for signs.

"Almost there," Kane said as they turned onto a street lined with architecturally ornate 19th century buildings. "Edmar lives in the Podil neighborhood. Pretty historic area."

"Where are we?" Jonathan had no sense of reference.

"North-central part of the city. Some good bars and restaurants, a bit bohemian. Not your kind of area, I'd imagine."

"I'm from New Orleans. There's no place that city doesn't prepare you for," Jonathan said as he observed the buildings on his side of the street. Many were recently painted, some yellow, a few blue, others beige, but the rest appeared uninhabitable.

Kane began explaining how the Great Podil Fire of 1811 had destroyed more than half the area's dwellings when suddenly his cellphone chirped. He pulled it from his shirt pocket and checked the message. "Sounds like Edmar might be ready to leave soon." Kane slowed the car and pointed at the corner up ahead. "He lives on the next street." He pulled to the curb and stopped but left the engine running. He reached into the glove compartment and retrieved what looked like a GPS navigation device. He turned it on and waited a few seconds before raising it for Jonathan so see. "We've got his van tracked at all times."

Jonathan leaned in. A flashing green dot appeared a quarter-inch ahead of their relative position on the device's digital map. The dot's location appeared to place them about a block south.

Kane turned onto the small street and then took another right at the next corner. "It's coming up on the left. There, a second-floor apartment above the restaurant with the brown awning." Kane sped up a bit. "Look straight ahead as we pass it. And close the laptop."

The narrow street was packed with cars parallel-parked on both sides.

"How long have you been keeping tabs on him?" Jonathan asked.

"Coupld days only."

Jonathan closed the laptop and held it on his lap. He again studied the inside of the car and began to add things up. The lack of diplomatic plates. Partially armored sedan. The strange glance two local employees gave Kane in the embassy hallway as they headed to the conference room. He fixed his gaze on Kane.

"What?" Kane asked.

Jonathan grinned. "You're CIA, aren't you?"

Kane pitched his head back. "You've seen too many movies, Mr. Brooks." His voice stayed stern. "I would think that an attorney with your experience would stay clear of the world of fiction."

"Tell me I'm right."

"I'm a Foreign Service officer—Second Secretary, to be exact—with a broad portfolio of responsibilities. And frankly, I'm doing you and your client a favor."

"You're CIA and this Edmar fellow is already on your radar for some serious reason, I imagine." Jonathan could feel his temper rise. He sensed that no one was telling him anything truthful. Not Cramer. Not Kane. Perhaps not even the attorneys at Soykis & Kharenko. "Do you know where Wyatt is? What are you holding back?"

Kane shook his head. "Don't be difficult, dammit. I have no idea where your guy is. None whatsoever." He then quickly stopped the car. "I'm here to help—so its counterproductive to piss me off, don't you think?"

Jonathan shifted his body to face Kane. "You can put lipstick on a pig, but it's still a pig. I've dealt with your kindred before. In Russia. In Venezuela. In Nicaragua. Elsewhere. There's nothing genuinely honest about any intelligence officer I've ever encountered, and—trust me—I've interacted with plenty of them. So, don't take me for a fool."

Kane's lips began to curl as her returned a pensive, unfriendly gaze.

"And I don't think it will go down well," Jonathan continued, "when my client reports back to Senator Jordan that the U.S. Embassy—and you, in particular—withheld key facts from me and impeded my ability to find my client's missing executive."

Kane turned his gaze to the street ahead and seemed to weigh a response. "I don't know whether to laugh or punch you in the face."

"A man's life is on the line—an American."

Kane lobbed an annoyed look at Jonathan, then quickly texted a message and waited. His cell rang again.

"Yeah," Kane said into the phone. "Uh-huh. I'll explain later. Head back to that Desna address, and wait there. He may head there tonight. I got him for now." He hung up and eyed the row of parked cars on Jonathan's side of the street.

Suddenly, a compact car quickly pulled out of a parking spot and sped away. "My colleague," Kane said. He just as quickly slipped the Volkswagen into the freed spot, turned off the engine, adjusted his side mirror and reclined his seat by a few inches. "Okay, now we wait."

Before Jonathan uttered a word, he heard his own cellphone ringing in his jacket. He quickly answered. It was Elya, and her voice was shaking as she said his name.

"What's wrong?"

"The airport commander—you know, the one we met. He just called me. The videos are gone."

"Gone?"

"He said a city police investigator—a man he'd never seen before—was in the surveillance room and probably took the DVDs."

"Jesus Christ!" Jonathan slammed his fist onto the dash. Nothing was going well, and the one key piece of evidence that could show he and Elya weren't hallucinating about Wyatt's abduction was now missing.

Kane nodded for an explanation.

"No sense going to the airport," Jonathan said, clenching his jaw. "Someone with clout stole the footage." He felt his rage return, his heart racing, the arteries throbbing. He turned and glanced over his seat in the direction of Edmar's apartment at end of the street. "Edmar's all we've got for now."

12

"I TAKE IT YOU'RE NOT MARRIED," MAX SAID NOT TWO minutes after Linda sat down at the dinner table.

This wasn't quite a topic she'd expected to come out so soon in the meeting, if at all. *Why would her marital status matter?* she wondered. *Sounds like a more loaded question than mere small talk.* She took a breath and reassured herself that he was a master in the profession and didn't intend anything by it. But when she didn't answer, hoping to move to another topic, he asked her pointedly, "You're not married, right?"

She looked down, concerned. Perhaps that's why he had chosen Da Giorgio, the smaller and more intimate of the restaurants at the Grand Hyatt. And possibly it was not for convenience that he'd selected a restaurant here, where she was staying. She hoped this "job offer" was not going to include a quid pro quo component.

But she also wasn't going to play victim, whether he had ulterior motives or was merely displaying friendly inquisitiveness. She met Max's gaze. "I'm divorced, and I still feel the shrapnel from it." Her tone was deliberately stern.

He nodded with a close-mouthed smile that told Linda her response might have worked.

The waiter arrived, and she ordered her drink.

"Orange juice?" Max asked, surprised.

Linda hadn't had a drop of alcohol in weeks. She nodded. "I'm just tired."

"Wine would help your tiredness."

"No thanks."

The small talk over appetizers was better. He spoke about the growth of the media business in China and his experiences in the industry. But Linda was worried that Max hadn't yet mentioned anything about his earlier offer. She wanted to be polite, waiting for him to say it, but every minute that went by made her more nervous. And by the time the waiter brought the main course, Max was no closer to giving a straight answer.

"I hear you took a leave of absence from anchoring."

"You did?" Linda hesitated. "Yes, I needed a break." She didn't want to explain.

"I've seen your work," Max added. "A buddy of mine sent me some of your segments back in New Orleans."

"From Hurricane Katrina?"

"No, older stuff. From when you were at Channel 6."

Oh god. Linda didn't want to remember. Not because she wasn't proud of her work she did back then.

But rather, it was an uncomfortable reminder of how confident she used to be.

"You're good. Real good. Your eye contact, your voice, your wit...your beauty. I think you still have all this today."

Linda nodded, unsure why he had taken the time to dig into her past.

"I've been in this business now..." Max looked up for a moment, chewing his lip, "for twenty-eight years."

"Long time."

"You're a veteran journalist, too, Linda. One thing time has taught me is to spot the winners. To differentiate between those who simply like this job from those who love it and thrive on the challenges. That's what makes the Dan Rathers and Anderson Coopers of the world so good. Passion."

Max sat back in his chair, his shoulders erect. "You know, it's probably not my business, but I was curious about something. You have a scar there," he said, pointing at her chest from across the table. "Did you take a break because of that incident?" He seemed to work hard to make his tone sound innocent and well-meaning.

Linda suspected that he knew about the scar, the fire, the whole ugly past. *Perhaps he just wants to test me? My stamina. Or my patience.* Regardless of the motive, the question rubbed in her face the single most painful experience of her life—the house fire she'd barely survived. Despite multiple cosmetic surgeries, the burn marks on her chest, lower abdomen and thighs had not vanished. Every day the mirror reminded her of the inferno, of the agonizing and long recovery, of the parts of her body that de-womanized her. And this man now sat facing her with the same honest harshness as her bathroom mirror.

"Max," she said, trying to avoid being combative. "You have to understand. I've gone through a lot over the years. You can't imagine the lows."

He nodded. "Fine, fine. Let's change the subject."

All of Linda's doubts and concerns were now bouncing wildly in her head. *Am I even good enough for what he had previously offered?* Or was it just to get me to dinner. She couldn't bare the silence about the reason she'd agreed to meet with him. She leaned forward. "What's the plan?"

He shrugged. "What do you mean?"

"Do I have the North Korea gig tomorrow or not?"

He chose to put a piece of bread in his mouth instead of answering, his eyes meeting her gaze.

"I'm not sleeping with you for it," she said.

He stopped chewing. "Oh, my goodness. That is not my intention. At. All."

"Because I'm not looking at this assignment as a license to have fun. Only a month ago I was still barely able to stay sober, tiptoeing across the boundaries of my sanity, some days not even wanting to live. That's the Linda I escaped from, but only a short while ago. My career now is all I've got keeping me from collapsing. And I'm putting into it every damn spark of energy I have."

Max shook his head as his cheeks began to glow red. "Linda, I didn't mean to—"

"Just tell me, are you giving me the job?" Either she would leave tomorrow for Pyongyang or for Hong Kong. In any case, she wasn't about to beg for the North Korea gig—and certainly his bed sheets would stay dry, at least from her, if indeed that possibility was still lodged somewhere in the back of his mind.

After a long silent stare, Max laughed. "Boy, you are a mood killer. But I like you, your strength...your directness. That's why I brought you here. I think you're among the best."

She took a sip of her juice and surrendered a mild smile. "I'm a bit skittish, I hope you understand. I've only recently jumped back into media, and simply am being cautious—there are a lot of sharks out there, but I realize you're not one of them."

"I'm not. Please don't mistake my curiosity for anything else."

"Okay. Thank you for understanding me." She felt relieved. "I'm very, very appreciative of everything you've done for me in the last few days. I really am. I'm simply not in a frame of mind to think about other things. It's all been a bit overwhelming for me."

"I understand," he said, his voice diminishing. "You're going, but without Tommy."

"But he's a good cameraman."

"I've already assigned another. And I've arranged something else for Tommy, anyway."

"Okay."

Max pulled out an envelope from his jacket pocket and handed it to her. "Just need your signature on a few forms, and you're good to go."

"Thank you," she said.

"Our flight leaves for Pyongyang tomorrow just before noon."

"*Our* flight?"

He smiled. "Yes, I'm going along, too."

Persistent fella.

13

Northern Ukraine

A RANCID STENCH SEEPED INTO KEVIN'S LUNGS AS he suddenly jolted his head back from unconsciousness. He tried to open his swollen eyelids. The left one was impossible to move, but he managed with his right one, barely. He was still in the same room. The same single light bulb hung from the concrete ceiling. But the thugs were gone. *Thank goodness.*

He scanned the bare cement walls of the dimly lighted room just as the nerves around his wrist regained the excruciating burning sensation from earlier. He was sure the rope had peeled through the skin of his wrists, perhaps to the muscle tissue below. And it was no looser than it had been the moment his ruthless Asian captors had tied his hands to the back of the chair.

His head throbbed from within, and the needling agony that stretched across his scalp and the upper part of his face returned in full force. There was still a small puddle by his feet, though now it was a mix of blood and urine.

He had no perception of time, but he guessed he'd been here two to three days, and that he was about two hours from Kyiv. He then realized he'd defecated in his pants. He'd gone in and out of consciousness at least three times, each time after they struck his head, apparently tiring from beating his limbs and abdomen. They had also injected him with drugs that had made him hallucinate. Every part of his body ached.

The sound of footsteps came through the closed metal green-tinted door. The lock rattled loudly as someone inserted a key. A figure appeared, slowly pushing open the door halfway. The silhouette appeared unfamiliar. The prior torturers were short and bulky, but this one appeared to be a large white man.

Kevin blinked his right eye several times, trying again to clear the fluid that blurred the limited vision he had left.

"You look like shit." The man's voice was deep, and the Eastern European accent heavy.

Fuck you. Kevin didn't have it in his lungs to reply out loud. He saw the light dim around him. He was under the man's shadow. A large man. Dress shirt. Formal slacks. Dress shoes. But it was too painful to look up at the man's face.

"If you want your family to see you alive, you have to talk."

"Ah!" Kevin cried as the man kicked his shin.

"If they take you away, you'll certainly die."

Kevin didn't know what he meant. *They? The Asians? And who the fuck are you?*

"You don't have much time, Mr. Wyatt. We only want some information. It will have no impact on you or your family. You will go home. You will be the hero who survived an international kidnapping. You will live your life in peace. Just give us the information. We are only asking for a few codes and some details on IT infra- structure. Quite simple."

Kevin kept his eyes on the floor. The ripping pain bolted across his thorax as he struggled to breathe. He gulped for air, gathering the strength to speak. "It's not just codes, motherfucker. You're asking me to betray my country. In any case, much of the programming, secured access and information have changed."

"Good, you have found your tongue." The man took a step back, his shoes exiting the murky puddle below Kevin's chair.

Kevin found his only strength—a collection of mental snippets of his wife's voice and his son's face. But the continuing pain dissipated the thoughts. He imagined what was in store for him. More excruciating abuse, no doubt. He'd already endured so much. And through all this torture, he'd tried his damnedest not to spill anything of value. The pain again prompted him, albeit as briefly as it had before—to weigh the wisdom of resisting. After all, he'd left the NSA five years ago. What he still remembered of these government networks was indeed deep, but the intelligence agencies and the Pentagon had surely changed much of the source code, protocols, firewalls, encryption and other security features since he took Cramer's offer to join Southern Seas Logistics and reap the benefits of the private sector.

What his captors wanted was not trivial. They knew exactly what to ask for. Kevin knew the questions could only have come if they'd already hacked partly into the networks. He'd listened to their every word. He'd told them to pound sand. And his body had taken the ensuing beatings. There was nothing new now. The thugs would simply repeat the cycle, he assumed.

The man stayed hovering over Kevin as two people suddenly entered the room. Kevin struggled to look up. From what he could tell, they were the same two who'd abused him before.

A massive shock pounced his head. Kevin propelled left and screamed out his lungs. The large man had punched Kevin in the temple. He hadn't caught the man's arm swinging his way. Not that it would have helped him to do anything other than flinch. But as futile as that would be, he simply wanted to know when the blows were coming. But his field of vision had narrowed to a mere sliver. He sat barely upright, battered, unclothed and shivering, waiting for this man and his cohorts to unleash another session of their cruelty.

"You must talk, *blyat!* Tell us about SIPRNET, JWICS, and NSANET and you'll live through this! Or my friends here will start removing parts of your body."

"I told you," Kevin said, his voice cracking, his lungs gasping for whatever air his exhausted diaphragm could scavenge. "I don't know. I have no idea what these networks are. I'm only a—"

"You lie!" Another blow came from the left. Kevin's head swung and hit his own shoulder, the pain exploding uncontrollably. He feared his neck bones might snap if this beating continued. His already swollen left eye felt as if it had turned inside out. Fluid drained down his nose and lips—most likely blood.

"If you don't talk, we will take you to a place where there is no return," said a voice with a strong East Asian accent—perhaps Mandarin or Korean.

Kevin breathed in and slowly stretched his head backward, looking right up at the white man's squarish face and boxy build. The man held a handkerchief over his mouth and nose. Despite the minimal lighting, and his bad eye, Kevin examined the shape of the man's head, brow, hairline and plump-shaped jaw. He blinked again as a spike of excitement came to mind. His eyes focused further on the man's facial features. And then it hit him. *It's not possible*, Kevin instantly told himself. He suddenly looked down, disturbed, his muddled judgment bouncing in his head. *Bodrov?* For a split second he ignored his pain. *Goddamn Artem Bodrov?* He'd seen the CEO's face on ScorpionCloud's website and in a marketing video less than a week ago, in preparation for the negotiations at the law firm. He again looked up at the man. There was no mistaking it. The handkerchief did little to hide Bodrov's face. Kevin assumed it was simply to lessen the smell.

The man quietly stepped back as the two thugs moved in closer, one of them grabbing Kevin's jaw.

It now dawned on Kevin that Bodrov wasn't trying to hide his identity. That meant no one intended for Kevin to leave alive, no matter what secrets he revealed. His heart sank. For the first time since he'd been thrown into a van at gunpoint near the airport, he understood his impending fate. His chest tightened. The thought of never seeing his family again suddenly hijacked his every thought.

14

Podil District, Kyiv

"THERE HE GOES," KANE SAID TO JONATHAN, PROPPING himself upright and turning the ignition key.

A black, windowless Mercedes van passed them at high speed.

"He's alone," Kane added. A few seconds later he pulled out of the parking spot.

"I'm telling you," Jonathan said, "if this guy is any good, he'll know he's under surveillance."

"We'll stay a block or two behind," Kane replied, grabbing the tracking device and shaking it at Jonathan.

Kane did as he'd said; they stayed well back. Over the next fifteen minutes Jonathan briefly caught sight of the van only twice.

The sky's remaining yellowish-red hue from the earlier sunset were now about to fade to darkness. Kane continued to drive, occasionally glancing at the tracking device. They passed several rows of shabby eight-story, Soviet-era apartment blocks that lined both sides of the road. The street veered right, past a park and its old, rusty swing set. The neighborhoods appeared more rundown as they continued away from the city toward the southwestern outskirts.

"Any clue where he's headed?" Jonathan said.

Kane shook his head. "I'm not aware of any ScorpionCloud facility in this part of town."

The four-lane road narrowed to two. There was now much less traffic and many more industrial buildings than residential ones, but all the structures were equally dilapidated, with crumbling cement walls and rusting, damaged property fences. The uneven sidewalks were cracked and overgrown with weeds. Ungroomed greenery seemed to fill up the space between buildings.

The van driven by Edmar came nudged sight again some distance ahead, its turn signal flashing. It pulled to the left at the next intersection.

"We're too close," Jonathan warned. "And there's little traffic to blend into."

"I see that." Kane said, his voice stern. "Chill. I'll give us more distance. I know what I'm doing."

Yeah. Jonathan had heard this confident word before—in Moscow, in Panama City, in Washington, in New Orleans, in Caracas, among other places—and things often didn't end well. He didn't really care whether Kane was CIA or not. The most talented humans make mistakes, particularly those who over-rate their skills, he thought.

Kane took the following left rather than follow the van. He crossed the opposite lanes of traffic onto a smaller street that led into an industrial park, where the buildings—mostly made of brick—appeared to be warehouses or perhaps small assembly plants or factories. Some looked in use, while others seemed ready for demolition.

At that moment the van crossed their path about a hundred fifty yards ahead, heading to their right. It also had turned its lights on as darkness set in. Jonathan began suspecting that Edmar had no good reason to be in this area except to gauge whether he was being followed.

Kane checked the tracking device and continued straight to avoid turning behind the van.

"I think he knows," Jonathan said.

Kane didn't respond and simply followed the van on a parallel route to the end of the block. Jonathan glanced down at the tracker and then peered ahead. The van had once again turned and appeared to be heading back to the main road from where it had entered this industrial area. Kane turned at the next corner since the path ahead was a cul-de-sac.

"Slow down," Jonathan said, looking at the dot that represented the location of the van. "Okay, now turn."

Kane veered onto another long, deserted path between two warehouses. They crossed one alley, then another. Suddenly, from the corner of his eye Jonathan spotted something moving fast toward Kane's side. He turned his head half-way and flinched. "Oh man!"

A massive object barreled into them from the cross street. The thundering sound of crushing metal and smashing glass burst through the air, and shards sprayed violently over Jonathan as he was thrown airborne across the car's front compartment. His upper body collided with Kane's and ricocheted back into his own seat.

Jonathan gripped the back of his seat with his left hand and the dashboard with his right hand, his eyes fixated on a huge, mangled front grill of a truck that had pierced half-way into Kane's side of the car. Kane didn't move. His face a bloodied mess.

The grinding sounds of gears shook the air. The truck began reversing, its engine revving and belching hard, and completely dislodged Kane's door as it pulled back. The tearing metal sounds blended with the deafening rumble of its diesel engine operating at full power. As the truck backed up some more, Jonathan heard the squealing wail of belts, which he realized came from Kane's car. Damn, it's still running.

Kane was slumped motionless, his head and neck bleeding profusely. As Jonathan scrambled to right himself, he saw that the assaulting vehicle, a garbage truck, had stopped its reverse path some thirty yards away. Both its doors flung open, and a man jumped down from each side. The driver had a weapon—bigger than a handgun but smaller than an assault rifle. He then raised it at Jonathan.

"Shit!" Jonathan threw his left leg over the center console and stomped on the gas pedal while also lunging sideways to grab the steering with both hands. The car propelled forward as a volley of gunshots rang out, and Jonathan heard several bullets hit the car.

Now it was too dark to see well ahead. He toggled the headlight switch, but it was pointless—the lights were dead. He glanced in the rearview mirror just as five or six more rounds hit the rear windshield, which created crackled shapes resembling oversized snowflakes, but they didn't penetrate the glass. Kane was right, Jonathan thought. The Volkswagen was indeed bullet resistant—but not garbage truck-proof.

Jonathan, half-seated on Kane's lap, was barely controlling the car as he sped through the darkened street at about forty or fifty miles per hour. He kicked Kane's feet off to the side to have more room while attempting to gain better control of the pedals with his left leg—his other leg was still sprawled across the center console and passenger side. Using his shoulder, he pushed Kane's body further back into the driver's seat but not so much that Kane would fall out of the opening left by the missing door.

The road was in bad shape, judging from the sounds of debris and the potholes he felt as he raced forward. He glanced to his left. The pavement was whizzing by rapidly, the beleaguered wail of the battered Volkswagen filling his ears. He swerved into a narrow alley between other buildings. He was sure the truck was in pursuit but hadn't seen it yet. He gripped the steering wheel hard, his eyes stabbing the darkness in search of obstacles. Only a faint glow in the distant sky, remnants of the sunset, helped him make out faint silhouettes of buildings.

He again glanced over his shoulder. There was no way of knowing how much of a lead he had over his attackers. He assumed the truck's lights also were likely damaged.

Jonathan swerved around barrels and old industrial equipment that had been left in the alley. He steered the car as best he could from his contorted position. But then the path ahead became so dark, he could barely see anything. He kept his foot firmly on the accelerator but leaned farther over the dash to try and see better ahead. He eyed a dim sliver of light that momentarily stretched across the distance, but he couldn't make it out before it disappeared. He looked right and left but had no working streetlights to give him any sense of direction. There were now no buildings on either side of the road, but he couldn't see anything ahead. He tried to move his right leg over to the driver's side but unintentionally kicked Kane's laptop under his butt.

Suddenly the car hit a rough spot on the road. The jolt threw him sideways and almost tossed Kane out of the vehicle. Then Jonathan heard the pelting sounds of gravel. Before he could press the brakes, the car rocketed through shrubbery, burst through a fence, and he instantly felt the ground give way. *The car's airborne!* One second. Two. Bam!

"God!" Jonathan's body smashed into the dashboard as water burst through the mangled windshield and completely doused him. More water instantly rushing into the car from every direction. He quickly pushed Kane's body off of him as the car rapidly sank. When he tried to jostle his legs free from under the steering column, Kane's laptop swirled up with the rough torrent of water and hit his neck. He grabbed the laptop with one hand while trying to free his leg with the other. Perhaps his pant leg was caught in something. He knew every second mattered. He kicked and twisted violently, trying again to free himself from whatever had trapped his left leg. The rushing water had now reached eye-level. He jolted up, taking a big gulp of air. His head pounced the roof. He gripped the steering wheel and pushed again. Harder still. He screamed, pushing. Finally!

He was free. He inhaled one more air and dove into the water, quickly twisting his body to exit through the opening on the driver's side. He kicked his legs and swung his left arm to push himself faster to the surface, while clutching the laptop with his right arm. The car had submerged deeper than he'd thought. Barely able to hold his breath any longer, he kicked harder. Just as his lungs were about to surrender, he burst through the surface, gasping and coughing. He looked around and guessed he was in a pond or lake.

He scanned for any sign of Kane floating on the water. There were a few bubbles and waves coming from the spot where the car had gone under, but then the surface became still within a few seconds. He thought of diving back into the water to search for him, but it was futile. It was too dark, and by now the car was likely too deep to reach in a single breath.

Jonathan took in deep breaths as he treaded water, careful not to make noise. His eyes adjusted to the dark surroundings. The assailants were surely not far, and with flashlights they could easily spot him in the water. He turned on his back and began swimming in the opposite direction from where the car had plunged into the water. At that moment he felt a ripping pain twist around his chest. Something was wrong. He continued swimming in a half-backstroke, the pain inside him growing. For a split-second he feared it was a gunshot wound. He'd been shot before. But soon he realized the pain was not comparable.

Scanning the surroundings as he swam, he suddenly spotted silhouettes at the bushes lining the ridge where the car had gone airborne before plunging into the water. There were two people, both with flashlights, and they began pointing searching the surface of the water. They were likely the assassins from the truck, but the vehicle was nowhere in sight.

The water was cold, certainly below 60 Fahrenheit. By now Jonathan had swum about a hundred yards from the men and was about to reach to opposite bank of the pond. The darkness had completely set in, which gave him cover. But the pain in his chest was so profound that he was beginning to lose his grip on the laptop. His knees and back also were excruciatingly painful—but less than his chest. He began to feel dizzy. He knew he'd hit his head in the initial collision, and the impact with the water probably made it worse. As long as he was still in the water, his survival depended on staying conscious. He suddenly remembered the similar frightening crash into the water at night just weeks ago in Nicaragua. What damn luck. Except this time, it was a car rather than an airplane.

He scaled the muddy, graveled edge of the pond, his limbs aching as he crawled and then stood. He grabbed the thick shrubs to help him stabilize as he walked through the wooded area, heading towards a distant glow of lights and faint sounds of traffic.

The pain didn't let up during the ten-minute trek over uneven ground in the dark. But he finally reached a busy road with fast-moving cars. He strolled along the narrow curb, squinting as he faced the bright lights of oncoming vehicles. He lifted his arm to flag down the next car coming his way, but suddenly his vision began to twist. His vision blurred and limbs went numb. He collapsed onto his knees. The sound of screeching tires drilled through his head. He fell forward, and everything went dark.

15

Solom'ynsk District, Kyiv

A SHARP PAIN SHOT UP JONATHAN'S ARM. HE INSTANTLY cried out and opened his eyes. He blinked several times until his vision became less blurry. There stood a woman near him wearing a white apron and a tall white hat, like a chef. He examined her. He blinked again and realized this wasn't some kind of kitchen. She was a nurse and that hat was a trademark of Eastern European medical staff.

The middle-aged woman glanced at him, returning a lukewarm smile, but said nothing. She finished adjusting the needle of the IV that was attached to his bandaged forearm.

Jonathan was surprised he was alive, but that momentary gratefulness passed as quickly as it had popped into his mind. He scrutinized the surroundings: well-worn drapes on each side of a small, partly-opened window that showed a dark sky, two empty hospital beds to his right, and some sort of old, non-functioning monitor on a cart next to his bed. The door was wide open, and he could see an empty nurses' station a few feet down the corridor. He then realized that whoever had attacked him might not have trouble tracking him down here. That's when he spotted what looked like the sleeve of his jacket hanging out of a burlap bag that had been set on a chair against the opposing wall. He knew he had to leave as soon as possible.

"Where am I?" he said, his voice cracking. The slowness with which he felt is words leave his mouth told him sedatives were still in his body.

She seemed surprised he'd spoken in something other than her language. "No English," she said, shrugging, and began heading for the door.

"Wait, where are we?" With his right hand Jonathan motioned the international sign for here, pointing downward. "What is this place—which hospital?"

"Ah." The nurse seemed to understand. She grabbed the clipboard at the foot of his bed and pointed to the top of the paper chart. There were four words followed by "No.6." She read them out loud while tapping her finger over them.

"Hospital Number Six?" Jonathan said, after which she nodded.

He pointed at her wrist, and she turned it so that he could see her watch. It was twelve-ten in the morning. He guessed he'd been here about three hours.

Soon after she left the room, Jonathan removed the IV needle and replaced the taped cotton swab over the spot. He got up slowly, tossed the blanket to the floor and threw his legs over the edge of the bed. His thighs and calves were bruised and scraped in several places, and just about every muscle and bone in his body was in agony, especially his right chest. He stepped barefoot over the cold tile floor, and that's when a ripping pain bolted through his ribs. The same pain he'd felt when he escaped from Kane's sinking car. *Dammit.* He pressed his chest with his palm and understood what had happened. Just like one unlucky afternoon playing football in high school, he had fractured a rib. He was sure of it. He walked slowly, his legs wobbling. He grabbed each bed's metal footboard as he continued toward the door, which he then closed. He returned to the burlap bag and pulled out his shirt, pants, underwear, undershirt, and shoes, all of which were still damp and cold and reeked of mildew.

At the bottom of the bag he found Kane's laptop. The top half that had the screen was missing, but the bottom portion containing the hard drive appeared fine, albeit a bit bent and missing several keys. He also found his passport, watch, and wallet. He assumed his cellphone was at the bottom of the lake, along with the car and perhaps Kane's body.

When Jonathan was dressed, he stuffed the three pages of his medical chart into his pocket and went into the tiny bathroom. After splashing water over his face, he looked into the mirror and noticed two large bruises, one on his forehead and the other on his neck. His chin was scraped, too. All in all, though, it wasn't so bad after having survived such a brutal attack.

He cracked open the door and waited until the hallway was quiet and clear before heading to the stairs with Kane's laptop tucked under his arm. The pain in his chest and soreness in his limbs made the three-story walk to the ground floor excruciatingly difficult. Breathing alone felt like someone was stabbing a knife into his ribcage.

The lobby was empty. A lone security guard meandered in the other direction. He peeked through the glass doors at the entrance and eyed a phone booth under a street lamp on the other side of the hospital's entrance. He quickly got change from a vending machine and walked out in the cold air.

His hands shook as he grabbed from his wallet Elya's business card, which included her handwritten cellphone number—it was smudged but still legible. He dialed, and after six rings she finally answered.

"It's Jonathan," he said, his voice hoarse. "I know it's late but—"

"I've been trying to reach you all night," she said, her loudness forcing him to tilt the phone away from his ear for a moment. "Where are you?" Her voice was stern and sharp. Clearly, she hadn't yet gone to sleep.

"Hospital Number Six," Jonathan said, his chest continuing to ache so much it was difficult to speak full sentences. "I was attacked. By Bodrov's men, I'm sure."

"What do you mean? Artem Bodrov?"

"I was with Kane, the man from the embassy. They shot at us and chased us, and we drove into a pond. I made it out, but Kane's dead."

"My God," she gasped. "It was you?"

"What?"

"I saw on television—on the evening news—that a car fell into a lake. But they didn't say anyone was injured or killed."

"I'm not safe here. If they targeted an American diplomat, they'll have no problem killing me in this hospital."

Jonathan told her everything he could remember about the attack as best he could, his agonized breaths and pain cutting his sentences into short phrases.

Her voice was now shaky. "I'll pick you up in fifteen minutes."

"Be careful. Make sure you're not followed. I see a restaurant about fifty to sixty meters from here. It has a red and green neon sign. Meet me there."

*   *   *

Jonathan had waited about ten minutes behind a dumpster a half-block away from the hospital entrance when suddenly he heard an engine roaring. A dark Range Rover rapidly turned the corner and sped toward the medical facility, where it abruptly stopped under the lighted entry canopy. Three men got out, two of them quickly disappearing into the building. The other was the driver, a large man wearing a thick jacket. He seemed to scan the surroundings and then leaned on the vehicle, its lights on and engine running.

Jonathan's heart rate shot up. This was no normal hospital visit. And the fact that it was nearly one in the morning told Jonathan they were probably there to kill him.

He ducked further behind the dumpster and turned to eye the restaurant where he'd told Elya to meet. It was only about seventy yards from the SUV. But he had no way of reaching Elya to tell her to pick him up further away. He had no choice now but to wait for her. Every few seconds he glanced at the bulky man next standing at the hospital entrance.

Jonathan shivered in his damp clothes, sockless feet, and wet shoes. He replayed the attack in his head, trying to recall any distinctive features of the two assailants in the garbage truck. But everything had happened so quickly, they were some distance away, and it was dark.

He finally spotted Elya's Saab pass through the quiet intersection and stop at the other corner of the restaurant. Jonathan glanced back at the man next to the SUV. Good. Only the back of Elya's car was visible from Jonathan's angle, and even less so from the hospital entrance. The man now appeared to be on his cellphone facing the glass doors, seemingly unaware of Elya's car.

Jonathan quickly got up and crossed the street, hoping not to get spotted while passing under the lighted neon sign of the closed restaurant. The gripping pain in his chest had worsened. Whatever sedatives he'd been given had now worn off. He waved at her as he approached.

"Oh my," he heard Elya say as she quickly opened her door and began stepping out of her idling car. She wore jeans, a green t-shirt and black blouse, and now looked younger without the makeup she'd worn at the law firm.

"Get back in the car," he said in a loud whisper, nearly out of breath as he momentarily leaned on her car's trunk to secure his footing.

"But you're hurt."

"I'll manage. We need to leave now."

She quickly got back into the driver's seat and closed her door.

"Go, go." He sat down in the front passenger side, and the car took off. "They're at the hospital now, looking for me."

"This is completely crazy!" She shook her head, her gaze never leaving the street. She turned the car at a high rate of speed onto another road.

He looked over his shoulder at the empty pavement behind them. "I think we're okay. They didn't see us." He then leaned back in his seat, trying to find a position that lessened the needling ache in his chest and limbs.

"I'm so sorry, Jonathan."

Jonathan chuckled. "I'm embarrassed to tell you that this isn't the first time I've had this happen to me."

She glanced at him with eyes wide open but said nothing.

"I have something big," he said, holding up Kane's damaged laptop. "If you can find a smart codebreaker, we may have a lot of answers from this hard drive."

Jonathan looked back once more to make sure no one was trailing them. They then turned onto a well-lighted four-lane street that had some traffic.

"You need medical care." Her voice was still shaky but less than when they'd spoken on the phone.

"Not now. And I can't go to my hotel," he said. "Bodrov's people are probably tracking down every place I could possibly be."

"Then my place."

"No, you're probably on his list."

"Maybe the embassy?"

He thought about this for a moment but then realized that embassy officials would likely involve local police, or worse yet, they'd treat him as a suspect. He sighed. "No, forget that—it's not an option."

"I have keys to a flat—a friend of mine who is on holiday this week. Bodrov cannot possibly know this."

"Here? In the city?"

"Yes, she lives in a nice area—in the Pozniaky district, on the east side of the river."

Jonathan considered her offer. He held his chest as the level of pain ebbed and flowed with the car's movements.

"Do you have a better option?"

"Fine, take me there."

"But you'll need fresh clothes. What about medicines?"

"Painkillers would be nice," he said, trying to suppress the discomfort to sound as normal as he could so as to not frighten her more than she already appeared to be.

"We're crossing the Darnyts'kyi Bridge," she said. They drove fast on the middle lane of the three eastbound lanes. A train passed them going the opposite way on the rail line that occupied the center of the bridge.

Jonathan looked out his window. There were few lights along the west bank of the Dnieper river. A lot more lights came from the opposite side, where they were headed.

About five minutes after reaching the other side of the river, Elya pointed at an apartment block that looked at least twenty stories tall and took up more than two city blocks. She turned onto Oleny Chilkiy Street and then pulled up to one of the building's entrances next to a ground-floor pharmacy. He looked up at the building and sighed. Here he would be safe, at least he hoped.

Elya helped Jonathan walk from the car and up the two flights of stairs. Once in the apartment, he washed his face, inspected the rest of his bruised body, got out of his wet clothes and wrapped himself with a towel and blanket. He walked to the living room, eyeing the chairs to determine which would be the most comfortable.

"I texted Vanko," she said from the kitchen. The sound of a boiling kettle accompanied her words. "He'll be here soon with men's clothes for you. And he can help with extracting the files from the computer hard drive."

"Thank you."

Jonathan sipped his tea in a plush leather chair, his feet propped over a pillow on the coffee table. He gazed at Elya, who was reading the medical chart that he'd taken from the hospital. She studied the pages, at times appearing to reread some sections before she put the papers down. She then walked to a bookcase behind the sofa.

"I don't know how to translate these words," she said, eyeing the shelves. "Good, she has one—an English dictionary." She flipped back and forth between several pages and after a few minutes returned to the couch to face Jonathan. She crossed her arms and frowned. "Want to know what you have?"

Jonathan wasn't keen to hear it but nodded.

"Two fractured ribs—right side, numbers 4 and 5. Also a fracture of the right scapula, another small fracture of the...I don't know how to pronounce this...i-l-i-u-m—"

"Ilium, the pelvic bone." Jonathan said softly.

"Yes, and a concussion."

"Fantastic." Jonathan shook his head. "Anything else?"

"Nothing else serious."

Jonathan slowly twisted his body to test whether the listed injuries were all true. "Ahy! Yep, I feel it...and here too. Dammit."

"What?"

"My shoulder blade, my hip. The pain in my chest must have drowned out the pain from other parts of my body, but not now. I feel it all."

"I'm sorry," she said, gently laying her hand over his, her eyes sedate. "Consider yourself lucky that you didn't get shot, rupture an organ, or drown."

"Uh-huh, what amazing luck I have."

A knock at the door suddenly made Jonathan's heart jump.

"It's okay," Elya said, quickly walking to the door. She looked into the peephole before opening it. "It's Vanko."

He came in, nodded a nonchalant hello at Jonathan and gave Elya a duffel bag.

"Some clothes for you," she said, turning to Jonathan.

Vanko stayed near the door talking with Elya, who then handed him the laptop. A moment later he left, and Elya locked the deadbolt and returned to the living room.

"Here, use my phone for whatever you need. I asked Vanko to get you a new cellphone in the morning."

"Thank you," Jonathan said. "Thank you for everything you're doing to help me, and to find Kevin, too."

She smiled, got up and went to the kitchen.

Jonathan dialed Cramer and was happy he picked up. He told him everything about the attack, and everything he'd learned from Kane. Cramer was angry and shocked. He had insisted on flying to Kyiv, but Jonathan managed to convince him otherwise, at least for now. It would only complicate things, and Jonathan was already up to his eyeballs in trouble.

16

2:45 A.M., Pripyat, Ukraine

"DMITRY, OPEN." EDMAR KNOCKED AGAIN ON THE METAL with his other hand pointing a flashlight at his black dress shoes, which were half-immersed in one of the many puddles that covered much of the concrete basement passageway.

He heard hurried footsteps and a clanging noise. The door opened, and Dmitry's pale face and disheveled golden hair peeked out. Edmar quickly shoved the door wide open.

"You're late," Dmitry said with eyes wide open, his hands rubbing his stubbled chin.

"I was delayed," Edmar replied tersely. Coordinating with Dmitry's crew was difficult enough since they were isolated in this underground shithole, but when Edmar was without his cellphone—it was necessary each time he made these clandestine commutes—it really set him off.

But it was Edmar's own rule. Everything had to be done to ensure an adequate air gap—in this case, a sufficient physical barrier—between this secretive location and any possible connected computer, device or communications network. This basement was the most secure remote facility he could find in the entire country. Not only was it relatively isolated by being in the Chernobyl Exclusion Zone, it was located in the abandoned town of Pripyat that once housed over 50,000 people until Chernobyl's Reactor Number 4 blew up two miles away. And there were also no cell towers in the immediate vicinity. The facility was as disconnected from any device, whether a smartphone, tablet, or even something as benign as a fitness monitor, as one could possibly find, except perhaps in the middle of the Sahara. Without this buffer Dmitry's crew risked being discovered by ever-more sophisticated law enforcement cybercrime units each time they turned on a connected device.

Dmitry shut the door, closed the double bolts and turned back to Edmar. "We have problems."

"We all do now."

"No, I mean...the Asians. They are here again."

"So what?" Edmar dropped his large briefcase, took off his soaked trench coat and tossed it over the wall of an adjacent cubicle.

"They tried to take him."

Edmar felt his blood pressure rise. "Artem is going to slit my throat. Why did you let them in before I arrived?"

"You told us to give them access."

"*Ebat!*" He waved his fist at Dmitry. "This is different. They can talk with him, but not remove him."

"How should I know?"

Edmar felt like punching the man, but he realized Dmitry was a twenty-year-old spineless nerd, good only at programming and breaking codes, not one for common sense.

"They tried to remove him from the room," Dmitry went on, "but I stopped them. They had dragged him all the way here, to the door. I argued with them...told them to wait until you arrive. So, they took him back to the room, and they have been in there for the last hour beating him nonstop."

Edmar shook his head. He had little time to think this through. He needed Artem Bodrov's advice, but they were cut off with no way to call or message him. The "farm," as Bodrov called it, was concealed deep in the windowless, barely ventilated basement of a concrete building that once housed Pripyat's Elementary School No. 5. The structure was surrounded by dilapidated apartment blocks, radioactive soil, and overgrown greenery, all of it uninhabitable for the next hundred years.

"Look, I don't like what I'm seeing here," Dmitry said. "You hired us as computer experts to write programs and break codes."

"And to train a few North Korean software engineers, remember?"

"Yes," Dmitry said, his eyes shifting. "But *not* to help them torture people, nor to fight them."

Edmar met Dmitry's gaze, his heart rate now sprinting. Dmitry and two other programmers worked fourteen-hour shifts, slept in sleeping bags, ate canned food, and only stepped outside at night. And they didn't seem to mind that just about everything outside the basement was contaminated with enough radiation to shorten their lives by several years. Despite all this, Edmar didn't have the patience to deal with the fuss that Dmitry was beginning to make.

"Well?" Dmitry said, shrugging and waiting for Edmar's instructions.

Edmar clamped his waist with his hands. *What to do with them?* He peeked above the cubicle wall and spotted Dmitry's two hacker colleagues glued to their monitors, one of them a North Korean trainee. "Yes, they saw everything, too," Dmitry added.

Edmar sighed. "Which of them are in the room?"

"All three assholes."

Edmar sensed his pulse quickening even more. "Maybe we've got worse problems," he said. "I was followed."

"Here?" Dmitry's jaw dropped.

"No, in the city earlier."

"What do you—"

"I took care of them. But I'm not sure who they were."

"Police?"

"I don't know. Artem just told me to get rid of them quickly."

"What did you do?" Dmitry's face seemed to turn arctic white.

"Don't ask. It was on the news."

Dmitry shook his head. He ran his fingers through his messy hair and bit his lips. "The police might find this place."

"We're safe, I am telling you. It happened in the city. No one followed me here."

Dmitry was now pacing.

The last thing Edmar needed was some sort of mutiny from the hacker crew. "Take the briefcase and get back to work."

Dmitry frowned. "I can't believe this is happening." He took the large black case and laid it flat on a bench near the entrance. He turned the dials of both combination locks to the predesignated code and opened it. He began counting the USB thumb drives, each partially buried in grooves cut into the thick foam padding that filled the case. "Twenty-four this time, is that correct?"

"Yes," Edmar said. He didn't care about this delivery as much as he worried about the three North Koreans at the other end of the basement. He gazed past Dmitry, at the space that consisted of two large adjoining rooms, each about the size of a three-car garage. The first room had a half-dozen cubicles on one side, and on the other, three rows of tables were filled with enough computers, monitors, and other hardware to rival a call center. In the next room, dozens of server racks stood from floor to ceiling, with streams of wires and ventilation piping spread throughout the space. A loud humming noise from the multitude of active components and their cooling fans came through to the first room.

"I will talk with them now," Edmar said. "They can't take him." That was because Bodrov had not yet received the money. Edmar didn't know how much, nor was he privy to Bodrov's negotiations. But he had discerned the arrangement. "Until Artem gives me the go-ahead, no-one will take the American."

"They're animals," Dmitry said in a whispered voice, shaking his head. They brought tools...like medical tools...to destroy the guy. There's blood everywhere in that room."

"They still need him alive, not dead."

"I don't know what Artem is up to, but doing that here just puts this whole operation at risk."

"It's not your business. It's Artem's decision. And don't forget whose hand is feeding you." Edmar grabbed Dmitry's shoulder and yanked him closer. "Get back to your fucking computers." He then shoved Dmitry back toward his cubicle.

Edmar briskly walked through the server room and headed to a small corridor that led a half-floor down. It was an underground tunnel connecting to an adjacent wing of the same school building whose basement once doubled as a bomb shelter. The air became stuffy and warmer—perhaps from the heat in the server room. He now felt sweat dripping down his back.

He wasn't worried only about the North Koreans. Bodrov's rash decision to attack the men trailing him was now eating at him. He felt the whole operation might well unravel despite his efforts.

Bodrov had entrusted Edmar to make this hideout completely secure. They had bribed two government officials with luxury cars for their wives. They had made handsome cash payments to a handful of security guards manning the checkpoint into Pripyat to look the other way. One of Bodrov's other companies had also become an official vendor of telecommunications infrastructure for the project to build the new sarcophagus over Chernobyl's nuclear reactor, which allowed him to isolate Pripyat from cell tower coverage and to have advance notice if any law enforcement operatives were to begin eavesdropping on the construction site or other areas of the Exclusion Zone.

Outfitting the *farm*—the name Bodrov had given for the secret basement—with high performance servers and all the software a team of hackers could dream of having had taken about a month. Within the first six months, Dmitry and his colleagues had developed some of the most sophisticated hacking programs on earth that were then used by proxies to steal over 320 million dollars in funds by cyber-attacking bank and insurance accounts, running ransomware operations, and even diverting funds from two of the European Central Bank's own depository accounts. It had become a cash cow, with higher earnings than Bodrov's other five businesses. And for that, Edmar was proud. But he was resentful that Bodrov allowed a North Korean hacker into his prized lair. To train him, Bodrov had said. But over the following months, there were two other North Koreans coming and going. And then a third. And they weren't engineers. Just shady people whom Bodrov simply called "diplomats." Edmar feared these interlopers would loosen the security protocols he'd put in place.

Everything seemed in jeopardy now, at least until Edmar could speak with Bodrov. The closest possible option was to use a payphone in the village of

Chernobyl, some twelve miles away. But using a public, unencrypted phone line was out of the question.

Some fifty feet into the passageway he began hearing sounds. Thumps. Then a scream—a man in pain. He grabbed his pistol from his underarm holster, racked the slide and then slowly lowered the hammer. He reached the door, which was left cracked open. He listened to the tortured sounds a moment longer and then pushed it open with his elbow.

Dmitry was right. All three North Koreans were there, two of them huddled over the bloodied, naked American, whose barely conscious body was propped half-seated on a wooden chair—the only furniture in the concrete room. The men turned to Edmar, gazing non-chalantly at him, but said nothing.

"Visiting hours are finished," Edmar said in his near-perfect English. He kept his hand tight on his weapon, which butted against his right thigh. He could raise the weapon and take them all down in three seconds flat. *If I have to.*

The two short men doing the dirty work eyed his weapon and each let go of the American's arms, at which point he fell to the wet floor. And the one supervising—a skinny fellow with a stubby neck and drooping shoulders whom Edmar knew only by his first name, Han-bin—crossed his arms and frowned.

"I am serious. Out. Everyone out." He pushed the door open wider and pointed at the corridor with his weapon.

Han-bin stepped forward, his fists clenched. "He is our property." He appeared to remain calm, but his eyes told Edmar things might turn ugly. "And we can do whatever we want. In one hour, we will take him with us. We will not bother you after that."

"Not until Bodrov gets paid."

Han-bin tilted his head.

Edmar didn't understand why he might feel surprised. After all, this North Korean was the most senior guy and was without doubt more aware of the exact arrangements than Edmar.

Han-bin then loosened his fists and cracked a grin. "Put your gun away. We paid Bodrov two hours ago. Leave us now."

17

6:49 A.M., Kyiv

JONATHAN AWAKENED TO ELYA'S VOICE. SHE WAS NEXT to him, seated on the large armrest of his chair.

"Here, take this," she said, handing him a white pill and a glass of water. "A Ukrainian painkiller."

"Does it work?"

"For some of us here, it's like a vitamin—makes us stronger to handle the problems in our country."

"And hopefully my problems, too." He downed the medicine and began stretching his body but immediately felt the same excruciating pain bolt through his chest, right arm, back, pelvis and thighs. "I'm destroyed."

"No, you'll be fine."

Jonathan saw daylight filtering through the closed window shades. "What time is it?"

"Seven," Elya said, standing again. "Want breakfast?"

"I'm not hungry."

"Vanko will be here very soon. He worked through the night with a friend of his—a computer expert—to extract files from the laptop. Apparently, they were successful; he will show us."

Jonathan smiled. "Let's hope." It meant either that Kane was sloppy at securing the data on his computer or the U.S. government encryption wasn't so good. Either way, Jonathan felt a badly needed rush of energy pump through his veins.

Within about twenty minutes, the painkiller began to have the desired effect. Jonathan felt comfortable enough to get up from his chair and walk to the kitchen. The pain in his chest and limbs seemed to have diminished by eighty percent. Now he was mostly fighting the drowsiness that came with the pill.

Vanko arrived and set up his own laptop on the kitchen counter. He'd also brought the hard drive from Kane's laptop. Jonathan and Elya huddled around him as he started up the computer.

"The access password was easy to break," Vanko said, pointing at the various folders in the directory. "We found about sixty files with no encryption. The rest was encrypted using different tools—and there are many, many folders and files. My friend cracked two of the encryption programs but not the others. So, we now have about two hundred files that we can see—most are reports, photographs, and some emails that were saved as .pdf documents."

Jonathan was eager to dig into the contents.

"It's here, in this new folder," he added and moved the curser over the folder named *2005-J*.

"What about email?" Jonathan said.

"Sorry, no. The laptop did not have any email folders."

"Then he used other devices to communicate," Elya said. "I suppose it's at the bottom of the lake."

"Open that folder," Jonathan said, pointing at the screen.

"Please, go ahead." Vanko moved out of the way and motioned for Jonathan take control of the mouse.

Jonathan scanned through a first batch of pdf formatted documents. These were bank account records, including several statements from one account in Vienna, others from two different Ukrainian banks. Then he opened another group of files. There were scanned images of several pages of Edmar's Ukrainian passport with various European arrival and departure stamps and a European visa issued by Germany. He opened several image files.

"Birth certificate," Elya said softly over his shoulder. "He was born in Kharkiv, near the Russian border."

Jonathan opened the first document of another set of files. "Hmm," he uttered and leaned more closely at the screen. "Check this out."

"What is it?" Elya asked.

"Looks like diplomatic cables—to and from the embassy here."

Jonathan quickly read the first five cables in the subfolder, all of which were two to three pages in length. He had seen "secret" and "top secret" U.S. government documents before. These had the typical markings, including the classification levels and SCI control systems headers, dissemination controls and code words. "Damn."

Elya leaned into his shoulder.

"Edmar has been under surveillance for at least two weeks," he said, summarizing for her benefit. "This means the U.S. authorities have wanted him for something else, long before Kevin was abducted."

"What for?" Elya said.

"Not sure. Kane had implied this but didn't give me details."

Jonathan opened another diplomatic cable, this one from the U.S. Ambassador in Kyiv to the State Department headquarters in D.C. and a recipient at CIA headquarters in Langley. Half-way into the third paragraph he threw his hands in the air. "The British."

"Yes, I see that," Elya said.

Her soft voice so close to Jonathan's ear gave him a strangely unexpected sense of comfort. It was as if he finally realized he had a partner in all this.

He read the next paragraph and then said, "Edmar may be involved in some fraud or conspiracy relating to the Chernobyl Sarcophagus Fund."

"Yes, sounds like it," she said. "The fund was set up mostly by the European Union, since Ukraine alone can't afford to put a new protective shield over the reactor. In fact, my firm was briefly involved in a procurement matter related to this fund two years ago. The European Bank of Reconstruction and Development hired us for advice on contracts dealing with local suppliers."

Jonathan continued reading to the end, then opened and read the last three cables. When he was done, he stood back from the kitchen counter and turned to Elya. "So, there's a Mikhail Zhuk—who appears to be an information source. He dies in an accident, and the Brits think it's foul play. Then Edmar pops up as a potential suspect."

"Yes, and then Kevin goes missing." Elya said.

"I still don't understand any connection. Kevin had nothing to do with the Fund. And neither does Cramer's company. So, I don't get it."

"Perhaps they went after Kevin for different reasons. And if Edmar can kill a diplomat and try to kill you, he can certainly kidnap an American businessman."

"Somehow, we must find Edmar."

"This is getting bigger than we thought, Jonathan," Elya said, her voice moving into a hesitant monotone. She took a step back and crossed her arms. "A fraud with this fund will most likely involve government officials— it can get ugly. Dangerous. In the last five years, Ukraine has become deadlier and more corrupt than ever before. And Artem Bodrov is from a handful of families that are untouchable here. They have powerful allies."

"Then why should we even have negotiated with them in the first place? Soykis should have told Cramer to look elsewhere for business."

"It's not so simple. Bodrov's business empire—his father's, that is—has many legitimate operations and you can still deal with them. But I fear there may be a darker side that we don't know about." Her brows turned in and her shoulders drooped. "I'm sorry. I hope you don't think that—"

"No...no." He met her gaze and shook his head. "I didn't mean to be accusatory."

Vanko got back in front of the computer. "You must also see these documents." He turned the laptop to Jonathan's direction. "They are surveillance reports, I think. Look."

Vanko again stepped back and let Jonathan scroll through the files. He and Elya resumed reading them together.

"Amazing," Elya said, pointing at the screen. "Do you think Edmar might return here?"

"Yep." Jonathan nodded. "Let's go there now—to Ivankiv. Today is Monday, so he might go there, just as he has the last two Mondays and Fridays—at least according to this report."

Elya checked her watch. "It's a small town about an hour north of here by car."

The document was apparently typed by Kane. Either he or someone in his team had followed Edmar to a gas station. Jonathan reread the middle two paragraphs of the report. "Sounds like a dead drop."

"A dead drop?" Elya said.

"Yes, when a person secretly places an item for someone else to pick up," Jonathan said, and then began reading out loud the paragraph that described the most recent sighting of Edmar—referred to in the report as "the target"—prior to the day Jonathan and Kane were attacked. "The target parked his vehicle in a parking spot adjacent to the gas station's convenience store building. He exited the vehicle carrying a black briefcase he had taken from the backseat and walked into the store. He appeared to have used the restroom but did not make a purchase nor speak with the cashier. He returned to his vehicle carrying a briefcase that at first appeared to be the same as the one he had taken into the building. But upon closer, later inspection of photographs taken at that moment, the briefcase seems to have a slightly different exterior trim and locks. Likely a similar but not identical model to the one he had carried into the store. We were not able to see anyone retrieving his original briefcase because we left shortly thereafter to continue surveillance on the target, who drove back toward Kyiv using the same road he had used to head to the gas station. We are investigating the management and ownership of the gas station and running ID checks on license plates of the nine vehicles located on the property at the time of the target's presence. These included five cars, one van, a minibus, and two motorcycles."

"Interesting," Elya said. She turned to Vanko and spoke with him as the two of them headed off into the living room.

Jonathan continued reading the report, then opened another, and another. He skimmed every document Vanko had made available in the master folder. And when he was done, he realized the morning hours had passed quickly. It was nearly nine-thirty. A first surveillance report showed Edmar arriving at the gas station at 11:48 A.M. one day, 11:25 A.M. another day, and 12:10 P.M. on a third day. If Edmar was likely to show up today, Jonathan had little time to get there.

Elya returned to the kitchen. "How are you feeling?"

"My pain?"

"Yes."

"Almost gone, but I'm as high as a mountain goat."

Elya tilted her head, her brows raised.

"Never mind. An expression," Jonathan said, smiling.

"We're leaving in twenty minutes, if you still plan to go there," she said, checking her watch. "Vanko will drive us, and maybe we can spot your guy. But are you sure you don't want the police or your embassy involved?"

"For now, no cops, no diplomats, no FBI—nothing until we know more," Jonathan said, straightening his back. "At this point, I don't know whom I can trust. And you're not coming with us. It's too dangerous."

"I want to be useful, Jonathan. I'm already very deep into this problem."

"There are other ways you can help without adding to the body count."

She shook her head. "Besides, Edmar knows he was being followed when he attacked you, so why would he go back to the same gas station?"

"You have a point. But I must try. We're thin on clues; Edmar is the only big lead we have so far. And maybe he doesn't think he was followed before. Or he may simply change vehicles. Who knows? But I can't just sit here and wait for answers to fall on my lap."

18

Odessa, Ukraine

KEVIN WYATT TURNED TO HIS SIDE ON THE VAN'S HARD metal floor as every corner of his head still throbbed and his arms and legs ached, as if they were still being beaten on the wooden chair in that dreadful basement cell where he'd been held captive for days.

The hood over his head rubbed uncomfortably over the fresh cuts and swollen skin on his face. They'd placed the hood the moment they yanked him from his basement prison and had only lifted it once during the drive for him to sip water, which he refused. The taste of dried blood blended in his mouth with vomit from the motion-sickness he'd had over the past hour. He ran his tongue gently across the bottom of his mouth and noticed another tooth had fallen out. That made it three in total since his captors had started their brutal inter-rogation. But now he couldn't even tell where his pain was greatest. Perhaps it was his wrists, which felt raw from the zip-tie and previously from being bound by a rough rope, which had eaten into his flesh. Or maybe it was his head that hurt the most. They had hit him hard and enough times that he suspected the awful pain came from fractures in his cheekbones, temple and jaw. And it surprised him that he was still somewhat lucid after such harsh treatment.

He guessed that he'd been in the van for four or five hours. The last thirty minutes he'd heard sounds of bustling traffic and felt more frequent stops and turns than earlier. He assumed they had arrived in a large city, probably far from Kyiv. He felt the van turn a few more times, speed up, and then it stopped and idled for a few minutes. He now heard people speaking, but the voices were too faint to make out if they were his Asian or Ukrainian captors. Then the loud rattle of a metal fence opening—perhaps a gate of sorts—came his way. The van sped forward and then again slowed for some distance and stopped.

A ship's horn blared just as Kevin heard the van's rear doors swing open and someone hop inside. He felt hands grab him by his arms. They yanked him off the floor and rushed him out, his feet dropping to the pavement. The ripping pain instantly followed, and he let out a gasp.

"Stand!"

Kevin recognized the skinnier Asian's voice—the only one who hadn't beaten him, choosing instead to instruct the others to do the dirty work. "I can't. It's too painful," he said, his voice trembling and weaker than when he'd last tried to speak.

"Stand now or I'll break something on your face."

"You already have, motherfucker," Kevin mumble. He took in a deep breath and gathered every bit of strength he had to stand, but his limbs and back were frail. He gently twisted his head to try and see through a small tear in the hood. He heard the chirping of seagulls, and nearby the sound of a small motorized vehicle—perhaps a forklift. There were again men speaking; this time he could make out an Asian tongue. As he began to stabilize under his own strength, the men holding him loosened their grip. That's when he managed to glimpse through the slivered opening and spotted the bow of a ship, its black paint worn to reveal rusty metal. He held his head high to see a bit more. They moved along the dock. The men around him spoke fast, their words sounding harsh. Perhaps they were even arguing, but he wasn't sure.

Just as Kevin heard the van pull away, a captor slapped his head from behind. "Faster, hurry," he said in broken English.

Kevin felt another hand grab the back of his hood tightly and push him forward almost more quickly than his legs could keep up. He felt his feet leave the pavement and step onto a metal gangway that clanged loudly as he heard at least three pairs of feet marching behind him. They pushed him again along the a steep climb to the vessel. Kevin did his best to ignore the aches across his entire body and focused on two things: not falling down and not provoking further beatings.

Seagulls chirped and another ship's horn blasted, but this time from a more distant vessel. Kevin struggled to walk the remaining steps up the incline until he was on board the vessel. There it seemed different people took a hold of him by his arms and pushed him forward, his shoulders hitting both walls of what seemed like a narrow corridor. They then stopped him. Suddenly, the hood was pulled off his head. He could finally see, albeit only with one eye. The other was still swollen shut.

"Go down," demanded a short Asian man in overalls as he seized Kevin's collar and pulled him towards an opening in the floor.

Kevin glanced down. There were stairs. Tight, steep stairs descending to a darkened deck below. And the strong smells of mildew and fuel. He stumbled forward, almost falling. Then another man bumped him sideways as he barged past Kevin and slid down the stairs using the railing. He then turned and, with a hostile glance, waved at Kevin to follow suit.

Kevin turned and gingerly made his way down, every movement needling more pain through his nerves. His captors pushed him through another passageway, then down two more decks deep into the belly of the cargo ship. Kevin began hearing the pulsating, humming noises of the engine room, which felt quite near— perhaps only one or two compartments away. The men shoved him forward again, opened a steel door and manhandled him into a cramped, darkened room. Kevin was pushed down into a seated position on the floor. One crewman grabbed his arms, cut his zip-tie and then handcuffed his right wrist to a metal pipe running from floor to ceiling. The men then briskly left the room, the last one throwing a piece of bread the size of a fist and a plastic water bottle, both landing near Kevin's feet. The door shut, and Kevin was left gazing into complete darkness.

19

Near Ivankiv, Ukraine

JONATHAN, HOLDING A PAIR OF BINOCULARS ON HIS LAP, leaned over the dash and glanced out the windshield at the gas station across the street. He checked his watch for the umpteenth time. It was now two-thirty in the afternoon. A light drizzle began to fall and with it came an unpleasantly cool breeze.

"He should have been here by now," Jonathan said, glancing at Vanko, who sat calmly in the driver's seat of the Nissan van they'd rented soon after leaving the apartment. "Perhaps Elya is right. Maybe Edmar is so spooked that he's hiding somewhere that no one will find him."

Vanko, whose enormous biceps and chest would easily tear apart his undersized t-shirt with a simple move, shrugged and took a last drag of his cigarette before tossing it to the pavement. "You know, Elya likes action." He rolled his window up. "She is not happy when someone stops her."

"This is no place for her. She's safer in Kyiv."

"But Bodrov can find her there, too." Vanko took out his pack of Priluki cigarettes from the glove compartment. He started to slide another one out but instead tossed pack onto the center console. "I must quit. Elya tells me all the time."

"Maybe today?"

Vanko laughed. "In another life, I think." He turned his armoire-ish body half-way toward Jonathan. "You know, her father was a colonel in the Soviet Army. In Afghanistan for some time, too. He came back with two missing fingers and a broken leg, but he still stayed in the army. She has his fighting genes."

"Is that a warning?" Jonathan said, chuckling.

"No, I just want to say that she is stronger than you think."

"I've seen her driving, so I agree."

"And one time, she broke a man's arm when he tried to steal petrol from her car."

"Oh." Jonathan had already gathered that Elya was not the quiet, shy, delicate lawyer he'd first met at the law firm. But it was a bit hard to picture her as someone who busts bones.

"It was her boyfriend."

Jonathan leaned back in his seat. "Okay, I won't mess with her. I only told her 'hell no' to protect her," Jonathan added. When Vanko had arrived at the house to pick up Jonathan, Elya had again insisted on coming along. But Jonathan refused. He didn't want Elya to risk the same fate as Kane if Bodrov's thugs somehow used the gas station as a trap. In any case, Jonathan had asked her to speak with Soykis this afternoon and find out whether the Chernobyl Sarcophagus Fund could potentially be linked to Wyatt's disappearance. From the looks of it, Jonathan saw the fund as a key nexus to Kevin's kidnapping, the garbage truck attack, and Edmar's apparent dead drops near the Chernobyl Exclusion Zone, though the hows and whys remained elusive.

Vanko had positioned their van on a dirt path about eighty yards south, and across the street, from the gas station mentioned in Kane's surveillance report. Two trees, a dilapidated wooden fence and a large, stationary propane tank belonging to the neighboring car repair shop gave them additional camouflage. The location seemed like an acceptable vantage point to monitor the gas station without giving themselves away.

"What about this one?" Vanko asked, nodding.

A small sedan driven by a man wearing a hat passed by on the main road and began to slow down. It turned into the station, edged forward to one of the four gas pumps and stopped.

Jonathan looked through the binoculars as the man exited the vehicle. "Nope. Unless Edmar has aged twenty years and grown a mustache since Friday." He lowered the binoculars and sat back in his seat, stretching his back. He was glad the second dose of Elya's pills had completely taken away the pain from his fractured bones, though the lightheadedness that came with it was disconcerting.

"Give me," Vanko said suddenly, grabbing the binoculars out of Jonathan's grip. He jerked forward, propping his elbows over the steering wheel and peered through the device.

"What is it?"

"*Blyat!*" he barked, adjusting the sights. "Damn this! I did not see it before."

Jonathan quickly sat upright.

"There is a car parked behind the gas station," Vanko said, his words now flowing fast. "I think someone just got out of it."

The rain was coming down harder now. Jonathan leaned over to Vanko's side and flipped the switch that sped up the windshield wipers. He then aimed his gaze in the same direction, to the right of the gas station's building. "A white car?" he asked, only able to see what appeared to be the upper half of the vehicle, since the rest of it was obstructed by shrubs that separated the adjacent properties. Kane's report had mentioned Edmar had used two different vehicles on his excursions to the gas station: a blue Honda and the black van they'd followed the evening Kane was killed. But not a white car.

"Look for yourself," Vanko said, handing the binoculars back to Jonathan.

"It could be an employee."

Vanko shook his head. "Why park in the back when there is so much room in front?"

Jonathan pulled the handle and cracked open his door. "I'll go see—"

"No, he may know your face," Vanko said loudly, grabbing Jonathan's elbow. "I will go. You can drive closer if you need to, but stay in the van." He quickly stepped out.

Jonathan kept his eyes on Vanko, who briskly crossed the wet road before slowing to a casual stroll along the edge of the gas station property. He slid into the driver's seat and revved the engine, his focus still trained on Vanko, who had stopped behind a tree about ten feet from the suspect car. Vanko then seemed to take his cellphone in hand.

Jonathan's cellphone, which was on his seat, began buzzing. He grabbed it. It was Vanko.

"It's a Mercedes with a Kyiv license plate. I think the person is now in the gas station building, but he got in from the back. There must be a door there, but I don't see it from here."

"Be careful," Jonathan said, scanning the gas station's front lot.

Vanko was almost out of sight behind the bushes closest to the property dividing line. "It's parked on the grass. I will wait."

A minibus filled with passengers pulled into the station, somewhat far from the pumps, just as the car that had been at the pump pulled away. Jonathan scoped out the bus. Lining its side was a bright yellow banner with the words "Chernobyl Tours" painted in black, above a shorter phrase in Ukrainian and a website. Several passengers and the driver exited the vehicle and casually walked toward the store.

Jonathan dialed Vanko. "Go inside. There are enough people now that you can blend in."

"Okay, I will text you from the store," he said and hung up.

Jonathan's pulse quickened. He drove forward a few feet until he reached the shoulder of the road in front of him. He held his phone over the steering wheel and waited.

Vanko walked across the lot and entered the gas station's store at the same time as the tourists. A moment later, a text came in to Jonathan's phone.

Edmar is here. Walking out of toilet.

This confirmed that the white Mercedes was indeed Edmar's ride. He'd sneaked into the store from the back. But why?

Jonathan texted back. *Is he carrying anything?*

No.

A few seconds later another text hit Jonathan's phone. *Other man went into toilet and came out with bag. It is bus driver.*

Jonathan needed to see this with his own eyes. He drove across the street and pulled into the far edge of the gas station's paved lot, his eyes now fixated on the glass storefront ahead of him.

Another text from Vanko came in. *Driver leaving store.*

Before Jonathan finished typing his reply, he saw the storefront door open. The driver, a short fellow in his mid-twenties, wearing jeans and a white sweatshirt, walked out carrying a large, black briefcase. The glass door closed behind him. There was no doubt Edmar had deliberately left it in the restroom for this man to take.

Jonathan looked down at a new text. *Edmar now leaving from back door.* He then looked up and saw Vanko heading back to the van. He quickly moved to the passenger side to free up the driver's seat as Vanko pulled open the door.

"You were right," Jonathan said the moment Vanko sat down.

"Yes, and Edmar waved at the cashier on his way out."

"Clearly he's paying the staff to help him." Jonathan felt a rush of excitement. "We must follow the tour bus."

"But what about Edmar?"

"No, I think for now the bag may be more useful."

Jonathan leaned forward and observed the driver, who opened the undercarriage compartment of the mini-bus and pushed the briefcase deep inside, behind back-packs and duffel bags. He then closed it and entered the vehicle. The tourists trickled out of the store with drinks and snacks in hand and soon were all back onboard. The driver pulled out of the lot.

"That is not good!" Vanko said.

"Why not?"

"They are going north. And there is a checkpoint. We must have permission to enter."

"A checkpoint for the Chernobyl Exclusion Zone?"

"Yes. The guards will not let us in."

"But they'd let a tour bus just drive in?"

"I am not sure. But it appears to be where they are going. But I imagine the tourists' documents have been pre-approved by the authorities."

"Fuck!" Jonathan fumed. Nothing was ever simple. He immediately dialed Elya. Told her about the driver and the briefcase. About Edmar. Then he asked how to get into the Exclusion Zone.

"I think Mr. Soykis can help us," she said, her voice sounding like she was as thrilled as Jonathan that they had finally grasped something potentially useful. "He knows many government officials. I'm sure one of them can help. I will call him now."

20

JONATHAN TURNED AND SAW ELYA'S SAAB APPROACHING fast. The car screeched across the wet road's shoulder, its tires locking up and spraying gravel and mud until it came to a complete stop just a yard from Vanko's rental van parked on the same side of the roadway. The rain had stopped but the humidity lingered with the faint scent of grass and manure from the surrounding fields.

She quickly got out, waving a paper in the air. "Here it is!" She also carried a small bag in her other hand.

Jonathan glanced at Vanko. "I'm impressed." Elya had acted fast. Barely two hours had passed from the time Jonathan called her.

There was excitement painted across her face as she joined Jonathan and Vanko, both of whom were leaning on the side of the van. She handed the note to Vanko, said something in Ukrainian and then thrust her shoulder into Jonathan with a wide smile.

"Can you believe how lucky I was?" she said. "I got Mr. Soykis the exact moment he finished playing tennis with the number three bureaucrat at the Ministry of Transportation."

Jonathan peeked over Vanko's shoulder. The note was short, had all their names and ended with two signatures and a circular red stamp. "You're awesome," he told her, raising a thumbs-up.

"And I brought you sandwiches," she added, handing the small bag to Jonathan.

He suddenly realized he'd barely eaten anything in the last three days. The pain, the stress, and the painkillers had stifled his appetite. But he'd force himself to eat, he thought. "Let's eat while driving. We have to find the tour bus—*now*."

"But how?" Elya said raising her hands to her head. "The Exclusion Zone is huge."

Jonathan had this covered. "I called the tour company." He had indeed spoken to the manager, whose English was perfect and who also tried her best to sell him a tour package.

"Don't tell me—they take people into Reactor Number 4 until their eggs explode," Elya said, her brows raised.

"Eggs?"

She gestured at Jonathan's groin.

"Oh, balls," he said with a chuckle. "They take tourists three times a week to the old power plant, and then to a town called Pripyat."

Elya frowned. "Pripyat is abandoned—a town more radioactive than the area around the reactor. I don't understand how anyone would pay to see it."

Jonathan shrugged. "Recreational radiation—no prescription needed."

She rolled her eyes.

"The tour starts with a welcome meal in the village of Chernobyl. The whole thing takes about three and a half hours, she told me."

"But I'm sure the bus driver already gave the brief-case to someone."

"Yes, I'd like to see that briefcase," Jonathan said. "But the bus driver could be just as useful. We need to find him before he leaves the zone."

Elya had left her car in the parking lot of a board-ed-up grocery store and jumped into the van. Vanko downed his sandwich while gunning it northbound along the isolated, two-lane road.

"Look, there," Vanko said, pointing over the steering wheel. "See it?"

Jonathan ate the last morsel of his food and squinted. "The checkpoint?"

"Yes."

There was a gap in the wooded horizon that showed the roadway widening. Seconds later, Jonathan spotted three small buildings—one of them a single-story struc-ture on their side of the road facing a candy-striped, gated barrier. They passed two large signs with the universal radioactive symbol, and an even larger, bright yellow sign with the words *КПП ДИТЯТКИ*.

"What does it say?" Jonathan asked.

"Checkpoint Dyatyatky," said Elya. "It's the name of a nearby village."

Vanko then pointed at a billboard next to the sign. "And that map shows the area of contamination."

An armed security guard dressed in dark blue fatigues and combat boots stood at the center of the expanded pavement and signaled at Vanko to stop.

Vanko rolled down his window, as did Elya behind him. The guard spoke briefly, and Vanko quickly put the van in park and turned to Jonathan. "We must get out and go to the building."

"I will talk with them," Elya said, not wasting any time. "Give me your passports."

"How well do they like Americans?" Jonathan then said, his hands beginning to sweat.

Elya grabbed his passport. "They are low-paid, administrative employees not trained to think independently. They will not question this letter, even if it has a foreigner's name on it."

"I hope."

With all three passports in hand, Elya walked up to the check-in window that faced the exterior of the building. Before Jonathan and Vanko reached her, she was already heading back. She winked. It was done.

"Here," she said, handing them their documents. "And I borrowed this from the guard." She held out a small yellow device that resembled a flip phone.

"A dosimeter?" Jonathan guessed.

She nodded and slipped it in her tote bag.

Once back in the van, Vanko pulled forward to maneuver the vehicle within a white rectangle painted on the pavement. The security guard came around, lifted the van's rear door, briefly examined the luggage compartment and then signaled for Vanko to proceed. Some ten yards further, another guard pushed down on the counterweight of the candy-striped barrier and waved them through.

"Not so bad," Jonathan said and turned to Elya in the back seat. "But are you sure we don't need protective gear?"

Elya tapped Vanko's shoulder. "It's safe, right?"

"Umm, generally yes. But stay on the road or sidewalks only, as much as possible. Do not touch the ground or anything wet. Do not go too close to..." He started gesturing a square-shaped pattern with his hand, searching for a word in English. "You know, the metal thing on the street."

"*Kanalizatsiyna reshitka?*" Elya blurted.

"*Tak.*" Vanko chuckled.

"He means a hole for the sewer."

Jonathan nodded. "Sewer grates."

"Very radioactive," Vanko said. "Because the ground is very bad, very dangerous, especially in Pripyat."

"Then let's see if our eggs explode," Jonathan said, winking at Elya.

21

ONLY THE SUBTLE, MONOTONOUS HUMMING OF TIRES could be heard as the van proceeded north from the checkpoint, and this gave Jonathan time to further ponder the somber significance of Chernobyl's Exclusion Zone. An uncomfortable eeriness seemed to cloud the most benign things in sight. A lone concrete bench at an old bus stop. The lush trees lining the right side of the roadway, some of their trunks painted white to aid motorists. On the left, the uncut yellow-green fields that flourished, displaying the warm colors of fall. Mundane and tranquil if it were any place else.

But everything in view was contaminated with a level of radiation somewhere above normal. And that *normal* ended abruptly at 1:23 A.M. on Saturday, April 26, 1986, when an explosion tore off the thousand-pound lid atop the power plant's Reactor Number 4.

"It hasn't changed," Vanko said, holding the steering wheel with two fingers and glancing at Jonathan on the passenger side. He was the only one in the van who'd been to this restricted area before, back in the late '90s. "Same road. Same abandoned farms. No one can build anything new in this place." He shook his head.

"Why were you here?" Elya said.

Jonathan was surprised Vanko had never told her.

"My older brother was an electrician in the army," Vanko said, "and on my birthday, he gave me a uniform to wear and took me into the area for a few hours."

Elya craned forward and rested her elbows on the shoulders of both front seats. "My uncle was a fireman in Kyiv when the accident happened. He was part of the next wave of rescuers that hurried north that morning to help."

Jonathan turned and met her pensive gaze. He was curious but reluctant to ask about her uncle's fate.

"He told me years later how difficult it was. How some in his team got very sick. One died that first week. Another a few months later at a hospital in Moscow." She frowned and added, wagging her finger in the air, "The government in Moscow never told the public the real number of casualties. The radiation hurt everything and everybody—men, women, children, animals, trees, soil, lakes, rivers. There was more cancer, not only in this area but also in Kyiv and western parts of the country. And many other health problems." Her voice cracked, and tears began welling in her eyes. "My uncle died four years ago from lung cancer."

"I'm sorry," Jonathan said.

"And he never smoked."

"That was..." Jonathan interrupted himself when he felt Vanko applying the brakes. He pivoted forward and quickly read a sign that flashed by his side of the road. "Did it say Chernobyl?"

"Yes, we are here, but it is only the village," said Vanko, his demeanor turning introspective. "The nuclear station is more north."

A few small buildings came into view as they entered the village. They passed two more road signs, indicating a lower speed limit of 40 km/h and that no trucks were permitted on the short, pristine two-lane stretch of road with perfectly aligned trees in the center medium—what appeared to be the hamlet's main street.

Vanko passed a small intersection and proceeded slowly through a second, larger one, where he turned left. A lime-green, two-story building sat kitty-corner from a smaller, one-story structure with colorful, patterned murals facing the street. The first building was a cafeteria, Vanko said, the other an administrative center to pay workers. This was Chernobyl's unimpressive main square.

Jonathan continued to observe the village out the window. A spacious, ungroomed park took up the other corner, where a young woman strode with groceries in hand. On the right a man pedaled his bicycle, a relaxed grin brightening his face. The ordinariness could easily be confused with any sleepy town in southern Louisiana, he thought. "People still live here?"

Vanko looked at him as if he'd said a bad word. "Of course. There is a lot of work to do here."

This was not the image Jonathan had expected. "I thought, if there are residents, they would wear some form of protective gear or at least face masks—especially given the dangers you told me about."

"A client told me recently," Elya said, "that they are now forcing workers to have shorter rotations in the zone—about 15 days in, and 10 or 15 days out. Some of them are here to build the new sarcophagus. Construction will start soon, when the European Union finally sends us the money. But most of the work for now is to decontaminate the old reactors—the last one was still active until 2000."

"What?" Jonathan was stumped. "They still used the plant *after* the disaster?"

"Uh-huh," replied Elya, shrugging. "Reactor Number 2 had a fire in 1991, around the time Ukraine became independent, so they closed it. A few years later they closed another."

"Reactor Number 1," Vanko butted in. "And then the last one, Number 3."

Jonathan shook his head in disbelief.

"When your government has no money to build something new," Vanko added, his voice stern, almost angry, "you keep using what you have."

"Even if it kills you," Jonathan whispered.

"I suppose they just think no person can die twice from the same thing," Elya said and sighed loudly. "We each have our time to go, I guess..."

Vanko turned onto another street, where a middle-aged couple stood on the sidewalk facing a five-story concrete housing unit. There were several such structures, all of them with dilapidated facades and balconies that looked as if they could suddenly fall to the ground. They appeared similar to the old apartment blocks he'd seen in Russia years earlier.

They had crossed the village of Chernobyl in less than three minutes and were again northbound on a lone two-lane road, its surface scarred with patches of sloppily repaired asphalt. They passed by a few abandoned homes, more like large shacks. But the area was rural, with fields and woods dominating the surroundings.

Elya's phone rang. She answered. By the time she'd spoken a handful of words, her expression flattened. She plunged back into the rear seats and just listened. Jonathan could barely make out a woman's voice speaking firmly on the other end of the line.

Jonathan turned to her and mouthed the word, "Okay?" accompanied by a matching hand signal.

She shook her head, her lips as straight as a ruler. The call lasted another minute before she flipped the phone shut and glared at Jonathan, high-browed and bothered. "We have a problem."

Jonathan groaned. He was tired of problems. But by now he'd become accustomed to something going wrong any time things appeared to be progressing nicely. "Tell me."

"Men in suits were at the firm looking for Mr. Soykis and me about three hours ago."

"Who?" Jonathan said. "Bodrov? His thugs?"

"No," Elya said, looking puzzled, her fingers fiddling with her necklace pendant. "The FBI—at least that's how they identified themselves to my assistant. She said they definitely were American—one of them was black."

"Three hours ago! Why didn't she call earlier?"

"A partner at the office told her not to. And he also refused to alert Mr. Soykis."

How bizarre, Jonathan thought. If foreign law enforcement officials arrived at any legal firm back home, he mused, there'd be messages going out on bull-horns, pigeons and camels, if need be, to make ensure all managing partners knew about it. "You should tell Soykis now."

"I will text him."

The long, straight stretch of road began a wide left-ward bend.

"The next checkpoint is coming," Vanko said.

Ahead were two small shacks that faced each other across the road, and between them were candy-striped barriers similar to those that greeted them at the first checkpoint.

Two guards dressed in dark blue fatigues with hol-stered side arms, their backs emblazoned with the word "*Militsya*," got up from a bench and signaled Vanko to stop. Vanko rolled the window down and spoke, hand-ing them the letter Elya had brought. It was simpler than before. No one had to leave the vehicle. The guard lifted the barrier open, and Vanko drove off.

Dense forest covered both sides of the road for about five minutes, and then the horizon opened up to grass-land and a canal that skirted the right edge of the pave-ment. Ahead, Jonathan saw what looked like a cooling tower, except it was shorter and wider than ones he'd seen before, like the Grand Gulf Nuclear Station on the Mississippi-Louisiana border. What resembled a rusted crown of thorns ringing its top edge told him the tower wasn't fully constructed.

"The cooling tower for Reactors 5 and 6," Vanko said.

"But you told me there were four reactors."

"They were under construction when the accident happened." Vanko then pointed to an adjacent structure about ten stories high whose shape and color resembled a giant bathtub topped with a crate of bricks. "The unfinished reactor building." Then he pointed dead ahead, beyond where the road veered right, following the curve of the canal. "And that...is the monster. The building with the towers."

"Reactor Number 4?" Jonathan craned his neck over the front dash. He felt as if he were tracking a large, dangerous, rare mammal out in the wild. Past the canal, beyond the low line of trees and complex maze of electrical poles and transformers that seemed to cover the area facing the reactor, the beastly rectangular frame rose ominously from the ground. Two chimneys, one wider and taller than the other, pointed at the heavens. Below them, the surface of the power plant's gray metal roof was weatherworn and rusted.

Vanko had explained earlier that in the hours and days following the explosion, hundreds of helicopter flights dropped thousands of tons of sand, lead, clay, and other materials onto the burning reactor to contain the radiation leaking from the ruptured core. The containment efforts were expanded by placing concrete and lead slabs around and on top of the structure as a temporary sarcophagus. No one thought at the time that "temporary" would mean twenty-plus years. *When a country has not money...,* Jonathan silently replayed Vanko's words.

Jonathan gazed back at the reactor until the roadway veered into a wooded area. As he turned in his seat a sharp needling pain crossed his chest. *My ribs.* He reached into his pocket for another dose of painkillers, which he quickly downed. Since the time Elya had given him the drugs, he was willing to accept the drowsiness they produced in lieu of the agony from his injuries.

"We are two minutes from Pripyat," Vanko said, now holding the steering with both hands. He seemed agitated, or perhaps angry.

Jonathan hoped it wasn't because of something he'd said.

"And one more checkpoint," Vanko added, "there, that metal cabin."

Jonathan noticed the tiny guardhouse, a white barrier and an overweight officer standing next to it, stretching his arms behind his head as if he'd just woken up.

They repeated the drill. Vanko rolled down his window, as did Elya, who also held the official authorization letter and all three passports. As the van crawled to a stop, she leaned forward from the backseat, ready to jump into the looming conversation.

The guard's gut was about as wide as it was tall, his white undershirt nearly in full view behind his half-buttoned blue-patterned camouflage jacket. Given his unhealthy physical attributes, Jonathan mused, the man was likely incapable of stopping anybody trying to get in or out of the abandoned town—except perhaps if he used the holstered semi-automatic partly covered by his love handles.

The guard lazily scanned the letter before barking words at Vanko. His demeanor was aggressive, and certainly rude, Jonathan guessed, though he didn't understand a single word of it. The three began a back and forth that quickly escalated into raised voices and disturbed gestures. Jonathan wasn't sure if bullets might soon fly or if he'd have to call Cramer to get his ass out of a Ukrainian jail. Suddenly Elya shouted, her decibel count far higher than theirs, and pointed menacingly at the officer through her window.

Jonathan's heart skipped a beat. He leaned down a bit to have a full view of the man's face as Elya continued to speak with him loudly. He eyed them both, hoping cool heads would soon prevail. But he feared the guard's temper was escalating and Elya wasn't the kind of person to back down easily. He glanced at Vanko, hoping he might intervene to calm things down.

The guard suddenly seemed to place his hand over his holster, but Jonathan wasn't sure—it was below his line of sight. The man chewed his mouth, his nostrils flaring. He took a step back and mumbled something. Then spat on the ground, threw the letter back into the van and walked off.

Vanko glanced at Jonathan as if nothing out of the ordinary had happened and stepped on the gas.

"What was that all about?" Jonathan said, his eyes still locked on the guard, who had entered his cabin and immediately pick up a wall-mounted phone.

"I don't know," Elya said. "He didn't want to let us in. I finally told him that if we were forced back to the main checkpoint, I would report him to the commanding officer and to the Ministry of Transportation."

"I guess you scared him," Jonathan said, laughing, but more out of nervousness than humor. He remained troubled by the guard's scowl. And there was no telling who the guard was now calling.

"In this country, sometimes bitch-power works," Elya said, raising her fist.

"And in America as well," Jonathan said with a chuckle, immediately thinking of Linda—brave, beautiful, brainy, brash, and sometimes, as she'd laughingly labeled herself on occasion, a raving apocalyptic bitch. *But damn I love her*.

As Jonathan turned to face forward, he opened his eyes wide. "What the…" It was as if he'd landed on another planet.

"Lenina Prospect—the main avenue," Vanko said, glancing at Jonathan with a raised brow, perhaps as if he was curious to see an American's reaction.

Jonathan didn't say a word. He scanned the surroundings. Everything in sight reflected a glaring, ghostly, apocalyptic absence of human life. The avenue was lined by abandoned nine- and twelve-story apartment blocks on both sides, most with missing or broken windows; cracked, weed-filled sidewalks; pavement covered with dirt and leaves; overrun vegetation; and rusted light poles.

"Crazy, isn't it? Fifty thousand people once called this place home," Elya added.

Jonathan immediately thought of New Orleans' devastated Ninth Ward after Hurricane Katrina destroyed the levy. There were eerie similarities. "I can only imagine the fear...the panic. People desperate to get away. Just awful."

"The government waited to order the evacuation until two days after the explosion."

Jonathan couldn't help but think of the parallels with the warnings about Katrina. In the Big Easy, the evacuation order had been delayed. And lives were tragically lost as a consequence. Here in Pripyat, the delay ensured that the death sentences were given, though the actual deaths came later in the form of cancers and other long-term ailments.

Elya continued, "So before the busses finally came to get them out, most people were exposed to radiation equivalent to a thousand x-rays, but others had even more exposure."

"Look!" Vanko shouted.

Jonathan turned. Straight ahead, three hundred yards away, was the minibus. But the driver and tourists were nowhere in sight.

"They parked at the main square," Vanko said, slowing down the van. "That is the Palace of Culture behind it, and that white building over there, on the right, is the old Hotel Polissya."

Jonathan read the large, rusted metal Cyrillic letters atop the seven-story former hotel. From its prominent size, location and modern exterior design, he imagined it had served as a respectable address in its heyday.

Elya leaned forward. "What should we do?"

"Turn right," Jonathan said. "I'd rather stay distant from the bus, since the tourists will return at some point. So, stop there, across from the hotel."

Vanko followed Jonathan's advice and parked partly on the sidewalk a hundred yards away from the bus.

"Any news from Soykis?" Jonathan asked Elya.

She brought her phone to her face. "Looks like...I have no signal. None."

Jonathan checked his own. "Neither do I."

"Pripyat is a dead zone," Vanko said.

Jonathan gurgled. "Yes, in more ways than one."

The van's engine went quiet as Vanko shut it off. He took a flashlight from the glove box and got out, as did Jonathan and Elya.

Jonathan followed Vanko to the back of the van. Vanko lifted the rear door and then jolted open the carpeted floor panel to access the spare tire compartment. He stretched his hand under the back of the tire and pulled out a firearm—the same one he'd loaned Elya back at her friend's apartment soon after Jonathan had sought refuge there.

Jonathan eyed the weapon in Vanko's hand and then met his gaze. He instantly felt they shared the same momentary thought. Neither of them wanted to be in a situation where they'd actually have to use it.

Vanko lifted his chin, his forehead creasing. "Insurance." He lifted the back of his shirt and tucked the weapon behind his belt.

Jonathan turned, examining the pavement around his feet, then gazed at the other side of the street before turning to Elya. "Give me the dosimeter."

She raised a brow but quietly went back in the van and pulled it out of her tote bag, which she'd hidden under the driver's seat. She turned on the device and handed it to Jonathan.

He strolled to the other side of the road where he had spotted a sewer grate. Holding the device lengthwise about two feet off the ground, he slowly approached the grate. About five feet from it, the dosimeter began to chirp intermittently, with a digital reading of 2.80 microsieverts per hour, or uSv/h, popping on the screen. Jonathan wasn't sure what a bad reading should look like, but he'd seen enough movies to know that any chirping or beeping wasn't good. The chirping became more frequent and louder as he moved closer to the grate, and when he held it a few inches over it, the device convulsed as loud as it could. The chirping had turned to a constant, intense whine, and the screen now read 19.40 uSv/h.

Vanko leaned over his shoulder. "That is about three to five times higher than normal."

"Not so bad." Jonathan lowered the device further, and the reading rose to 21.60.

Vanko cleared his throat. "I mean normal for the Exclusion Zone."

"Oh." Jonathan stood upright.

"Which is already eighty to a hundred times higher than normal for the rest of the world," Vanko said, his mouth twisting.

Jonathan winced. "Great."

Elya took the dosimeter from his hand. "He told you, the ground is bad. The water below ground is even worse."

"That is why people normally don't stay long in Pripyat," Vanko added. "Maybe two or three hours, not more."

"We don't have that much time." Elya said, frowning. "The curfew here is eight o'clock. And my letter will not stop the Militsya from arresting us if they catch us here after that time. And that fat guard would love nothing more than to find us here at 8:01."

"We can go in different directions," Vanko suggested as he tested his flashlight.

A faint murmur came from a distance, past the tour bus, somewhere near the Palace of Culture. Jonathan scanned the darkening fringes of the main square. Then he spotted a person in a white shirt, quickly followed by two others.

"Tourists," Vanko said. "They're coming from the old grocery store."

Jonathan felt a rush of impatience, but there was no need to head straight for the tourists. "Let's go there, but through the covered walkway, and see if we find the driver."

He gazed up at the cloud-filled sky. Nightfall was about thirty minutes away, he guessed. He crossed the street and hiked up several concrete steps to an expansive area that probably was a pleasant place for pedestrians back in the day. Elya and Vanko followed about twenty yards behind.

The muttering of chatty tourists became more audible. English words, mostly. Jonathan examined them in search of the driver. Reaching the cover of the walkway, which curved from the Hotel Polissya to the Palace of

Culture, he turned and shook his head at Elya. He'd hoped the driver would be there.

Two of the six tourists took pictures of one another, the flash of their cameras lighting up the front of the grocery store. They barely noticed Jonathan. By the time he had taken the roundabout way to the store, three more tourists had emerged from a large opening that used to be floor-to-ceiling glass.

Jonathan entered one of the store's aisles. The metal shelving units stood empty, decaying and twisted. He stepped over a broken lighting unit strewn across the floor.

He stopped upon hearing a faint noise of laughter and footsteps that came with the whistling breeze from the other end of the store. The darkness only let him see the most immediate surroundings. The laughter morphed into two male voices chatting boisterously in English, one of them with a strong Russian or Ukrainian accent.

He stepped forward, careful to keep his footsteps as quiet as possible over the debris-covered floor. Turning the corner, he suddenly faced two men, one of whom he immediately recognized as the bus driver. The other was likely a tourist.

That very moment Elya and Vanko popped out of another aisle behind the men, who fell silent, their smiles evaporating.

"Go away," Jonathan said to the tourist, who instantly scurried off.

The driver stood still, wide-eyed, with his hands on his waist.

"Where did you take the briefcase?" Jonathan asked, approaching him slowly.

"What briefcase?"

"The one Edmar gave you." He carefully eyed the man's jacket to see if he might be armed, as improbable as it seemed for a minibus driver. "The police will get him and everyone else he's been working with—including you."

"So, you better talk," Elya shouted from behind the man with her arms crossed as she approached him.

Vanko was next to her with one hand behind his back, no doubt gripping the firearm in case it was needed.

The driver turned sideways and glanced back and forth between Jonathan and the others. "I don't know what you are talking about. I am only—"

"Stop lying!" Jonathan's patience had long run out. "We saw you take the briefcase at the gas station. Edmar helped kill a diplomat two days ago. Can you imagine how much trouble you're in? Talk—now!"

The man seemed to swallow hard, his eyes shifty. His hands began to shake as Vanko took another step forward and shouted something in their native language.

The man raised his hands in the air and bit his lip, his eyes turning back to Jonathan. "I did nothing. I don't know what he gave me today. I never know. I only deliver and pick up. Nothing more. I am not involved."

As the man turned again to Vanko, Jonathan lunged at him, grabbed his collar and threw him against a shelving unit face first without letting go. "Tell us where it is, or my friend here will pull out your teeth one at a time."

The driver collapsed to his knees and burst into tears, wailing like a child. "I know nothing."

"Where did you take it?"

He waved his arm out without looking up, his voice shaky and hesitant. "Over there...on the north side...near an old school."

"You know where that is?" Jonathan asked Vanko, letting go of the man.

Vanko shrugged. "No idea. I think there were five or six schools in this town."

Jonathan kicked the man's leg. "Which school?"

"I don't know...past the amusement park."

Vanko leaned down and slapped the driver's head and shouted at him as he fell to his side, his hands covering his face.

Jonathan looked down at his feet and noticed liquid oozing over the floor. "Vanko, you made him pee his pants!"

"Huh." Vanko seemed to hold back laughter. "Where is this school?"

"School Number 5, across from the stadium, on the other side of Sportivna Street."

"Let's take this piece of shit with us," Jonathan said, "to make sure he's not lying."

"No, he's a liability." Vanko straightened his back. "I know how to get there."

The man wiped his face with his sleeve. "I told you the truth."

"We can tie him up," Elya said. "If he's telling the truth, we can let him out when we get back."

"What about the tourists?" Jonathan asked. "We don't want them running off to the guard shack to report this." He motioned to the driver. "Give us the keys to the bus."

The driver went to reach in his pocket, but Vanko stepped on his wrist. "Keep your hands where I can see them! I'll check your pocket for the keys."

They marched him out of the grocery store through the back doorway and up a set of stairs in the neighboring building, where they tied him up to a set of water pipes with wire that Vanko had grabbed among the debris on the floor of the store. Elya then shoved her scarf in the man's mouth, and Jonathan looped the lengthy wire in it like a bridle bit.

"If you yell, we'll come back and beat you, understand?" Jonathan said, waving his fist in the air.

"But we must to something about the tourists," Elya said. "I'll be back in a few minutes. Wait for me." She quickly headed back down the stairs.

Moments later Jonathan heard her speaking loudly outside but couldn't make out exactly what she was saying. About three minutes later she returned a bit out of breath.

"What did you tell them?" Jonathan asked.

"That the driver lost his keys and had to walk to the other side of town to get spare ones."

Jonathan shrugged. "Not bad, but that won't buy us too much time."

"I know," Elya said. "Let's hurry. We only have until eight and it's already six-fifty."

The headed back downstairs. Vanko quickly led the way through the ground floor of the Palace of Culture, which was also littered with debris, including broken chairs and shattered desks and lamps. It was a shortcut to the amusement park, he said.

Darkness continued to bleed into the abandoned town as Jonathan kept up with Vanko, whose flashlight cast a wide beam ahead of them. Though there was still enough light to see basic objects with the naked eye, the town would turn pitch black very soon, as it had no electricity and no working lights.

"We are in the amusement park," Vanko whispered loudly.

Jonathan gazed at an old carousel, its damaged plastic horses left abandoned on the surrounding pavement. The dormant, rusty fixtures served as a reminder that whatever joy this place was intended to bring had been sucked out of existence the moment the reactor blew up. The contrast struck him as he wandered past a ticket booth at the base of an immense Ferris wheel, its twenty open-air gondolas shaped like Reese's peanut butter cups. He imagined the sounds of cheering kids, their parents waving from below. How quickly life can take a turn for the worse.

"Sad, isn't it?" Elya gently placed her hand on Jonathan's shoulder. "The park never opened. It was supposed to on May 1, International Workers Day."

Jonathan shook his head, recalling the date of the accident: April 26.

The breeze had turned into a sturdy wind, bringing with it the loud rustling of leaves on the trees and squeaking, creaking sounds of metal from these carcasses of rides.

They passed a bumper car circuit, its dilapidated, scaffolded roof swaying slightly with the wind. The cars sat idle, their yellow paint chipped and peeling, their rubber bumpers wilted and left to rot in the elements.

The three crossed another weed-filled street and headed around a flat, windowless concrete structure that at first appeared like a wall. They walked around it through a thick mass of trees.

Suddenly, Jonathan noticed something strange. He squinted. From this side, it was a very different structure. Not a wall. His mouth dropped. "We're in the stadium."

He stopped and gazed at concrete stands rising from the ground—a dozen rows, all topped with wooden bleachers. The top of the stands had a small set of enclosed press boxes and above it a concrete awning that covered maybe a fourth of the seats. But the past thirty years had turned the soccer field facing the stands into a small forest. They were standing in the center of the stadium, surrounded by tall trees. Jonathan had never seen anything like this.

They approached the bottom of the stands, and Jonathan noticed Elya was also in awe at what they were witnessing.

"Yes, Avangard Stadium," Vanko said, pointing his flashlight at a faded metal sign lying on the ground about five yards from the first row of seats. "It says 'stay off the grass.'"

Jonathan chuckled.

Vanko again led them northward, out of the stadium. They crossed another street that also had been overtaken by the powers of nature.

"Straight," Vanko said. "Because those two tall buildings on the left are apartment blocks—not a school. But that one," he said pointing in the two-o'clock direction, about a hundred yards ahead, "could be."

Suddenly, a loud metal clanging sound shattered the sound of the wind. It was as if a metal door had closed.

"Get down," Jonathan whispered. "And turn off your flashlight."

Vanko huddled next to Elya behind an old concrete bench, about ten feet away from Jonathan, who'd hidden behind an overturned garbage dumpster.

Jonathan peered ahead and saw something move next the building, most of which was surrounded by thick brush and trees. A dark figure moved slowly away from the building, about forty yards away. Now it was too dark to see faces, but Jonathan eyed the silhouette as it crossed from his one-o'clock to his ten o'clock.

He signaled Vanko to join him, which he quickly did, ducking as best he could for such a large man.

"Follow the guy," Jonathan said in a restrained tone despite the excitement pumping through his veins. "Elya and I will go into the building—I hope it is the school." Splitting up now was the best option, given that it was nearly quarter past seven and the curfew would spell trouble for them. And Vanko was armed, thus better equipped to follow the stranger.

Vanko nodded, and keeping a ducking posture, stepped away. Seconds later he was nearly out of sight, moving discreetly through the dark thickness of the wooded area.

Jonathan joined Elya and told her the plan.

She looked up at him and frowned. "I hope you know what you're doing."

22

16 Miles Southwest of Pripyat, Ukraine

"GOT'EM! THERE, YOU SEE?" BLURTED A GREEN-CLOTHED operator to his colleague seated next to him as both zoomed in on three grainy, bright figures that appeared on their monochrome flat screen displays. The thermal imaging camera—mounted on their unit's heavy but compact, man-portable winged drone—fed the live images to their surveillance van. "I'm sure it's your guy and his companions," the man declared over this shoulder.

"Finally." George Porter moved his bulky, six-foot-three frame to face the screens and patted both operators' shoulders. He leaned in for a closer look.

The three figures on screen moved slowly along the periphery of a mid-rise building.

"Yeah, it's probably him," Porter said. "But zoom in closer?"

"It's as good as it gets," the operator said, showing Porter that he was pushing the button on his joystick all the way.

"Slant range is now 600 meters," his colleague said.

Porter eyed the targets, which were intermittently obscured by foliage of trees as the drone moved stealthily through the airspace in a circular pattern. "I need a better visual. If it's not him, we're wasting our time."

"Okay, but..." The main operator pitched his joystick forward and pressed a few buttons on his keyboard. "It's quiet over Pripyat; they might hear the drone if we go below 300 meters—"

"Then don't descend," Porter cracked and slapped the man's seatback. "Guys, we're not playing a goddamned video game. I need to see more clearly—what they're carrying, where the fuck they're goin' and what's in their immediate surroundings." Porter stretched his neck, scrubbed his cheeks with both hands and rubbed his sore eyes, which had been bloodshot for hours. He knew his body couldn't take much more exhaustion. He'd pulled two all-nighters already since Kane was killed. The first murder of a CIA officer working under Embassy cover in Europe in over two decades had turned his week upside down. A battalion of intel and military brass was pressuring him to chase all leads and get results. And if he screwed this up, he might as well kiss his prized new posting in London goodbye.

His three-man UK-based drone crew were tired as well, but for different reasons. They'd endured torturous logistics over the last twenty-seven hours that had begun with a late-night flight from an airbase at Lakenheath, where they had boarded a C-130. They landed briefly an hour later at Ramstein Air Base in Germany, where the surveillance van and the two-drone package were loaded aboard. Then they were off again for a ninety-minute flight to *Baza Aeriană 95*—the Romanian Air Force base at Bacău, in the north-eastern part of the country. Using the van, they drove three hours north to the village of Climăuți, a stone's throw from the Ukrainian border. There, under cover of darkness, they slipped into Ukraine undetected, maneuvering the van with difficulty over a muddy, unpaved path that cut through a corn field before joining a paved rural road for an eight-hour drive to Kyiv, where Porter and a three-man CIA tactical operations team joined them. Just prior to that, Porter had accompanied the resident FBI's legat (legal attaché) for a visit to the law firm of Soykis & Kharenko.

The last leg of their journey to get prepared for the surveillance operation was north of Kyiv. The team split in two near the town of Sukachi. Porter, his drone crew and his team's secretive high-tech gear headed forty-five minutes west to their current location just clear of the Exclusion Zone: a rugged dirt road at the edge of a forest about 500 yards from the Uzh River and two miles from the hamlet of Cheremoshna. This complied with two simple rules the head of Operations back at Langley had given Porter: First, "Don't get the fuck caught." Second, "If you do, don't get nailed in the Exclusion Zone or on other Ukrainian government property." But Porter didn't apply the rules to his heavily armed three-man assault team. They had driven their SUV through dirt trails in mostly forested areas and sat on standby just three miles southwest of the former Chernobyl reactors in the heart of the Exclusion Zone.

A digital topographic map appeared on the operator's left screen. It outlined the Exclusion Zone with a red dashed line, a form resembling the head of a claw-shaped can opener. Their location was marked with a blue triangle, which barely touched the red line. Porter's crew had picked this remote spot not only for its ideal woodland cover, but also because it was roughly equidistant to several key positions: the village of Chernobyl, the nuclear power plant, the abandoned town of Pripyat, the southern checkpoint into the Exclusion Zone, and the northern border with Belarus. This gave them the most flexible vantage from which to surveil the gas station, where they'd expected Edmar to appear. At least that was the original plan. But when Porter got word from his team in the UK—who in the meantime had been scouring intercepted phone and data traffic—that Jonathan might also be there, it changed everything. The drone had soon spotted Jonathan in a van across from the gas station. And for Porter, from that moment on, the movements of the New Orleans lawyer immediately became just as interesting as Edmar's.

Porter glanced at the red numbers of the digital timer on the corner of the screen. "Only forty-one minutes," he said. That was the fuel time left on the drone flying over the target, and it needed about thirty-five to return to the surveillance van. There would be a ten- to twenty-minute gap in the video feed before the second drone could take up position, since the distance was slightly over the threshold needed for nonstop coverage using these types of drones to relay each other. When one drone was out over the target, the other flew back to the surveillance van to get batteries swapped out and refueled, and this cycle continued. They'd been doing this for three and a half hours.

"They're following someone," the operator said, his voice now pumped with energy. He pointed to the top of the video feed as he zoomed out first and then zoomed in on a new spot. "That's what they're following. That person. See it?"

"Uh-hum." It wasn't a very clear image, but Porter could still see a small figure contrasting with the gray background, moving briskly through a wooded area just south of a large apartment block.

"They're splitting up," the other operator said.

The target Porter suspected was Jonathan went in one direction with what looked like his female companion, their images clearer now that they were in the open. The larger man accompanying them headed down a flight of steps near a swing set and turned onto the same path as the new person they'd just spotted.

"Follow that guy for a moment," Porter ordered. He knew the operator could quickly zoom out again and track Jonathan in no time. At least for the next couple minutes.

"There you go," the operator said, zooming in on the large figure who'd split from the group. "He's the only one following the new guy."

"I see that," Porter said, trying to piece together what all he was seeing and what it meant.

"Look now," the operator said, his finger pointing at the most recent target. "He looked back for a second and now just ducked behind that wall. And I think I saw a weapon." He turned to his colleague and said, "Rewind on your screen."

He quickly rewound a twenty-second loop of the video recording. "A knife. It's got to be a knife."

"Maybe." Porter tilted his head. The stranger had indeed pulled out something from his backpack, but he wasn't as certain it was a knife. And now the man was barely visible in thick shrubs next to a wall.

Porter leaned in. The larger target paused near the shrubs, apparently searching for his quarry. And the other man concealed himself further. "Knife or not, this could get ugly."

The larger, bright figure again was on the move and was fast approaching the other in hiding.

"Damn!" Porter barked.

The man behind the wall suddenly jumped out with an object in hand that he immediately thrust into the upper body of the figure who'd been on his trail.

"Call the others," Porter snapped. "Get them in there!"

The operator turned, his look bewildered.

"You heard me," Porter said sternly.

On-screen, the larger man buckled over—clearly, he'd taken a hit. But he quickly regained his footing and leapt at his assailant. Porter fixated on the violent brawl fed live on-screen as the operator zoomed in further.

The two glowing figures twisted, punched and then rolled over the ground. Both landed a few blows to each other's heads.

"Knife is down," said Porter, taking a deep breath and expelled it, running his hand over his scalp. The weapon went flying a yard away as the figures continued to battle on the ground. "Gun! They're wrestling over a gun. Look."

One man quickly flopped backward on one knee, while the other grabbed his foot but remained on the ground. He stabilized his footing and turned to his opponent below.

"One of them's gonna die," Porter said.

Suddenly a flash lit up the space between the fighting figures.

"That's gunfire," the operator said.

23

Pripyat, Ukraine

A HELL OF A SOUND. EVEN THE STALWART BREEZE THAT swayed the trees didn't hide it. The deep muffled cry resembled a bear's growl, ricocheting off the nearby uninhibited apartment blocks.

Jonathan turned to Elya. "What the..."

"Vanko?" she said in a loud whisper, her face twisting.

The noise had come roughly from the same direction where Vanko had gone to follow the stranger minutes earlier.

"An animal?" Jonathan said.

"No. We didn't even see a squirrel since we came into the Exclusion Zone."

They had reached the dense brush at the base of what Jonathan believed to be the old school—the one that the tour bus driver claimed he'd gone to on Edmar's behalf.

Elya glanced at the woods. "Should we go check?"

"We should go inside," Jonathan said, pointing at a row of steps leading up to a set of double-doors. "With so little time before curfew, we need to get in and back out as fast as we can."

A loud bang rang out.

Jonathan jolted and Elya grabbed his arm. A hollow echo followed. Unquestionably a gunshot. *Vanko's?* Something was terribly wrong.

Elya pushed him forward. "Let's go."

She was off like a shot, running fifty yards to the nearest road with Jonathan close behind. As they passed he spot where they'd last seen Vanko, they slowed to a brisk walk but stayed on the pavement where they could move silently, rather than crunching across the leaf-covered ground of the adjacent wooded area.

"Stop," Elya said suddenly, panting slightly. "Listen."

Jonathan stood still.

"You hear that?"

He tried to tune out the wind. "Yes." A faint groaning came from the woods.

"We have no light." Elya's voice was shaky.

He wasn't about to call out Vanko's name. "Be careful. There could be someone armed and waiting."

"What if...that man attacked Vanko?" She said, her words jumping.

Jonathan hoped that whatever happened, Vanko would have the advantage with his physical size and firearm. But if something had happened to him, he and Elya couldn't just stand there and wait.

Jonathan took a deep breath. He walked off the pavement, scanned the ground around him. He spotted a long, dark object, though it wasn't clear to him what it was until he picked it up. "This will do," he said. The yard-long, two-inch thick branch was a better weapon than his bare hands. "Follow me."

As they ambled deeper into the timbered blackness, at times bumping into tree trunks and shrubs, the scratchy groans had morphed into deep, monotone moans. Jonathan drew closer. He now understood it was a man in great pain.

"Vanko!" Elya cried out. She darted ahead and dropped to the ground near a darkened silhouette at the foot of a large bush.

"God, no..."

"What happened?" Elya said, her voice frantic, as she hovered over Vanko looking for injuries. "Vanko?" She then spoke in their language.

Jonathan kneeled next to them. There was almost no ambient light but barely enough to see Vanko lying on his back, his neck and face blood-soaked.

Vanko's moans diminished in strength. His inconsistent breaths were accompanied by an odd gargling, which told Jonathan there was likely a severe injury to his lungs or airway.

Elya squeezed Jonathan's arm for a second. "It's really bad." She quickly patted Vanko's chest and shoulders in search of the wounds. "Here, his chest."

Jonathan grabbed the flashlight lying on the ground a few feet away and turned it on, aiming it Vanko's upper body.

"You see," Elya said, pulling Vanko's shirt collar wide open.

"Damn." A crimson stream ran from his lower neck to his left shoulder. "Probably a knife."

Elya began pulling Vanko's shirt up. A smaller wound on his other side of his chest, below his armpit, also oozed blood. "Another stab wound," she said, her unsteady voice sounding as if she was on the verge of tears.

He aimed the light downward, along Vanko's abdomen until the beam of light hit a large crimson stain just above his groin. "Oh man, here too, and I think it's from a gunshot." The blood loss was heavy, draining over Vanko's jeans and flowing over the leafy ground beneath him.

Suddenly, the moans ceased. Jonathan checked Vanko's neck for a pulse, and then his wrist. Nothing. He leaned over his chest. "He's not breathing."

"*Blyat!*" Elya shouted. She realigned her body partly over Vanko's and immediately began chest compressions.

"Stop, stop." Jonathan grabbed her by the sleeve. "There's nothing we can do to save him. Nothing anyone can do."

She fought off his hand. "I must try."

"Stop." He grabbed her wrist again, tighter. "He's dead, Elya." He tried to sound rational. He tried to calm her down. They needed to think clearly. His heart was pounding like a war drum.

She began sobbing, her face now buried in her hands.

He shifted to her side and gently wrapped her with his arms, bringing her into his fold. "Please, we have to stay quiet, go find the briefcase, and then leave."

"It's not fair. This shit is not fair."

"I understand."

"He did nothing wrong. He didn't deserve this."

Jonathan had seen death before. An enemy was one thing. But an undeserving victim simply made him angry. He thought of Bodrov. He thought of Edmar. They would pay. They would pay dearly, and he needed to figure out how.

He reached into Vanko's pockets and retrieved the keys to the van and the tour bus, along with his wallet and passport. With the flashlight in hand, he then scoured the ground around Vanko's body.

Elya was breathing heavy. "What are you doing?"

"Looking for his gun."

The beam of light scanned over the leaves and twigs and into the bushes. But there was no weapon in sight.

He turned off the light, held her hand and pulled her up. "Let's go back to the school."

24

JONATHAN AND ELYA STOOD AT THE TOP OF A CONCRETE staircase on the exterior of the building. He pointed the flashlight at a sign on the wall next to the large metal double-doors.

Jonathan was still shaken by Vanko's death but relieved they were apparently at the right place. He pulled on the door handles, but they didn't budge. Unlike the abandoned buildings they'd seen throughout Pripyat, where most had missing or shattered doors and windows, these were locked.

"Strange, right?" Jonathan said and then shone the light at the windows one floor above them. "They're all boarded up. And look at the plywood—pretty good condition." The windows on the next two floors were not boarded up, however.

Elya gazed above. "Someone did this recently."

Jonathan again pointed the flashlight down at the lock where the two doors connected. "They're not only locked," he said, surprised, after leaning in closer. "They're welded shut."

"But how did that man get out?"

Jonathan turned off the flashlight. "I don't know. Another door, somewhere."

"Perhaps he didn't come from this building. We only saw him walking in front of the school."

"But remember, right before we first saw him, we heard the sound of a metal door closing." Jonathan turned and briskly walked down the steps. "Let's look for another way in on the other side."

He went ahead. The building was three stories high and seemed to be a rectangle shape with its longest side about eighty yards long, he guessed. They soon found another door. It was also metal and, like the other ones, also welded shut. They continued searching along the shrub-filled base of the building for any other means of entry, be it window or door. The windows on the ground floor and the next floor up were also boarded, just like on the other side of the building.

"Come here," Elya said in a loud whisper.

Jonathan walked a few feet back, pushed the shrubs to one side and leaned down to where she knelt.

"Try opening it. It's moving a little, but I'm not strong enough."

"Not exactly a door," Jonathan said, his flashlight circling the edges of what looked like a metal hatch about three feet by four feet that was hinged at the top.

"It must go to the basement, I think," Elya said, again pulling on the handle to no avail.

Jonathan shifted into a better position, sitting himself down on the ground. He placed his feet on the side wall, grabbed the handle with both hands and pulled with all his strength. A ripping pain shot through his chest, and he let out a groan, letting go of the handle as his feet slid to the ground.

Elya laid her hand on his shoulder. "Please be careful. I know you're hurting."

Jonathan caught his breath and tried to ignore the pain. "I'm doing my best." He straightened himself as well as he could, repositioned his feet on the wall and began again to pull the handle.

The metal hatch squeaked as it moved about an inch. He pulled harder still. The opening widened a few more inches, and he felt a gentle warm draft on the back of his hand. "There must be power in there. I feel warm air." A few more seconds of effort and the hatch opened wide. It weighed about twenty pounds, and Jonathan held it up as Elya peeked in. She took his flashlight and pointed the beam of light into a dusty confines of the space. There was a cement wall a few feet in front.

"You're right. The air feels warm here." She pointed the light to the left and then right. "Looks like a corridor."

"Let's go inside."

Elya squeezed through hatch and climbed down into the space.

Jonathan followed, carefully closing the hatch as quietly as possible.

"Which way?" Elya said, handing the light back to Jonathan.

He dimmed the glow of the flashlight by covering it partially with his hand and then led the way into the dark passageway. "Careful, steps coming up."

The floor was littered with debris, making it difficult to walk stealthily. He assumed the grit came from the decayed walls and ceiling. They descended some steps, and the corridor now narrowed to about four feet in width. As he reached the last step, a loud, hollow clanging sound broke out behind him.

"Shit!" Elya said in a shouted whisper.

He quickly turned and pointed the light down behind him. Elya had accidentally knocked over a fire extinguisher. "Dammit, you're going to give me a heart attack."

"Sorry."

Jonathan continued his careful strides along the littered concrete floor. They turned a corner. The floor was now paved with small white tiles, many of them cracked or missing. He began hearing a steady whining noise, like the sound of an air conditioner.

The moment he turned the next corner, he saw a light in the distance—a dimly illuminated room about twenty yards away.

"Looks like server racks," Jonathan whispered over his shoulder.

"I'm scared," Elya whispered, tugging at his sleeve. "What are we going to do?"

"Bring me the fire extinguisher." At least it was something he could use. But he wasn't sure what to expect. He waited as she ran back around the corner to retrieve it, his mind racing.

Elya returned and handed him the extinguisher. "We should leave. This is too risky."

Jonathan was tempted to follow her advice. After all, he thought, he had used up more than his nine lives in recent days and weeks. But they'd come this far. Kevin was gone. Vanko and Kane were dead. And whoever was ultimately responsible for their deaths—be it Edmar, Bodrov or someone else—these misdeeds could well have been staged from this building. Turning back now was not an option. He had to discover the truth, and this basement likely held the answers.

"If we leave now," he told her, "we may not have the opportunity to return. Just stay close to me."

She nodded.

He carried the extinguisher firmly in front of him as they treaded cautiously toward the lighted room, the open doorway of which was only a few yards ahead.

"Jonathan!"

A force threw him into the wall as he heard Elya scream his name. He bounced off the cement and spun his upper body, smashing the extinguisher into his assailant. Jonathan regained his footing and swung again, the metal clanging loudly as it hit what sounded like a gun in the man's hand.

The weapon clattered to the ground and skidded along the tiles. The man lunged at Jonathan's chest, his head ramming his already damaged ribs. The two crashed into the wall again. As Jonathan tried to grab the man's arms, he saw Elya's silhouette flip over them. She had jumped into the fray, pouncing on the man's head as Jonathan tried to tackle him to the ground. They all fell to the floor.

But the man abruptly twisted out of Jonathan's grip and lunged forward, crawling quickly along the floor with his arm stretched toward the weapon. Jonathan dove at him, but it was too late. The man's hand grabbed the weapon.

A loud blast boomed.

Jonathan landed chest-first onto the man's legs. He lunged forward, twisting and trapping the man's arms as the gun again fell to the floor.

A subtle cry echoed. From the corner of his eye, Jonathan saw Elya collapse. Before he could turn, the attacker grabbed his shirt and kicked his waist.

Jonathan threw himself down on him again, and gripped his face with his right hand, burying every finger into his cheeks—the man's instant cries told him he might now have the upper hand. Jonathan's left arm was locked around the man's thin waist, his fist clenching a leather belt.

Jonathan tried to wrestle into a more favorable position. He struggled, trying to shift his body above the man, but his grip loosened. They again slammed hard into the wall of the tight hallway, bounced back and into the opposing wall, their legs tangling. Jonathan felt the man's hardened grip at his neck, his thumb prodding deep into his carotid. Jonathan head-butted the man and then smashed his elbow into his sternum.

"Ahh!" Jonathan yelled as a sharp thrust cracked the back of his head. His shoulders drooped. He fell to his knees, the light at the end of the corridor suddenly spinning and fading at the same time. He struggled to stay conscious. He gazed up and saw a second man hovering over him. A punch came fast. He dropped to the floor.

Two seconds later arms had wrapped around Jonathan—both men, he guessed. They lifted him violently to his feet, but he could not stand on his own. The back of his head was throbbing, a pain so strong he thought his skull was being pried open. He tried to speak but couldn't. His jaw began shaking. His legs turned numb. He briefly saw Elya's prone body below him as the aggressors quickly carried him into the lighted space and tossed him to the ground.

Jonathan cringed. His eyes closed. The excruciating pain was nearly unbearable.

"Who are you?" one of the men shouted in broken English.

Jonathan reopened his eyes and took a deep breath.

An Asian man knelt before him, his hand clenched hard on Jonathan's collar. His eyes were rabid, his face dripping with sweat.

"Let me kill him," said the skinny man who was now standing, a pistol in hand. His English had a Ukrainian or Russian accent.

"No. We wait for Edmar." The Asian man tightened his grip. "Who sent you?" He yanked Jonathan by the collar.

"I'm not..." Jonathan had no energy to finish his words. His vision narrowed and blurred as he gazed around the room. The space was filled to the ceiling with servers that were connected to ventilation pipes, with

dozens of cables snaking across the floor and above the
server racks.

"Answer!" The man gave another harsh tug of the
collar, jolting Jonathan's head backward.

"Motherfucker—"

The agony needled through every muscle and bone
in Jonathan's body. *Who are these men?* Jonathan
thought. *Why do they speak English with one another
if it's not their native language? And what are all these
sophisticated computer servers doing in the basement
of an abandoned school in the middle of a deserted,
contaminated town?* Nothing made sense. But the pain
exploding from the back of Jonathan's head had intensified. He couldn't think. He couldn't speak. He couldn't
construct a single idea for how to save himself from this
dire predicament.

"Put him in the cell," said the man with whom
Jonathan had wrestled in the hallway.

The Asian man shoved Jonathan's face to the floor
and then quickly tied his hands behind his back with
tape. "Someone else will make you talk," the man said,
his voice harsh, hate-filled. He then propped Jonathan
against a server rack and began wrapping tape around
his head until his mouth was fully covered.

The two attackers picked Jonathan up and dragged
him into a passageway at the other side of the server
room. They descended a few steps and a short distance
later, the Asian man opened a metal door, threw Jonathan
onto the floor and left, locking the door behind him.

Jonathan lay on the floor motionless. His eyes
scanned the room, which was illuminated with a lone

bulb dangling from the ceiling. The space smelled like rotting animals. He noticed blood stains on the floor and on a wooden chair nearby. But the blood wasn't his. *Wyatt's, maybe?* he pondered.

*   *   *

More than two or three hours passed, Jonathan guessed. He struggled to listen for a noise that might indicate what was happening with Elya, but he hadn't heard anything but his own breathing. He lay on the floor accompanied by his unrelenting aches and pains. His throat was so dry that each time he swallowed it was as if it were lined with sandpaper. His wrists had been taped so tightly that his hands were half-numb. And the pain throbbing across his head, spine and chest had only gotten worse.

Suddenly, the walls and floor shook, like the beginnings of an earthquake. Then a deep thud echoed. And another. He twisted his head and stared at the metal door. Another explosion shook the walls. Then deep cries. Men yelling. Another explosion.

"Get down! On the ground, now!" he heard someone yelling in English.

Jonathan twisted further, bending his knees and trying to pivot his body in such a way that he could get up. But his restraints made it impossible.

The ruckus beyond the hallway was loud, with voices bellowing and the sounds of things being thrown about.

Jonathan wasn't sure if this was good news or not. But he decided to take a chance. Lying on the ground, with his arms still tied behind his back, he jostled forward, twisting and turning until his feet were just about at the door. He then kicked the bottom of it as hard as he could. On the fifth kick the door unlocked and flung open, hitting his knees hard.

The pain made Jonathan scream through his taped mouth, and sooner than he had blinked, two assault rifles with silencers were pointed at his head. The men wore black helmets, fatigues, body armor, balaclavas, night-vision goggles and knee- and elbow-pads.

"Speak English?"

Jonathan nodded and signaled with his head to free him of the tape.

"Are you Kevin Wyatt?"

Jonathan shook his head, again groaning through his taped mouth.

"Are there other prisoners like you elsewhere in this place?" barked the closest man, his barrel still pointed at Jonathan's forehead.

Jonathan shook his head violently and then grunted loudly, until the other man strapped his weapon over his back and knelt, took out a knife and began slicing the tape loose from his face. But his colleague continued to point his assault rifle at Jonathan.

"Who the hell are you?" Jonathan asked the moment his mouth was free to speak. "And stop pointing that at me. I think we're on the same side."

A third man in black camo walked in holding a pistol. "That's not important," the man said, holstering his weapon. "You American?"

"Yes?"

"What's your name?"

"Jonathan Brooks."

The man spun around and headed out into the passageway where it sounded to Jonathan as if he was calling someone on a radio. Jonathan tried to listen but could make out only scattered words. "Target... missing...captured...assets." Clearly, Jonathan reasoned, they were U.S. military or law enforcement, and given that they were in Ukraine, he realized that this was no trivial operation—and one that was likely being done without approval of local authorities.

"Will someone please tell me what the fuck is going on?" Jonathan shouted. "Are you FBI? Special Forces? What are—"

"Calm down, sir!" shouted the man who still hadn't taken his weapon's sights off Jonathan.

"I'm American. I was taken prisoner. I have nothing to do with the people running this place. So, untie me."

"You just stay put until we figure this out."

Jonathan was getting angry.

"One female...checking IDs...suspects down...," the man said, having again stepped out into the corridor, his words still not fully audible. Then he reentered the room, put his arms on his waist and stared at Jonathan. "You're Brooks, right?"

"Yes, dammit. My passport's in my back pocket."

"Untie him," the man said and gestured to his colleague kneeling on the floor and with his hand lowered his other teammate's weapon. "Let's get cracking. Exfil in ten minutes."

"Is she alive?"

The man's brows lifted. "Who?"

"My friend in the hallway."

He shook his head. "Sorry, no."

Jonathan's breath caught in his throat. As he shook his head, he realized there were more sounds coming from elsewhere in the basement. Men talking loudly—one with an accent sounded as if he was arguing.

"You've got one of them?" Jonathan asked as he slowly stood up, straightened his back and wiggled his arms to let the blood flow back into his hands.

"Yeah, an Asian guy. We'll take him with us."

"What is this place?" Jonathan asked.

"You've been here longer than us, so you tell me."

Jonathan wasn't up for wiseass remarks. "They caught me soon after I crawled in here. And they killed her. So, you tell me what you know, because clearly I'm the one with less info here."

The man took off his helmet but kept his balaclava, below which he had a throat mic. "This place looks like a hacker's wet dream. There's a server room and a control room with more computers than I've seen at military command centers."

One of his colleagues left the room, while the other took swabs of the blood stains on the chair and put the specimen in a clear plastic bag.

Jonathan looked at the soldier taking another sample off of the seatback portion of the chair. "It's probably Wyatt's blood—he must have been here at some point. There's more blood on the floor—it's not mine. And there's a bloodied shirt there in the corner, over there behind you. Wyatt was my client, and I've spent the past few days tracking down the men who likely kidnapped him.

"Yeah, we know."

"Do you know where he might be now?"

"That's above my paygrade. I just need to get you and our detainee out of here. And then someone you already know wants a word with you."

"Who?" Jonathan could not imagine who he was talking about.

"Let's move to the other room now," the man said assertively. "You'll find out in due course."

25

Pyongyang, North Korea

SOMETIMES THE TINIEST THINGS CAN TRIGGER A MOUNTAIN of pain, Linda admitted in silence, her eyes fixated on a jade ornament carved in the form of a tiger. It sat at the center of the circular conference table, next to a small vase of purple orchids. The longer she gazed at it, the more her chest constricted. This simple, barely conspicuous ornament, coupled with the forty-five-minute delay for her interview with Ri Yong-nam, Deputy Minister of Foreign Affairs, had pried open a door she had subconsciously bolted shut for a long time.

What a roller coaster it had been.

She quickly counted the years, her gaze melting deeper into the jade's matte pink surface. The tiger was virtually identical to a gift she'd received from Jonathan's father.

Twenty years.

Linda shook her head and closed her eyes. Jonathan's father had given Linda the gift upon his return from a business trip to China, soon after learning that Jonathan had proposed to her. But later that same day Linda's mother shared some awful news: her cancer was back, and it was terminal. Linda had stayed up for hours talking with Jonathan that night. He'd listened. He'd embraced her as they wept together. Held her hand. Said all the right things. She was bursting at the seams with conflicted emotions—the happiness of knowing she would spend her life with Jonathan, her high school sweetheart whom she adored, and the sadness that the greatest woman she'd ever known, and who'd brought her into this world, was dying. Jonathan had held Linda together.

She continued to eye the ornament as the memories of that night began hemorrhaging a larger archive of thoughts: a younger, invincible, spirited Jonathan. The memories flooded back in snippets that further tightened her chest. The gentle, supporting expression that swept over his face when he tried to help build her confidence before her first job interview. The moment he'd swept her off her feet and carried her down the steps of Old St. Patrick's Church in New Orleans minutes after they'd celebrated their nuptials. Their tranquil, 4 A.M. barefoot walk along a desolate beach on the first night of their honeymoon in Key Largo. The aching grew as the mosaic of crystal-clear recollections flowed uncontrollably.

Linda felt the tears welling in her eyes. She took a sip of water and tried to curb the stream of memories. But they kept coming, and her sadness deepened as she recalled the months-long treatment for her burns after the house fire. And the follow-up plastic surgeries to diminish the prominence of the scars across her body. She remembered Jonathan's unwavering support; his guilt born of his feelings of responsibility for the circumstances that had caused the fire. He was there all along, through the countless doctor consultations, procedures, recovery, rehabilitation, counseling and psychiatric sessions. Every step of a long, arduous journey that never seemed to have an end in sight. And for all that, she gave him only resentment in return. She recalled his apologies, his attempts to make amends for what had happened to her. And then later, his empty stares, his defensiveness, his anger, his tears. All the arguments she'd incited when their marriage began to unravel. When she'd turned to drinking. When she'd lost her job at the news channel. When there was nothing left in their relationship for her to cling to as she descended into her own abyss. Those happier days might as well have been a past life. Or simply somebody else's.

I was so unfair. She flickered her eyelids, opened her eyes wide and looked up at the ceiling, trying to stop the first tear from breaking free. She now felt confused at this sudden deluge of pain. Perhaps it was guilt. Or maddening regret? Or love? She looked down and with her index finger gently wiped the liquid off her eyes, careful not to smudge her eyeshadow and mascara. *Do I still love him?* she thought, abruptly feeling uncomfortable that the question even came to mind. *Even now?* She sighed. Goosebumps ran up her spine.

Suddenly, a loud thump shattered the quiet and the door flung open.

She jolted, the abruptness halting her recollections of Jonathan. And whatever sentiments lingered, she expunged quickly. She now had a job to do. And do it well, too.

A gray-suited man lumbered into the room. "Sorry we are late," he said with an accented English while holding the door open, his eyes turning to the corridor. An Asian man in a navy-blue suite followed behind him.

Linda immediately recognized the deputy minister, a seemingly fit, salt-and-pepper-haired man in his late-forties. She jumped to her feet and extended her hand. "Very pleased to meet you, your Excellency."

He nodded and returned a soft handshake and a lukewarm smile, making the briefest of eye contact with her.

Deputy Minister Ri was a tough nut to crack, Max had told her on the flight into Pyongyang. Once the director-general of the ministry's North American department, and prior to that a diplomat at the North Korean mission to the U.N. in New York, and before that in Geneva, Ri had acquired an unusually solid understanding of Americans, or at least the diplomats and policymakers he'd met over the years. This made him the single most experienced member of Kim Jong-il's foreign policy team to have worked with Americans, and far more so than Ri's boss, the Minister of Foreign Affairs, whose career had been built through postings in Beijing, Moscow and Warsaw.

Though Max had asked Linda to hammer Ri about North Korea's tarnished record of prior nuclear nonproliferation commitments, Linda preferred a different angle: How well did he really know America and its official intentions and hopes for these strategic negotiations? Perhaps, she thought, his answers would be the best indication of whether the regime intended to deceive the West again or, on the other hand, put some pressure on his own policymakers to back up the lofty nonproliferation aspirations they'd trumpeted unstoppably over the past few months.

Linda and Ri sat on the same half of the conference table in full view of each other as the bodyguard stood in the corner behind Linda, facing Ri. Once they had exchanged formalities, Linda was ready to unload her questions. She had submitted them in writing the night before, as Ri's minions had demanded, but she had mentally prepared several more prying questions that she intended to throw in like a touch of hot sauce to make things exciting—regardless of whether he would answer them. In any case, there would be no way to capture his reaction on camera. His staff had rejected the use of any recording device. Linda had to rely only on her notes.

She took a quick sip of her water and pulled the trigger. "Why should anyone in Washington believe you? Your government's promises, that is?"

"The same can be said of your government, right?"

"I understand," Linda replied slowly. "Trust me, we ask the same tough questions back home. But I'm here now, in your country, trying to assess whether this talk of nonproliferation is real or not."

Deputy Minister Ri's brow lifted slightly, his lips straight as a hyphen. Perhaps he was gauging her stamina, she thought. Or he simply wasn't used to anyone—a woman, especially—speaking to him so candidly that it could be mistaken for a cross-examination.

"Our commitment is solid. We see mutual benefits," he said dryly.

She quickly noted his response in shorthand and moved on to the next question. Five were about recently published statements from Kim Jong-il. Twelve of them were politically focused, and she hoped to get them all out in the time remaining. But she'd also thrown in a couple personal ones—about his family and how he mastered his mostly flawless English, which was really a curious blend of Canadian and British English with the occasional word or phrase that sounded like a New Yorker.

Halfway through the interview, another suited man came in and brought them two cups of ginseng tea. Linda finished her water and began sipping from her mug, keeping her eyes on Ri but saying nothing. He appeared to be deep in thought. She wondered if he, with his calculating, analytical mind, was worrying about how his responses would play out to a Western readership.

She resumed the discussion, soon reaching the last question on her sheet. The interview had gone over by about ten minutes. She watched as Ri took another sip of his tea.

She smiled, put the sheet face down on the table and sat back in her chair. "I'm not going to write your answer to this last question." She ran her fingers through her hair. "What if this all happens?"

He shrugged, his forehead glistening, his hands unmoved from their interlocked position on the tabletop. "What do you mean by 'this'?"

She took the last sip of her tea. "If your government's nuclear disarmament actually happens, where you give up your research, testing, production, and stockpile of weapons. You reintegrate the physicists, chemists, mechanical and electrical engineers into civilian industry. You reallocate the funds to infrastructure or healthcare, for instance. Let's say all this happens, and a formal peace treaty is signed...how will all this really benefit the peninsula if the border... still...stands? If families remain separated? If nothing else changes except the lethality and readiness of the weapons that are pointed at each other? In other words, what's the point? There will still be two Koreas—or more like two completely different worlds—despite the two populations speaking the same language. And one day in the future, someone writing history books might ask, Why didn't Deputy Minister Ri do something about it? Why didn't he make a difference? Why?"

His forehead wrinkled, and his eyes locked onto hers.

"I'm not asking this for my readers," Linda continued. "You can see that I have set my pen down. I'm asking because I want to know, personally. And I think anyone in this room with an ounce of empathy for humanity would ask the same thing."

With his finger, Ri cleared a droplet of perspiration from his brow and crossed his arms, his face twisting. Linda noticed a vein on his temple pulsating. No doubt he was pondering the best response he could give, but he'd have to be a magician to spin something positive out of the fact that the heavily militarized border standing since 1954 wasn't going to change anytime soon, if ever.

"You know, Mrs. Brooks," he said, his voice turning cold. "I will—"

"Ms. Fabre," she corrected. "Brooks is my former married name."

"Uh...yes...Ms. Fabre," he said, the tautness of his tone undisguised. "I hope you...I mean, we all have a role to play. But let's not forget that each one of us is less important than the bigger causes we fight for. And far less important than the people who lead us or control us." A closed-mouthed smile crossed his face as his gaze intensified. She now saw only hate in his eyes. "Cemeteries are filled with dreamers who were either untimely or unwise."

She quickly replayed his words, trying to extract a coherent meaning.

He quickly got up, buttoned his suit jacket and nodded at her. "We're done, I think."

She was still deciphering his word salad, and then it hit her. Did you threaten me? she asked silently. A chill crawled down her spine.

He walked out without shaking hands.

26

THE SHARPLY POINTED PYRAMID-SHAPE OF THE RYUGYONG
Hotel pierced the dark stone sky like a dagger thrown at
the heavens. Some, however, might say it was a middle
finger thrown at the world, as the massive one-hundred-
five-story tower, with its planned revolving restaurants and
entertainment facilities, remained a ghostly, unfinished
structure for the last two decades and symbolized the
dictatorship's unaccountable, unrepentant and unforgivable
excesses. From the backseat of the government car, Linda
glared at the stacked, lifeless concrete floors. Only a few
lower floors had their intended exterior glass panels
installed. And with over three thousand rooms, no one
in their right mind could imagine every filling it with
tourists. Political prisoners, maybe.

Linda had been in the city only thirty-six hours but
already sensed that journalists were not to be trusted.

In fact, she was sure that North Korean society was structured on distrust and lies. The government lied to its people, the people lied to each other, the minders lied do foreigners, the foreigners lied to their hosts—all of it forming an elaborate web of deceit. Her interview with Deputy Minister Ri only reinforced this feeling. And everything else about Pyongyang appeared cold and deceptively staged.

With about three city blocks in sight ahead of her, she saw only one bus, two cars, a handful of laborers unloading a 1950s-vintage flatbed truck and a few schoolchildren in uniform strolling the sidewalk. How odd it was for a city of nearly three million to seem so absent of life, she thought. *It's two-thirty in the afternoon, on a Tuesday, for God's sake.* She passed several patriotic billboards that decorated the sidewalks—their bright colors stood out in contrast to the bland, weatherworn grays of the architecture. One of them made her chuckle. It showed an oversized Korean worker's fist crushing a soldier's helmet that was inscribed with a white star and the initials "U.S." She'd seen many more propaganda posters, billboards and murals the previous day, when a squad of overly polite English-speaking minders took the visiting Western press corps on a ten-monument bus tour of the city, the climax of which was a brief visit to the open-air deck of Juche Tower that faced the riverfront.

More dreary facades of large concrete government buildings and insipidly designed apartment blocks, many of them dated showcases of socialist urban planning, passed by. But the capital was a bubble, Max had told

her, far better than any place else in the communist country. No civilian could live in Pyongyang if they weren't
a trusted member of the "songbun" social caste system.
And most North Koreans only dreamt of making it here,
where the standard of living was relatively livable compared to rural towns and second-tier cities, all of them
suffering from shortages of food, medicines, power and
other necessities of life.

Her government driver sped the late model Mercedes
down a nearly deserted six-lane boulevard, occasionally
glancing at her in the rearview mirror. She was certain
he only knew two words in English: hello and hotel. She
would know soon if he knew a third—goodbye.

Linda again thought about her interview with Ri.
She'd thrown a few good curveballs at him, but he was
articulate, well-prepared. Except for the last question.
What he said unnerved her, though she wasn't certain
what he'd meant. For sure, the words weren't lost in
translation—Ri's English was impeccable. Maybe he
wanted to be provocatively ambiguous and nothing
more. *No*, Linda thought, shaking her head. She was
convinced he had woven a cryptic threat into his parting
words? It now left her wondering if she'd crossed a line
to deserve it? Perhaps in this culture, she had.

As she deconstructed more of their dialogue, another
detail jumped out at her, and it was even more disturbing.
Why had Ri called her by the name Brooks—her ex's
surname? She'd given it up four or five years ago,
choosing instead her maiden name that has since become
as prominent as her wavy blonde hair. It was printed in
her passport, on all her visas, her press credentials and

mentioned on every TV channel that had aired her reports since she plunged back in the media industry. There was no trace of the name Brooks except in her soul.

The driver turned, and Linda instantly recognized the landmark on the righthand side: Pyongyang Station, the city's main railway hub. The car sped up along Yokjon Street, which was as dormant as the other avenues. She knew the road would turn ahead soon and cross a bridge that connected the west bank of the Taedong River to Yanggakdo Island.

As the car raced over the water, she recalled her arrival the prior day, when she crossed the same bridge for the first time. She sat in a bus with twenty-five other members of the international press corps, and that very moment the government minder took the microphone and explained that their hotel was situated at the north tip of a small island in the middle of the river and reminded everyone that no one was permitted to leave the hotel's premises unless accompanied by his staff or other government officials. While it drew chuckles and laughs, the message was clear. Foreign journalists were isolated and any venturing from the hotel would be either in a fish bowl or a coffin.

The car turned onto a two-lane road surrounded by well-groomed foliage and headed past the city's International Cinema Hall—a place she'd been told played mostly locally produced patriotic films, but only on nights when the electrical power was expected to work past seven in the evening. The winding road ended at the large paved parking lot of the Yanggakdo Hotel, an austere 1980s era 47-story concrete and glass monolith.

Linda walked briskly into the hotel, ignoring her fellow foreigners in the immense marble lobby. Her eyes felt glassy and her muscles were tight and sore. She assumed her travels, including a string of recent late nights and early mornings, were finally catching up with her. She entered the elevator ahead of two Australians she'd met during the flight into Pyongyang. As the doors began to close, a hand poked rapidly between them and pushed them open again. The suited hotel manager moved in, greeted the guests with an impassive nod and pressed a button.

"Care to join us at the rooftop?" the heavier-set Aussie asked Linda.

"I'm really tired, but thanks," she said.

"Please join us," his colleague added. "Brad here is as Australian as a boomerang. He'll keep circling back until you finally say yes."

Linda smiled. "Maybe I will." She pressed the button for the 18th floor, glanced down and did a double-take. "That's odd!" She craned her neck toward the lower row of buttons. "Your engineers forgot number five."

The manager turned briskly, his brows joining. "The most important floor you should notice is yours," he said, his voice slightly raised.

Linda glanced at the Australians and shrugged. Everyone remained dead quiet until the eleventh floor, where the manager stepped off.

When the doors closed again, Brad leaned into Linda and whispered, "A Chinese journalist told me something quite unpleasant about the fifth floor."

"How so?"

"I'll tell you more over a cold North Korean beer."
He winked and crossed his arms.

"Ok, I'm hooked. See you up there shortly." She was
too tired to venture a guess about that missing floor.
She'd already seen countless bizarre things since landing in Pyongyang. Like an official poster with approved
haircuts, or the red lapel pin worn by all adults, or radios
tuned to patriotic hymns that can't be turned off, or a
customs official confiscating a pair of jeans—they are
illegal in the country.

The elevator stopped on her floor, and Linda headed
to her room. She still found it odd that she, Max and the
only other two American journalists were on the same
floor, while other nationalities were scattered over several higher floors.

*   *   *

Linda had thrown on a bit of makeup, a pair of comfortable slacks and a squeeze of her favorite Dolce &
Gabbana perfume. She got off the elevator on the hotel's
circular top floor and immediately spotted Brad and his
buddy, Terry, sitting by the windows, their shirt sleeves
rolled up and smoke rising from their cigarettes. Brad
had flung his sandaled feet over the coffee table.

"There you are!" Terry shouted and raised his half-
filled glass in the air the moment he locked eyes with
Linda.

Taking a chair between them, Linda counted four
empty one-liter beer bottles on the table. "You have a
heck of a head start, I take it," she said, smiling.

Brad put down his glass. "Taedonggang beer," he said pointing at the green-labeled bottles. "The waiter promised us it's not piss. So...a cold one for you as well, right?"

"She seems more the wine type, Brad," Terry said, his words a tad slurred.

"I am," Linda said, trying to gauge whether it was such a good idea to join them. "But I imagine they won't make the same promise about North Korean wine."

The waiter soon brought her a beer, opened it and poured a glass. But she hesitated to pick it up.

"Really, it's quite safe," Brad said.

Her reluctance had nothing to do with safety or taste. She hadn't had a drop of alcohol in weeks, and after spending years mired in a state of self-destruction aided by vodka and Vicodin, she understood taking a sip now was no trivial thing.

She glanced at Brad and again stared at her glass. *One drink*, she thought. *Just one, dammit*. And why not? Killing time in the middle of this weird country, she felt her own rules were loosening. And everything had changed so fast. After all, just a week ago she'd been reporting from hurricane-ravaged towns in southern Louisiana. A week later, she was in the Chinese capital hob-knobbing with the country's political hierarchy and foreign media elites. And now, she thought quixotically, she'd stepped into an entirely different dimension—the most repressive nation on earth. *Who would have guessed.*

Brad raised his glass, and the three toasted, the loud noise of pinging glass turning a few heads at nearby tables.

Terry took a long drag of his tobacco, exhaled and said, "Did you notice you're the only Western woman journalist?"

"No, there are two others," Linda said, frowning. "One from Chile and the other from..."

"No, no, no." Terry's eyes were becoming bloodshot and his cheeks reddened, too. "Did you see them? They're not women."

"Oh, be nice, you drunk fool," Brad said and glanced at Linda. "You must excuse him."

"No, I'm serious," Terry said, his body slumping to the left in his chair. "That one from Chile is hairier than a koala."

"Skull it down and shut up before Linda slaps ya head to the ground."

She sat back in her chair and looked out the window at the cloud-filled dusk skies and the flickering lights of radio towers in the distance. That's when she noticed the view hadn't changed since she sat down. "I thought this floor revolved."

Terry sneered, almost spitting out his beer. "You'll have to wait. Apparently, they ran out of spare parts last year."

"Besides, the view will get very boring, very quickly."

"I understand," Linda said. The previous night, most city lights had gone out at around eight, and the remaining ones—mostly to light up monuments—turned dark an hour later.

Linda had barely finished her beer an hour into her mostly slap-happy chat with the boys from down under. But her stomach had begun to ache. Perhaps it was the alcohol or the fatigue. But she had little energy in her to leave.

As Brad slipped a cigarette to his lips and lighted it, he turned to her. "Fancy checking out the fifth floor?"

Linda tilted her head back. "Oh, you were going to tell me more about it."

"It's easier to see it in person,"

Terry crunched his eyelids and then opened his eyes wide. "You're joking?"

"No."

"You heard what the Chinese mate said. It's for their spooks."

Linda straightened her shoulders. "Spies?"

"Yes, there's some sort of surveillance operation down there." He turned half-way round. "And...you see...that man in the blue shirt?"

Linda nodded.

"He's with France 1 news channel. I heard he went down there last night, through the fire escape stairwell."

Brad raised a brow. "Well, can't let a Frenchman have all the fun. Let's go."

Linda didn't think this was such a good idea. "Brad, we've been warned many times to behave," she said, as Terry slapped thirty Euros on the table.

"Don't be so uptight," Brad said, grinning. "We're only exploring the hotel; we're not overthrowing the regime."

"The beer is making you brave," she said.

"Brave and curious," Terry added, reaching into his pocket. He pulled out a miniature flashlight attached to his keychain. "And fully prepared."

Linda sighed and shook her head. She'd had only one glass of beer but felt as if she had downed three bottles. And her stomach was aching more than before. As interesting as it might be to explore a secret floor of the hotel, she was now equally interested in taking two antacids and going to sleep.

The men were standing, both with arms crossed and blank gazes.

"Fine, dammit, but I'm only staying two minutes on that floor," she said, starting to feel annoyed by their insistence. "And not a second longer."

"Promise," Terry said, raising his straightened palm mockingly.

She got up and put her fleece jacket back on. She felt strangely nauseous but ignored it as best she could.

Brad led the way down the normal stairwell one floor below the non-revolving restaurant and then traversed the hallway to the other side of the floor toward the fire escape stairwell.

He pushed the door and held it open. "Your highness," he said, motioning with his hand an exaggerated prostrating gesticulation to Linda as she passed him in the doorway.

She rolled her eyes, her lungs taking in his alcohol breath accompanied by the musty air of the emergency stairwell. She followed Terry, whose less than steady descent down the steps of the dimly lighted space told her he was more intoxicated than she'd previously suspected.

Without uttering another word, the three journalists headed down floor after floor, each time passing a large door—some had a floor number painted on it, some didn't.

Terry's pace slowed. He then stopped at a door facing him. "This is it, I think," he said excitedly. He shone his tiny flashlight at the upper center of the door. The faded number five was barely visible on the grayish-green metal door.

Brad clumsily walked around Terry and pulled the handle. "It's open!" he said in a loud whisper.

Linda hissed. "If it's so secret, why is it unlocked?"

"Who cares," Terry replied, pushing Brad out of the way with his shoulder and entering first. "Come on." He first craned his neck out into the hallway and then motioned for the others to follow.

The three were now in the corridor, which was illuminated by low-wattage incandescent lights, unlike the other floors of the hotel. In both directions there were doors, but there were fewer than on other floors.

"Check out the low ceiling," Linda said, glancing up. It was barely a foot above Terry's head—he was of average height.

"It's a false ceiling so they can run wiring and cables," Brad said, his voice low.

"And what's with the poster, mate?" Terry said, pointing to the wall on their left. The large propaganda poster depicted an armed pilot, a nurse, a rifle-carrying soldier and an armed sailor, all aggressively peering down at the bust of a long-nosed, helmeted head that wore a dented, green helmet with the letters "US" painted on its side—the entire scene set on a red background with bold wording in Korean written at the top. The ridiculous image reminded Linda of a similar billboard she'd seen in the city earlier in the day.

Brad toggled a doorknob, but it was locked. He and Terry moved ahead to the next door, tried it, but it too was locked. At the next one, Terry reached for the handle and turned it. He slowly opened the door, and both men took a step into the room.

Linda strolled in, squeezed her way between their shoulders and stepped ahead of them. She was surprised the moment she saw at the center of the brightly lighted, windowless room a long wood-paneled workstation that resembled the many TV news anchor desks she'd used over the years. There were two worn cloth office chairs behind the desk and four spotlights trained at the desk from a track lighting unit on the ceiling. But that's where the similarities ended. There were no cameras. No teleprompters. No LED or LCD screens. No platforms or staging. Instead, at one end of the desk sat a bulky electronic device the size of a suitcase, with various dials and symbols that she guessed was a military-style radio transmitter. Lying at the center of the desk were two sets of large earphones with long, twisted cables winding their way to the device.

"Jesus," Terry whispered. "A radio station?"

"No, a listening post," Linda said, her words coming out slowly as she scanned the room in detail. "We should leave," she added the moment the smell of fresh cigarette smoke entered her lungs.

"There's no one here," Brad whispered.

Linda glanced at a wide, doorless opening on the left that led to a darkened adjoining room. Her heart began to speed up. She swallowed hard. Whoever was in this room had left only a short time ago.

Suddenly a man's voice blared from the darkened room—angry words in Korean blasting in rapid succession.

"Fuck!" Brad said as he stumbled backward into Linda as he leapt for the door.

Linda jumped back and darted out into the corridor with both Aussies in tow. They ran fast down the corridor toward the fire escape as the Korean man's yells echoed from behind them.

Another door ahead of her suddenly flung open and before she could stop an arm came out and grabbed her by the arm of her fleece jacket and spun her into the wall, after which she tripped forward and fell to the bare concrete floor.

"Sorry, sorry," Brad said to the man who'd grabbed Linda.

Terry also apologized loudly but the Koreans' voices were louder. Seconds later a third Korean—this one in green military dress uniform, unlike the others in plainclothes—came out of nowhere and joined the fracas. He first shoved Brad to the wall, then raised his hand threateningly at Terry but didn't strike him. He then turned to Linda, who was still on the floor, and speared her with a vicious gaze.

Linda tried to get up, sliding her back upward along the wall to stabilize herself.

"Sit down!" the soldier barked, pointing angrily at her.

His accent was milder than the official minders who'd shepherded the press pool, which indicated to

Linda that he was a military linguistic or an intelligence officer.

He took a hard step towards her and in a loud voice said, "You're the American, right? Linda?"

Her eyes widened. She felt her heart was about to beat out of her chest. Linda nodded but the rest of her body froze.

"Sit back on the floor!"

She did as she was told. She glanced at her two Western colleagues about ten feet from her. Terry was still protesting at the other Koreans. "We're hotel guests! We didn't mean to—"

Both plainclothes Koreans grabbed him by his shoulders and shoved him into the wall.

"Stop this," Brad said loudly. "We'll leave."

The military officer turned to them, quickly pulled out something from his belt pouch and pointed it at Brad. A liquid shot out at his and Terry's faces. Pepper spray, most likely.

Linda cried out, then covered her mouth. She began to feel nauseous.

"Fuck!" Brad yelled, twisting and feverishly wiping his face, as did Terry. They both staggered backward along the corridor.

The officer then spoke into his radio and turned back to Linda. "You, get out!"

Linda was too terrified to move.

He quickly gripped her upper arm and pulled her up. She yanked her arm free. "Okay, okay!"

"Out!" He pushed her toward the door that led to the emergency stairwell.

She raced down one flight of stairs and darted through the hallway of the fourth floor in under six seconds, terrified about what might be in store for Brad and Terry. She took the glass elevator up to her floor, all the while wondering why they'd let her go. Because I'm a woman? she wondered. Or an American? Her pulse was still racing, her fleece jacket was torn and her shirt soaked with sweat. When the elevator doors opened, she ran to Max's room and banged on the door until he unbolted it and ushered her in.

"You have to do something," she sputtered, nearly out of breath.

"What's wrong?" he said. "I was just looking for you as well. Seems your ex-husband has been trying to locate you."

Linda reared back. "Jonathan? Is he okay?"

"He's in some sort of trouble in Ukraine. My staff in Beijing forwarded his message to our hotel."

"What kind of trouble?"

He shook his head. "No idea. As you know, our phones don't work here and we can only receive emails on the hotel computers in the Guest Services office, but they're closed for the night."

Linda leaned back into the door frame and exhaled deeply. Her nausea and dizziness had not subsided. "I don't feel well." She looked up at Max, whose face suddenly blurred. Her knees gave way, and she collapsed into his arms.

27

Southwest of Chernobyl, Ukraine

"WE'RE CLEAR!" SHOUTED THE DRIVER, WHO WORE night-vision goggles connected to his helmet, as he steered the vehicle in complete darkness with head-lights off.

"Clear of what?" Jonathan asked from the third row of seats at the back of the large SUV, his words trembling from the rough ride. He held on to a handle to avoid being thrown about as the vehicle moved over one of the roughest terrains Jonathan had ever ventured across.

"The Exclusion Zone."

Loud thuds and squeaks came from the SUV's suspension. The armed Americans who'd rescued Jonathan from the school basement in Pripyat had left the abandoned town in a different direction than the way Vanko had taken Jonathan. They chose a route that avoided the security checkpoints, which meant mostly going off-road.

The team leader was in the front passenger seat, his two colleagues sat behind him, and in between them was the Asian man they'd taken into custody at the school. Their prisoner was hooded, with a crimson-stained bandage wrapped around his right arm, and appeared to be asleep. His head and body swayed back and forth between his captors with each rough movement of the vehicle.

Jonathan tapped the shoulder of the American closest to him. "Who is he? Chinese?"

The man glanced back. "North Korean, dude."

That's when the leader up front quickly turned. "No more questions, you hear me?" he shouted at Jonathan and then raised his hand at his colleague, adding, "Just ignore him, dammit."

Jonathan was surprised to hear the prisoner's nationality. He'd imagined that an Asian involved in a cyber-hacking lab would likely be Chinese. "What did you give him?" Jonathan asked. "A strong sedative, I bet."

"We should have given you the same," the leader shouted back.

"You sure it's strong enough? You know he's going to be pissed when he wakes up. Probably wants to kick your asses."

"Don't worry about how we handle our job. We know what we're doing."

Jonathan didn't find this kind bravado so convincing. No matter how tough this special ops team appeared to be, they didn't have complete control of the circumstances as long as they were still in Ukraine—a country that would not take kindly to having armed Americans trespassing, firing weapons and taking prisoners on their soil.

They'd also told Jonathan that the other two suspects in the cyber-hacking lab were both dead, since they had drawn weapons when the ops team stormed in, though Jonathan hadn't seen their bodies when he was quickly hustled out of the school and taken to the SUV parked a quarter mile away.

Jonathan gazed out the window into the near total darkness. His mind was filled with the ghastly sights of his bloodied companions, Elya and Vanko. The reality of their deaths was sinking in more deeply, washing him in guilt for having involved them in the search for his client. His heart constricted. He thought of Elya, everything she could have achieved in her career. A life now stolen. And for what?

Distraught, his veins began pulsating with anger. The terrible night had brought much senseless violence, and the reasons behind Wyatt's kidnapping were still opaque—and more importantly, he had no idea who the puppeteers were in this affair.

The SUV dipped hard into another large pothole, throwing everyone to one side and then the other. Jonathan gripped the handle firmly, stabilizing himself. He then gently touched the back of his head, feeling the large bump from when he'd been knocked almost unconscious in the basement. The pain had only slightly subsided and just about matched the discomfort from his fractured ribs.

"We'll be at the rendezvous point in about ten minutes," the driver said as he turned the vehicle a sharp right, after which the road surface felt smoother but still not paved.

They finally arrived. Jonathan slowly exited the vehicle through the back door and into the pitch black, cold air. He heard the faint sounds of water—a nearby river or stream, he guessed.

As he turned away from the SUV, the powerful beam of a flashlight pierced his gaze. He covered his eyes with his arm.

"Well, well, what have we here?" The voice was deep. African-American. And laced with sarcasm.

The beam moved upward, and then the man pointed it briefly at his own face.

Jonathan's eyes popped wide open. "Jesus Christ!" He immediately recognized the man—George Porter, the CIA operative who'd gotten him out of a jam only weeks ago in Venezuela.

"Uh-huh," Porter said, now pointing the flashlight at the ground. "You *should* call me Jesus now that I'm again saving your skinny, white ass."

Jonathan shook his head. He knew that this meeting could hardly be a coincidence. And he suddenly feared that Porter might not be as empathetic as the last time around.

"Get in there," Porter said, turning and pointing his flashlight briefly at the back of a van parked some ten yards away. "I'll lead the way."

Porter slid open the van's side door. "Gentlemen, I need some privacy for a few minutes."

Two men in green fatigues facing monitors got up from their seats, and both eyed Jonathan as they stepped out. Jonathan apprehensively followed Porter into the vehicle.

Porter closed the door and glared at Jonathan. "Why the fuck are you meddling in CIA operations again?" he barked, wagging his finger inches from Jonathan's face. "You know law enforcement back home could come up with some kind of charges. I'm tempted to call them to get started on it. And that certainly wouldn't be good for your law license."

"I'm not looking for problems," Jonathan said. "Problems came to me—and to my client. It's been a nightmare the last few days. Don't get me wrong, I'm very appreciative of your help tonight, though your team came too late to save my colleagues."

"We're not in the saving business," Porter said, shaking his head. "Especially not for an adrenaline junkie playing Jason Bourne."

"My client's a U.S. citizen, a former intelligence official, and he was kidnapped. What am I supposed to do? I simply asked an American diplomat for help and all hell broke loose. But if anything, I've helped you rather than interfered. I found the hacker lab, didn't I?"

"I'll ask the questions, thank you." Porter's brows tightened down. "You better be straight with me, or I'll throw you in that radioactive river just outside."

"I'll tell you everything I know. But I need to send a message."

"To who?"

"My ex."

"Why?"

"Because I want to let her know I'm okay."

"Kinda strange to care for an ex, right?"

"Not for me. And she's in China, so I worry about her being so far away."

Porter returned a look of surprise. "China?"

"Yeah."

"She ain't in China, man. She's in Pyongyang. With a bunch of Western journalists."

Jonathan's muscles stiffened. "What the hell are you saying?"

Porter pulled out his cellphone and scrolled through content. "There." He held it up with the screen facing Jonathan and then flipped it and began reading. "She landed two days ago with three other Americans, twenty other foreign reporters and support crew."

"Why do you know this?"

"We did our homework the moment I saw you were roaming wildly in Kyiv."

"Roaming wildly, huh," Jonathan snapped, feeling his anger resurging. "If my client hadn't been kidnapped, I'd be comfortably back in New Orleans minding my own business."

Porter shrugged like he really didn't care.

Jonathan sighed. "I need to call Linda. She never mentioned to me that she was headed there. I only heard her say China."

"You should be a happy man," Porter said and then chuckled, adding, "I wish to God my ex would end up in North Korea."

"You don't understand our relationship."

Porter sighed and crossed his arms, returning a

smug gaze. "I'll let you message her but only after you cooperate and we're safely out of this country."

A sudden, frightening thought burst into Jonathan's mind. His pulse quickened as he gazed at Porter. "You mentioned she's gone to North Korea. What if someone lured her there? What if they knew I was homing in on their hacker lab and Wyatt's hostage takers, and they took her as bait or leverage?"

"You've got a wild imagination, Brooks. Gotta give you that. But she wasn't taken. As far as I understand she joined a select group of Western journalists covering the disarmament negotiations. Nothing's happened to her. Besides, I doubt the North Koreans even know she was married to you. She doesn't use your last name."

Porter had a point. But Jonathan couldn't be sure. He wasn't going to sit idly by, hoping the North Koreans wouldn't connect the dots. "I need to talk with her to make sure she's safe. Can I use your phone?"

"You can't just call her there. Westerners can't use cellphones, and her hotel doesn't connect calls directly to rooms."

"How do you know this?"

Porter tilted his head, his brows raised. "It's my business to know. But there are other options. I'll have my team send her hotel a message—don't worry, I'll figure something out. In the meantime, you'll come with me. I've got a plane picking us up in two hours."

"Where are we headed?"

"A command center." Porter put on a baseball cap. "Right now, my main concern is finding Wyatt. We intercepted emails referencing Odessa."

"The city on the Black Sea?"

"The port, to be exact. Perhaps a ship. We'll know more very soon once we interrogate our detainee and scan through the half-dozen servers we took out of the old school."

Jonathan now had only Linda on his mind. He had to find a way to warn her that she could be in danger in North Korea, no matter that Porter didn't seem concerned.

28

Pyongyang, North Korea

"HOW ARE YOU FEELING?"

Linda slowly opened her eyes. Max leaned in, eyeing her with concern from two feet away.

"What happened?" she asked, feeling groggy.

"You passed out."

She glanced around. She was seated on a chair in his room. "How long was I out?"

"A few minutes."

She wiped her face and swept her hair back with her hand.

"Take some," Max said, handing her a glass of water, which she slowly sipped.

"You said something about my ex, Jonathan...but I don't remember, exactly."

He stood back, crossing his arms. "He's been trying to reach you somewhat urgently—but he didn't give details."

"I must get up." She pressed her elbows down on the armrests, trying to muster the strength to rise to her feet.

Max leaned in closer, wrapped his arm around her and helped her lift herself off the chair.

"How are the Australians?" she asked, stabilizing herself as her wooziness had not eased much. "There were—"

"Yeah, I heard what happened. They are fine but are being deported later today."

Suddenly, a fast, painful, nauseous feeling gripped her stomach. She started to spasm and immediately threw up the little food she'd eaten. It spilled over the parquet floor.

"You're really not well." Max eased her back into the chair. He quickly got a wet washcloth from the bathroom and handed it to her. "Should I get a doctor?"

Linda struggled to catch her breath. "I don't know what's happening to me. I feel weighed down. My mouth tastes like metal. I'm dizzy as hell, and now my stomach."

"I have the name of a local UN doctor. I'll go downstairs now and ask the reception to call him." He stepped out.

"Please do." Linda leaned forward over her lap because her stomach was too painful to allow her to sit upright.

Her ears began to ring, and she barely heard Max when he returned to the room.

"All good. The front desk called the doctor," Max said. "Hopefully, it's just something you ate earlier tonight."

"I skipped dinner."

"Or at lunch."

"I ate a salad."

"Well, there. Don't eat uncooked vegetables in strange places."

"I've had food poisoning before. This feels different. So much pain and my head is spinning."

"You need to rest."

*   *   *

The knocks on the door were loud and rapid. Linda heard several sets of footsteps rumbling into the room. They mumbled in Korean until one of them—a dark-haired middle-aged man wearing thick-framed glasses—kneeled in front of her.

"What are you feeling?" the man asked in thickly accented, barely understandable English.

She sighed, looked up and described her ailments, feeling the nausea and shortness of breath increase with each word she uttered. The man then spoke quickly to his male assistant.

"Are you the UN doctor?" Max said from somewhere behind her.

The man waved his hand dismissively. "We will take her to the clinic."

"Which one?"

"Very close. Twenty minutes by car."

Linda vomited again, this time on the washcloth, after which Max brought her a hand towel.

"Can you come with me?" she asked Max.

He frowned. "I have a breakfast meeting at six-thirty with an important official. And it's already three-twenty. You'll get good care."

"I'm not comfortable going alone."

Max leaned in again, rested his hand on her shoulder and looked into her eyes. "I'll check on you right after that meeting. I'm sure you'll be back here at the hotel by then."

Linda didn't want to leave the hotel with these strangers, and she was tempted to stay put, except that she also worried that her condition could worsen.

The Korean doctor and his assistant helped raise Linda off her chair. Max then strapped her purse around her shoulder. "Your passport is in here as well."

Soon Linda was in a vintage ambulance, heading across the river. She occasionally glanced up, but the intense cramping of her stomach forced her to immediately curl forward. She briefly spotted the Juche Tower on the left, but that was the last landmark she recognized for the rest of the ride. They drove further north, she guessed, along wide, nearly-empty streets and past myriad drab, Communist-style multi-story apartment buildings. As she clutched her stomach, her thoughts shot back to Jonathan, and she hoped she could get in touch with him soon.

29

Somewhere over the Black Sea

DESPITE WEARING A HEADSET, JONATHAN WAS WORN OUT from the deep palpitating sounds of the helicopter they'd been on for nearly two hours. While he was relieved to have been secreted out of Kyiv on a CIA Learjet that Porter had summoned, he was exhausted, his head, face and chest aching from multiple injuries. They had flown directly to an airbase in Romania, and from there, without a moment to rest, they'd boarded the U.S. Navy *Sea Hawk* helicopter.

Jonathan silently eyed Porter, who sat across from him with his satellite phone in one hand and a half-eaten sandwich in the other. Porter had not told him much along the way, except that their next destination—that he still kept secret—would help Jonathan to reach Linda and be useful to follow-up on leads regarding the whereabouts of Kevin Wyatt.

"Ten minutes," a voice came through the headset, presumably from someone in the cockpit. The helicopter's throttle pulled back a bit and he felt they began a smooth, speedy descent.

Jonathan glanced out the window. The skies were dulled by thick cloud cover overhead. He then looked down. "We're still over water," he told Porter. "Will you tell me now where we're going?"

Porter checked his watch and brought the mike of his headset closer to his lips. "Look out the window again. You'll see it soon, I think."

Jonathan gazed out, scanning past low-lying clouds that hovered over the grayish waters. But he saw nothing but the vastness of the Black Sea. "Where are we landing?"

"The USS *Mount Whitney*."

Jonathan then overheard the cockpit crew confirm they were in the pattern to land on the vessel.

Porter continued, "The flagship and command vessel of the Sixth Fleet, and it happens to be right here in the middle of the Black Sea."

Jonathan observed the ship coming into view. The helicopter banked left as it circled into position to reach the landing zone at the stern of the ship.

"A very fine vessel, sir," said a Navy crewman seated next to him who leaned in, having overheard his conversation with Porter. "Its communications capabilities are second to none. It functions as a C4I center."

"C4I?"

"Command, Control, Communications, Computer, and Intelligence," the crewman added. "It can receive, process and transmit enormous amounts of secure data from any point on earth through HF, UHF, VHF, SHF, and EHF communications, enabling the Joint Intelligence Center and Joint Operations Center to gather and process all their information to manage a battle environment."

"So, we're going to war?" Jonathan joked, glancing at Porter.

The helicopter turbines grew louder as it slowed its descent in the last few hundred feet. Jonathan spotted the landing deck, and seconds later the aircraft touched down. He unbuckled himself as the engines wound down and followed Porter out of the chopper. They headed quickly to a waiting sailor, who led them across the ship's expansive, mostly flat deck toward the central structure that rose like an island several stories above the main deck. There, they descended two flights of stairs and walked through a maze of corridors.

"This is our man," Porter said, pointing his thumb at Jonathan, as they approached two men waiting at a closed metal door emblazoned with large white letters "JTF" and below it the words "Restricted Access." The uniformed man was a Chief Petty Officer, Jonathan thought from glancing at his uniform, while the other man had a disheveled beard and wore casual civilian clothes.

The CPO opened the door and led them all into the Joint Task Force command center. The darkened room looked like something out of Star Wars and reminded Jonathan of his brief meeting with Cramer in the command center onboard the USS *Iwo Jima* back in New Orleans the prior week.

This command center was larger and had a dark ceiling cluttered with hanging lights, wires, cables, speakers and other gadgets. The walls were painted light blue and were also filled with electronic devices and smaller monitors. Jonathan noticed a set of six bright-red digital clocks showing the time in several zones. Large, flat-screen monitors took up most of the back wall, and below them was a row of manned computer terminals. Behind that were several manned workstations, perhaps for communications.

A uniformed naval officer, who appeared to have the rank of Lieutenant Commander (LCDR), approached. He shook hands with Porter and the civilian man but glanced uncomfortably at Jonathan.

"It's okay, he's with us," Porter said.

"Very well," the LCDR said, his frown fading. "Come with me." He led them to the monitors at the far end of the room.

"How's it looking?" Porter asked.

The colonel turned, pointing at a red dot on a large screen mounted on the wall. "We're tracking it now." The screen displayed a map of the southern half of the Black Sea, with Turkey's northern coast appearing at the bottom. "We've been following this vessel," the colonel continued, "the *Mu Du Bong*, a 430-foot North Korean bulk-carrier, for the past three hours. But we don't believe it came from Odessa."

"Then it's the wrong ship," Porter interjected, frowning and crossing his arms. "I'm telling you, we have strong evidence that a North Korean-owned ship docked in Odessa in the last few days."

"This ship's path is consistent with coming from further east, perhaps from Ukraine's port in Mariupol, which means it had to cross the Kerch Strait."

"No, we think it's Odessa," said the civilian, who Jonathan now suspected was a CIA colleague of Porter's.

Everyone again looked up at a red dot on the large screen. Porter then said, "You're telling me, Lieutenant Commander, that this ship is the only North Korean flagged vessel in the Black Sea?" Porter's tone gave away his frustration.

"*Currently* in the Black Sea, yes," said the LCDR.

"What about in the Bosphorus or the Aegean?"

"We can get the data in a few minutes."

"Please do."

"I'll be back."

Porter turned to Jonathan as the senior officer walked away and angrily shook his satellite phone in the air. "We found coded references to Odessa, dammit. The port specifically. And also a specific reference to an unnamed North Korean commercial vessel. My team's still looking into Ukrainian systems for lists of ships that docked there recently. I'm also waiting on imagery."

"Satellite?" Jonathan asked.

"Yes. I should have that soon."

Porter's CIA colleague added, "What if they docked unannounced?"

"Difficult to do at such a major port," Jonathan said, not because he knew much about the port in Odessa, but as a maritime lawyer, he had a good understanding of protocols ships were required to follow. "But it's possible if they turned off their transponders and paid off the right people at the port. Or they hacked into the port authority's systems to scrub any electronic records. Whichever way, it's not so easy."

"This is shit." Porter banged his fist against an adjacent railing.

Jonathan stepped closer to Porter. "If it's really the North Koreans, why did they take my client? What does he know that's so valuable to them?"

Porter's bearded colleague butted in, "That's not your business."

Jonathan had no patience for that kind of response. "You hustled your asses to Ukraine either because of Wyatt's background in intel or because your dead embassy guy was also CIA. I'm willing to bet on the latter, but perhaps both."

Porter tilted his head, his upper lip curling as his colleague returned only a stony stare. "You're a goddamned pain in the ass, Brooks."

"I need to be," Jonathan said. "And now I need to contact my ex." He pointed calmly at Porter. "You promised."

Porter looked indignant. "I told you, she's fine. And we already emailed her hotel. She'll respond soon, I'm sure."

Jonathan wasn't having it. "Now! I want to contact her now!"

30

Negev Desert, Israel

GWEN STEFANI'S *HOLLABACK GIRL* ECHOED FAINTLY from the CD player atop Ji Yung's desk, next to her clustered three-monitor display panel and her framed photo of her South Korean mom and Israeli father. Music always kept her company when she stayed after regular hours.

She sat alone at her cubicle. A blue balloon hovered above her as she scrolled through translated communications intercepts on the center screen. Coworkers had tied the balloon to the monitor as a friendly gesture to celebrate her first anniversary with Israel's esteemed Unit 8200—the country's electronic intelligence arm, akin to the U.S. National Security Agency.

"Staying late again, Corporal Ji?" The raspy voice came from behind her. She spun in her chair, looked up and stopped herself from frowning. It was Omer, her supervising officer.

"I haven't been paying attention to the time," she said in flawless Hebrew. "But it's okay; it's not like I have better options." As soon as the words exited her lips, she regretted them, fearing that Omer might wrongly take her reply as an invitation to "improve" her evening. "I mean, you know, there's so much data to review."

At twenty-five, Ji was a few years older than most Israeli Defense Force conscripts in Unit 8200. As the only Korean native-speaker analyst with a background in data sciences, her skills put her in a unique class of experts. But that meant working at the unit's main facility near Urim, at the northern edge of the Negev Desert. The secretive base was a long way from her family, friends, nightlife and other pleasant distractions that she previously enjoyed in Haifa. She'd have to wait eighteen more months for her military service to end, and if everything worked out, she'd probably land something big in the private sector, as had many Unit 8200 colleagues. Maybe she'd even move to London. Perhaps Silicon Valley or New York. That bright horizon gave her energy and patience to deal with the relative seclusion of her current duties.

"You don't get extra balloons for the overtime," Omer said, his hands rubbing his large belly.

His attempted humor used to annoy Ji. Now she simply ignored it. She knew he was harmless, despite his propensity for creepy weirdness. She gave him a mock smile, but her mind was too focused to wander off into useless small talk. "Since you're here, I want to show you something I found."

"What is it?"

Her eyes scanned his round, bespectacled face. "I looked at various auto-translated transcripts, but they seemed to have errors. So, when I listened to the recordings, I stumbled upon a bizarre conversation in the stack."

Omer took a step forward, the movement straining the threads of his beige military uniform to its limits. "Tell me." Ji took a breath. She felt uncomfortable each time he squeezed into her cubicle; he always seemed to hog most of the available air.

"An intercepted satellite phone call."

"From where?" Omer said.

"One caller is on a ship I believe to be the *Chong Chon Gang*—a North Korean bulk-carrier."

"North Korean?"

"Yes."

"Are you certain? We've rarely seen them use satellite phones."

"Sometimes they acquire them in Europe or South America through their various front companies," Ji said. "The geolocation data and our analysis of the satellite signal in this call are both conclusive—someone on that ship used one. And this ship has previously transported arms, drugs, precious metals and other illicit goods— at least occasionally—when it's under the control of Bureau 39, the North Ko—"

"Yes, yes, I know their intel services."

"At the time of this intercept, which was five or six hours ago, the ship was leaving the Aegean Sea bearing east, about a hundred kilometers west of Cyprus."

Omer nodded and leaned in, resting his pudgy knuckles on the desktop next to her keyboard, the scent of cheap cologne filling her workspace.

Ji turned to the monitor on her right and clicked the link that had the actual recording, the end result of a complex encrypted process that relayed voice and data captured by one of several listening stations scattered along Israel's coast and, as needed, from its naval vessels in the Mediterranean and reconnaissance satellites.

"This first voice is the person on the ship," she prefaced before muting her CD player and then clicking the play button on the screen. A male voice accompanied by patchy interference came through the computer speakers. She quickly adjusted settings on the program interface that made the voice slightly clearer, then rewound it to the beginning of the clip, but this time she interpreted simultaneously. "I am sorry, sir, that we could not answer sooner. But I must tell you, the package is not well. I do not know if it will make it." Ji clicked Pause. "Now, the other man says, 'What do you mean?'"

"Who are the callers?"

"Don't know."

"Did you run voice recognition?"

"Yes. But nothing solid so far for either caller. This second guy used a simple cellphone, and the registered account is unknown. But our signals analysis shows he took the call from within, or very near, As Salam Park in downtown Damascus, and he—"

"That's close to the North Korean embassy, right?" Omer interrupted.

"Correct."

"Hmm, strange for embassy personnel to call a satellite phone, knowing they can get intercepted."

"Perhaps because it was urgent. Both callers sound anxious." Ji again clicked the play button and went on interpreting the audio recording. "'What do you mean?' the man in the park says again, and he sounds angry now. 'We paid the pigs over a thousand leaves to bring you the package in good condition...'"

"Leaves?" Omer said, chuckling. "As in leaves of a tree?"

Ji pressed Pause again. "Sorry, a 'leaf' is North Korean slang for a hundred-dollar bill." She then continued the recording. "The man on the ship again says, 'It was not in good condition at all' and then the other guy says, 'Sail as fast as you can. They will pick him up.' So, here he pauses, contemplates. I think he realizes he said something he should not have mentioned, then adds, 'I mean, you understand, do not let this get worse.'"

Omer shrugged. "So?"

"Don't you see what's going on here?" Ji said. "The package is a *person!*" She was annoyed that Omer hadn't gotten it on his own.

He lifted his hand from her desktop, took a step back, and frowned. "Hmm."

"Remember the notice from this afternoon?" Ji said. "The one from Langley requesting any information about North Korean-flagged vessels calling on Odessa? Remember?"

"Yes, of course."

"The *Chong Chon Gang* crossed the Bosphorus thirty-two hours ago—I checked. So, I believe it's possible, even probable, that the ship came from Odessa and sailed through the Black Sea before coming to the Mediterranean. And the timing—"

"You're just guessing now," Omer interrupted, shaking his head. "Besides, the Americans are looking for a ship, not a person."

"Maybe they're looking for one because it's carrying a person—someone of interest."

Omer huffed and raised his brow. "I suppose you have a fair point."

Yes, I'm full of fair points, Ji thought, *perhaps you should come up with a few yourself.* She was still riding high on her most recent find: the clandestine importation of North Korean-manufactured nuclear reactor components into Syria. She'd spent the past two months tracking North Koreans in Syria in order to find where these components were either stored or assembled, though this still remained a mystery. Her initial find had earned her accolades from higher-ups, though she was irked that Omer tried to take a greater share of the credit, when in fact he'd been a skeptic throughout her investigation.

Omer checked his watch. "Come with me."

Ji followed him down the corridor to the first of several small secure conference rooms. Omer dialed the speakerphone at the center of the table, and a deep voice soon resonated from it. The man was Colonel Aharon Shoval, whom Ji had met briefly a month back. She knew little about him, however, other than he ranked high up in the Mossad and had close ties to U.S. intelligence services.

Omer informed Shoval about the intercepted call and the North Korean cargo ship and then glanced at Ji. "Anything I may have missed?"

She cleared her throat. "I want to emphasize how unusual it is for North Koreans in Syria to communicate like this, carelessly. They typically avoid smartphones of any kind or satellite phones. They are methodical at masking their calls, and they most often prefer to use shortwave, coded communications—even though it's not the timeliest method. I can only guess that the caller in Damascus is either a novice or, more likely, he was so worried about the 'package' that he knowingly breached protocol."

"Or their normal communication channel had technical issues," the colonel offered. "I will tell the Americans. If indeed the package is a person of interest, does it have any value to us, or any risks for us?"

"I don't think so," Ji said.

"Or any connection to your reactor components investigation?"

"No," Ji said. "I think this is something very different. Someone is on that ship, and it matters to at least two unknown North Koreans."

Colonel Shoval let out a short humming sound and then said, "Where is the ship headed?"

"I'm still hunting for customs documentation and electronic notices. So, until I find that, my best guess is Syria."

"Where in Syria?"

Ji chuckled. "Ships that size typically dock at Latakia or Tartus." She glanced at the clock on the wall and quickly recalculated the geographic distances she'd already figured out earlier. "By now the Americans have at best about five or six hours to board the ship before it reaches Syrian waters."

Shoval scoffed. "They're not going to raid a North Korean ship in international waters. Nothing I have heard so far tells me this is something urgent. But perhaps I will offer them some of our eyes on the ground. Let's see. In any case, good work."

31

Latakia, Syria

"THERE IS NO TIME TO STOP," FAROUK KAMFAR SAID loudly in Arabic as he sat in the passenger seat. He had just arrived from the Maldives and was still feeling nervous after passing through Syrian passport control using his alias, Yusuf Abubakar, and wearing simple Western attire: a long-sleeved polo shirt and khakis. "I am already late."

"It will only be for a minute," the van driver snapped back as he exited Bassel Al-Assad International Airport.

"No!"

"I only want a falafel," the driver insisted.

"First, get me to the port." Farouk couldn't care less that the man was hungry. His only priority was to pick up the sensitive "package" from a cargo vessel and securely deliver it two hundred miles south to Damascus, where it would board a plane at 11:30 P.M.—in about seven hours. The drive to Damascus would take at least four hours, he'd been told. And he knew damn well that if he failed, he'd be a dead man in no time.

That fear is why Farouk had asked his Al-Qaeda superior back in Malé, Ibrahim Jafal, why the connecting aircraft could not simply land at Latakia instead, making the transfer far easier. But it wasn't possible, Jafal had said. The North Koreans had dispatched an Air Koryo Illyushin-76 cargo plane, which was for all practical purposes a military transport aircraft except with civilian markings and the paint scheme of their national airlines. It had flown several times to Damascus over the past year, so it didn't attract the kind of attention that would surely come if it were to land in any other Syrian city for the first time. That would invite scrutiny from Syrian security forces, and scrutiny was exactly what Farouk and the North Koreans wanted to avoid.

Farouk checked his watch. There wasn't a moment to waste. His other concern, he hoped, would be eased with the eight thousand dollars in large bills he'd hidden in a false-bottom compartment of his suitcase. The money was to be used to grease palms as needed to ensure the package's smooth transfer. There was no telling what any official—whether a customs agent, a policeman or any other person of authority—working for the Assad regime might do. The Syrian dictator was vehemently anti-Al-Qaeda, as much as any Western government. So Jafal's arrangement with this local franchise of terror operatives entailed huge risks.

The driver, jerking the van to pass a slow-moving car, glanced coldly at Farouk and said, "I have been so busy I did not eat yet today. That is why I am asking."

"Just drive!"

The driver turned sulky but stayed silent for the remaining twenty-minute journey through downtown Latakia and on to the commercial port, Syria's largest. The dense five-o'clock traffic was loud, with sounds of blaring car horns and sputtering mufflers and the stench of exhaust fumes.

"We're on Yarmouk Street," the driver mumbled.

"Good," Farouk said and gulped a deep breath, knowing he was now near the rendezvous point. His mouth quickly became dry. His heart began to race.

"It's on Gamal Adbel Nasser, across from the port's south entrance gate," Farouk said, referring to the street that ran along the waterfront.

"I know. As soon as we cross 8th Azer. One minute more."

Farouk perched forward, scanning the buildings ahead for a café he'd been instructed to go to first, before heading to the ship.

"That one?" the driver asked, pointing right. "The Sport Café?"

"Yes!" Farouk felt the rapid thuds in his chest.

They pulled up to the curb, and Farouk quickly stepped out and glanced in all directions, looking for a man wearing red Adidas shoes. As soon as he turned to face the café a second time, a man barely in his twenties with black, curly long hair approached him while nodding discreetly. His shoes were red with white stripes.

"Are you looking for gifts?" the young man asked in Arabic.

"Many," Farouk said hesitantly, acknowledging the coded greeting that confirmed it was the right contact.

The man nodded once more and said, "I will get you in now."

"You?" Farouk imagined an older person would take on this risky task.

"Yes, me." The young man's brows narrowed; his voice was stern. "Is there a problem?"

"This is a very important affair. Maybe there is someone else I should meet?" Farouk suggested politely. But he was troubled that such a sensitive mission—and his own life, too—depended now on the actions of this likely unseasoned Al-Qaeda operative.

The young man scoffed. "I know exactly what to do."

Farouk then saw his driver exit the van, leaving the engine running, and head nonchalantly into the café after glancing disapprovingly at Farouk. He turned to his red-shoed contact and asked, "And where is he going?"

"I will drive now." The young man took out from his back pocket what looked like an envelope that had been folded twice over. He then lifted his chin in the direction of the port's canopied checkpoint gate directly across the wide street. "We'll go in this entrance. I will hand this to one of the guards. He's the only one who will let us in; the others will arrest us."

Farouk didn't like the sound of that. "Really?"

"Yes, God willing, but the guard is leaving in forty-five minutes."

Farouk sighed. "*Yallah*." They had to hurry.

They drove around the block, turning away from the café and into the driveway leading to the checkpoint. The young man stopped the vehicle under the shade of the large canopy and threw the transmission into Park.

Farouk counted six guards in all, two of them wearing military camouflage with Kalashnikovs strapped around their shoulders, and the rest dressed in tan outfits with only holstered sidearms. Two lightly armed guards begin walking to Farouk's van, but as they drew nearer, the larger-framed guard patted his thinner colleague and seemed to wave him off in the other direction.

While still seated in the front passenger side, Farouk glanced at the young man at the wheel. The man sat expressionless, staring at the guard. But his hand appeared to grip the steering wheel so tightly that his knuckles whitened. That only made Farouk more nervous. The guard came to the young man's door, but the transaction took a mere second. The guard simply walked past the driver's window, snatched the envelope in a way Farouk barely noticed and then tapped the hood with his palm before waving them through.

"That's it?"

The young man loosened his grip on the steering and laughed. "*Akeed*."

Farouk frowned and exhaled loudly. "This kind of thing can make a man shit his pants."

About three hundred yards away, the young man turned towards a docked vessel. "This is your ship," he said.

"The *Chong Chon Gang*," Farouk whispered to himself as he leaned forward to examine the entire length of the long, gray-hulled vessel as they approached. The hull had large patches of surface rust, and the tall funnel behind the white bridge castle had a stretched version of the North Korean national flag painted across its top.

"You must hurry," the young man said, rechecking his wristwatch. "We have to exit from the same entrance, and with the help of the same guard—but he's leaving soon, remember?"

Farouk nodded and quickly got out.

*   *   *

"You can't be serious." Farouk was livid at the condition of the "package." He stared down at a pale-faced man with bruised cheeks and dark sunken eyes, who was barely conscious, coughing violently, and lying on the floor in his own vomit. "What did you do to him?"

"Nothing!" the Asian man nearest Farouk said gruffly in heavily accented English.

"This isn't seasickness."

The Asian recoiled. "We didn't do this, I tell you." He appeared more agitated than he had the moment he met Farouk on the dock ten minutes earlier. "This is exactly how they gave him to us in Odessa."

"Has he eaten?"

The Asian shook his head.

"Has he had water?"

"Very little, I think."

Farouk felt his heart drop to his stomach. "He cannot die, you understand me?"

The Asian's face twisted and avoided meeting Farouk's angry gaze.

Farouk sucked in a lung-full of stale air and exhaled slowly, his mind racing through available options. *Should I summon a doctor? Should I alert Jafal? What to do?* But there is so little time.

The Asian man barked instructions at the other two crewmen in the room and then turned back to Farouk. "All I know is you must take him now."

The men quickly lifted the frail man.

"How are you feeling?" Farouk asked the captive in English. With his eyes closed and his head bent over his left shoulder, the man replied only with a barely audible mumble.

The crewmen carried the sick prisoner out into the corridor.

"Be careful!" Farouk said, nearly shouting. He followed, watching closely as the men kept the prisoner propped up while they climbed two narrow staircases to the ship's main deck. A third crewman waiting at the top then leaned in and placed a hat and a pair of glasses onto the ailing man's head.

"You want him in the van?" the Asian said, pointing to the dock, past the descending gangway.

"Yes, but do it gently. And give him some water once you have him settled."

Within ten minutes, Farouk and the red-shoed driver were back in the van with their package lying motionless on two blankets in the back. They had exited the port checkpoint with the help of the same cooperative guard, sped through several intersections, and circled halfway around the large roundabout at Yemen Square.

From there, they were about to join the M1 highway when Farouk, after checking over his left shoulder to make sure that the prisoner was still breathing, turned back and noticed something strange in his side mirror: a white Volvo sedan with two, perhaps three people in it. He remembered briefly spotting the same car when they had stopped in front of the Sport Café. He turned to the driver and announced, "We're being followed."

The young man at the wheel glanced twice in his own side mirror but remained calm. He picked up his cellphone, dialed and spoke to the other person on the line. "We have eyes on us—a Volvo, white. Check them, and if it looks bad, get rid of them. I will slow down now so you can catch up."

Farouk felt a chill run down his spine. His palms began to sweat. This was the riskiest assignment he'd ever been given, and now he had no idea whether he'd live long enough to look back on it.

32

Pyongyang People's Hospital Number 2, North Korea

LINDA SAW BRIGHT INCANDESCENT LIGHTS RAPIDLY passing by. The sound of a wobbly wheel rattled the quiet air. She blinked to clear her foggy eyes until she could more clearly see where she was: on a gurney, face up, being pushed along a corridor by a man wearing green scrubs, a face-mask and a matching head cap.

"Where are you taking me?" she asked, her lungs barely strong enough to force words out her mouth.

The man ignored her as he maneuvered the gurney into another corridor. Seconds later she felt and heard a thud. He had used the gurney to bump open a door and wheel her into a poorly lighted room. The man spun the gurney one hundred eighty degrees, locked the wheels and walked out.

Linda, still feeling groggy and nauseated, slowly raised her head a few inches and spotted a short, skinny woman standing with her arms crossed at the door of the room. She wore a white lab coat over a set of scrubs.

"Where am I?" Linda said and then breathed in deeply to continue speaking. "Do you speak English?"

The woman bit her lip, turned her gaze away from Linda and exited the room, closing the door behind her.

The room was weird for a clinic, she thought. The only furniture was a small tabletop with long metal legs and an old wooden chair in the corner. The walls were raw cement. There were no blinds or drapes on the small window. No other beds. No wall-mounted equipment or plugs for monitors, medical devices, or oxygen that she'd seen in hospital rooms back home. And perhaps most strangely, there was a large window next to the door that looked out into the corridor.

Linda glanced down her body. She was covered by a wool blanket, but her feet were bare. Her skin felt cold and clammy, and she had trouble keeping her eyes steady on any object in the simple room.

She mustered the strength to sit up, but it took a minute. The spinning in her head only made her nausea worse, and when she managed to prop herself upright, her stomach felt like it was being shredded. She pulled the blanket down to her thigh and lifted her gown to massage her abdomen with both hands. The sharp pain continued unabated.

Linda lowered the gurney's steel railing and slowly spun to the side, her legs dangling, and then stretched her left tip-toe to touch the floor, then her right. She stood while holding the metal edge of the gurney.

Her muscles were weak. It felt as if she weighed two hundred fifty pounds. She took small steps, her feet swishing over the cold, gritty tile floor. She looked up and gazed through the large window into the hallway, and seeing no one, she continued to walk slowly toward the door. She glanced at her feet, feeling shocked at how difficult it was to maintain her balance.

Suddenly a loud thump shook the room. As her eyes swiftly rose, another thump came from the window, the glass shaking violently. She jolted and let out a muffled cry. A man in a green military uniform, wearing a large hat, angrily stared her down. He pulled back his fist and banged the glass once more. She froze, feeling her pulse quicken.

The man pointed hostilely for her to return to the gurney. Behind him another soldier walked briskly along the corridor to join his colleague at the window. Neither man opened their mouths, but their eyes and gestures were enough to terrify Linda. Their harsh stares followed her every move as she carefully walked in reverse back to the gurney, gripping the metal railing to hoist herself up. After covering herself with the blanket, she saw the men turn away and speak with each other. She lay confused. *Am I a patient or a prisoner, or both?* she asked herself as the thought momentarily choked the breath from her lungs. She tugged her hair in frustration, feeling her eyes welling up. And as the first tears raced down her cheeks, Jonathan jumped into her mind. *Need you. Need your help.* A wave of dizziness coursed through her as she closed her eyes.

*   *   *

A sturdy breeze swept across the endless acres of corn stocks that surrounded her. Linda's ears filled with the ruffled sounds of fall in Iowa. A distant throttling of a combine's engine told her the harvest was underway. The breeze glided over her face, her eyes staying closed but seeing it all as if they were wide open. Her hair fluttered with the wind, the pleasantly cool tickle tingling her scalp. The scent of freshly cut stalks filled the air. She felt a sense of peacefulness, but there was something odd about it, though she refused to let it go. She breathed in deeply and allowed this comfort to embellish her senses, while also wondering how bizarre it was for her to stand there again. Back to an infrequent refuge. A serene farm in Wapello county. A place that cleansed her mind of reality. An escape.

The ruffling noise and the distant belching of the combine's motor tapered off, replaced by something grittier, yet more muted, like if a crowd were to whisper—an austere, deep undertone. It grew louder. The stale odor of concrete displaced the aromas of nature. The murmurs grew louder. The fields were gone. The breeze had died.

Light suddenly filled her eyes. *The room. The same goddamn room.* She jerked up from the gurney, her head spinning worse than before as she tried to hold herself upright. Two men and the woman she'd seen earlier stood nearby, all of them wearing white lab coats. One of the men hung an IV bag onto the top of the pole next to the gurney and turned to the metal table and began unpacking the tubing set.

"Will someone please talk to me, dammit," she said as fiercely as she could. "Does anyone speak English?"

The woman, whom Linda presumed was a doctor as she now carried a stethoscope around her neck, approached as her colleague continued to prepare the IV. "You are not in good health," the woman said in broken English.

No shit. "I feel dizzy, short of breath, nauseated, with pain in my stomach. My vision is blurry. I have a horrible taste in my mouth, like metal or old milk. And I'm so weak I can barely move."

"Lie down, please."

Linda did so slowly, all the while blinking rapidly as she struggled to keep her vision focused.

"May I?" the doctor asked, raising her bare hands over Linda's abdomen.

Linda reluctantly nodded.

"Does this hurt?" she said as she quickly jabbed Linda's tummy with her fingers.

"Ahh...Jesus, yes!" The pain was sharper than before.

The doctor instantly pulled back.

Linda was tempted to ask if she'd earned her medical license at a mortuary. She took a deep breath and said, "I want to call Max, the American at my hotel."

The doctor turned halfway and glanced oddly at her male colleague who stood stiffly poker-faced by the door.

"And I'd like a pillow, too, if possible."

The doctor nodded and stepped aside to make room for her other colleague to connect the IV tubing.

The doctor's lab coat suddenly waved out of Linda's line of sight, and she spotted a young Asian man with

short dark hair, round cheeks and a chubby neck peeking into her room from behind the window next to the
door. He seemed to be in his late teens, or barely twenty
at most. His face was almost pressed against the glass,
but as soon as she met his gaze, he sprung back a step,
frowned and looked away, adjusting his thick-framed
glasses—perhaps embarrassed she'd seen him. The
soldier that stood guard outside her room was still there,
half-visible from her angle.

The stout young man took another step back and
crossed his arms. A man in a suit approached and nodded after something the young man said. And then, as
the mysterious man caught the soldier's glance, the soldier immediately bowed to the young man.

Linda kept her gaze locked on him as he walked
away, until he had turned the corner at the far end of the
corridor. She chewed on her lip, her mind attempting
to decipher the young man's possible identity. He was
portly for his age, which, given North Korea's mostly
malnourished population, meant he had money. But
he was too young to have earned it himself. *Perhaps a
general's son*, she mused. *But why come to ogle me like
I'm some exotic fish behind glass?*

She returned to her thoughts about her predicament.
Sick with an unusual illness. Taken from her hotel
after learning Jonathan had run into problems and was
reaching out to her. It was all quite odd. And then she
pondered the strange young visitor. Perhaps she was the
weird fish after all. The thing you come see when trouble
is really brewing. *Is he in Kim Jong-il's family? One of
his sons, perhaps?* She'd heard they lived secretive lives

both here and abroad. She recalled the serious guard's expression and his deferential bow to the visitor. And the suited man's bow, as well.

The doctor's assistant straightened Linda's arm. She felt the prick of the needle and, a second later, that cool fluid from the IV. She gazed up at the ceiling. Things were not right. Not right at all. But she had no idea what to do now.

33

Mashrou Al Baath district, Latakia, Syria

"YOU'RE SLOWING DOWN TOO MUCH," FAROUK SHOUTED at the young driver, thinking the opposite would be more effective—to speed ahead and try to lose the Volvo trailing them. "And we're not even armed."

"We are," the driver replied as he eased the van into the right lane along the wide Abdel Qader Al Hussaini Boulevard. "Open the glove compartment."

As Farouk quickly did so, a revolver fell out, hit his shins and dropped to the floor. His heart jumped. In the years since he'd sworn allegiance to Jafal and other senior Al-Qaeda leaders, like Abu Ubaidah al-Masri and Abu Hamza Rabia, he'd never had to hold a weapon, let alone fire one. He'd always been told his brain was more valuable to the organization, not his war-fighting skills. But more importantly, he'd never felt before today that a bullet might come his way.

"Take it!" the driver said before picking up and dialing his cellphone again.

Farouk ground his teeth. He picked up the weapon with both hands, rested it on his lap and then eyed the side mirror, spotting again the white Volvo that kept pace with them three vehicles back. "Where are the others? You said they were near."

The driver spoke briefly on the phone, but Farouk didn't listen. His attention was fixated on the car following them. He squinted, attempting to discern whether there was a third person in the car.

Just after they passed a sign for Tishreen University, Farouk looked across the grassy median and the opposite lanes and noticed three parked military trucks with soldiers disembarking. "Be careful," he said.

"*Khallas!*" the driver blurted, waving his hand dismissively. "Stop worrying! That's the entrance to an army base. Nothing more."

Farouk again glanced at his side mirror. "Are your friends coming or not?"

"Calm down. They will meet us near the Mohammad Hadi Mosque, a few minutes from here. There will be a gas station on the right very soon. We must turn there."

"Who do you think they are? Police?"

"No."

"How are you so sure?"

"My boss has good connections. No one from Syrian authorities is looking for your prized package."

"*Kol khara,*" Farouk said loudly.

"Eat shit yourself."

"This is our package."

"No. I'm only responsible for taking you and your prisoner to Homs—not for protecting you against your enemies."

"What? We paid for safe passage to Damascus."

"True, but someone else in Homs will take you there."

None of this was reassuring to Farouk. And if the Syrians weren't aware of the kidnapped American, then who the hell was following them? *CIA, perhaps, or Israelis?* he asked himself. The prospect of an encounter with such operatives began to sink in. *Perhaps a drone was circling overhead*, he wondered. *Or a squad of special forces in helicopters*. He glanced up at the skies as is mind exploded with terrifying scenarios.

Farouk looked ahead and saw that they veered right, following the sign for the M1 highway. "I thought you were not going to take this road."

"I'm not." The driver swept his mop of curly hair off his face. "The gas station will be on the right very soon; we'll go back south from there."

Thirty seconds later, they turned and cruised down a desolate paved road that appeared to cut through an area filled with warehouses, many of them with large trucks and trailers parked in front lots behind fences and high walls.

As they then merged into a small treelined neighborhood with quaint homes surrounded by lush orchards, Farouk again glanced into his side mirror. "They are still behind us."

"I see them." The driver turned hard right. "This is Zabadani Street. We will be at the mosque in two minutes."

A large orchard took up the space on the right side of the road, and small, run-down apartment blocks were positioned on the left side. Farouk swallowed hard. He had no idea what the driver and his colleagues were going to do about the Volvo. He simply wanted the problem to go away.

The street became narrower in this part of the city, with clustered three and four-story residential buildings and busy retail spaces at street level.

"You see the mosque?" the driver asked, slowing the van. "Over there, on the right."

Farouk squinted. The mosque was a simple, three-story concrete structure with large open windows. There was no minaret, nor any overly ornate external décor.

"The blue and white cars are our helpers," the driver said.

Farouk eyed the vehicles, one on each side of the narrow street. Several men were seated in them and three more, carrying poorly-concealed weapons, stood on the sidewalk immediately in front of the place of worship. There were numerous pedestrians nearby as well.

The van proceeded past the two cars for about thirty yards and then stopped. In the side mirror, Farouk observed the Volvo begin its turn. The blue car immediately spurted out of its parking spot, its tires squealing. It cut in front of the Volvo and stopped, blocking its path. Instantly, the Volvo's occupants drew weapons that protruded from their windows. As the Volvo sprinted in reverse, Farouk spotted muzzle flashes coming from the blue car—they'd fired first. He flinched as loud, rapid thuds of automatic weapons rang out from both cars.

The armed men on the sidewalk fell like dominos, as did two unlucky pedestrians who were crossing the street. Farouk assumed they were all hit. Those in the blue car weren't moving either. The others ran for cover behind the white car and continued to fire at the Volvo, which zigzagged clumsily in reverse, scraped several parked cars along the way and finally slammed trunk first into a stationary pickup truck. The sound of crashing metal mixed with the ongoing sounds of gunfire. Two men in the Volvo darted out, ducking as they dashed to take shelter behind the damaged truck.

Popping sounds suddenly shook the air from somewhere near Farouk. They were loud metal-bashing clunks, unlike the rapid automatic fire ringing out in front of the mosque.

"They are shooting at us!" Farouk shouted as he ducked for cover on center console, realizing the attackers in the Volvo were aiming for his van.

The driver floored the van, propelling it forward as several more rounds pierced the metal skin. Farouk then heard the shattering of glass echo to the front of the vehicle. He was breathing so fast, he was afraid he might pass out. About a hundred yards ahead of the firefight, the driver stopped, threw the van in Park, grabbed the revolver off of Farouk's lap and jumped out.

Farouk hesitantly opened his door and looked past the back of the van at the scene in the shadow of the mosque. The shooting had ceased. Three armed men with guns drawn ran toward the Volvo, which now had smoke spewing from its hood. Two men looped around to the pickup truck and fired some more rounds. A few *coups de graces*, Farouk imagined, for good measure. One man then signaled to the others with a wave of his Kalashnikov. His companions-in-arms quickly pulled up alongside in the white car, shouting something as he got in. The engine revved, tires squealed, and they disappeared into a side street.

"I will call them," the driver said to Farouk, his voice panicky.

Farouk assumed the men in the Volvo were neutralized. He rubbed the sweat off his face with both hands. "This is crazy." With his heart still racing, he briskly headed past the side of the van, his eyes scanning everything in the distance to gauge whether the danger had really passed. He heard the driver speaking on his cellphone as he reached the rear of the vehicle.

"They are saying it is all good," the driver said, his voice still shaking as he turned off his phone. He patted Farouk on the shoulder. "Are you fine?"

Farouk nodded. The shock of the armed exchange had still not completely passed.

"We must go now, before the police arrive."

Farouk glanced at his hands and noticed they were shaking. He then spotted shards of glass on the ground. He turned to face the van's closed rear doors and saw the shot-out rear windows. He glanced down and spotted a bullet hole in the metal, and then another. He silently began to count them. *Three, four, five...Oh, no.* He lunged at the handles. "No, no, no!" He flung open both doors and jumped inside, crawled forward, grabbed the blanket that covered the captive and threw it to the side. "No!"

The American that Farouk had been trusted to keep safe at all costs lay motionless, blood gushing from his head and left thigh. With both hands Farouk rolled the man onto his back. The crimson stains soaked nearly every inch of the man's clothing.

Farouk touched the man's neck but couldn't find a pulse. He wasn't breathing, either. The bullets had fortuitously hit their mark. Farouk leaned back, almost unable to breathe, and stared at the lifeless body. A sudden feeling of nausea gripped his stomach as he turned to the driver who stared blankly at him from just outside the van. "We are dead."

34

Aboard the USS Mount Whitney, Black Sea

THE DOOR FLUNG OPEN AND GEORGE PORTER, FOLLOWED by his bearded CIA colleague, barged into the small room. And both looked equally annoyed.

"Got answers for me yet?" Jonathan asked, his hands on his waist, his voice about to get louder. And for good reason. They'd had him locked in here for the past hour with no news whatsoever.

Porter faced Jonathan, resting his large hands over the back of the only chair in the room. "Looks like there's an issue after all."

Jonathan tilted his head. "What exactly?"

"We've been told that your ex was taken ill and transported to a clinic."

"In Pyongyang? Are you kidding me? A hospital in goddamn North Korea? And after what we've uncovered, don't you now see this as more than a mere coincidence?"

Porter's mouth twisted as he seemed to ponder a response that wouldn't make him look like a liar or a fool.

Jonathan felt vindicated but that mattered little now. "Where exactly is she?"

"I've tasked teams to listen in on every signal coming out of Pyongyang and report back. We'll find her."

"Not good enough!" Jonathan kicked the chair that Porter was leaning on. "You need to find her and get her out. They've taken her hostage, probably because of me. And I don't give a crap if you have to wake up some general or the Secretary of State to get this done."

"Whoa, man," said Porter's colleague, raising both hands in the air. "You're in fantasyland now. Her boss emailed us saying she probably had a food illness, nothing more."

"Did you talk with him?"

"No, only email."

"Then how are you certain it was from him?"

"We confirmed. He's American and the email he sent to us also had his secretary in Beijing copied. Nothing malicious that we can see, so far."

"Then you're blind." Jonathan shook his head. A frustrating feeling of helplessness came over him. He was in the middle of the Black Sea, a continent away from Linda, and in the company of CIA operatives who didn't appear to believe his suspicions. If there wasn't anything more to gain from being here with Porter, Jonathan thought, he had better get the hell out and find an alternate way to reach Linda.

"Let me work the phones," Porter said, now showing a sliver of compassion. "I have some ideas."

Too little, too late, Jonathan thought. "Get me off this ship."

Porter shook his head. "Where will you go? And who else has this kind of power to help? We're in the heart of one of the world's most advanced intelligence centers."

Jonathan rapidly contemplated the meager options he had available. Asking for help from Cramer in New Orleans would take too long. Dialing up old contacts in Washington could get him access to key policymakers, but that too would burn through time inefficiently. And going to the press might only further endanger Linda.

He turned away from the two men and glanced at the floor, brainstorming at full-throttle. He sighed, realizing that there was really only one option. And as insane as it sounded, the more he deconstructed it, the more he imagined how it might work.

He sucked in a deep gulp of air and silently recapped the decision he'd just made: He would use whatever leverage he could muster to go to North Korea and bargain for Linda's return out of the country. And if Kevin Wyatt was also there somehow, he'd try to get him out, too. And to do so regardless of whether he'd get any help from Porter or anyone else in the U.S. government.

"What are you thinking, man?" Porter's colleague asked Jonathan with a condescending tone.

Jonathan turned to them and glared at Porter. "Can you at least get me to Vienna or Berlin so I can fly home?"

Porter stood and stretched his back. "You're not going to work with us on this?"

Jonathan stepped forward. "Do you need anything else from me? Because if not, I need to get going."

Porter stepped aside and smiled. "As you wish. But you know we'll be watching you."

35

"WHAT EXACTLY ARE YOU SAYING, ASTER?" THE question came forcefully from the president, who sat back in his chair, his hands crossed behind his head. "I can understand Goss because he's clear," he added, referring to his esteemed CIA Director. "But you, no. Please get to the point. Either there's a problem, or there isn't."

"I'm saying, Mr. President, that it's possible, perhaps even probable," Aster Clayland, Deputy CIA Director, said hesitantly. He was still uncomfortable that he'd been the only one in the room willing to broach the topic. And even more so now that the president hadn't missed another opportunity to belittle him with a reminder that he served as a "deputy."

"What does your boss think?" the commander-in-chief asked.

"I haven't discussed this with him yet," Aster said, edging forward on the couch. "But I will as soon as he's back from vacation."

"And you? You believe this stuff?" the president said as he shifted his gaze to his National Security Advisor, who sat on the sofa across from Aster.

The man raised his brows, shrugged and nonchalantly uttered, "News to me."

Aster swallowed hard and cleared his throat. "Like I said, Mr. President, there's growing circumstantial evidence that this man was kidnapped by thugs running the cyber-hacking business we discovered—in an abandoned, radioactive town, of all places."

The National Security Advisor sighed loudly.

Aster continued, "The Ukrainian connection seems pretty damming. Let's not lose sight of the fact that Kevin Wyatt was, only a few years ago, leading some of the most innovative projects at the National Security Agency. The guy's a genius. A top technical strategist, and one of the agency's most talented and inventive engineers as well." Aster glanced at the man across from him. "Ask your folks. Many know his name and impeccable reputation."

The commander-in-chief leaned forward, clasping his hands over his desk. "I'm inclined to think this is more about kidnapping an important American businessman for ransom."

"But that's not—" Aster blurted.

"Hear me out here!" the president said, cutting him off. "Even if this guy was kidnapped, it's probably the Ukrainian mafia. Perhaps they knew his background and wanted to take him for his engineering skills—or perhaps, let's say for argument's sake, because of his NSA experience in cybersecurity or encryption." He pushed his chair back and stood up. "But I'm not going to accept leaping to a farfetched theory that somehow North Koreans in Ukraine are involved."

Aster gazed in frustration at the yellow walls of the Oval Office until the president was done. He suspected that the commander-in-chief hadn't even read the paragraph Aster had inserted into this morning's Presidential Daily Brief (PBD).

The president crossed his arms, his chest inflating with confidence. "You know very well I don't think much of Kim Jong-il. I don't trust him one bit. But he's not a tactician. And he's not a huge risk-taker, for sure. He dresses like a gardener, for goodness sakes. And spends more time with porn and hookers than his generals."

Aster looked down.

"I'll be damned if I'm going to lob some unsubstantiated accusations at this guy. Who knows what he could do? He could just say screw it and go on a nuclear warhead manufacturing spree. Who knows? And especially now that the ink hasn't even dried on our new agreement. The Chinese would raise a huge stink. The Russians, too. And I can just hear the angry calls coming in from Tokyo and Seoul. So, I don't want to hear a whisper of this so-called kidnapping unless and until you find some new evidence that is as air-tight as the Pope's butthole. Got it?"

"With all due respect, sir, we have a North Korean hacker in custody who's admitted seeing a man fitting Wyatt's description being interrogated and tortured. We have email messages implying Wyatt was smuggled into a North Korean ship in the Black Sea. We have a word the Israelis observed a white male detainee being taken off a North Korean cargo ship at the port of Latakia, Syria.

The president sat down again, rubbed his bristly cheeks and frowned at Aster. "Not enough. Add further details in tomorrow's PBD if you get anything more specific. Otherwise, I'm not about to scuttle our Six-Party talks and the freshly signed denuclearization deal. Besides, who's leading this investigation?"

"Operations. A solid team."

"Well, tell them to get better evidence or else stop the investigation all together."

"Oh, I forgot to mention," Aster said. "There's...uh."

"What?" the president said, the impatience in his voice almost toxic.

"There's this lawyer by the name of Jonathan Brooks."

"And?"

"A small-time attorney from New Orleans. He's had run-ins with the CIA before. Kind of a troublemaker, but he helped find the cyber-hacking lab. But now, he may be a complicating factor."

The president leaned his chin over his clasped hands.

"Really bizarre coincidence, but his wife happens to be a reporter, and she's in North Korea as we speak."

"What are you saying?"

"Seems she's ill and was taken away by local authorities. We've asked the Swedish embassy to pay her a visit. To see that there's nothing nefarious going on."

"A lot of coincidences."

"Yes, sir."

"Don't let these coincidences reach the press."

"I understand."

"Where is this lawyer?"

"With our team."

The president tilted his head. "Okay, good. Then tighten his leash. I don't want him taking these wild coincidences to the media. Make this problem go away, fellas. I don't want angry Chinamen and Ruskies blamin' me for ruining a vital agreement with the most difficult regime on the planet." He nodded at Aster. "Anyway, thank you and keep me posted. Now please let me have a chat in private."

Aster fumed inside. This was only his third time sitting in for his boss at an Oval Office meeting. He walked past the president's executive assistant, all the while brooding that no one in that room was really listening. And that lawyer Brooks was a loose cannon who could make this whole thing blow up in the president's face.

36

Residence No. 55, Pyongyang, North Korea

A BURST OF ANGRY WORDS TOO QUICK TO CATCH IN their entirety resonated through the dark walnut office door about five yards to Deputy Minister Ri Yong-nam's right. He jerked and turned his eyes to the door, expecting someone to barge out red-faced at any moment. A loud thud followed. An object hitting a wall, Ri guessed.

Ri ran his fingers in the space between his neck and collar and was surprised to feel sweat on his skin. He'd been sitting in the cold hallway for thirty minutes. He leaned back into the wooden bench and realized his whole back was drenched, too. He glanced at his hands. They were shaking slightly, so he quickly tucked them under his thighs.

Ri's heart continued to race, as it had the moment he'd been summoned to this building in the Central

Luxury Mansion complex, which was the sprawling personal residence of North Korea's Supreme Leader, Kim Jong-il, and his extended family.

He tried to dismiss the tension building inside him. He was sure he'd done nothing to warrant anyone's anger. He reassessed every significant action he'd taken in the last few weeks. Nothing had happened without the prodigious bureaucratic wheels of the government of the Democratic People's Republic of Korea grinding through each printed character of his requests, proposals, statements and the like. Nothing he'd done, said, wrote, or gestured could be considered controversial to the regime, he assured himself. He also tried to remember all the important discussions he'd had with fellow government officials, subordinates, friends, relatives, even the neighbors across from his spacious high-rise apartment. He reviewed in his mind his interview with Linda Fabre a day earlier. Again, he was certain he'd said nothing blasphemous—nothing that would in any way question his loyalty to Kim Jong-il, the Workers' Party, the Ministry of Foreign Affairs, or any other part of the labyrinthian collectivist and nationalist ecosystem that sprang from the nation's *Juche* ideology.

Another loud voice briefly came through the door, and he caught the last few words: "No, not good enough!"

What is this all about? I have done nothing wrong. After all, Ri was the second highest ranking official dealing with foreign affairs. A seasoned diplomat. The most revered expert on the United States. He was smart. Had a clean track-record. As far as he knew, he'd made no enemies during his ascent in this highly stratified, opaque regime. And the Supreme Leader liked him. He was sure of it. *But if this was all true, why am I here?* he asked himself silently. *Why does the Supreme Leader's son need to speak with me so urgently?* He swallowed hard. *I barely know him.*

Ri glanced to his left at the long stretch of desolate white marble flooring that ran some fifty yards to the ornately engraved glass doors—the only source of light in the hallway decorated with a dozen paintings commemorating the war against the Japanese and the Americans.

He now heard quieter, muffled voices coming through the door. He tried to make out how many people were in the room, but the sounds were too garbled to count accurately. Minutes ticking by only brought more uncertainty and angst. He sensed his breathing accelerating, feeling perplexed that he'd not been given any clue as to why he was called to meet with the Supreme Leader's son—a person he'd only briefly encountered once, during a military parade. And as far as he'd heard, the young man was still only a student at the Kim Il Sung National War College and had no official duties. Besides, everyone in the know seemed to think his older brother, Kim Jong-chul, was likely the eventual heir, having already reached a senior position in the Workers' Party.

The door suddenly opened, and three men in military uniform stepped out hurriedly—one of them Ri recognized as a colonel in the Ministry of State Security, one of the DPRK's main intelligence services, but Ri couldn't recall his name. The other two were a Korean People's Army officer and a *Sangsa*—a master sergeant. The officer and the colonel walked briskly down the hallway without making eye contact with Ri, but the *Sangsa* walked straight to Ri, bowed and said, "*Kim Seonsaengnim* will see you now."

Ri hesitantly entered, stepping into a small anteroom with clean white walls and gold-framed portraits of Kim Il-sung and Kim Jong-il, which were mounted above a black leather sofa. The *Sangsa* exited and closed the door behind Ri.

Ri took a deep breath and eyed a dark brown wood wall in the adjacent room. The matching wood floor was partly covered by a sumptuous, deep red Oriental rug. As he stepped into the room, he spotted a large desk and behind it the Supreme Leader's twenty-two-year-old son, Kim Jong-un, who gazed over his shoulder at Ri from a contorted position on a footstool next to a bookcase built into the back wall. The young Kim wore a black double-breasted blazer with wide, peaked lapels, a black shirt and gray slacks and was holding a book that appeared to have a damaged cover.

"Welcome," the young Kim said, motioning toward one of two plush black leather chairs next to where Ri stood. "Sit, please." Kim stayed standing on the footstool and positioned the book next to a signed, mounted basketball, which seemed to serve as a bookend.

Ri bowed deferentially and sat down, quickly glancing around the room. The oversized wood desk at the center was larger than his own boss's, he thought. The entire room, in fact, was adorned with the kind of expensive furnishings he'd only seen in ministerial-level offices overseas. Near the large, single-pane window was a lavishly carved wooden cart filled with whiskey, gin and vodka bottles and a collection of crystal glasses.

Ri then scanned the surface of Kim's desk, on which lay only three items: a black telephone, an ornate black and gold desk lamp, and a closed file folder thick enough to make Ri fear it was his career dossier. He suddenly sensed his seniority withering away. The young man facing him was the Supreme Leader's flesh and blood. Ri felt even more vulnerable as he recalled rumors that the young Kim was prone to temper tantrums and irrational behavior—rumors dating as far back as when Kim had been sent to school in Switzerland.

"I'm deciding where to put these," Kim said, his back still half-turned as he shifted several large, green hardback books from one shelf below the one with the damaged book to another adjacent shelf. "Maybe here is best," he said, tilting his head, and then eyed Ri. "What do you think?"

Ri swallowed, his mouth dry. "I suppose..."

"It's the newest collection of our Great Leader's biography—volumes one through six," Kim said excitedly as if Ri should know. He picked up one volume and brought it to his nose. "The leather smells amazing—published only last week. Written by better authors, who have finally added many more details about his extraordinary life. There are also newly discovered letters showing his wise counsel to other world leaders and their grateful responses."

"That's wonderful," Ri replied.

Kim stepped down from the stool and casually walked to his oversized leather chair at his desk and sat down. "Do you have them, too?"

"I will make sure they are in my office this week," Ri answered.

Kim's face puckered into a frown. "You should get them even sooner. Today, if you can. And read them carefully. It will help with all the work you're doing. My grandfather was a wise man who transformed this nation from a collection of American craters to a prosperous, powerful country revered the world over. And my father has continued this important mission, and perhaps one day I shall lead this effort, too."

"I understand," Ri said calmly, suppressing his surprise that the young Kim aimed for an ambitious future. "Of course, this history is important for all of us in our great motherland. I have read two older editions."

Kim nodded, raising his chin and sucked in a deep breath that inflated his chest.

Ri didn't dare ask why he'd been summoned, so he waited apprehensively, hoping the topic would soon surface.

Kim clasped his small, pudgy hands together behind his head and flashed a patronizing grin at Ri. "I want your assistance. My father seems to have a high regard for you. He trusts that you do things intelligently. That you know the Americans very well and how to deal with them effectively."

"That's very kind of you to say."

"I'm not trying to be kind." Kim's expression turned serious, which only made Ri more uneasy. "For the last year, my father has given me...oh, how would I call it... experimental powers." He briefly snorted.

Ri leaned forward a bit and discreetly wiped his perspiring hands on his lap.

"I took on a portfolio of disruptive operations," Kim went on. "All of them quite small, but interesting. Some with the help of the General Staff Operations Bureau; others in the domain of the Reconnaissance General Bureau, Third Department, and more recently their newest team, Unit 180."

"I am not familiar with that."

He raised his brow and puckered his lips. "Of course not. The team is still being built. But something has gone wrong. Not my fault, but wrong nevertheless. And you need to clean it up. And clean it well, in a way that my father will never hear of it. Ever."

Ri said nothing as his mind digested Kim's words. He quickly realized something was being asked of him that would test his loyalties. He bit his lip before saying in a soft voice, "I have always been honest with your father—"

"I'm demanding an exception in this case—for our country...and for your own good."

Ri clenched his pantlegs with his fists. He could hardly believe what he'd just heard.

"This is important for all of us," Kim said, his words flowing faster, impatience mounting in his tone. "If you use your skills wisely, everything will go smoothly."

"I feel very uncomfortable about your request."

Kim scowled. "Then I will throw in an incentive," he said, now pointing his thick index finger at the other side of the room, over Ri's left shoulder. "You see that briefcase?"

Ri turned and spotted a black satchel, its leather flap quite worn, on the floor leaning upright against the wall. He turned back to face Kim but stayed silent.

"It contains thirty thousand dollars and ten thousand Euros, all in cash. If you do your work properly, the money is yours." Kim leaned back in his chair, crossing his arms. "But if you don't succeed—or you refuse to help—I will report to my father that the security services discovered the money in your apartment."

The words came to Ri like bricks thrown at his face. The young man was threatening him with something that would send Ri to a firing squad. He swallowed hard and, as if guided by survival instincts alone, emitted a simple "I understand" as his heart pounded in his chest hard enough to make his words jump. But he didn't understand. The very idea that a potential future leader of his country could stoop so low as to menace a faithful servant of this regime left him horror-stricken. A cocktail of anger, terror and disgust started to sluice through his veins. But as much as he longed to stand up and tell Kim to go screw himself, he knew that he could do no such thing.

Kim's dark eyes pierced him with malice. Ri immediately thought of his young daughter, his wife, and even his aging parents in Kaesong. Snippets from his entire career, in the form random mental images, began bolting through his mind. All of it could be destroyed by a regime that not only kills its enemies, it also expunges their entire legacy, eviscerates every known achievement, uproots every seed planted. Ri now understood that there was nothing he'd done to deserved punishment. This meeting was about damage control.

"What about asking General Hyon—"

"No." Kim shook his head, his brows bent hard.

"Perhaps there are others in the intelligence field who are better—"

"No!" Kim snarled and slammed his fist on the desk top. "I don't want generals or anyone else from the military or security services. They are naïve and stubborn. I can't trust them to do the job well or to keep their mouths shut. They are all sucking my father's nipple. But when the day comes, I will make sure they will remember where they went wrong."

He gathered that Kim had likely already queried higher-ups in the military but had been rebuffed.

For a moment, Ri contemplated speaking with the young man's father directly, but that option was paved with danger. He was not close enough to the Supreme Leader to ensure he'd be protected against his son's recklessness.

Kim composed his face into a placid expression. "I have chosen you because I know you can solve my problem."

Ri's heart began beating at a fevered pace. Whatever the request, he knew he'd be powerless to refuse it. "How exactly can I possibly help?"

Kim leaned his elbow into his left armrest. "A few months ago, I sent our best computer engineers to Ukraine to have them trained by experts—the very best computer hackers the world has ever known. But they have gone silent, along with their trainers. Completely silent."

Ri again rubbed his sweaty palms over his lap, feeling his fingers shaking. "Were they arrested?"

"I don't know. I have no one on the ground there to look into it. There have been no messages whatsoever for two days."

Ri was still puzzled, since this seemed far more suited for intelligence operatives. "Who was training them?"

"A group led by a powerful, local businessperson. But there is a more serious complication, and that's where you can help." Kim spun his chair around and opened the lid to a humidor on the credenza behind him. He pulled out a cigar and quickly sliced the cap with a cutter. He then lit a wooden match, began heating the other end of the cigar and slowly rotated his chair back to face Ri. "A few weeks ago, I learned that a top computer scientist named Kevin Wyatt—who was also a former official at the U.S. National Security Agency—was traveling to Kyiv. It seemed to be a perfect gift for our country. With his knowledge we could penetrate their systems for the first time. The NSA has been probing and disrupting us for years, and we finally had the opportunity for payback."

"An American," Ri mumbled to himself, now anxious to hear what imprudent thing the young Kim had done.

Kim took a few short drags of his cigar and exhaled a thick plume of smoke that slowly rose up to the room's high ceiling. "We took the man, interrogated him, tried to bring him here...but..." He held the cigar over the desk with both hands and stared at it for a moment. "Wyatt is dead."

Ri's breath caught in his throat. "How?" A chill ran down his spine as he thought about the high-profile Six-Party denuclearization agreement he had helped negotiate over the past six weeks.

"In Syria. We used intermediaries to transport him from the port in Latakia to our plane in Damascus. But he never made it out of Latakia alive. It's a mess. A real mess."

"Do the Americans know?"

Kim shrugged. "I have no idea."

"The Americans are very cooperative now," Ri said. All this could change. A dead American could lead to more severe sanctions, or even military intervention. *You young, irresponsible idiot*, Ri thought. *What have you done?*

"That's why you need to fix this, somehow, and fast. I can't imagine what my father will do if this gets out." He leaned forward and patted the closed file folder on his desk. "All the information you need is in here."

Ri shook his head. "This is going to be very difficult."

"We have one thing that can save us."

"Oh?" Ri said, noticing that Kim had used the word "us" to reframe the problem as theirs, and not just Kim's.

"The last communication we got from Kyiv is that an American lawyer named Jonathan Brooks started to cause problems soon after Wyatt was taken."

Ri straightened his back. "Wait, I know that name." His mind spun quickly. "You mean it's—"

"Yes." Kim grinned. "The woman who interviewed you. It's her ex-husband."

Ri breathed out a lungful of air. "Did you arrange the interview?"

Kim laughed and took a drag of his cigar. "More than that," he said through a smoky exhale. "I had our Chinese friends pay an American media executive in Beijing to bring her here. I think she's an intelligence operative. Working for the Americans, perhaps, or the Brits...or maybe she's a rogue agent, a freelancer working for private interests."

"How do you know this? She acted like a professional journalist during our interview."

"Yes, that's her background, but she's been absent from the media for several years...and suddenly she's doing high-profile news coverage in Beijing, and now here? Don't you find this strange?"

"Perhaps," Ri muttered, but he was reluctant to trust this young man's logic.

"So now you can use her as bait, or to trade her, perhaps. Whatever might work to stop them from pursuing Kevin Wyatt. What do you think? Pure genius, right?" Kim had an excited, childlike smile that contorted his puffy cheeks.

Ri didn't know what to say, so he simply nodded. He realized what Kim had done was likely foolish rather than a masterful act of negotiating prowess.

"How would she be helpful?" Ri said. "It seems to only add to our problems."

"It might be important to lure that lawyer here. And then either negotiate with him or kill them both."

"And then what?" Ri asked, trying hard to decipher the young man's apparent strategy.

Kim frowned as if it was an affront to be questioned.

Ri wasn't trying to poke holes in Kim's logic. He was simply questioning something that appeared to lack any semblance of logic. Ri continued but tried to tread lightly. "The real problem is if the White House gets involved. And your father will surely be informed."

Kim took another hit of his tobacco. "I'm hoping they don't find out. That's why dealing with the lawyer may be our best choice—but we must act fast."

"But Linda might leave soon."

Kim barked out a laugh. "She's not going anywhere. I saw her today at the hospital."

"Is she sick?"

"Yes, you could say that," the young man said, his tone unexpectedly laced with pleasantness. "We put polonium in her tea cup during your interview with her."

Ri's eyes widened. *Reckless bastard*, he thought. *I could have accidentally sipped from it.* "A second dead American will not help our situation."

"I'm told it was a very small dose."

"But it's radioactive, right?"

Kim rolled his eyes. "Not nearly enough to kill her." With both hands, he thrust the file folder across the desk's surface toward Ri. "Make this problem go away."

Ri's heart began pounding even harder than before. "I will need resources. And what will I tell my boss, the Minister? Why will anyone agree to do things I tell them to do?"

"Open the folder."

Ri removed the string that tied the folder closed, flipped the cover open, and stared at a letter atop the stack of documents.

"It is signed by my father. Show it to anyone who gets in the way."

Ri's chest tightened. "But it's fake."

Kim shrugged. "Of course, it is. But no one will know."

37

Vienna, Austria

JONATHAN GAZED OUT THE LEARJET WINDOW AT THE distant terminal buildings of Vienna International Airport, darkened by heavy gray clouds though it had stopped raining. The aircraft taxied for several minutes until it reached the far end of the airport and parked on the wet apron next to other corporate jets and a wide hangar.

He disembarked alone and was met just outside by a tall, slender man in a beige trench coat. "Mr. Porter asked me to drop you off at a hotel of your choice," the man said.

"No thanks," Jonathan said, walking towards the terminal.

"His treat."

"You know him well?"

"He's my boss."

"My condolences." Jonathan didn't slow his pace, but the man walked faster and stepped in front of him.

"We're just being courteous," the man insisted. "You've gone through a lot."

Jonathan stopped and sighed. "I've cooperated enough; I don't want anything more to do with Porter or anyone else."

"It's simply his way of showing gratitude. Besides, you need a place to stay—your flight back to New York isn't until noon tomorrow."

Jonathan thought about it. Porter had arranged commercial airline tickets for him to return to New Orleans via Vienna and New York, but only after Jonathan had agreed to an hour-long debriefing aboard the *Mount Whitney*, where he'd given Porter and his colleague every detail he knew about Wyatt's disappearance. Jonathan surely merited something for his cooperation.

The man smiled. "He asked me to persist if you said no."

Jonathan was tempted, realizing that the corporate credit card Cramer had given him was likely maxed out. And the cash in his pockets probably amounted to no more than two hundred dollars. In any case, accepting the offer would not prevent Jonathan from moving ahead with his plans.

"Well?" the man said.

"Porter's paying?"

"Yes."

"Fine, but we're done after that, right?"

The man nodded. "So, where to?"

"Isn't there a hotel in the city center known for its chocolate?" Jonathan said, recalling that a client once had given him the delicacy years ago. "But I don't remember the name."

"You must mean Hotel Sacher."

Jonathan shrugged. "That sounds vaguely familiar."

"Known for its chocolate pastries and for being one of the oldest grand hotels in Vienna."

"Okay, take me there."

The man laughed. "Very well, I'll call for a room from the car. Get the best out of Uncle Sam while you can."

Jonathan followed the man through the airport's VIP terminal, cleared the arrival formalities by presenting his mangled but still legible and valid U.S. passport, and headed to a car with diplomatic plates outside.

The thirty-minute drive to the hotel in the city increased the restlessness that had been building in Jonathan during his hour-long flight aboard the CIA-chartered plane from Romania and the prior helicopter ride back from the U.S. military command ship. His mind stayed focused on one disturbing issue: Linda's safety. Despite Porter's efforts, Jonathan still had no news of her condition in Pyongyang. But now that he was out of Porter's control, he could follow the plan he'd loosely put together in his head over the last few hours.

*   *   *

Shortly after nine in the evening, Jonathan slipped out of the hotel, whose entrance faced the Opera House.

He needed a cab, but the area was simply too busy to tell if someone was about to follow him.

He began to walk, all the while glancing occasionally over his shoulder. After about fifteen minutes, he had reached a much quieter part of downtown, where there were few people, and almost no traffic or street lamps. He turned onto another equally quiet street and again observed his surroundings. The moment the last pedestrians on the block turned a corner, he reversed his path, headed briskly to the prior intersection and, finally confident that no one was tailing him, flagged down a taxi.

"Beckmanngasse, number 10, please," he told the driver. A short while later, the cab turned off the busy road and onto a narrow, mostly residential street. Jonathan leaned forward, searching for street signs.

The cab turned again onto a tight, one-way street that had a few parked cars on one side and then pulled over at the curb. "This is the place," the driver said in heavily accented English, pointing to his left and nodding at Jonathan via his rearview mirror.

Jonathan glanced out at a white two-story, baroque-style embassy building with a yellow painted roofline, pediment and window frames. As he stepped out of the cab, he noticed for the first time how hard his chest was pounding. He was nervous but determined to do as he had planned.

He strolled along the sidewalk in front of the embassy as the cab drove off, discreetly scanning each street-level window as he passed alongside. But the blinds were closed, and the rooms behind them appeared to be dark. He glanced up. No lights were visible from any of the windows on the second floor either. He continued a dozen yards farther, to where the building ended but the property continued behind an eight-foot perimeter wall that was partly cement, partly wrought iron fencing. He peeked through the metal slats and spotted two black Mercedes sedans parked in the small, gravel-surfaced lot. He walked a few more feet until he reached a large green-colored, solid metal gate. He glanced up and noticed the North Korean flag fluttering gently atop a pole, and behind it, there were trees and a triangular shaped shortwave radio antenna perched on top of another pole.

As he stepped back to get a better view of the side of the building, he noticed a dim light coming from a second-floor window overlooking the parking spots behind the green gate. Jonathan eyed it intently. Suddenly, something moved across the room that made the light momentarily flicker. There was surely someone inside.

Jonathan reached into his pocket and pulled out what he'd concocted back at the hotel: a handwritten note folded multiple times and taped to the bottom of a heavy, glass ashtray embossed with the Hotel Sacher's name and logo. He stepped back to the edge of the sidewalk, glanced at both ends of the street, and seeing no one, aimed for the window. He threw the message-laden ashtray as hard as he could.

The sound of splintering glass burst through the quiet air as the ashtray smashed into the bottom right window pane and then tumbled toward the ground. Jonathan rushed to peek through the slats of the fence as the object hit the closest Mercedes, cracking the windshield, and wedging itself between the wipers and the hood.

"Eh!" a man shouted, gingerly raising the window as a shower of glass fell onto the cars. The man pointed at Jonathan and shouted again as another man joined him at the window.

Jonathan stepped away from the wall and pointed in the direction of the parked cars. "Read my message!" he shouted.

One man disappeared into the room, while his colleague continued to yell at Jonathan from the window.

Jonathan raced to the corner and sprinted the length of the narrow residential street that faced the treelined portion of the embassy grounds, which he estimated to be a bit larger than an acre. He continued to run until the pain in his ribs became unbearable, at which point he slowed to a light jog.

He eventually reached Penzinger Street, where he quickly turned the corner, crossed two sets of tram lines and a five-lane boulevard, and headed as fast as he could into the dense cover of a forested park. About a hundred yards in, he stopped for a moment at a bench, leaning a knee onto the wooden seat while he caught his breath.

Jonathan looked back. There was no sound of police sirens, and no blue lights on the streets. Perhaps the embassy personnel had read his note, he thought. But it was equally possible that the police had not yet dispatched patrol cars to the scene. In any case, he couldn't stay where he was for long. He hurriedly headed to the other end of the park, crossed a busily trafficked street and turned onto Schwendergasse, a wide boulevard with tram lines running in the median. He passed a tram depot on the right and soon after, when he was again nearly out of breath, he waved down the first cab he spotted.

From the backseat of the taxi, he thought about what he'd just done and the note he'd written. If his hunch was correct, there would be no police waiting for him at the hotel. Instead, he expected a North Korean diplomat would track him down, perhaps as soon as early morning.

38

Incirlik Air Base, Turkey

"WHAT IS IT, DAMMIT?" GEORGE PORTER SHOUTED INTO his satellite phone the moment the screen signaled an incoming call. The sound of the helicopter turbines was deafening as the aircraft hovered toward the landing zone.

"Joe here. Got your computer handy?"

"I'm about to land." Porter glanced out the window and spotted the top of Incirlik Air Base's control tower dead ahead as the chopper completed its descent. He checked his watch and frowned. "And it's five in the morning for Christ's sake. Can't it wait?"

"I don't think so."

"Then hold on." Porter rested the phone on his lap as he waited for the chopper to touch down. The rear ramp lowered, and he stepped off the aircraft, carrying his heavy briefcase. "Okay, tell me."

Porter picked up his phone and heavy briefcase. "Okay, tell me."

"Looks like your pal Jonathan has been quite busy tonight."

"Why am I not surprised that he's suddenly not on his way stateside?"

"I've just sent you video I got minutes ago from Austrian intel."

Porter shook his head and sprinted his oversized body across the tarmac to a pickup truck parked nearby. He pulled out his secure laptop from his briefcase, flipped it open on the hood of the vehicle and waited for the signal to authenticate. Seconds later, the feed came through.

"You see it?"

"Yeah," Porter snapped. He rewound the grainy, black and white night-vision footage. "That's Brooks, right?"

"Yes, in front of the North Korean embassy, here in Vienna."

"Son of a bitch..."

"Looks like he's thrown a message to them."

"Or a grenade that didn't explode." Tapping his laptop's touchpad, Porter froze the image of Jonathan with the object in his hand just before throwing it. "Yep, he's starting a dialogue, all right. But how could this happen? I thought you had your eyes on him."

"He took your hotel offer. Seemed quite mellow. Exhausted, in fact. I didn't think he'd get a second wind and do anything crazy."

"It isn't crazy; it's smart as hell." Porter wiped his tired face with his sleeve. "He's played us. And now he knows a lot. There's no telling what he'll spill if he talks to them."

"What do you want me to do?"

Porter shook his head, brainstorming, though he wasn't sure a good answer would come to him fast. He had so little sleep that he could barely stand. "Pick him up, Joe."

"But on what basis? What can—"

"Just do it."

"George, this is Austria, not some shitistan."

"Just fucking pick him up. Now!"

39

SLEEPING IS A NEAR IMPOSSIBILITY AFTER HAVING BEEN attacked by killers, beaten by thugs, interrogated by the CIA, shuffled across four countries, forced to witness friends being murdered, and compelled to poke the eye of a rogue regime, Jonathan mused, checking his watch. He'd tried resting for almost two hours but finally gave up, got dressed and grabbed a cold sandwich at a 24-hour convenience store near the hotel.

He now stood on the top steps of the Opera House under a clear, dawning sky that had turned a shade of mauve. The morning air chilled his skin through the light jacket and sweat shirt he'd been given onboard the US Navy command ship. He had nothing warmer, since Porter had refused to let him retrieve his luggage from his hotel in Kyiv before whisking him out of the country.

He pretended to read a newspaper to conceal his face while he surveyed the entrance of his hotel across the street. The Hotel Sacher's red-coated bellman stayed inside the lobby, occasionally peeking out at the street through the glass doors. There was barely any traffic, and the sidewalks were clear.

Jonathan hoped the message he'd thrown at the embassy had triggered a willingness to talk, but he had no way of knowing, except that no police had yet shown up at the hotel—a good sign.

At a minute shy of four-thirty, a black Mercedes came around the corner. Jonathan immediately recognized the cracked front windshield and the diplomatic license plate. The mild growl of its diesel engine grew more distinct as it crawled past the burgundy awnings of the hotel entrance, turned off its lights, and stopped at the end of the block. The car idled, the exhaust steam continuing to belch from its pipes.

Jonathan stepped down to the sidewalk and headed in the opposite direction to give him more distance from the vehicle. He stopped at the corner and again raised the open newspaper but didn't let the Mercedes out of his sight.

A figure suddenly emerged from the car's passenger side and hurried to the hotel's front doors but hesitated before entering.

As he glanced back at the Mercedes, Jonathan heard the sound of an engine over his shoulder, turned, and half-lowered the newspaper. A dark van with blackened rear windows had eased to a halt at a vacant bus stop on the opposing side of the street. Neither of the two men in the front seats were Asian, nor did they make eye contact with Jonathan—a bit odd, since he was the only person on the sidewalk this early morning.

Porter's men? Jonathan guessed. He feared there were more men inside, which would reduce his chances of fighting them off to zero. And if they were indeed CIA, and intervened, Jonathan knew he'd have no way to communicate with the North Koreans.

Jonathan's pulse quickened. He had to think fast, or else he was likely to end up in the back of the van with some broken bones. He closed the paper and began walking back towards the hotel, glancing twice over his shoulder and attempting to appear as relaxed at possible. But the van crept forward, touching the street's centerline. He jaywalked to the opposite sidewalk and strolled under the hotel's extended awnings toward the entrance and the Mercedes beyond.

The van's engine revved slightly. A second later, the clunking sound of a manhole cover rang out as the van's tire no doubt rolled over it.

Jonathan estimated the distance to the car that was still idling at the next corner. Twenty yards. I can make it, he told himself. He tossed the paper and darted forward.

The van's engine suddenly roared loudly behind him.

Now in full sprint, Jonathan extended his arms to cushion the blow as his body collided into the Mercedes. He banged on the passenger glass with his fist. "Let me in. Quickly!"

An Asian driver leaned over the steering wheel, his eyes wide open.

"Now!" Jonathan yelled, pointing frantically at the fast-approaching van behind them. He yanked the door handle. "Open!" He heard the clicking sounds of unlocking doors and pulled once more, jumping into the seat. "Get out of here!"

The driver hesitated.

"They will kill us!" Jonathan said, hoping this would do it. "Hurry, just go!" As the last word exited Jonathan's mouth, the driver floored the gas pedal and Jonathan was thrust back into the seat as the car shot forward, its tires squealing like a pig being skinned.

Jonathan whipped around to eye the van, which was close behind and about to pull alongside. "Go faster!"

The driver swerved left, then right, and leaned into his door as he fishtailed the car through a screeching left turn.

"Jeez!" Jonathan said, grabbing the handlebar, his face almost pressed flat on the glass.

The Mercedes skidded to a halt, but the van had spun out over the sidewalk and was now facing the wrong direction. The embassy driver again stomped on the gas and maneuvered the car through another sharp turn, with Jonathan still holding himself upright. They sped through two more quick turns before hurtling into the left lane of a large boulevard.

"You are Jonathan?" the driver shouted in English with a dense Asian accent, pronouncing the name without the "h".

"Of course."

"The deputy ambassador is in your hotel, looking for you."

"Well, I don't think we'll meet for tea in the lobby." Jonathan turned and looked for the van but didn't see it. "Keep your speed up."

The driver's eyes shifted rapidly between the road ahead and his rearview mirror. "I don't know what you did, but everyone at the embassy is very nervous."

"Why?"

"That is not important now. We must get away from that van." He turned another corner, running through a red light, this time without burning rubber over the pavement. "Where do I go?"

Jonathan considered the options. "Your embassy?"

"No," the driver barked just as Jonathan realized his suggestion was a bad idea.

"No," the driver barked just as a bright flash lit up the area around them. Jonathan jerked and whipped around.

"What was that?" Jonathan said.

"A radar camera."

Jonathan smirked. "I'll pay the ticket."

"Our diplomats never do," he said, grinning.

As they turned onto yet another street, Jonathan glanced back again and waited. The van, if it was still in pursuit, was too far behind to catch them.

The driver, his eyes fixed on the road ahead, raised a finger in the air. "I have an idea."

He slowed the car to a speed that seemed within the legal limit, made a hard right onto a small two-lane street, passed through a narrow alleyway between two commercial buildings, and emerged onto a tree-lined avenue.

"On the next turn," the driver said, "I will pass in

front of a white apartment building on the left and stop for a second." He stretched his arm and opened the glove compartment. He took out a small, square device, handing it to Jonathan. "You will get out and use this to open the garage door. Hide behind the cars until someone comes to get you."

"Whom should I expect?"

The driver raised his brows. "You will know. There are not many Asians in this part of town."

"How long will I wait?"

"Thirty minutes, maybe more. It's safer than if you stay with me in this car."

As the vehicle made the final turn, Jonathan grabbed the door handle, waiting for the driver to stop. Seconds later, Jonathan stepped out, sprinted down the short ramp of the underground garage and waved the device across the reader attached atop a metal pole. The garage door rose as Jonathan heard the Mercedes accelerate down the street.

For now, he was safe, the North Koreans seemed willing to talk, and Porter's cronies were out wasting time learning Vienna's roadways. But his plan still remained a long shot. The note he'd thrown at the embassy had bought him time, but he had no way of knowing if it would also get him closer to Linda.

40

Pyongyang, North Korea

PRESSURE SUDDENLY BORE DOWN ON LINDA'S FACE. SHE opened her eyes and saw the hand of a male nurse covering her nose and mouth with something. Her lungs pushed out a cry, but the sound was muffled.

She jolted, turning her head to one side. "What are you doing?"

"*Jibeaochiwo!*" the man barked, jerking back but still pressing what looked like an oxygen mask over her face.

"Leave me alone!" She tried to seize his arm, but her hands locked up almost instantly—her wrists were tied to the side of the gurney. "I don't want your help!" She twisted her left shoulder upward, bumping his elbow out of the way. He withdrew the mask and glared at her.

She had no idea what treatments they'd already given her, and she wanted none more. "Let me out of here! Call the doctor!" She yanked on the wrist straps repeatedly, the sound of rattling metal resonating through the room.

Suddenly, the door flung open. The soldier who'd been posted outside stormed in, followed closely by two clinical attendants.

"Take me to my hotel." Linda realized her feet were unrestrained, so she began kicking. The wool blanket covering her went flying. She continued to kick, hitting the metal railing. "You hear me?" She sprang skyward from her elbows, swung her waist to the right, and kicked once more, striking the nurse in the groin with the ball of her foot.

He curled over, stumbled and fell to his knees, groaning.

"I am an American! A journalist!" Her legs swung again as she tried to hit the nurse's head, but the soldier yelled and seized her leg in mid-kick. He forced her limbs back into a straightened position and threw his weight onto her knees.

"Get off me!"

The soldier pressed down harder, as if he were attempting to snap her legs in half.

She tugged her arms violently, trying to free them from the restraints. "You can't hold me against my will."

A female aide darted at Linda out of nowhere and clamped her forehead with both hands, the woman's fingers painfully pinching her skin. Linda shifted her eyes left, the view partially obstructed. The male nurse rose from the floor and grabbed her with one hand clutching her left arm where the IV needle was taped in place, and the other clasping her neck. He shoved her hard into the gurney's thin mattress just as another woman brushed by him and lunged at Linda with a syringe in hand.

Linda tried to lurch sideways but was now immobilized. "Leave me alone!"

The aide squinted as she test-squirted fluid from the needle and then angrily jabbed it into Linda's upper arm.

"God!" Linda cried in pain, feeling as if the needle had gone straight through her arm. She prepared to scream once more but as she gasped for air, she suddenly felt a cold, tingling sensation rapidly ooze through her shoulder. It spread to her chest, neck and face as she ended her next breath. She knew what it was. "Fuck you," she blurted, the words slurring, her voice waning. She filled her lungs, but her next words didn't exit her lips with any sound. Her jaw and cheeks became numb. Her shoulders sank. The sedative they'd injected into her began to dull the rest of her body.

The soldier and staff talked loudly with each other, perhaps arguing, as they continued to restrain Linda. She battled with every neuron in her head to stay alert, to keep her eyelids open, to resist as best she could. But the strength she'd had moments earlier had melted away. The distant edges of her room began to blur. Her eyelids lowered and her breaths slowed, though her mind remained tormented but helpless. The rough voices around her fused into an indistinguishable garble. Her head felt cold and heavy. And everything went dark.

*   *   *

A sharp, musty, malodorous stench crept into her lungs. Again and again, it infected her slow breaths. The acrid scent sharpened further. Linda opened her eyes slightly, gaining her senses, though her fatigue and wooziness seemed potent enough to throw her back into her dreamless sleep. Her eyes felt sore and puffy. She assumed the painful stiffness in her hips and spine came from the hard surface over which she lay.

She lifted her head a couple inches and examined her surroundings. A bench faced her, its wooden surface cracked and decaying, as were the matching benches on the other side of the aisle. "A train car," she whispered, wondering how long she'd been knocked out.

She felt wetness below her waist. Glancing down, she noticed she now wore a faded, maroon-colored men's sweater. Her legs were fitted into loose olive-green pants that had a wet stain at her groin. "Jeez." She'd urinated on herself. The shoes on her feet were oversized, well-worn moccasins. Her legs were stretched toward the large window, whose grime-coated glass glowed with strange opalescence as the bright daylight came in through the dozen exterior metal bars.

As she slowly propped herself up, a cold, sharp tug pulled her left wrist. She was handcuffed to a rusted metal railing at the top edge of her bench. She slowly sat upright, her hand raised over her shoulder as it couldn't rest any lower. Suddenly, her stomach needled with pain—the same tormenting agony that had begun when she'd gotten sick at the hotel. Her heartbeats seemed sluggish. As the twist in her stomach subsided slightly into nausea, she looked at her uncuffed right hand. It was pale, her joints achy as she unclenched her fist.

Linda scanned both ends of the aisle. The train car was empty, the metal floor smeared with dried mud and littered with plastic bags, cigarette butts and a few grubby rags, one with crimson stains. If train services had a fourth class, this would be it, she decided. And judging from the smell, it was fit only for livestock.

"Where the hell am I?" she whispered, her heart sinking. She thought of Max. He hadn't checked on her, as he'd promised. How could I have been so naïve? She blamed herself for having misjudged his assurances that all would be fine. It was his responsibility to ensure his staff's safety in such an inherently dicey country and apparently, he'd shirked that responsibility. And now that she was nose-deep in the dark side of this reclusive regime, Max's absence both appalled and frightened her.

She turned to the window again, observing what she could through the filthy glass from three feet away, her handcuffs preventing her from getting any closer. A rudimentary shack with wooden walls and a rusted corrugated steel roof stood between two trees. Beyond it was an ungroomed field, and farther away a forested hill topped with coniferous trees. There was nothing else in sight. No soldiers. No people. She suspected the train had ventured far from Pyongyang, but it was only a guess.

The piercing silence calmed her a little. She hoped someone was looking for her—if not Max, someone else from the press corps. She briefly convinced herself that the North Koreans couldn't simply kidnap an American without someone making a stink about it. Perhaps diplomats were already searching for her or negotiating for her release.

She took a deep breath and stared at the closed metal door at the far end of the car. The sharp pain returned to her stomach, and as Linda, doubled over, she spotted a yellowish object protruding from a crack adjacent the metal footing of the bench across from her. She took a deep breath and stretched her foot in front of her, stroking the object with the tip of her moccasin until it edged out of the crack. It was a cigarette lighter. She extended her uncuffed arm and picked it up, then flicked it a few times until a weak flame struggled out of its tip. An idea came to her, but she'd have to wait until dark to try it.

She slipped the lighter into her right shoe and sat back on the bench, brushing the hair from her face. But when she moved her hand away from her head, she gasped. "What the..." A clump of hair was caught between her fingers. At least ten follicles, maybe more. She quickly touched her head again, and more strands came out with only a modest effort to pull them. Three clumps of hair lay on her pants. She began to perspire, and her heart sped up. She'd never had anything like this happen to her before.

41

Vienna, Austria

THE DISTANT SOUND OF A DOOR OPENING AND QUICKLY closing pierced the stuffy, pitch-black air. Several overhead incandescent bulbs began flickering before glowing steadily, illuminating the garage where Jonathan had been left in the dark for nearly an hour.

He swiftly sat up from the cold concrete floor where he'd been lying in between two parked cars and cautiously crawled to the back of one of the them. He peeked around it, scanning the main gallery that housed some twenty vehicles, mostly compacts and a few SUVs.

Footsteps resonated from the far end of the garage. He listened, guessing the sound came from more than one person. Two men, both Asians, emerged from behind a station wagon and stopped in the middle of the gallery, peering in all directions.

"I'm here," Jonathan said, crawling forward to the back of the car with one knee still on the floor.

The broad-shouldered man wearing a mid-length black coat—which Jonathan suspected looked bulky enough to conceal a firearm—marched toward him. The man's suited colleague followed closely behind.

Jonathan leaned onto the car's bumper as he mustered the strength to stand. But before he could lift himself up, the black-coated man grabbed his shoulder and held him down with one hand while quickly patting Jonathan's jacket and digging into his pockets with his other.

"Looking for ashtrays?" Jonathan said.

The man finished his gruff inspection and stepped back, his hawkish stare unflinching.

"Get up," said the man in a suit, his facial expression as caustic as his tone.

"Who are you?" Jonathan said, standing and brushing the dirt off his pants. He ignored the sharp pain in his chest and the discomfort just about every place else in this body as best he could.

"Mr. Pak, deputy ambassador," he said matter-of-factly, his hands slipping into his pants pockets. His accented English had a strange infusion of both Korean and German. "I read your note."

"Good."

The diplomat raised a brow. "I have nothing to say about it. Neither does our ambassador. We don't understand why you chose our embassy. It's not our business. It's incomprehensible."

"Incomprehensible?" Jonathan said, confused, given that the diplomat was highly versed in English, regardless of his accent. "I was very clear." Jonathan quickly recalled the few sentences he'd written on the note he'd taped to the ashtray. He'd made a calculated bluff after everything he'd learned from Kane's laptop, the hacker lab in Pripyat, and from Porter, including his time on the U.S. Navy vessel in the Black Sea. He'd told the North Koreans that Bodrov had double-crossed them, having successfully extracted from Wyatt information worth millions on the black market. Jonathan claimed to have the data on a flash drive and would trade it for Linda. He was confident that the ruse offered the best chances of keeping Linda alive, at least in the short term.

"We know nothing about the names you mentioned," Pak said. "Nothing about Mr. Wyatt or Ms. Fabre. Nothing."

"My note wasn't really meant for you."

"Obviously. After we cabled your message to our Ministry, we received very odd instructions."

"Odd in what way?"

The diplomat squinted at the ceiling. "I have been told to help you," he said. "Though I would much prefer to kick your teeth in and throw you in the river with lead weights."

"I've had worse things happen to me."

Pak exhaled loudly and shook his head. "Because that was my car that you vandalized."

"Ashtrays are temperamental creatures."

Pak approached, his angry, squarish face close enough for Jonathan to spot a vein pulsating on the man's temple. "You are foolishly brash, Mr. Brooks. Unless you have lived in a cave all your life, you should know we are not a country to be taken lightly." The faint scent of tobacco glided out his mouth and into Jonathan's nostrils.

"I'm trying to make a deal, Mr. Pak. As simple as that."

The deputy ambassador said something to his big-shouldered armoire standing near Jonathan. The man took off his coat, revealing a pistoled holster under his arm. He threw the jacket at Jonathan.

"Put it on," Pak said. "And wear the hat, too. It's in the left pocket."

Jonathan removed his light jacket and slipped into the coat, which felt two sizes too large. He pulled a black baseball cap out of the pocket and placed it on his head. "So, how do I look?"

Pak nodded at him coldly.

"Like a Korean rock star?" Jonathan turned to the armed man. "You can wear mine, but I'm afraid you'll tear the seams." The bodyguard stared at him but did not respond.

Pak crossed his arms. "Who was chasing you tonight?"

"I don't know."

"Americans?"

"No, not likely." Jonathan didn't want to risk scaring off Pak and his puppeteers back in Pyongyang by mentioning the CIA. "Probably Ukrainians, I'm guessing. They've already tried to send me home in a casket."

"You're lying!" Pak said. "I'm sure they are Americans. And if that's true, it's going to be a problem to get you from here to China."

"I'm not going to China. I told you, I want you to fly me to your country."

"You are better off going through Beijing." Pak moved back a step but the antagonism in his tone dropped a notch. "If you're wanted by authorities, American or otherwise, there could be an Interpol red notice out for your arrest. Or, if they are very bothered by you, they may even invalidate your passport. Either way, you will not make it through passport control at Vienna airport."

"I told you, there's no police or intelligence services after me. Only criminals. Thugs. Gangs. People like your pal here."

"Do not push your luck."

Jonathan understood that Pak was no ally, but the man hadn't yet ruled out that some solution could come of this. "What do you propose?"

Pak turned pensive, his eyes shifting away from Jonathan as he took another step back. A half-minute later he looked up at Jonathan. "We have a way, but I cannot guarantee that it will be free of trouble."

"Trouble is my middle name these days."

The diplomat tilted his head slightly, his expression muted. "Whatever you have done, or whatever you are trying to do, I can only assume you have lost your mind. Indeed, you are trouble, Mr. Brooks. The sooner you leave this city, the better. Come with us now."

42

"YOU CAN GET UP NOW," PAK SAID IN ENGLISH, THE condescension in his voice slightly diminished from when they'd left the clandestine meeting in the garage nearly an hour ago.

"Where is this?" Jonathan rose from his prone position across the backseat of the Audi A4, which had rental car stickers on the rear windows.

"The Vienna suburbs, a peaceful place where a person like you can have a chance to live a bit longer."

"You're funny, Mr. Pak. I didn't realize North Korean diplomatic school taught such wicked humor."

Pak's heavy-build colleague turned off the tree-lined rural road and eased through an opened gate between high cement walls. The car rolled into a commercial storage site composed of two long single-story structures, both with a dozen garage doors facing each other across the paved path. He revved the engine hard, sprinting toward a man standing at the distant end of the building on the right, all the way to the last garage door.

The car stopped and the two North Koreans got out and joined a short man outside, who also appeared Korean. A moment later Pak's guard lifted the garage door open and summoned Jonathan with a brisk wave of the hand. Jonathan got out of the car and entered the unit, scanning the space. It measured roughly ten by twenty feet, with high ceilings and corrugated steel walls. A printer, scanner, and laptop rested on the surface of a foldable table and an opened suitcase sat next to several cardboard boxes. As the door closed behind him, Jonathan glanced at the short man, who circled the room and turned on portable standing lights in each corner until the space was almost too bright on the eyes.

"Sit," Pak instructed, pointing at two empty chairs at the center of the space, as the short man, his back turned to Jonathan, riffled through the luggage.

Jonathan selected a chair. "What's he doing?" he asked Pak, indicating the short man.

We have to change your appearance. And this man is a magician."

Jonathan drew in his breath. "The last time I heard that word, I just about ended up at the bottom of a pond," he said, recalling the negotiations in Kyiv, when Artem Bodrov bragged about the title on his business card.

The short man took the seat next to Jonathan and set a basket containing several small objects at his feet. "What exactly will you change?" Jonathan asked.

"He doesn't speak English," Pak interjected.

The man wiped a wet rag over Jonathan's face. Then he massaged a gel into his hands and rubbed them through Jonathan's hair. He used the rag again to wipe away some excess gel that had dripped onto Jonathan's forehead. He lifted Jonathan's chin a bit, pulled something out of a plastic wrapper and lifted it toward Jonathan's nose.

"A mustache?" Jonathan gazed down without lowering his head but was on the verge of laughing. "Are you serious?"

"Let him do his thing," Pak said. "We're changing your look for a new passport."

The man placed the fake mustache over Jonathan's lip, adjusted it slightly and pushed on it hard. The adhesive burned his skin for a solid minute.

"It's not superglue, is it?

Pak ignored him.

"Is it from North Korea?"

The diplomat ignored Jonathan, instead watching his disguise specialist in action.

"And, just so you know, I'm allergic to raccoon hair."

The short man turned his attention back to Jonathan's gelled hair, grimacing for a moment. He then took a small, unmarked plastic tube and squeezed a whitish goo from it into a paper cup. He turned, said something to Pak and then lowered Jonathan's head.

"He's going to gray your hair."

"That should happen naturally when I go to your country, don't you think?"

The man mixed the liquid with a mascara wand and slowly applied the product to Jonathan's strands of hair in repeated swaths that each felt about an inch wide. After about ten minutes, he pushed his chair back and observed Jonathan, who glanced at Pak.

"Not really a Korean rock star, but good enough," the diplomat said before turning to the short man and switching to Korean. The man nodded and walked back over to the luggage area.

After a few minutes, the man returned and aimed a Canon digital camera at Jonathan's face, motioning silently for Jonathan to raise his chin. The camera clicked six or seven times. The man went to the laptop on the table and pulled up the images. Jonathan got up and approached the screen, as did Pak.

The man selected one of the stills. He then made minor adjustments, cut and pasted it onto another image that looked like an existing passport page.

As Jonathan leaned in to inspect it, he noticed the image that his headshot was being added to was the information page of an American passport. "Bradley Kriegermann?" Jonathan said. "Seriously? Couldn't you have chosen a name that won't leave me tongue-tied at the wrong freaking moment?"

"It's perfect," Pak said. "A real person. Jewish."

"I'm not Jewish."

"Doesn't matter—he was white, and you're white. And only a few years older than him. He died in 2001 somewhere in Arizona."

"How good is this fake? I don't want to spend the next ten years in an Austrian prison."

"You won't," Pak said. "You're flying out of Munich."

"Okay, then a German prison."

"You do not understand, Mr. Brooks. Our counterfeiters are among the best in the world. Especially for passports."

"What about biometrics?"

Pak scratched his jaw. "Yes, those will be challenging, but we have a few years to tackle that. Until then, it's easy—most passports are just machine-readable, not biometric. We have also mastered fake currency, like superdollars."

Jonathan had heard of these high-quality counterfeit hundred-dollar notes in a maritime seizure case his law firm had worked a few years earlier.

"And British pounds, Euros, Russian rubles," Pak said proudly. "Also birth certificates, cigarettes—you name it."

"Nike shoes?"

Pak frowned. "No, the Chinese are better with apparel."

Jonathan shrugged. Pak's assurances carried little weight. "So why Munich?"

"Leaving out of Vienna is too risky. So Munich is next closest city that has a direct flight to Beijing. You are booked on the five-twenty flight tomorrow afternoon. Whoever is after you is probably tracking every major transportation hub here in Vienna. And if the intelligence services are involved, they will—"

"I told you, only Ukrainian mafia is after me."

"Intelligence services can monitor traffic cameras, private security cameras and webcams and they have other electronic means of finding you." Pak turned and patted his guard's shoulder. "My assistant will drive you there. Same rules: you lie down across the rear seats until he tells you it's clear to get up, and then catch your flight. They have great meals on Lufthansa."

"Uh-huh, you make it sound pleasant and simple when you avoid mentioning passport control. The German authorities are not stupid. I'll be handing them a goddamned fake passport."

"We are not amateurs, Mr. Brooks. We've done this more times than you can imagine." Pak checked his watch. "You will head out in six hours. In the meantime, you must stay here, out of sight."

The newly minted passport page came out of the printer. The short man picked it up and cut it precisely to size. He set a U.S. passport on the table, opened it, separated several of the pages, inserted the new one and, within thirty minutes, had restitched the document to its natural state. Pak picked it up and set it in Jonathan's hand.

"You cannot get cold feet," Pak said. "You know what will happen if you don't go."

"And you know damn well if anything happens to me, all the information I have will go public."

Pak shook his head. "I assure you, we have cleared German passport control with similar documents."

"What if we—"

"No," Pak barked, interrupting him. "Our plan is your only option. I've been patient enough with you. Sit down and wait till it's time to leave." He grabbed the passport back from Jonathan's hand.

*   *   *

Jonathan caught his breath and wiped the sweat off his brow the moment he slumped into seat 27A. His overheated, perspiring skin now felt chilly and clammy. As the Lufthansa widebody Airbus taxied away from the gate, he scanned out his window for signs of the runway. Until the aircraft was airborne, he wasn't yet out of Germany's grasp. He imagined briefly a police car racing across the tarmac, cutting off the plane's path and sending stormtroopers into the aircraft to grab him out of his seat and off to a prison cell.

The red sign for Runway 19 emerged, partially obscured by uncut grass next to the pavement. The engines roared, the plane accelerated and moments later, it rotated. He understood that the risk was diminishing further but was not exactly over. His eastbound plane had to clear the airspace of the last NATO country. He smiled to himself. The irony didn't go unnoticed—that he'd feel *free* once he crossed into Russian airspace. From there, no German or American could stop his onward journey to Beijing and Pyongyang.

Jonathan leaned back in his seat and quickly came to the realization that his freedom would be fleeting. Perhaps merely as brief as the eight-hour flight ahead. His survival depended on the leverage he'd hastily created: the information on the note to the North Koreans, and the letter he'd sent via air mail that would arrive at Cramer's office within a week, at which time Cramer would, he was certain, immediately reach out to law enforcement and the intelligence services. But Jonathan understood there were many loose ends to his plan. Where all this would ultimately lead remained opaque and depended ultimately on who would deal with him in Pyongyang. In any case, there was nothing he could do to change the circumstances now. He needed sleep—there was no telling if he'd have much of it later. Even a few hours would suffice to keep him sharp for his arrival in the Chinese capital at around noon.

43

Thirty miles north of Pyongyang, North Korea

LINDA TRIED TO CATCH A GLIMPSE OF THE MOVING scenery outside her window, but it was blackened by night—too dark even to see the outer metal bars. But this absence reduced her sense of confinement an infinitesimal amount. She had no idea about where the train was headed as it lumbered slowly, with no working lights in her car and no light from outside. If there were fields, mountains, hills, rivers or coastline nearby, she had no way of knowing.

Having spent much of her career facing television cameras with rigid guidelines for moving from one topic to the next, she had acquired a knack for precisely tracking the passage of time, even when, like now, she had no wristwatch or clock to use as reference. But this night she sat less confident of her skills. After all, she'd endured excruciating pain in her stomach. His heart still felt sluggish, as were her breaths. The clumps of hair she'd pulled from her head left her immensely disturbed. And whatever sedative they'd given her hadn't worn off completely, leaving a dizziness that made it difficult for her to sit upright on the bench. And she'd gone without food for two days—assuming that she hadn't lost any full days while unconscious—and had drank only a single cup of water that a nurse had handed her earlier at the hospital. But she tried anyway to deduce the time. The train had traveled an hour or more since dusk, when it had left its earlier extended stop, so she guessed it was nine at night by now.

Suddenly the brakes screeched loudly, and the train slowed to a complete stop—only the second time it had done so since she'd woken up after her drug-induced sleep. When about ten minutes had passed in complete silence and darkness, during which she reviewed the Morse Code she'd learned as a Girl Scout, she pulled out the lighter from her shoe. This was as good a moment as any to try what she had planned.

Linda leaned as close to the window as she could, though her handcuffed hand held her back by about a yard from the glass. She held the lighter up to the center of the window and began flicking it to signal "SOS." Each sparked flame illuminated the grimy window. She did it a second time, and a third. She then gave her thumb a rest, letting the lighter's roller cool. She thought for a moment and then hummed the monotone sounds that made up the five letters of her name in Morse Code. She signaled again with the flick of the lighter, repeating her name's code three times.

As she started to signal a fourth time, a loud boom pounded the window, and a man shouted in Korean. She withdrew the lighter and slid it under her thigh. The thump echoed again, only louder, and this time she saw the faint silhouette of a hand pressed flat on the glass. It hit once more, and a stern voice again echoed.

A door somewhere near the back of the train slid open, and she heard footsteps clattering her way. The metal door at the far end flung open. She heard men bellowing and saw a flashlight aimed in her direction, bobbing up and down as it approached quickly through the dark. She squinted, partly blinded by the light, and spotted two uniformed soldiers darting towards her. One of them leaned in and yelled at her in Korean from a few inches away, spraying spit over her face as he shouted.

She choked in mid-breath. They could easily kill her, she thought, but they hadn't yet. "I want to speak to—"

A firm slap knocked her head sideways. Linda cried out and raised her arm to shield her face as the skin of her left temple began to throb from the hit.

The other soldier patted her down roughly, then grabbed her wrist, and with both hands tried to pry open her clenched fist. She yanked her arm back as hard as she could and screamed, with all the air in her lungs, "Let me go!"

The soldier slapped her again, and once more, harder still. She dropped the lighter and fell sideways, perched over the bench but avoiding the floor only because her other arm was fully stretched and handcuffed to the bench. He kicked her feet away, picked up the lighter and slipped it into his pants pocket, all the while cursing her. She hesitantly lifted herself back up to the bench, saying nothing, her eyes locked onto the soldier who'd hurt her.

The train car shuddered briefly and began moving forward again at low speed. The men straightened their backs. One checked his watch, and the other unclipped a handheld radio from his belt and called in. The voice on the other end screeched with static. They spoke for under a minute. Then both soldiers moved to the window, each crudely shoving Linda's knees out of their way, and peered out briefly. The soldier closest to her turned off his flashlight, and both men sat down on the opposite bench. They occasionally glared at her as the train continued slowly into the night. She understood they would not leave her alone again.

About an hour later, a strong light suddenly beamed through the steel cage outside the dirt-covered glass, momentarily illuminating the car as slim shadows from the metal bars slid across the benches and the faces of two angry, man-spreading warriors seated across from her.

Linda again touched her face, delicately sensing the skin where the soldier had made contact. It still burned, though less now. But she was less afraid of them, too. Any uniformed man who hits a woman is no warrior, she realized. Just a coward, using physical strength to overcome what they lack in every other sense. She hoped she'd have a chance for payback. But for the time being all she wanted to focus on was trying to survive long enough to confront someone with real authority. Someone who might be reasonable enough to understand it was not in their country's best interests to harm an American civilian. Someone who'd agree to let her get the hell out of the country.

The train continued in complete darkness for a while longer. Then another source of light glowed past and faded away. And another. The train stopped again, and a few words came through the soldier's radio. Both men abruptly stood up, one of them quickly unlocking her handcuff. They lifted her by her arms.

"Where are you taking me?"

"*Ibdagchyeo!*" the soldier glued to her right screamed into her ear, raising his hand as if he were about to pounce on her once more. Both men jostled her forward through the long, darkened aisle, her moccasins slipping off her feet in the commotion. Her stomach pain returned in force. She curled forward in agony, but they forced her upright, dragging her roughshod out of the car, down three steps and into the chilly air—much colder than in Pyongyang. She saw her own breaths and felt the jagged rocks of the train tracks scraping her toes. The men carried her over another set of tracks and onward toward a man wearing a thick parka and a military cap who stood with a lighted cigarette under a dimly glowing streetlamp. Behind him was the beginning of a narrow dirt path, not wide enough for a vehicle, and the chirping noise of crickets.

Her stomach retched as the soldiers carried her forward, approaching the stranger under the light. She heaved twice more, but only phlegm came out. She had nothing left in her stomach to throw up. The soldier stopped about five feet from the man. Their painfully tight grips under Linda's arms were the only thing stopping her from collapsing. She raised her head and looked up at the man with the cigarette.

"Ms. Fabre," the stranger said. "We meet again."

"What?" Linda squinted, scanning the contours of his face that remained obscured under the shadow cast by the lip of his cap. She replayed his flawless English and when he took another drag of his cigarette, it hit her. He was Deputy Minister Ri, whom she'd interviewed only days earlier. A wave of hope washed over her. Had the second most powerful official in the country's diplomatic service intervened to help her?

"Thank God you're here," Linda said. "I'm not well and these soldiers have detained me against my will. I assume you're here to clear this up and get me on a plane home."

"Whether or not I can do that remains to be seen," Ri said coldly. "I now have a better sense of why you've come to our country."

She inhaled deeply, confusion mingling with the pain. "I'm just a journalist trying to do my damn job.

Ri nursed his tobacco, the cold breeze dissipating the smoke over his shoulder. "Who sent you to Beijing?"

"I was hired on a freelance assignment to cover the summit for several U.S. and Canadian networks."

"I would have thought by now you would be truthful."

A wave of fear began to wash over her. "I...I don't understand."

"If you don't help me with real answers, there are others who may simply feed you to the pigs."

"There must be some misunderstanding." Linda suddenly felt cold, but the adrenaline beginning to course through her system gave her the strength to stand on her own. She stabilized her bare feet on the sandy ground and straightened her back, tugging her arms away from the soldiers, who loosened their grip. "I've done nothing wrong. I completed my assignment in China, and then Max—the bureau chief whom I'd never before met—convinced me to come here for a London network that wanted interviews and post-summit coverage. I have no clue what the hell you're suspicious about."

Ri barked something to the soldiers, and one of them sprinted back to the train. He then pointed at her with the fingers that held his cigarette. "A good starting point would be for you to admit your ties to intelligence services. Just like your ex-husband. You both have an agenda. That's why you are risk-takers, and sometimes..." He interrupted himself with a drag of his tobacco. "Sometimes, risk-takers die at the hands of their own arrogance."

She swallowed hard, wondering how on earth she could prove her innocence. "You've got the wrong person, I swear. Have you talked with Max?" Then she thought of Jonathan and what he might have done. After everything he'd told her from his near-fatal escapade in Central America in recent months, she suddenly locked her thoughts on one possibility. He might have lied to her. Perhaps what he'd gone through in Panama and Nicaragua was not accidental at all. But even so, she couldn't grasp why anything he had done in Central America could have any connection to her reporting in Pyongyang or Beijing.

She heard the crushing of stones. The soldier returned from the train tracks with her moccasins in hand. He tossed them in front of her. "Where is Jonathan?" she asked, balancing from one weak leg to the other to slip on her shoes.

"He's a foolish man. And I have no doubt your divorce is a ruse."

"He has nothing to do with my work here. But why are you implying that he does?"

"Ms. Fabre, you disappeared from the media for over six years. That's plenty of time to be recruited by our enemies and trained in the art of deception. Then, suddenly, you surface of all places in Beijing's corridors of power, prying into the Six-Party talks—"

Linda felt the pains begin to stab her abdomen. "I. Am. A. Reporter. Nothing. More," she said.

"I am certain you spent your time keeping tabs on Russian and Chinese delegations, as well as our own, while you were in Beijing."

"I was there barely three days, for God's sake."

"Yes, right. And then your husband miraculously uncovers one of our most secretive operations in Europe. Do not try to convince me that you and your ex are victims of coincidence. We are America's greatest enemy, and that reality means we do not leave things to be explained by chance."

Linda had no idea how to respond. His claims were as farfetched as if he'd called her an alien. But what if this was in fact somehow connected to Jonathan? The possibility that Jonathan might have lied to her all along made her feel as though a rug was being pulled from under her.

"I hope this camp will convince you to start speaking truthfully. Then, we'll talk again."

"What camp?"

Ri smiled for the first time. "Behind me." He threw his cigarette to the ground and crushed it with his shoe. "Bukchang Concentration Camp. Some make it, some don't. I hope your survival instincts guide you wisely." He nodded at the soldiers. They grabbed her arms and hustled her forward onto the dirt path, past Ri and into the darkness.

Pyongyang, North Korea

LUCK IS THE WIND THAT HITS YOU ON LIFE'S HIGH-WIRE journey. Jonathan recalled the words—pretentiously uttered by his Constitutional Law professor in New Orleans—as he peered out the airplane window at the distant grass-topped hills. And the words seemed more prescient—and ironic—now that Jonathan had barely cheated death in Kyiv only to have the misfortune of arriving in the most dangerous nation on earth.

Jonathan had indeed been lucky. He'd made it to Beijing unharmed. He'd connected to this Air Koryo flight, again without incident. And now the only thought that stood out was the stark reality that he was alone—unfathomably alone—and that his luck-drenched journey to connect with Linda could be coming to an end, perhaps as soon as he stepped out onto North Korean soil.

The Soviet-era Tupolev Tu-154 continued its descent, passing over a wide, deserted, paved road. Then a barren pasture came and went, seconds before the airliner touched down like a brick. The roar of reversing engines merged with the loud clackity-clunk of tires rolling over the runway's uneven concrete surface until the plane had slowed to taxiing speed.

The main terminal of Pyongyang's Sunan International Airport stood in the misty distance under a cloud-filled sky nearing dusk. Jonathan's heart picked up its pace. He licked his dry lips, his mind jumbling with anxiety. Ahead of him stood the gravest negotiations of his life. His lawyerly prowess was about to be tested like never before, but his bargaining strength depended on one key factor: whether the North Koreans had fallen for his bluff.

The aircraft turned slowly towards a man on the tarmac waving yellow sticks, and then it stopped. Jonathan eyed the terminal building ahead, which was now close enough for him to spot the large, framed headshot portrait of the nation's founder, Kim Il-sung, mounted on its roof.

A flight attendant appeared in the aisle and timidly leaned over the two empty seats next to Jonathan. "Stay here, please," she said, nearly whispering. "After the other passengers leave, someone will come for you."

And that's exactly what happened. The other thirty or so people deplaned to a waiting bus, and within a minute, two gray-suited men with unfriendly faces and tightly shaved black haircuts marched to Jonathan's row and silently signaled for him to get up. With his duffel bag in hand, he did as he was shown, stepping calmly out of the plane and down the mobile stairs. The air was cool, humid and laced with the scent of jet fuel. He could hardly believe he had made it to Satan's *terra firma*.

The men, all of whom wore small red badges with the faces of their past and current leaders on their lapels, ushered him to a waiting olive-green jeep. A man in military uniform with a side-arm locked in his holster jumped into the driver's seat and chauffeured them to the far corner of the terminal building, on the opposite end from where the bus had dropped off the other passengers.

Jonathan's heart began to pound rapidly as he followed the men through a set of glass doors, careful to observe everything and everyone around him. The three men descended a flight of stairs to the basement floor. The confined surroundings began to feel constricting to Jonathan, and increasingly uncomfortable as they walked across the room. They stopped at the end of the room and one of the men motioned for Jonathan to sit on a plastic chair at the far wall.

Moments later, another man arrived. He wore thick glasses and a darker suit. "Passport," he said gruffly and held out his hand.

Jonathan reached into his pocket. "Yeah, your work of art." He handed over his counterfeit passport in the name of Bradley Kriegermann.

The man opened it, frowned and looked up at Jonathan as if he'd just been called a dirty name. "No! *Your* passport."

"Ah, that one." Jonathan unzipped his duffel bag and removed it from bottom of the bag, where he'd hidden it since his trip began in Munich. The man snatched it from his hand, inspected the identification page, scrutinized Jonathan with a hostile gaze and finally handed it back. He said something to his colleagues and glared at Jonathan. "Go there, change." He pointed at a door on the opposite wall.

Jonathan frowned. "Change?"

"Go!" He gestured again, more aggressively.

Inside was a small room not much larger than a walk-in closet, and neatly folded on a metal shelf were a beige sweater, a pair of gray slacks and white briefs. The soldier who had driven the jeep followed Jonathan into the space and stared coldly at him until he'd switched clothes. The soldier then pointed behind Jonathan at the floor, where there was a pair of worn, brown dress shoes with a black sock in each shoe. Jonathan slipped into them and tied the laces. He assumed that they wanted to ensure that none of his clothing had any kind of electronic device or visual tag. He left the room and returned to the suited men.

"I need to speak with someone senior," Jonathan said, making sure his voice didn't tremble from the nervousness streaming through his mind. He had to remain at least outwardly calm and display a semblance of confidence—without it, the fear of surrendering to their every demand would surely become self-prophesizing.

The men ignored him and continued to chat amongst themselves with their backs turned to Jonathan.

When Jonathan repeated his request, the bulkier of the men abruptly turned.

"No talk. One minute and we take you to city."

Jonathan didn't expect polite conversations or a welcoming party. After all, they let him come to Pyongyang because of fear. Fear of information. Fear of exposing their cyber-hacking ventures, their kidnapping of two Americans, or perhaps something worse that Jonathan still didn't know. While he was thankful that he hadn't already been executed, he also acknowledged that being alive in this hermit kingdom was a privilege, not a right—especially considering the potential threat he posed to the regime. As hard as it felt, he knew he was better off accepting the salient fact that his life could end at any moment. But in the meantime, he needed to make the most of this opportunity to discover what he could about Kevin. And most of all, to find Linda.

*   *   *

"Where are we going?" Jonathan asked from the backseat of the same jeep he'd ridden when he'd stepped off the plane.

"Quiet!" barked the suited man sitting in the front passenger seat. The other suited man, who was seated next to Jonathan, glanced at him derisively.

Jonathan's duffel bag lay behind the backseat on top of a two jerrycans and next to an opened bag of tools. Up front, between the soldier in the driver's seat and the man on the passenger side, was a Kalashnikov mounted upright within easy reach of either man.

The jeep turned without slowing, its tires screeching until it was heading straight again, this time on a narrower, well-paved road between large buildings whose monolithic design told Jonathan he likely was now in a government district. The road was desolate except for a lone bus operating with only a single working headlight. The sidewalks were sparsely lighted and desolate. They passed two apartment towers, their depressingly dilapidated facades resembling those he'd seen in Kyiv, and also in Moscow a decade earlier. Local architects must have gotten their inspiration from their Soviet mentors, Jonathan mused, and replicated their principal achievement: cramped, soulless, primeval communal housing.

A moonless, starless night now blanketed the skies. The driver turned into an alleyway and slowly edged into the underground garage entrance to a concrete edifice that had several colorful propaganda posters pasted on its exterior wall. Jonathan was escorted into the building and then shown to the window-facing side of a meagerly furnished office on the fifth floor. A portrait of Kim Il-sung and Kim Jong-il hung on the far wall.

A thin, thirty-five-ish man in a wrinkled white dress shirt with rolled up sleeves walked in. The two suited men quickly departed, leaving only the soldier standing by the door, his hand resting over his brown leather holster. The man glanced coolly at Jonathan, who reached out to shake his hand but was rebuffed.

"Sit." The man, who wore the same red lapel badge Jonathan had seen on others earlier, crossed his arms and half-sat on the edge of the metal desk, glaring at Jonathan with the same sneer a security guard might give to a newly apprehended shoplifter.

"Where am I?" Jonathan asked, gesturing toward the view outside the window, which featured a brightly lit, oversized statue about three football fields' length away.

"That is Mansudae Hill, the Museum of the Revolution, and in front of it the monument to Great Leader Kim Il-sung," the man said with pride creeping into his lightly accented English. "Because of our Supreme Leader, we are free from imperialists—first free from the Japanese killers and now free from you crazy Americans." He then twirled his finger next to the side of his large forehead—the international sign for crazy. "Completely free."

And free from progress, as well, Jonathan thought. He leaned forward, toward the window, for a clearer view of the monument. The bronze-surfaced statue looked to be at least six or seven stories high and featured the country's revolutionary founder wearing a light coat with his right, open-palmed hand raised toward the sky in a grand-standing pose. The bronze gleamed from floodlights positioned both at its base and on the roof of the large building behind it.

Jonathan turned to the man, examining him carefully, and asked, "And who are you?"

"Does it matter?"

Though Jonathan was relieved that the man was proficient in English, unlike the others who'd met him at the airport, he also sensed that he was not far up the food chain. Jonathan needed to speak to someone senior, someone with power, some who could fully appreciate the seriousness of the deal he was trying to make. Someone who could perhaps give him some information about Kevin. Someone who could reunite him with Linda.

"Tell me what happened in Ukraine," the man said, his unfriendly glare unflinching.

"I want to see Linda."

"Not for now."

"First, I must see Linda. Otherwise there's nothing else to discuss."

The man raised his brows, causing deep wrinkles to form across his large forehead. "Do you understand where you are? And who sets the rules?"

"Yes and no."

The man tilted his head.

"Yes, I know where I am. And no, you're not making the rules here. The kind of information I have could devastate your regime. So, tread lightly."

"You are just a man, seated in a chair. I can walk to this soldier, take his gun, shoot you now and someone will throw your body in the forest. It's that easy."

Jonathan's blood began pulsating wildly through his body. "I have deposited, in a safe place, detailed information about your operation with ScorpionCloud, including the facility in Pripyat. I have a flash drive with all the data your Ukrainian criminals took from Kevin Wyatt. That is everything I need to throw your country into the biggest crisis you've ever faced with the U.S. And all I have to do for that information to go public—and to the U.S. government—is to not come out of this country alive and well with Linda by next Tuesday."

The man shoved his sleeves a bit higher up each forearm as a frown crept across his face. "I am not sure I know what you are talking about."

"Don't fuck with me. I shut down your cyber-hacking center in Pripyat. I killed the Ukrainians and your Korean hacker working there. I know more than you can imagine. But my goal isn't to destroy your regime. I frankly don't care. I simply want Linda safe and out of this place. Then I will go on my way and you guys can continue your insane ways."

"Show me what's on the flash drive."

Jonathan shook his head. "Please. I didn't come this far by being an idiot."

"How else can I really believe you?"

"You are free to not believe me," Jonathan said. "But when one day next week your buddy Kim Jong-il turns on the television and the ugly truth hits him in the face, he's going to come after you and everyone else who could have prevented this crisis. You'll be the first to face a firing squad, I'm betting."

"Isn't there an expression in English...Seeing is believing?"

"How about another one: Walk blindly off a cliff." As his words kept rolling out his mouth, Jonathan began to feel the kind of confidence that would come to him when he was successfully arguing a case before a judge. The crucial factor was being able to correctly read your audience. "If Linda and I don't leave Pyongyang unharmed by Tuesday, I think you should start picking the clothes you'll wear for your last day on earth."

The man said nothing. His flat expression gave Jonathan little clue on whether he was making any headway but at least he was listening.

The man shifted his weight from the edge of the desk and stood up. "Linda is not well, as you must know."

"I want to see her now."

"Not possible. She is in a special clinic and needs medical care before she can travel or accept visitors. She is in good hands."

"I need to see her myself. Then you and I can talk."

"We have nothing more to talk about right now. I will discuss this internally and get back to you, perhaps in a few days."

Jonathan lifted his chin at the man. "You have five days to resolve this to our mutual satisfaction. Don't waste time."

The official shook his head and walked out of the room without saying another word. The suited men returned and grabbed Jonathan up from the chair by his arms.

Jonathan shook their hands off but followed their gestured commands to exit the room. This first meeting was not at all what he'd hoped for. He now feared, more than before, that they had called his bluff.

As the soldier and suited men escorted him into the elevator, Jonathan now wondered if the five-day deadline had any value. Maybe he had only hours left, not days. He needed a tailwind, the kind of luck that could give him something more than a bluff and a prayer. And he needed it quickly.

45

A MAN CAN DIE EITHER BY SURRENDERING TO AN ENEMY'S will or by standing honorably by his own rules. Only the latter would be acceptable to Jonathan. He was a lone warrior confronting a tyrannical regime, his life possibly hanging on one man's understanding of a few facts bundled into an enigma that Jonathan haphazardly concocted to buy time to save Linda's life.

Jonathan, again in the backseat of the jeep accompanied by his three guards, felt more like a prisoner now than when he'd first arrived in the city. He recycled what he'd said to the white-shirted man who'd interrogated him. He also recalled the man's every word, gesture, and facial expression—in an attempt to decipher whether his bluff had fallen apart. *Was I believable?* Jonathan asked silently through nervous, arrhythmic breaths. *Did I mess up? Or leave out anything crucial? Did I succeed in*

*scaring this man enough that he'd convince his superi-
ors to let Linda and me leave in peace?*

The jeep exited the parking garage, its engine gur-
gling, the clutch grinding, and the gasoline sloshing in
the jerrycans in the back as it maneuvered over uneven
pavement to reach the wide avenue ahead.

Jonathan sat wide-eyed and worried. There was
no telling where they were taking him, but he'd seen
a change in the faces of his guards, and it disturbed
him. And he couldn't count on anyone's help. Despite
the fact that Porter knew Jonathan was trying to get in
touch with Linda, he likely had no clue that Jonathan
had been secreted out of Europe, let alone that he'd
made it to North Korea. And in six days, Jonathan
thought, Cramer would act on the information he'd
mailed from Vienna, but by then it would be too
late—he and Linda could be long dead. With every
passing second, Jonathan's confidence withered. He
suspected that his ruse had unraveled, and that the
North Koreans were planning to kill him once they'd
realized he had no information of value to them. He
pondered this possibility as his heart thundered in his
chest. His hands, already clammy, began to shake. The
adrenaline sluiced through his veins as his growing fear
tormented his senses. Was he now being driven away
to be slaughtered? Perhaps in a forest, or a basement of
a secret prison, or an isolated field where they'd simply
toss his bullet-ridden body into a ditch? He regretted
not taking Porter into his confidence. A tragic end
that had been a possibility from the moment he landed
in Pyongyang now seemed all too probable. But he

refused to let it happen on their terms. If he was about to die, it would be by his own rules. His mind spinning, he quickly calculated his limited options.

From his rear seat, Jonathan spotted the illuminated bronze statue on Mansudae hill on the left as they shot past, and, about two hundred yards straight ahead, a smaller road that jutted downhill from the minimally lighted main road. No other vehicles were around. His eyes homed in on the driver's holstered firearm. He then scanned the narrow space between the driver's seat and the passenger seat—about a ten-inch gap. He lunged forward and yanked back the leather flap of the holster, clenched the revolver's grip and pulled out the weapon, all in under two seconds. The suited man who'd been seated next to him tried to grab his arm, but Jonathan elbowed his head and spun towards him, slamming the butt of the weapon's grip into the man's face. A loud cracking sound came from the man's nose, and he slumped to the other end of the backseat.

Both men in the front seats turned their heads, their faces bleached with panic.

Jonathan aimed the gun at the driver's head. "Turn right!" he shouted, swiftly pointing with his other hand at the smaller road. He spun once more and thrust the barrel into the neck of the injured man to his left, who had begun howling in pain, his nose bleeding profusely through his fingers.

"Turn right or I'll kill him!" Jonathan told the driver as he shoved the back of the injured man's head into the glass and again smashed him across the face with the weapon, causing him to collapse, unconscious, and slide halfway down his seat to the floor. "Now!"

The driver hit the brakes and abruptly veered onto the side road as Jonathan had commanded, but the vehicle jerked violently as its right tires caught the curb, propelling over the sidewalk and sending everyone airborne. Jonathan's head bounced into the vehicle's canvas top. The jeep then slammed back onto the pavement as the driver fought to regain control.

"Stop!" Jonathan yelled, trying to keep himself upright.

The soldier, gripping the steering wheel with both hands, slammed on the brakes. The jeep screeched to a halt, its tires locked up, with the sound of gravel pelting its undercarriage.

"Put your hands in the air so I can see them," Jonathan shouted to the men in front, his weapon again drawn on them. He wasn't sure if they understood English, but there was no mistaking good old gun-barrel dialect. "Up, up, motherfuckers."

The men grudgingly raised their hands in the air. They glanced at each other, perhaps sharing their disbelief at what was happening.

Jonathan pushed open the rear passenger door across from him, keeping his aim on both men in the front. He shoved the unconscious man out of the vehicle, his bloodied body twisting messily over the ground.

Jonathan opened his own back door and got out, too, and checked over his shoulder to ensure there was no one around to witness the chaos. Then, standing two feet from the front passenger side door, he aimed the weapon between the eyes of the suited man seated next to the driver.

"You, get out slowly!" Jonathan opened the man's door and gestured with his weapon. He realized the gun was shaking in his hand, but he did his best to keep his jumpiness in check.

The man scowled as he reluctantly stepped out, but his ashen complexion told Jonathan he was probably equally terrified. Jonathan took two steps back, signaling for him to get on the ground and lay flat. When the man had done so, Jonathan nudged his arms downward with a few gentle kicks, positioning them along his body. He then rested one foot over the man's back, just below the neck, while aiming the weapon at the disarmed soldier sitting in the driver's seat. "Your turn. Come here." With his free hand, he motioned for the man to hurry. The soldier scooted slowly across the seats and exited the vehicle, his hands raised over his head.

Jonathan grabbed the soldier's collar, spun him 180 degrees and thrust him into the side of the jeep, keeping the revolver's barrel planted in the man's neck. He frisked his pockets and took out a lighter, which he tucked into his own pocket. He then dug into the two leather pouches on the man's belt, discovering handcuffs with a set of keys resting in the lock. He snapped one end onto the soldier's right wrist, moved him rapidly to the other side of the jeep and attached the other end of the cuffs to the vehicle's door handle. He then grabbed the man's radio and the handcuff keys and threw them into the trees behind him.

Jonathan had to find a way to secure the other two men but he had little time, since someone was bound to come down this roadway at some point. He hurried to the back of the jeep, all the while keeping a close watch on the man lying on the ground. He opened the vehicle's rear hatch, grabbed the tool bag he'd spotted earlier next to the jerrycans and let the contents fall around his feet. There were three bundled ropes, a hammer, an assortment of screw drivers and wrenches, old wool gloves and a flashlight. He needed something that could restrain the man for at least twenty minutes.

He picked up two ropes and returned to the man on the ground just as the soldier began speaking angrily in Korean.

"Shut up," Jonathan replied loudly, holding the gun out over the jeep's canvas top, aiming it at the soldier's head. That silenced him.

Jonathan tucked the firearm behind his belt, keeping it easily accessible in case the man he was about to tie up made any wrong moves. He stretched the man's arms upward and over his back, tying them tightly with the thinnest of the ropes. Then he secured one end of the second rope around the knot and the other end to the nearest door handle on the opposite side the vehicle from the soldier. He looped the rope several times, then tied it into three knots. He then grabbed the third rope from the back of the vehicle and, using one end, tied the man's ankles together as tightly as possible and securing the other end of the rope by cinching it around the unconscious man's ankles.

Jonathan inhaled deeply and quickly gathered his thoughts. He leaned into the jeep and removed the loaded Kalashnikov that was mounted against the center dashboard. He then returned to the back of the jeep and shook the two jerrycans, taking the one with the most fuel—about half full. Clutching the revolver and jerrycan in one hand, and the assault rifle in the other, he crossed the road and sprinted up the slight incline to the main boulevard from which they had veered. Seeing there was still no one around, he sprinted to the other side, towards the brightly illuminated bronze monument, scanning ahead at the wide, paved space facing the statue and contemplating whether to go there as he'd originally thought, or to proceed to the building behind it. The square was wide open, with no shelter, and he feared he'd get spotted quickly. The roof of the building made more sense. He ran along the edge of the square, under the cover of trees and shrubs. He then spotted a door along the side of the large building, which he now remembered the white-shirted man had said was the Museum of the Revolution.

The additional hundred-plus yards to get there were exhausting. His lungs were nearly unable to pump breaths by the time he reached the door. He set the jerrycan down for a moment as he leaned forward, his hands on his knees, panting loudly and feeling his legs and chest ache. He had no strength to carry everything any farther. He removed the magazine from the assault rifle and threw it in the bushes to his right. He cleared the chamber and tossed the rifle behind a dumpster a few feet to his left.

The metal door in front of him looked heavy and thick, but it had a midsized window built into it. He took off his jacket, wrapped it around his right hand, and slammed his covered fist into the glass. The shards flew, some tearing his jacket but not his skin. He stood on his tiptoes, stretched his arm through the opening and pulled the latch.

He entered, holding the revolver in one hand and the half-filled can with gasoline in the other, and immediately noticed he'd penetrated a service entrance. An old elevator, with its safety cage closed, stood directly ahead in the darkened space, and to his right were stairs. He needed to reach the roof as quickly as possible before anyone arrived and stopped him. He raced up the concrete steps, barely able to discern their placement due to the low visibility from minimal outdoor light piercing the tiny windows along the way. His shoes stumbled into the risers and across the treads as he braved two-step leaps to climb the first floor and the second. As he reached the third floor his pace slowed to one step at a time. His breaths were harsh and loud, and his racing heart felt like it would pop out of his chest. He reached and passed the fourth floor, his mind intensely focused on not losing his footing as his exhaustion slowed him further.

When he arrived at what appeared to be the top of the stairwell, he spotted a door that likely led to the rest of the floor. Despite the near-obscurity, he suddenly caught sight of something shiny a few feet away, across from the door—a cage of some sort. Approaching it cautiously, his eyes now better adjusted to the dark, he noticed it was a shabbily positioned gated fence. He leaned in and eyed what stood behind it: more stairs. They were much narrower than those he'd just climbed, but stairs nonetheless. He assumed it was a restricted access to the rooftop—exactly what he wanted. But a large lock hung from the latch on the gate, and he knew it was pointless to try to break it. He took a step back, caught his breath and kicked the fence with all the strength his legs could gather. The gate shook loudly, and a bolt locking the gate's metal frame to the adjacent wall popped out and skated across the floor. He kicked again and the frame twisted slightly farther backward, with another bolt popping loose. He tried again. And once more. Finally, another kick knocked it nearly halfway down.

As Jonathan squeezed through the opening, pulling the jerrycan with him, his jacket caught on the fence's metal edges. He twisted himself free of the garment and jumped a step up. As he turned to continue upward, he heard sounds of a door bursting open, perhaps the door from which he'd entered the building.

He scurried up the nearly pitch-black stairwell, crashing hard into a wall as he navigated a sharp turn and clambered the last stretch of stairs. He leapt over the final step, stumbled and smashed head-first into a wooden door at the top, his body ricocheting and collapsing, the jerrycan and revolver clattering across the landing. He quickly spread his arms, his hands patting the floor in search of them. As the echoing noises grew louder, his fingers touched the revolver. He grabbed it, and a second later he found the jerrycan. He turned, searched blindly for the doorknob and turned it. To his surprise it wasn't locked.

He pushed the door and it gave way to reveal Pyongyang's nocturnal skies, the cool air rapidly filling his exhausted lungs. He ignored the throbbing ache in his ribs and ran onto the building's expansive, concrete rooftop, which appeared to be mostly flat. On the closer side of the building stood a faintly lighted urban landscape, with some highrise apartment blocks displaying a modest number of illuminated dwellings, while others presented only dark silhouettes. On the other, farther side of the building, the glistening bronze-colored raised arm of the Kim Il-sung statue dominated the view, while the rest of the body was hidden below the edge of the rooftop.

Jonathan quickly twisted-off the jerrycan's lid and with both hands tilted it to a forty-five-degree angle over the concrete. As soon as the gasoline began pouring out, he began walking rapidly in a slight arced path, and then beelined a route to the edge of the roof facing the statue, continuously pouring gasoline along the way. He then marched in a perpendicular direction, again dousing the surface with fuel, and quickly backtracked to finish forming a pattern that resembled the letter "J." He pulled out his lighter, knelt and lit up the puddle of gasoline nearest his feet. A whooshing sound came from the igniting fuel as the flames shot upward and out and spread rapidly along the combustible letter-shaped track he created. The fire was strong, with flames rising a foot above the surface. He only hoped it was bright enough to be seen from space—he was sure that America's electronic eyes were aimed at the heart of this cruel kingdom. Perhaps Porter's team would see this, he imagined. *Now they'll know.*

He walked to the edge of the roof and looked down. Dozens of soldiers were now racing across the square facing the statue, some looking up at him. "This is it," he whispered. He stood no chance.

A bizarre thought came to mind—a sort of ceremonial final act. He took out his revolver and aimed it at the statue's head. "Take this, dear leader," he said and pulled the trigger. The firecracker sound blasted, and a loud ding followed as the bullet ricocheted from the statue's metal exterior. He fired off more rounds until the weapon's last bullet blasted out and only benign clicks sounded from it. He tossed the weapon over the edge of the roof and walked away from the ledge, past the flames closest to him. He raised his hands and stared across the blaze at the door from which he'd accessed the rooftop. He waited.

The uniformed men quickly emerged, all of them armed, shouting and running towards him. A dozen of them, it seemed. They leapt over the flames, their barrels pointed at him, as he stood stoically, his hands still raised They hadn't shot him. They were planning to take him alive. This meant there was still hope; that there was a chance he could still get to Linda.

46

U.S. Embassy, Vienna

GEORGE PORTER, SITTING IN A SECURE EMBASSY ROOM, pressed his face into his open palms and groaned. He closed his tired, dry eyes, the frustration that had built up over the last twenty-four hours flooding through his system. He was tempted to bash Joe's eye sockets together. "I still can't believe you let him slip away."

"That's not my fault," Joe said sternly, no doubt tired of defending himself after this mammoth blunder. "And I could hardly predict that Brooks would actually do the impossible."

"How sure are you that it's him?" Porter mumbled through his hands before glancing up for the umpteenth time at an image displayed on the wall-mounted monitor. Porter was sleep-deprived and started to doubt even the obvious facts. After all, he'd hustled nearly non-stop since heading to Kyiv with his team. And a few hours ago, he arrived in Vienna from Turkey to join Joe at the embassy, just in time to receive the exasperating news: The BND—Germany's intelligence services—had reached out belatedly to the CIA Chief of Station in Munich to raise concerns about a U.S. passport used hours earlier at the city's airport. They'd found an anomaly on the identification page of the machine-readable passport (MRP), the Germans said. They'd also sent video stills from airport security cameras that allegedly showed the man they believed used the passport in question.

"Chelsea said it's most likely Brooks," Joe said, crossing his arms without even looking at the monitor.

"Of course it is. Do we have confirmation?"

"Yes, Pete agrees, too."

Porter didn't doubt the expertise of his imagery team in London, but it aggravated him that Jonathan was about to cause more trouble in some way that Porter had yet to discover.

"They probed the photos for over an hour. We can conference them in, if you want."

"Yeah, we need to make the ID."

Joe leaned over the table and dialed. The woman's voice answered on the third ring. "It's Joe. George is here."

"You want to chat about the images?" Chelsea said. "Or about something else I found?"

"Images first," Porter said. "I'm afraid to know what your 'something else' is."

At the same time Joe tapped keys on his laptop to rewind the images on the screen. "Chelsea, we're on image one." It was enlarged, grainy color picture of a man wearing a dark coat and eyeglasses walking into the airport terminal carrying a duffel bag. "That's when he first arrived. Look at his profile and body—"

"You mean to tell me Brooks grew a full mustache in a day?" Porter interrupted, examining the photograph. "And the hair here is gray. Brooks' is dark brown." As the words left his mouth, he conceded that a disguise was entirely likely. He'd done it himself and seen it done on many covert operatives throughout his career. But he was irritated with Joe and questioning the evidence felt like the right thing to do.

Joe, looking as though he'd rather be anywhere other than this room, took a breath and spoke up, "It's a disguise."

"Maybe, but the resolution sucks."

"It's the cameras," Chelsea chimed in. "The Germans haven't yet updated them. But look at the face—pretty similar."

Porter rubbed his jaw as he studied the screen. "Did Passport Control keep scans?"

"No," Joe said. "They only do that for biometric passports, not American MRPs."

"And the name again?"

"Bradley Kriegermann," Joe said, reading from a printout on the table. "No overseas travel in several years. We're still checking databases stateside. And it's the same name as on the Beijing flight's manifest."

"But there's no image of him boarding?"

"We've asked, and they're checking."

Joe clicked the next picture, which showed the same man walking to the Lufthansa check-in counter from a rear angle. "He got his boarding pass here but didn't check in any bags. And that counter was for the Beijing flight only, I'm told."

Porter shook his head. "If it's him, and he did board the plane, then he's using a counterfeit passport, which means it has a fake Chinese visa. So, who on earth could do this for him?"

"The North Koreans, of course."

"You're probably right, Joe." Porter conceded. "So, assuming it's him, and he took the flight, then he's going to meet a North Korean official somewhere in Beijing."

"Or he's on his way to Pyongyang," Joe said, hesitantly.

Porter tapped the table with his fingertips. "Where's the plane now?"

Joe glanced at the wall clock behind him. "It already landed. Maybe two hours ago."

"Get me Legal in Langley. We need to charge him somehow. Get red notices out. And revoke his passport. This may force the Chinese to stop him from boarding another flight. But we need to act quickly; to make sure he doesn't reveal anything to the North Koreans that he learned while he was aboard the *Mount Whitney*."

"What if we call Beijing police directly?"

Porter thought for a moment. "No. Without the legal part going first, they'll suspect something strange is going on. It may make it harder for us. Get someone out to the airport ASAP. Whether he's ending his journey in Beijing or has somehow gotten himself to Pyongyang, we need him located. And followed." Porter sat down again at the table and turned to the speakerphone. "What else you got, Chelsea?"

"You ready for something freaking insane, guys?"

"I hate surprises," Porter said, shaking his head.

"I just sent you ten pics."

Joe clicked the keyboard on his laptop. Seconds later new images popped up on the screen. "They're up."

Porter frowned. "It's farmland, right?"

"Only the first is zoomed out," Chelsea said, her voice raising with excitement. "Go to the next one."

Porter eyed the black and white night-vision image of what looked like a train on a single track. "Talk to me."

"I may be totally wrong, fellas," Chelsea said, "but, get this. NRO (National Reconnaissance Office) recently began using a new algorithm to scan satellite imagery for coded signals, like reflections from mirrors, flashlights, and so on. Since you asked me to keep watch on DPRK imagery, the East Asia team sent me these images. See the window at one end of the third car? It's the only source of light on the train, except for the engine at the front."

"Yeah, so?" Porter said.

"I looked at fifty-two stills, all of them taken a quarter-second apart. That light in the train car was not on constantly, but rather it was flickering. And it did so in a code—a coded message for 'SOS' and something else but I can't figure it out because of the time gap between each image."

"I'll be damned." Porter rose to his feet, his hands clutching his hips.

"I'm not done," Chelsea continued. "So that got me thinking. I checked a crapload of other imagery, from the various stations along the way, and going all the way back to Pyongyang. I tracked an ambulance at a warehouse near a military depot from where the train started its journey. And before that, the same ambulance was parked at the back entrance of Pyongyang People's Hospital Number Two. Click on the next image."

Joe tapped his keyboard and a new image popped up, this time in color and taken in daylight.

"See the patient on a stretcher? And the four men standing nearby?"

"Uh-huh," Porter uttered.

"I looked up the captured electronic footprint of the same general location at roughly the same time. We picked up seven cellphones, two of them assigned to the military—and it looks like one or two of the people next to the patient are in uniform."

Porter raised a brow. "Who are they, or to whom are those numbers tied to?"

"We don't know, but one cell number is tagged to an unknown user who only recently started making frequent calls to Ri Yong-nam, the deputy minister at their Ministry of Foreign Affairs. Ri's a well-known name among our State Department officials, by the way."

"Perhaps one of his officials is sick."

"No."

"Are any of his calls archived?"

"Hold your questions, George, and hear me out," Chelsea said. "Do I ever give you a presentation that doesn't deliver an awesome climax?"

Porter chuckled. "You have no idea how much I could use some awesome right now."

"I also ran an elint intercept and analysis in the vicinity of the train. One of the cellphones at the hospital made it onto the train. Also, coincidentally, Ri Yong-nam's own cellphone signal placed him on a road twenty miles north of the train at the same time someone signaled the SOS code from the train."

"You're telling me Ri is mixed up in this?"

"Well, jump to the next image."

Porter gazed at what seemed to be a close-up of the earlier picture of the patient on the gurney.

"It's a woman," Chelsea said, "And her right arm is hanging out of the gurney...and you see her bracelet? See how it has two gaps between the shiny parts?"

Porter squinted. "It's quite grainy now that you've zoomed-in so much."

"Ok, now flip to the last image."

Joe stood up. "Jesus."

Porter tilted his head. The image showed Jonathan's ex-wife holding a microphone while interviewing a person.

"Taken from news footage in Beijing last week."

Porter gazed at the brown leather bracelet on Linda's hand that held the microphone. It had two gaps between three flat silver accents. "She's on the fucking train." He puffed a lung-full of air. "Damn you're good, girl."

"I am," Chelsea said proudly.

Porter's mind was racing. The images apparently confirmed Jonathan's suspicions that Linda was in trouble. There was no reason he could think of to remove her from a Pyongyang hospital and put her on a train heading north. "Where is that train going, and why is she on it?"

"I'll need an hour or two more," Chelsea said. "There's a lot of imagery to check."

Porter turned to Joe. "Get me Aster. This is spinning out of control."

47

Near Kagam, North Korea

THE DEEP, MONOTONE HUMMING OF TIRES ROLLING AT high speed over a poorly paved road rumbled through the back of the truck where Jonathan sat shackled to a bench. There were more chains on him than what would have been used to restrain a wild animal. But he was thankful that death hadn't come, neither when his captors terminated his brazen deed on the museum rooftop nor thereafter. But although they hadn't killed him, they didn't leave him unscathed. His right eye was swollen from the vicious hit he'd taken from the first soldier who had knocked him down. And his sore back and already-injured ribs were left bruised and sharply aching after additional soldiers took potshots at him before throwing him into an armored vehicle sometime in the middle of the night.

Now nine soldiers, five of whom were hugging Kalashnikovs, sat surrounding Jonathan. They weren't about to give him a second chance to escape. He shivered in the painfully chilly air, missing the jacket he'd lost in the security gate at the museum.

The wind swirled violently. The back of the truck remained open, with parts of the canvas top flapping loosely in the wind. He gazed out of the opening at the road behind them. A desolate rural backdrop gradually came into view under the dawning skies. There were no other vehicles. The truck occasionally passed people walking along the dirt shoulder of the road, many dressed like farmers or laborers. One was walking an ox.

After another half-hour of mostly winding road, the truck pulled into a fenced area with rows of concrete and stone shacks spaced ten to fifty yards apart. The soldiers manhandled him out of the truck and pushed him forward, his arms and legs still fully shackled, across a patch of dead grass. A man in a grey uniform rushed up to him, said a few words in Korean, and pulled his arm, guiding him forcefully in another direction. All the soldiers followed.

Jonathan took small steps as he was led to another shack, its exterior walls browned by decay and its sloping corrugated steel roof almost completely rusted. The door opened and a guard in a simple olive-green uniform carrying a pistol in a leather holster stepped out from inside the concrete structure. He spotted Jonathan surrounded by guards and raised his eyebrows. He studied Jonathan for a minute and then waved at the soldiers to bring him inside.

Jonathan cautiously entered the cold, darkened space as a guard behind him barked loudly into his ear and then shoved him forward with the butt of his rifle. The building was even smaller inside than it appeared from the outside. His eyes darted ahead down the aisle that was lined on both sides by thick, floor-to-ceiling metal bars—there were four cells on each side. From the corner of his eye he caught something moving slightly. A person lay on the floor of the nearest cell to his right. He focused his eyes and saw it was a woman, curled in a fetal position over a small, filthy mattress. "My god," he choked as the realization hit him like a baseball bat to the face. "Linda!"

A hard, jagged object slammed into his back. He pitched forward, the shackles preventing his arms from cushioning the fall. He cried out as his body hit the concrete floor. The guards grabbed him by the chains that enveloped his arms, dragging him up the aisle. They opened a cage, and threw him inside, his left shoulder landing first. Another guard followed him inside the cell, barking and kicking him several times in the stomach and legs. Jonathan groaned and coughed loudly as he tried to will himself to absorb the excruciating pain.

"No talk!" a guard yelled.

"Linda!" She didn't answer. "Linda!"

The guard kicked him three more times in rapid succession. "No talk!" He stepped out of the cell and locked the cage door.

Jonathan could barely breathe; the pain from what he was sure were newly broken ribs slicing through his body with each inhalation and exhalation. But despite the agony, the shackles, the cold, the inescapable fear and the dehumanizing treatment, Jonathan was elated to have found Linda. Every bit of torture he'd suffered was now all worth it.

48

Andrews Air Force Base, Maryland

"YOU'RE NOT GOING TO BELIEVE THIS," THE WORDS CAME to Aster the moment he answered his cellphone.

"Porter, it'll have to wait," Aster said, "I'm at Andrews about to meet the president on Air Force One."

"It can't wait."

Aster peeked ahead as his driver steered the Suburban past the security gate towards the tarmac, where the tail of the aircraft came into view, the rest obscured by a large hangar. "You've got one minute."

"That Brooks fellow...he's in Pyongyang."

"What? Him too? You just told me about his ex-wife."

"I got word moments ago that he started a fire on the rooftop of a government building."

"How do you know it's him?"

"A fire in the shape of the letter 'J'."

"You for real?" Aster shook his head as the Suburban pulled up to a stop.

"They've arrested him. They were holding him at the building as of late last night."

"Brooks must have a death wish. Anyway, I gotta go. But I'll find out what we can do." He hung up, exited the vehicle, showed his badge to the Secret Service personnel at the bottom of the mobile stairs and climbed up to the plane. He then straightened his jacket and tie and stepped into the executive conference room.

"Better late than never," the president said as Aster entered. A few laughs echoed around the room.

"Sorry, sir. I wanted to catch you in person to discuss the situation about Ms. Fabre, our citizen detained in Pyongyang. We need to do something, and fast."

"Like what, bomb them?" The president stood up and frowned at Aster. "There's something fundamentally wrong with risking war over one person just because they hold a U.S. passport."

"It's actually three citizens, Mr. President," Aster said. "Kevin Wyatt, Linda Fabre, and, now I just got word her ex-husband arrived there too. And Wyatt is likely dead, based on what the Israelis are telling us."

"One, two or three makes no difference, frankly," the president said, his voice now raised. "I have three hundred million taxpayers to think about."

"With all due respect, sir," Aster said, "you asked to be briefed if better evidence came to light. Well, it has, as we added it in this morning's PDB." Aster knew he was up against a brick wall now that the National Security Advisor, the White House Chief of Staff, and the Director of National Intelligence—all of whom were presidential ass-kissers—had also assembled here. He had only a slim chance to convince the president to either go public about the Americans or privately threaten the regime. And he had little time to make his case, since the plane was about to depart for Houston.

"I read the PDB, Aster."

"Ms. Fabre was forced to leave Pyongyang and is somewhere in the north of the country, while Mr. Brooks is being held somewhere in the capital."

"They both went willingly," the president said, his hands on his waist.

"And what about Wyatt, sir?"

The president scowled. "Until we see a body, I'm not going to rely on rumors from Israeli intel."

Aster took a deep breath to tamp down his rising anger and stared first at the president and then at each of the men seated around the room. "There's been a long trail of evidence pointing to North Korean involvement in Wyatt's kidnapping and I know you've all seen it, too."

"Dammit," the president said, now crossing his arms. "We're on the cusp of curbing North Korea's nuclear program. Tell me what's better for our nation's security: Letting a crazy lawyer run wild in a wacky country in pursuit of an ex-wife, or irreversibly igniting the regime's ICBMs that could turn our cities into radioactive craters?"

Aster shifted his gaze to the patches of sunlight peering into the room through the half-dozen round windows. "He's not crazy. He's simply trying to save that woman."

"Answer my question," the president insisted. "What's better for our nation?"

"That's not my decision, sir," Aster said, restraining his instinct to reply more forcefully. "But there is no reason why this has to be an either-or proposition."

The DNI, standing next to Aster with his back leaning against the wall, cleared his throat and said, "Can we quietly negotiate their release?"

"Only after the disarmament negotiations have wound down." The commander-in-chief tilted his head. "The media catch any whiff of this yet?"

"Nothing," said his chief of staff. "I'm also sure Russians and Chinese have no clue either."

The president frowned. "Not yet, anyway."

"There is a remote risk in ignoring this," the chief of staff said. "People might react badly if they found out our government sacrificed three Americans for the benefit of the agreement, which ultimately is just an aspirational document."

"It's not a remote risk," Aster followed. "What if we stay silent about this and then North Korea for some reason decides to go public? If anything, you, Mr. President, would likely have tremendous public support if you took decisive, aggressive action against Kim Jong-il and forced him to release them and fully explain Wyatt's death." Aster scanned the room, waiting for some support, but all he saw were blank, noncommittal expressions.

"Ultimately, for decisive action to have credibility, you have to threaten a military response, and I'm not going to do that now," the president explained. "I'm not jeopardizing the negotiations. I'm not going to threaten anyone. We're already up to our eyeballs in Iraq and Afghanistan. And worse, I'm not going to taunt an unpredictable regime that could miscalculate and destroy half of Seoul and kill thousands of our men and women there. Of course, we'd eventually prevail, but it's not worth the risk." The commander-in-chief walked to the door and turned. "We'll see what transpires while we continue our negotiations. If they're still being held in a week or two, or if their lives are clearly in imminent danger, then we'll talk. Until then, we're done."

Aster was the last to leave the conference room, his anger and disappointment choking almost every other thought. As he stepped out of the plane and onto the top of the mobile stairs, he heard someone call out his name.

It was the chief of staff. "One quick thing," he told Aster, turning as if to check that no one else could listen in. He pulled Aster one step back inside the aircraft. "Look, the president knows this was not Kim Jong-il's shoddy work."

"Who said this?"

"Doesn't matter. We know the culprit is his idiotic son."

"Jesus, then why not bring this up in the damn meeting?"

"There's nothing to discuss. The president strongly believes that the youngest son is our best option for the future. Look, we were all young once. Everyone makes mistakes, especially in their twenties, right?"

"Mistakes?" Aster said. "Is that what you call it?"

"Drop it."

"Our president wants this idiot as the next leader?

"He's the lesser of two other evils."

Aster felt his face flush red. "So, it's not about the Six-Party talks, is it? This is all about protecting that young maniac."

"You're barking up a dead tree, while the president is protecting the forest. Let it go. If you want to get the Americans out, find a way that never goes public and never risks the regime's leadership, current or future."

"You're nuts."

"We're not taking down Kim's son, you hear me? Whether it's in two years or ten years, we want him in power."

Aster shook his head, looking over the chief of staff's shoulder at the president, who glanced eerily at Aster before turning to members of the press corps gathered behind him.

He walked down the mobile loading stairs, his soul dulled by the callous disregard for individual humans. As he stepped onto the concrete apron, his phone buzzed. He checked the screen and immediately froze in his tracks. A new text message arrived: "They're ready to talk. Bangkok. Tomorrow. Are we ready?"

"Mother of god," Aster whispered to himself. He clenched his fist in excitement. He headed across the vast tarmac as the presidential jet's engines wound up. He checked his watch and calculated the time zone difference before dialing. "Patch me through to Tucker in Bangkok—his cell number, since it's five in the morning there." Within seconds he heard the ring tone, and Tucker, the CIA Chief of Station in the Thai capital, answered.

"Aster here," he said to the man he'd only spoken to once before. "I know it's damn early, but there's something urgent I need you to do. And it's possibly the most important goddamned thing you'll do all year, and it has to be done exactly how I tell you."

49

Bangkok, Thailand

DEPUTY MINISTER RI YONG-NAM WAITED TENSELY, sipping his second cup of tea on an empty, queasy stomach at the Hello Strangers Café in Bangkok's Khlong Tan district. The air was quiet enough to hear a patron stir his mug a few tables away. From the window-facing counter, Ri eyed his driver standing at a small cross-street facing the coffee shop, next to the black BMW borrowed from the local North Korean embassy's fleet.

He picked up the burner phone he'd been given upon his arrival at the airport and quickly dialed. "Any news?" he asked in his native Korean. The man answered in coded phrases. The two Americans were now together in custody at the camp. "And how is the woman?"

"Very bad," the man answered.

Ri needed her alive, or else he'd have no leverage to negotiate an end to this madness. But the young Kim had insisted on her removal from Pyongyang and sent her to the prison camp, where there was no medical care for her serious condition.

The fear of Kim sending him before a firing squad had tormented him inescapably for days, infiltrating his thoughts as he'd swum with his ten-year-old daughter at the indoor pool, driven his parents to a cultural program and listened to his wife's soft breathing as she slept through his insomnia. Following Kim's orders was no longer like driving through fog at high speed but rather more like jumping off a cliff hoping a deep wave might whoosh by and save him from a rocky crash.

Ri felt the perspiration on his hands and back, despite the restaurant's well cooled air. He checked his watch again. The contact was already fifteen minutes late. And he wasn't completely sure the meeting was going to happen.

As he sipped his tea once more, a dark Chevrolet Caprice pulled up to the curb. A man wearing a sports coat and blue jeans got out, entered the coffee shop, and headed to the counter. After he'd ordered, he came straight to Ri and nodded. "I first need to know if you're going to record our conversation."

"I'm not," Ri replied, surprised at the question. "This would be bad for both of us."

"Much worse for you," Tucker said, his grin icy. He sat on the stool next to Ri. "I have exactly twenty minutes, and not a second longer, to give my boss a solid answer. And that answer will go straight to the top of the food chain, if you know what I mean."

"Whatever your constraints, I understand." Ri was sure Tucker was only bluffing. He'd seen many similar pressure tactics throughout his dealings with Western diplomats over the years. There was nothing alarming here as to form, but rather the substance of a possible deal was more important.

"Let me cut to the chase," Tucker said, his voice deep and authoritative. "Our government wants them back, alive and well. And within days, not weeks."

Ri raised his chin and crossed his arms. "If indeed we have them, we—"

"Dammit," Tucker barked, but then lowered his tone as a nearby patron turned her head. "Let's not play games, Mr. Ri. We know for a fact Brooks and Fabre are both in your government's custody, and you're entirely responsible for their well-being. Let me be crystal clear...our president will hold your government accountable for whatever happens to them."

"As I said, if we have them, we would like to return them." Ri wanted to keep the aesthetics of deniability for their detainment.

"Good."

"But only in exchange for silence."

Tucker leaned into Ri. "What do you mean *silence*?"

"The status quo. Nothing ever happened. Not a word to the press. No one looks back...and life goes on."

"That might be something we're willing to consider, but there's a far bigger problem." Tucker's face wrinkled.

"Wyatt. We believe your people had him killed. And that's not something we can overlook."

"We didn't kill him; it was the Mossad."

"But your thugs took him to fucking Syria. *Yours!* For goodness sakes, you guys kidnapped him, tortured him, threw him onto a ship and took him to Latakia. Don't start blaming others."

"The Israelis were on the ground. They messed up. They followed the men who were helping Wyatt's safe transfer, and they shot him, either deliberately or accidentally." Ri said this matter-of-factly, perhaps because he felt putting any spin on it was just a waste of time. He wanted Tucker to understand there was a subtle difference. "We really tried to keep him alive."

"Blood is on your hands," Tucker said, pointing at Ri's chest. "It's a real problem."

"So, what will it take?" Ri asked. "How can we wipe clean the Wyatt issue?"

Tucker puckered his lips and paused. He leaned in closer, stretched his elbow over the counter as his probing eyes met Ri's gaze. "There's a very quiet rumor going around that this whole shit-stinking-colossal-fuck-up wasn't under Kim Jong-il's watch. Rather someone else. Not military. Not intel. Someone careless, cocky, young. What do you think?"

Perhaps Tucker was simply fishing without a pole. Ri wanted to believe the young Kim had not thoughtlessly left breadcrumbs for foreign intel to sweep up. But as he remembered his taut meeting with the young Kim, the shock of the ultimatum and the decision he'd made when every belief he'd ever held seemed to twist upside down, as easily as an hourglass. "Mr. Tucker," Ri said, his hands beginning to shake as he lowered his voice. "I want to defect."

Tucker remained straight-faced, but Ri was sure the man was as surprised as he himself had been when he'd made the decision. It was likely Tucker already knew that Ri had been approached four times in recent years to defect and had refused to even entertain the thought.

"Did you hear me?" Ri added.

Tucker nodded and leaned forward. "Tell you what, give us information about Unit 121, and its subordinate organizations, like Unit 91 and Lab 110 and any other new groups. Give us that upfront as a sort of down payment, and I believe you'll be on your way to a deal, both for you and your slimy regime."

"I know of a new group—the one responsible for Wyatt's kidnapping and other activities over the last year," Ri said, wanting to strengthen his bargaining position. "But before I tell you more, I need guarantees. My family comes out first. I know you guys have done this for others recently."

"You would have to get them to the northern border. But once there, we can take them across the Yalu River and out of China."

"I understand." Ri felt a wave of sadness. He was betraying his country, a nation he'd defended with pride for so long. But if he took this step, he'd save the Kims from an international crisis, while also saving himself and his family. The CIA would welcome him with open arms, suck out everything he knew about the regime, give him a new identity, relocate him somewhere in the Midwestern United States, buy him a Subaru Outback. Hope crept back into his soul like a warm blanket. An escape from chaos now seemed at his fingertips. His wife, daughter and parents would be saved.

"Who ordered Wyatt's abduction?"

Ri was reluctant to say more. "I will tell later. For now, I need to know if we have a deal."

"A deal, Mr. Ri, would also mean many weeks of debriefing after you're free. We will want everything you know about the regime—unconditionally. And I must warn you, we won't tolerate any deception. If you don't meet your end of the bargain, your name will be leaked as the source."

"So I can be shredded by an anti-aircraft gun?

"Or charred by a flamethrower. Those are the most merciful ways your Supreme Leader eliminates his enemies. I am sure we both know some of the less merciful ways."

Ri raised his eyebrows. "Then you understand why I must defect."

"Aside from whatever we agree separately on the modalities of your defection, we still have to put in front of your superiors a workable and believable deal."

Ri nodded, worried that Tucker's proposal would be impossible to sell to the young Kim.

"This is what we want: First, you must take Brooks and his ex-wife to Panmunjom in the DMZ next Tuesday evening and allow them to cross the border. Second, transfer $4.8 million in hard currency cash, same location, same time. We will use the money to compensate Wyatt's family and secure a non-disclosure from them—so nothing goes public."

"And what about Brooks and Fabre?"

"We have ways to get their cooperation, too." Tucker crossed his arms. "Then, over the next week you'll clandestinely hand us the motherlode of info on all the Reconnaissance General Bureau units tasked with computer-hacking. In the meantime, we'll get your family out of the China border area while you travel once more to Bangkok. And we'll reunite you all in Seoul."

"That's reasonable," Ri said. But there was a catch. *Does the young Kim have nearly five million dollars at his disposal? And without alerting his father?* Ri had no idea. He got up and extended his hand.

"If I can get sign-off on the money, then I'm in."

Tucker paused and then extended his hand without getting up. "Don't take too long," he said. "It's all or nothing, and I'm not taking one step to initiate your defection until you can guarantee that we have it."

50

Bukchang Concentration Camp, North Korea

JONATHAN NOW UNDERSTOOD THAT THE TWO GUARDS who manned the shack would react with a Pavlovian response when he'd cry out for Linda. Each time, one of them would immediately run to his cell, unlock the metal cage door, and kick him senseless. He had provoked this response three times over the course of the morning, but Linda had yet to reply to his calls. On occasion during the prior night, he'd heard her groans through the hard rain that had trounced the metal roof, so he knew that at least she'd been alive. But at no time had she uttered his name or acknowledged his presence.

The stench of feces and urine continued to permeate the shack throughout the day, which explained why the guards stepped out so frequently.

Jonathan felt hungry, thirsty and nauseated, all at the same time. He struggled to rise up from the thin, rotten mattress that smelled like death, stretching his back and straightening his shoulders, accepting the pain that came with this effort. His left hand was shackled to a long chain that was bolted to one of the bars at the front of his cell and snaked across the floor to where he stood near the window. He touched the wall behind him and looked up at the light piercing the small window about a foot above his head. He reached up and held tightly onto the wooden sill at the bottom of the window and pulled himself up, while at the same time being careful to minimize the sounds from the chain.

He planted his feet onto the wall for balance and glanced out through the cracked glass. Tall sun-drenched grass, glistening from the recent downpour, separated his shack from another about twenty yards away, and past it he spotted a simple fence topped with barbed wire. Beyond that were trees and a forest-covered hill. There was no way of knowing what lay on the other side of his shack. Perhaps a similar landscape, or an army base, or a village. If he could find a way to escape, he thought, the wooded area ahead seemed like a good place to go, but it wouldn't be easy. Linda appeared to be in no condition to walk on her own. He'd have to carry her through the woods, uphill, and in the dark.

As he lowered himself back down to the cement floor, he felt the jagged surface of the wooden sill under his palms. Once standing, he continued to stretch his arms up to touch the wood surface, feeling every detail of its rough exterior. His fingers ran the length of what felt like a long splinter partly detached at one end, with a very sharp point. He gently slipped a finger under the loosened tip of the splinter. He pulled hard, harder still, trying to break it off as far as possible from the tip. As he added more pressure, he felt the space beneath it widening. Suddenly, the splinter snapped, the sound feebly audible. Jonathan froze, listening for any movement from the guards down the aisle by Linda's cell. He waited a few more seconds. There didn't seem to be a reaction.

He brought the splinter down to his chest and inspected it. Having the length of a pencil, but thicker at one end and thinner and sharper at the other, it would suffice as a rudimentary weapon, he thought. But he hadn't yet considered how to use it effectively. There were two soldiers in the shack, and he was unarmed in a cage with his wrist shackled by a chain. He was also injured and weakened by lack of sleep and food deprivation. He hid the splinter under the mattress and willed himself to concentrate.

* * *

Sometime after dusk, Jonathan got up slowly and quietly. His cell was not entirely darkened, as a faint light came in from the window—perhaps from a lamp outside, close-by. He reached under the mattress and retrieved the splinter. He then removed his right sock and immediately began to wrap the sock tightly around the thick end of the splinter. He did the same with his other sock, forming a sort of handle. He squeezed the bundled socks tightly together and pulled a loose string that had been hanging from the edge of the mattress.

He cut it free with his teeth and then started to tie it around the socks as securely as possible. Once he was done, he held the contraption in the air to examine it. He was satisfied that the makeshift dagger would serve its purpose.

For some time, he heard both guards conversing quietly at the end of the corridor, beyond his vantage. Then, when one of the guards stepped outside, Jonathan looked around his cell, staking out the best position for triggering another Pavlovian response. He clenched the makeshift dagger in his right hand and hid it behind his back. He had to move as quickly and accurately as possible, or the guard would have time to reach his holstered pistol and shoot him dead.

"Linda," Jonathan said faintly. He repeated the call a little louder.

The guard hissed and Jonathan heard the chair screech across the floor. Then fast footsteps. The guard appeared behind the metal bars, his angry glare barely visible with the ambient light bleeding through the cell's small window. Jonathan tightened his grip on the weapon.

"Linda," Jonathan said again, taunting him to enter the cell. He held his breath.

The guard unlocked the cage door, stepped in and, as he raised his arm, Jonathan lunged at him, hurling the sharp end of his makeshift weapon. The splinter entered the man's neck with ease as Jonathan crashed into his body, throwing his other hand over the man's mouth to silence him. The guard fell backwards into the cement wall just as Jonathan quickly plucked the dagger out and plunged it again into his neck. This time a stream of blood shot out. He'd hit the carotid dead-on. The man collapsed to Jonathan's feet without making a sound.

Jonathan grabbed the guard's pistol from his holster and set it onto the ground as he sifted through the man's pockets. He found the keys to unlock his shackled wrist as well as another set of keys that he hoped were for the cell doors. Once freed, he picked up the gun and headed to the front entrance, glancing briefly at Linda lying in her cell. He ached to go to her, to touch her, to check for breath, to reassure her that he was here, but he could not do that yet. He carefully positioned himself with his back against the wall behind the arc that the front door would rotate when it opened. And it would open soon when the other guard walked back in.

Jonathan tried to catch his breath, his heart still pounding as if he were running a marathon. That very moment the morbid thought sunk in that he'd just killed a man. A thirty-something-year-old guard who probably had a family. Living parents. Friends. A life outside this wretched prison. A man blindly following the orders of a repressive, militaristic regime in order to feed his family. Jonathan shook his head, his mind weighing the torment that had brought him here and forced his hand. There wasn't time to immerse himself in guilt, nor to rationalize that the killing was necessary to save himself and Linda. He also quickly understood another reality: he'd likely have to kill the other guard, and very soon.

He waited, his blood pumping. He gazed at Linda lying in the darkness behind the metal bars fifteen feet ahead of him. She deserved his every effort, free of any moral restraints. His rage and anxiety brewed. He waited impatiently for the second soldier to return.

51

A LOUD CRACKING SOUND SHATTERED THE EERIE quietness as Jonathan smashed the butt of the pistol into the back of the guard's head. Jonathan quickly closed the shack's door and jumped over the man, who had now collapsed on the floor. He knelt in the darkness, felt for the man's head and again pummeled it with the weapon until he began feeling a steady flow of warm fluid drain over the scalp. He could not allow the guard the chance to regain consciousness. Jonathan stood up and kicked the man's head three times more, dragged him back to the cell he'd been in and shackled him to the metal bars just in case he was somehow still alive. He then ran to Linda's caged door, unlocked it with the other keys he'd found on the first guard.

Once inside the darkened cell, he quickly approached Linda, looking for signs of life, but she was still curled up in the same fetal position she'd been in when he was first brought to the shack. He got down on one knee, gently placing his hand over her shoulder.

"Linda, it's me. Jonathan."

Only a faint murmur came from her. And she looked awful-grayish complexion, barely any hair, her body twisted into a ball. Her body twitched once as he reached out his hand and delicately caressed her face.

"I'm taking you out of here. There's a forest about five hundred yards away, and we need to get there as quickly as possible. But it won't be comfortable, and you can't make a sound."

She shifted her body slightly and spoke but too faintly for him to hear.

He leaned in, placing his ear over her mouth. "Tell me again."

"I'll do my best. Thank you for finding me."

"This may hurt." He took a deep breath, looped his arms around her and lifted her off the ground. He then edged her up and slowly bent her torso back over his shoulder. She groaned, her hands clenching the back of his sweater. His legs shook until he stepped forward and adjusted his balance.

"I'm lighter than before—they haven't fed me in days."

Jonathan was surprised she had any humor left in her, given how weak and ill she appeared.

He slowly opened the shack's door about an inch and peeked out. Several more concrete structures were visible some thirty yards away, but there were few lights in the distance and, thankfully, no guards in sight. He pushed the door further, took a half-step out and scanned a full hundred eighty degrees from his position. There was still no one in sight. Holding Linda tightly around her hips, while the rest of her body rested over his shoulder, he stepped out of the shack and turned right in the direction he'd seen from his cell window earlier in the day. Though the forested hill was invisible in the night, he knew where to go. Shielded by the darkness, he walked over the soggy grass, carefully gauging each step so as not to slip or trip.

He slowly made his way past another prisoner shack and at about fifty yards out, the metal perimeter fence came faintly into view. He half-staggered to its edges, his legs and upper body tiring from Linda's weight. As he lowered her gradually to a sitting position and she curled into a ball on the ground, he observed that most of the metal appeared dilapidated, much of it rusted and some links cracked and twisted. He glanced up at the spiraled pattern of the barbed wire along the top of the fence. There was no way he and Linda would be able to climb over it. He scanned the bottom of the fence and spotted gaps between the lowest point of the wire mesh and the muddy ground. It was their best option.

Jonathan lay on the wet grass and began pushing the wire mesh up slowly, attempting to minimize the clinking of metal. He pushed the mesh farther up and slid under the opening. He then stretched his arm towards Linda.

"I have to drag you to me," he said in a loud whisper.

She moved his way but only made it an inch or two. He pulled her outstretched arm across the grass until her upper body was mostly under the fence opening. He crawled fully to the other side while holding the wire up as far as he could and then got up on one knee. He lifted the mesh to the top of his knee and stretched his arms down to Linda. He clenched her right arm and right leg, and she dug in her left foot as though to push. He dragged her across the opening and then again picked her up and folded her body over his shoulder.

From there he carried her away from the fence, lurching through the dark as carefully as possible, so as to not make noise. Moments later, he felt thick gravel under his feet. Anticipating train tracks, he stopped, squinted through the dark and slowly crept forward, using his feet to search for the tracks. Falling here would be both dangerous and painful. And if he dropped Linda, the blow to her head would certainly kill her.

He navigated across the tracks, descended the gravel incline and continued straight, over muddy soil and patches of tall grass, through light but prickly shrubs and finally into the dense woods. He leaned on a tree trunk and caught his breath. He was thankful he'd made it this far, but there was no time to rest. Someone was bound to discover the guards' bloodied bodies and sound the alarm.

His first fifty- or sixty-yard trek into the forest seemed manageable, despite the rough ground and the uneven distribution of Linda's full weight across his body. But it wasn't long until he began feeling the terrain tilt upwards, as he'd expected. The tough walk became infinitely more arduous as he tried to keep the same pace heading uphill. He persisted, carefully positioning each step as securely as possible before shifting his weight forward.

Jonathan continued up the hill. The only sounds he heard were the rustling of leaves in the trees, the crushing of twigs below his feet, and his own harsh breaths venting every molecule of oxygen they could harvest. He ignored the pain and fatigue in his legs, the needling discomfort in his ribs, and the sore bruises on his back and face. His knees were on fire after hundreds and hundreds of steps. He stopped, slowly turned half-way around and glanced downhill through the trees. He shook his head, disappointed by the distance that separated him from the camp—he guessed he'd only trekked a mere quarter-mile at best. He turned and continued his strenuous journey up the steepening incline. Each step felt as if his shoes were filled with lead. He grabbed whatever he could to help him up—sometimes a tree trunk, others, meager branches from the shrubs he passed through.

Jonathan's front foot suddenly caught something in the darkness. He collapsed forward, but quickly twisted his chest and braced Linda with both arms to cushion her fall as he made impact with the muddy, leaf-covered ground. She let out a grunt, clearly in pain.

"I'm sorry," he said, panting, and reached his arms around her tightly, bringing her to his chest. "I slipped."

She patted his cheek lightly and mumbled some words he didn't catch.

"Shh," he said. "We'll be okay. Just hold on while we climb the rest of this hill."

As he turned, Jonathan again glanced down the hill at the camp through the mass of trees that surrounded him, but this time there was movement. He spotted what looked like flashlights blinking at different ends of the camp, and then a vehicle rushed across the center of the camp, heading rapidly in one direction, turning, and heading back the other way. The guards would soon expand their search outside the camp, if they hadn't begun already.

Jonathan was in pain, his body slowly draining of energy. But to reach a safe distance, he guessed they would have to go at least two miles through the night. He hadn't come this far to risk losing Linda once again. She moaned slightly, and he pulled her to him more tightly. And then he continued on through the darkened forest.

52

Pyongyang, North Korea

RI YONG-NAM BREATHED ERRATICALLY FOR THE duration of the elevator's descent down twenty-two floors as he held his daughter and wife tightly in his arms. He'd returned from Bangkok that evening, stopped by his parent's apartment and raced home from the airport as quickly as he could. He'd told his wife everything she needed to know and his daughter just enough so she'd not cry the entire night. He led them out into the lobby as quietly as possible, carrying only one large suitcase and a medium-sized vinyl bag so as not to raise suspicion. He accompanied them out of the apartment building under cover of darkness, turned the corner, and reached a military van that sat idling at the far end of the parking lot with his parents already in the back seat.

He kissed his wife and hugged his daughter, his eyes now tearing as they had hours earlier when they began separating out their most valuable possessions. For the next six hours his family would be incommunicado, heading north to the Chinese border as discreetly as possible. He'd armed the driver with four authentically stamped travel permits he'd typed on Ministry of Foreign Affairs letterhead. Once they reached a pre-designated location along the banks of the Yalu River, Tucker's contacts would take them across the water into China and then on to a safe house.

Ri watched as the van drove off, his emotions spiked with a chaotic cocktail of worry, sadness and joy. He was hopeful, if not confident, they would be safe as long as he could convince the young Kim to shell out the $4.8 million in hard currency. frightened him beyond anything he'd ever faced. Ri's proposition was Kim's get out of jail free card, but Ri feared the young man was too foolish to know when to take a good offer. If he refused to pay or simply had no access such large funds, Ri would forfeit his defection, and the American would likely betray Ri to the regime. He tried to comfort himself by acknowledging that his family stood a chance to be free. But there was no guarantee of that.

He returned to his apartment, plunged into his sofa, and pulled out a cigarette. But before he could light it, the phone rang. He turned apprehensively, glancing at the clock. There were few times the phone had ever rung after ten at night.

He took a deep breath and answered. The man's voice on the other end of the line was frazzled, his words loud, his breaths tense.

"How could this be?" Ri sprang to his feet. "When did they escape? And how?"

"They got out about an hour or two ago, we think," the man said. "I am assembling soldiers, and we'll hunt for them in the hills south and east of here—it's the only place they can be."

Ri felt his skin clamming with cold sweat. He didn't know the camp's commander well, but he feared that whatever the man was about to do would risk killing Brooks and Fabre. Without them alive, his deal with the American government to keep Kim's involvement quiet would collapse and Ri's family's defection would be discovered. Ri—and likely his family, too—would be dead.

"Do not send any people after them. That is an order."

"But I also have orders to detain them."

"You will obey me, or I will make sure you become a prisoner in your own camp."

53

Two miles south of Bukchang Concentration Camp

WITH LINDA FIRMLY IN HIS ARMS, HER WAIST BENT OVER his shoulder, he moved through the forest in the pitch-black night as if he were blindfolded. He tried in vain to find anything for his eyes to lock on to, but there was no moonlight, no stars, not a single source of light. The claustrophobia began to choke him. His racing heart pounded his chest. The forbidding darkness permitted no respite. He imagined that even in the dead of space an astronaut at least had distant light to give a sliver of hope. Here there was none. He wished he'd had a lighter, or a flashlight, to help him navigate. But no, in this deepest of blackness, each step meant he could again fall with Linda in his arms, and that would surely kill her. Blinded by the unrelenting sinister night, he etched a slow path forward using his other senses. The flutter of a bird's flight, the chanting insects, the fast-footed sprints of rodents, the breeze that carried a musty scent of foliage—these were sounds and smells that told him he was still somewhere in a forest.

Not before me, he thought. *You will not die before me*. The fear made him stop and raise his hand across her back. He felt her chest expand slightly. *Thank God*. She was still breathing. He clenched his jaw and lumbered on.

A feeble cough exited her mouth.

"Linda?"

She didn't answer.

"You'll be fine," he said, his voice trembling, a renewed surge of fight coursing through him. "You won't die before me, you hear me?" he added, chuckling for her benefit as he sniffled to himself, fighting back tears. "Men are supposed to die first. And dammit, you're going to outlive me; you're getting the hell out of here, back to New Orleans, choose from any one of the news channels who'll fight each other to have you. That's what's going to happen—your career, your life—you're only going to die peacefully an old, grumpy woman, on your rocking chair somewhere by the ocean. I will not accept anything else." He squeezed her closer into his grasp, the ache in his arms momentarily obscured by the rush he'd gotten delving deeper into his words. Tears began streaming down his cheeks. "I...I love you."

Not a word came from her; only a sputtered moan, like the ones he'd heard come out of her lips occasionally over the last few hours.

He began walking again. Slowly, precariously, as he mentally measured each step, sensing whatever obstacle lay in his path before solidly planting his next foot forward over the uneven ground.

Jonathan could not think of a more helpless and hopeless situation than the one they were in now, but he propelled himself forward with images of her from happier times. The blue cocktail dress she wore when he graduated law school. The embarrassing moment he spilled his glass of red wine on it. And how she laughed it off so comfortably, as only an extraordinary woman can. *This is why I am carrying you. Exceptional. Brilliant. Compassionate. Brave. Everything I ever dreamed my companion through life would be. I'm not worthy.*

Sweat and tears coated his face. His skin itched and burned from the mosquitoes that had gone after whatever blood he had left and the brush that had been scraping him raw since they'd escaped the camp. His lips were cracked and dry but stinging from dripping perspiration. They hadn't had a drop of water since morning. And no food for him in two days.

The forest seemed unending. It was like he'd gone on for countless hours. There was no telling exactly how long, but long enough to know his body would soon hit its limits.

Finally, he had to stop. His knees and legs were too weak to carry Linda any farther. He gently lowered her onto what felt like a patch of soft, wet grass. Once she was settled, he simply dropped to the ground next to her. His lungs vented deep breaths. He felt every part of his body throbbing in pain.

He didn't move. "I don't know if I can..." he whispered to himself, wondering if he could continue, even after a long break. And if so, for what purpose? To die a mile farther, or two, or three? His mind suddenly filled with worry. The dark, starless night made it impossible to navigate now that he could no longer see the camp from his former hilltop vantage point. Had he traveled in a wide circle? Would he suddenly find himself back near that camp again? He forced himself to take a deep breath and began to calm down once he realized that they had not descended for any length of time.

He looked up and saw only the solid darkness, not the leafy branches he knew crisscrossed high above. The breeze had picked up, chilling his limbs and chest. He huddled over Linda, rubbed her arms and legs, and rested for a short while. Then he struggled to his feet and took her up into his arms as before.

As the night progressed, a few brief, faint patches of clear sky finally let a little starlight filter through, revealing the silhouettes of trees above him—thin but tall trees on the sloping side of what was likely a tall hill. He carried her distances he measured roughly in paces, and it surprised him that he had been able to lumber this far.

Then the rustling of leaves and creaking of branches dissipated as he edged forward, caught by a sudden gust of wind that carried with it the fresh scent of grass. He guessed he'd reached a clearing—a field perhaps. With Linda still draped over his right shoulder, he continued ahead, the tall grass brushing his calves. He struggled forward, his legs burning, his arms clenched around her to keep her from sliding off his shoulder.

He walked farther, and farther still, his every append-age burning feverish with fatigue as the clearing lead up to another incline. Twenty paces in, the uphill trek grew even steeper.

The grass ruffled loudly in the strong air, but sud-denly a faint buzzing sound emerged. Jonathan looked around and pulled her more tightly into his shoulder, his every step calculated to avoid falling on the slope's moist, slippery grass. The buzzing rose in intensity. He stopped to listen.

"Linda, you hear that?" he gasped, his legs burning, his knees grinding. The sound deepened. "You hear it?" He was suddenly gripped by simultaneous fear and hope. *A chopper?* He felt his own winded breaths escape his body as he listened keenly.

There was no more power left in him to flee further, but he had to try. He sucked in a gulp of air and pushed himself forward, his arms still clenched around Linda's thighs and back side.

His foot slid sideways on the grass. "Jesus!" He stumbled forward but quickly corrected his balance, barely avoiding a fall. The weight pressing him down made every step more agonizing, the pain needling straight up his ankles toward his spine.

The wind and deafening noise of what was surely a helicopter blasted at him with the force of a hur-ricane. He could see nothing. Not a flash of riveted steel. Not a single light. Whomever they were, he thought, at least they hadn't yet shot him. He was still standing, squinting to see through the violent torrent of air. The noise and wind intensified. As he adjusted his footing, his right knee gave way. He collapsed but lunged sideways, trying to protect Linda's fall into the thick grass. The air blew his hair back hard, almost painfully. He huddled over Linda, covering her head with his hands.

Out of nowhere, a hand grabbed his elbow. Another grabbed his shoulder and pulled him back. He held on to Linda's arm for a second longer, until whatever phantoms had taken him pulled him loose of her.

"Let's go!" a loud voice pierced the air.

"No!" Jonathan shouted, but then realized he'd just heard a man yell in English. He tried to shake off the tight grips around his arms—he needed to get to Linda—but he felt as if he was floating, held up by the force of two or three people who'd dislodged him from her.

Suddenly, a horizontal green streak of light sliced open the darkness ahead of him. The light grew downward. *A ramp?* he guessed, his eyes glued to what was happening in front of him. *The back of a helicopter.* He noticed the steel belly of the aircraft. Four bulky men ran out, two of them coming straight towards him while the other two, who held assault rifles, took up positions on his flanks.

"It's just you two?" the first man's voice broke through the loud noise of engines and palpitating blades.

"Yes," Jonathan said, now able to see more clearly the camouflaged men on each side of him. They wore night-vision goggles and helmets, and their sweaty faces were painted brown and green. He assumed they were

U.S. Special Forces, and it brought him an immense feeling of relief. He spun back to Linda. "She's seriously injured," he told them. "You have to—"

"We'll get her right up," answered the man closest to him.

The men seated Jonathan down on the metal floor of the empty cargo bay. Another armor-clad man rushed toward him.

"I'm okay," Jonathan said as he waved off the man and turned again, trying to find Linda. "She's the one who's injured." He tried to stand but fell back down.

Three masked, helmeted men in camouflage, their assault rifles flung over their backs, shuttled back and forth from the helicopter to where Linda lay in the grass. Finally, one brought down a stretcher and within seconds they'd hustled her into the dimly lighted chopper.

The ramp began closing as the last soldier sprinted back into the aircraft. The turbines roared. The men secured the stretcher to a raised metallic bracket bolted onto the inside fuselage.

Jonathan stood, stumbled forward and held himself up near her side, gently taking her hand into his.

I will not let you die.

"Take a seat, sir," shouted the man who appeared to be in charge.

"She's my everything...and we've gone through hell." Jonathan barely had the strength to speak. He tightened his grip. A soldier—probably a medic—began shouting orders to his colleagues as he took Linda's vitals. Another soldier infused an IV into her arm.

Jonathan held on to her cold wrist, suddenly noticing the low temperature of her skin. His heart dropped. He could barely breathe. He wanted to believe she would make it. He raised her hand to his mouth, pressed it hard against his lips, and kissed it.

"Sit down, please!" a soldier said, pulling Jonathan back by his arm and pointing at the fishnet bucket seats on the other side. "We'll take care of her. But we've got four hundred miles to go, and the next thirty minutes are gonna be rough, treetop flying—sharp turns, steep dives, fast pullups—to avoid their radars. So, buckle up."

Jonathan reluctantly sat down and secured his belt over his lap, all the while keeping his eyes on Linda. His breath caught when he saw the medic place an oxygen mask over her face.

The medic suddenly began CPR, pumping her chest with his weighted force. Jonathan unbuckled himself and leapt up but another soldier pushed him back into his seat.

"Sit, dammit," the man said loudly. "They're doing everything they can." He scooted to sit next to Jonathan and pressed his shoulder back.

Jonathan felt his heart hammer through his chest, his eyes never leaving Linda. His soul filled with refusal, with despair that they'd come so far only to see her now on the verge of death. He would not accept this twisted fate. He gazed at the tranquil closed eyes that had captured his soul some twenty-five years ago. He watched the medic pump life into her, his motions hard. He studied the medic's expression and then, as her arm drooped over the side of the stretcher, he felt his eyes well up.

The piercing sounds of the turbine filled the cabin, and the aircraft swayed abruptly, pitching downward and then upward every few seconds. All the while the soldiers continued to resuscitate her, and Jonathan watched helplessly.

Please, live, live. God, please.

54

Desiderio Army Airfield, South Korea

JONATHAN SAT WITH HIS HEAD DOWN, STARING AT his feet, as the helicopter swayed violently through the stormy skies. He wiped the dried tears off his cheeks. He didn't have it in him to glance to his right at a lifeless Linda, covered by a blanket, but he held her cold hand in his. The medics and crewmen were seated across from him, their faces expressionless and shoulders sagging, just as they had been since they'd ceased their attempts to resuscitate Linda.

The chopper banked steeply, and one of the men signaled to Jonathan by tapping his watch and then waving three fingers in the air. The aircraft pitched forward, starting a rapid descent, the turbulent air still battering the fuselage. Within minutes it slowed, hovered some distance, and the wheels touched the ground. The whooshing of blades diminished in intensity, as did the whine of the turbines. The rear ramp lowered. Jonathan unbuckled his belt and immediately felt his eyes tearing again. He got up, doing his best to stand upright, and motioned for the medics to unhook her stretcher and move it to a gurney.

As he turned, he looked out the window and was surprised, although he somehow knew he shouldn't be, to see that one of the men waiting for him on the tarmac, next to the ambulance that was waiting to transport Linda's body, was George Porter.

He and Porter would have plenty to say to each other. And, once he returned to New Orleans, he'd have plenty to talk about with Cramer Banks. But for now, what he needed to do was to say goodbye to the love of his life. And he wanted to do that alone.

And so he motioned to the medics to step aside. And he began to walk her down the ramp himself.

Acknowledgments

I owe a debt of gratitude to my dedicated circle of authors, editors and proofreaders, any of whom have debated various twists and turns of this storyline, poked holes in the plot, swotted through early drafts, and pushed me to rewrite parts that needed strengthening. And this last step reminds me of Stephen King, who said, "revising a story down to the bare essentials is always like murdering children, but it must be done." And as uncomfortable as the making of a thriller can be at times, this invaluable circle of professionals gave me the encouragement and support I needed to write at my best. I must make special mention of Julia Borcherts, my editor. Having previously edited the first two books in the series, Tranquility Denied and The Serpent's Game, she holds the deepest knowledge of the protagonist and other recurring characters. But more importantly, her experience with crime fiction, sharp instincts, mastery of the English language and ability to logically deconstruct plots, are simply amazing. I'm also deeply appreciative of the entire team at Down & Out Books for their enthusiasm and professionalism. Ultimately, their collective efforts have made Jonathan Brooks a character you may want to invite into your homes, represent you in court in time of need, or even save you from a burning building or a sniper's vengeful aim.

I also extend my thanks to my multinational cadre of current and former military service members and law enforcement experts as well as members of the intelligence community and the diplomatic corps. Their insights and suggestions helped bring an added sense of reality to this novel. And many thanks as well to the lawyers and business consultants I have befriended in my twenty years of legal practice. There are too many to name, but almost every one of them played a part in my writing, sometimes by being the inspiration for characters—except for villains, of course—or by doing what lawyers do best: question everything, twist facts and circumstances to fit a particular point of view or purpose, and add a touch of cynicism.

Also, this novel required a significant amount of research—substantially more than I ever did for my prior books. This research included on-site visits to North Korea, China and Ukraine. I am immensely grateful to those who helped me on these interesting travels, including the great crew at Koryo Tours in Beijing who made it possible for me to explore Pyongyang, Kaesong and the heavily fortified North Korean side of the DMZ. I am also deeply thankful for the friendly, professional team at SoloEast Travel in Kyiv for their assistance in my visit to the Chernobyl Exclusion Zone, including Reactor No. 4 and the abandoned town of Pripyat, as well as other defense-related sites in northern and central Ukraine.

To my wife, Elena, and my daughter, Slava, a huge thank you for the endless love, support and belief in my literary endeavors, which I know at times requires a family to endure sacrifice. And this is especially true because my writing is in addition to a demanding legal career.

Finally, I'd like to thank you, the readers. Your feedback and support, both in-person and online, have helped sensitize me to reader preferences and also push me past boundaries I never thought I could cross. There is much more to come from Jonathan Brooks, and I'm delighted to take readers on these journeys, some of which at times may embody more reality than fiction.

Additional Information on North Korea

If you are interested in learning more about North Korea, you can purchase a copy of Frieden's photography book *North Korea: A Photographic Journey through the Hermit Kingdom* (Avendia Publishing), available at Amazon.com. This book provides a unique photographic journey through North Korea, one of the most isolated and least understood nations on earth. The pictures were taken by A.C. Frieden during his recent research trip to the reclusive nation. The images capture a wide range of North Korean life, from soldiers guarding the DMZ to farmers struggling to survive, from modern high-rises in Pyongyang to dilapidated housing in Kaesong, and many images the North Korean regime doesn't want the West to see.

Also, you may scan the QR code below to see a short video of Frieden's research travels through North Korea.

A.C. FRIEDEN

The Jonathan Brooks Series

TRANQUILITY DENIED

THE SERPENT'S GAME

THE PYONGYANG OPTION

LETTER FROM ISTANBUL

DIE BY NOON

Note to book clubs, bookstores, and libraries:

A.C. Frieden gives readings across the country and overseas, including fascinating presentations about his globetrotting research that goes into writing his books. If your book club, bookstore, or library would like to feature A.C. Frieden, please contact us. We would be delighted to co-sponsor such an event.

Please contact us at:
media@avendiapublishing.com

A.C. FRIEDEN

A.C. Frieden is an international author of mysteries and thrillers, including the acclaimed Jonathan Brooks espionage series (Avendia Publishing / Down & Out Books). Frieden is also an attorney, seaplane pilot, PADI scuba instructor, martial artist and former army sniper. He was born in Senegal and raised in India, Brazil, Switzerland and England before moving to the United States in his teens. Today, you'll often find him in a far-flung hotspot researching future books, like his recent investigative travels to North Korea, Russia, Cuba, China, Qatar, and India. He has faced the chaos of a Central American coup, piloted small planes over the Andes and the Panama Canal, explored remote underwater sites in the Indian Ocean, surveyed the damaged Chernobyl nuclear power plant, followed the Che Guevara trail in Bolivia, tracked down drug traffickers in Paraguay, investigated former Soviet missile bases, and much more across nearly eighty countries. Frieden is a member of Mystery Writers of America, International Thriller Writers, and the Military Writers Society of America and regularly participates in literary events in the U.S. and Europe. He speaks French, English, Portuguese, Spanish and some Russian, and carries several passports.